Also by Lucy Score

KNOCKEMOUT SERIES
Things We Never Got Over
Things We Hide From the Light

RILEY THORN SERIES
Riley Thorn and the Dead Guy Next Door
Riley Thorn and the Corpse in the Closet
Riley Thorn and the Blast from the Past

SINNER AND SAINT SERIES
Crossing the Line
Breaking the Rules

BOOTLEG SPRINGS SERIES
Whiskey Chaser
Sidecar Crush
Moonshine Kiss
Bourbon Bliss
Gin Fling
Highball Rush

BENEVOLENCE SERIES
Pretend You're Mine
Protecting What's Mine

BLUE MOON SERIES
No More Secrets
Fall into Temptation
The Last Second Chance
Not Part of the Plan
Holding on to Chaos
The Fine Art of Faking It
Where It All Began
The Mistletoe Kisser

WELCOME HOME SERIES
Mr. Fixer Upper
The Christmas Fix

STANDALONES
By a Thread
Forever Never
Rock Bottom Girl
The Worst Best Man
The Price of Scandal
Undercover Love
Heart of Hope

FINALLY

Mine

LUCY SCORE

Bloom *books*

Published by Bloom Books, an imprint of Sourcebooks
P.O. Box 4410, Naperville, Illinois 60567-4410
(630) 961-3900
sourcebooks.com

Originally published in 2018 by That's What She Said, Inc.

Cataloging-in-Publication data is on file with the Library of Congress.

Printed and bound in the United States of America.
LSC 10 9 8 7 6 5 4 3 2 1

To Andrea and every woman who left or stayed.

CHAPTER 1

This was the second stupidest thing she had ever done in her entire life. But since *this* stupid thing was going to remedy the first, Gloria Parker cut herself a tiny sliver of slack.

This was necessary, she reminded herself, running her hands down the front of her white T-shirt, wincing when she brushed bruises. Life and death. Hers.

Her rusty little car was packed with her meager belongings. She wouldn't be going "home" tonight.

"It's going to be fine," she assured herself, stepping onto the skinny front porch of the bar. Remo's was the favorite—and only—bar in the town of Benevolence. Built like a log cabin, the cedar-shingled exterior invited thirsty patrons inside with its hand-painted sign and cozy patio off the right-hand side. Its only view was the gravel parking lot, but if you were visiting Remo's, you weren't worried about ambiance. You were there to catch up with your neighbors. Enjoy a pitcher. Sample a plate of hot wings. Or, in *his* case, drink until you couldn't see straight.

She was twenty-seven years old and had never once stepped foot in Remo's. There were a lot of things she hadn't done. Yet. And one reason for all of it. Today, it all ended, and her life could finally begin.

It was spring, early enough that she could still feel a few curling tendrils of winter in the air. Spring meant new beginnings. As the sun went down over the town she'd been born and raised in, so would the curtain on ten years of stupid. Ten years of pain. Ten years of a history that she was ashamed of.

Gloria swallowed hard. "You can do this," she whispered. With a shaking hand, she pulled the thick wood door open, ignoring the purple welts around her wrist. She'd gotten good at that. Ignoring. Pretending.

She stepped through the doorway and into her future.

Cozy, not seedy, she thought. Wood-paneled walls showcased beer signs and pictures of Benevolence over the decades. There was a skinny strip of stage against the back wall. A crowd of mostly empty tables and chairs clustered around the pine floor. The glass door on the right led to a patio for warm weather socializing. But her attention was on the big man hunched over the bar.

Glenn Diller.

Judging from the slump in his shoulders, he'd either left work early, or he'd been laid off again from the factory and neglected to tell her. Either way, he'd been drinking for hours.

She took a shaky breath and let it out. It was now or never. And she wouldn't survive never.

The bartender, Titus, was an older man she recognized as the father of one of her classmates. His son had just finished law school in Washington, DC. And here was Gloria, still frozen in time. Titus spotted her, and his gaze slid uneasily to Glenn.

He knows. Everyone knows. It was part of the shame Gloria feared she would never shed. But she had to try.

Sophie Adler, crackling with energy, danced behind the bar, tying her raven hair in a tail. "Sorry I'm late, Titus. Josh hid my car keys in the toilet again."

Titus grunted and reached for the tip jar without taking his eyes off Glenn. He was expecting trouble.

Gloria prayed to God the man was wrong.

She cleared her throat. "Glenn." His name came out clear as a bell with a confidence Gloria didn't know she still possessed.

He turned slowly on his stool, an empty shot glass and a beer in front of him. His eyes were bloodshot already.

He focused in on her and lurched to his feet. "The fuck you doing here?"

That guttural growl, the threat of violence it carried, had cowed her for years. But not today. Today she was immune.

She wanted this, she reminded herself. She *needed* this.

She watched the man she'd fallen for at seventeen, the man she'd let systematically strip her of everything right down to her dignity, approach. Alcohol and a feeling that life owed him more had made his high school muscle bulky and bloated. It had dulled his eyes, sallowed his skin. He looked a decade older than his thirty years.

Glenn listed to the right as he shuffled toward her. Drunk but still capable of inflicting so much damage. That was why they were here. Not in the shabby trailer they shared where no one paid any attention to the sounds of fists and screams.

Here, there were witnesses. Here, there were people who might help.

She put an empty table between them, the hair prickling on the back of her neck.

"What the fuck are you doing here?" he demanded again. His bark drew the eyes of everyone in the bar.

"I'm leaving," she said quietly. "I'm leaving, and I'm not coming back, and if you ever touch me again, I'm going to the police." The words poured out like water rushing over the falls. They'd been lodged in her throat for so long they'd strangled her.

3

His once handsome face twisted into a gruesome grimace. His cheeks flushed red. The veins in his neck corded into a topographical map. But they weren't within the walls of his trailer. They had an audience.

It was a thin veneer of protection, and Gloria clung to it.

He laughed, a slow, dangerous wheeze. "You're going to be very, very sorry."

A chill ran through her body, lodging itself like an iceberg in her heart. She'd made a miscalculation. Her eyes flicked to Sophie behind the bar. The woman was watching her. She nodded toward the phone. A subtle signal.

Gloria gave a small shake of her head.

No. She needed to do this on her own. Make the break.

"Glenn. I'm serious. We're done. You're done hurting me. It's never happening again. If you try it, I'll take out a restraining order against you."

He'd been a king on the basketball court in high school. Big, mean, aggressive. He'd fought his way to win after win. She'd thought winning fueled him, that hero's adoration. But instead, it was the attention, the recognition that he was someone not to be messed with. A man. Respect through fear. Just like his father. His father drank and beat his wife…until his untimely death of a heart attack at forty-five. So Glenn drank and beat his girlfriend. Because that was what men did.

He reached across the table quick as a snake, his meaty hand settling on her arm in a painful grip. "Let's go have ourselves a little talk," he said pleasantly. But there was menace behind the words, laced like poison ivy around the trunk of a tree.

Gloria fought against his hold. It always started the same, that hand wrapping its way around her upper arm and choking the blood out of it. The last three months had been so bad she'd never healed. Just bruises on top of bruises.

"Stop it," she gritted out, desperate to yank her arm free. But it was a comedy, her small frame trying to deny his hulking strength.

He towed her toward the door like a man with a dog.

"Gonna settle up?" Titus called nervously after them.

Glenn didn't deign to answer, just shoved the front door open so hard it bounced off the wooden, shingled exterior.

She fought in earnest now as he dragged her toward his pickup at the back of the lot. Her sneakers slipped and stumbled over the gravel.

"Let go of me!"

He tossed her against the side of his truck. Her spine jarred at the impact. "You belong to me, Gloria Parker. You don't get to leave. Ever."

"You don't even love me," she shouted the truth in his face. He didn't know what love was. She wasn't sure if she did either.

"I don't have to love you. I own you," he hissed.

Every warning bell she'd developed to alert her to his changes in moods, to danger, clanged to life in her head.

"You don't," she told him. "You don't own me. You have to let me go."

"I don't have to do shit," he slurred.

The backhand caught her by surprise, stunning her. She shook it off as she had so many others and pushed him back. She had to fight now like never before. Her life was at stake.

"You stupid fucking bitch. Ungrateful slut," he breathed, shoving a hand into her hair and pulling it until she yelped. He liked when she cried. Liked when she was terrified. He wanted her to know that he had the power to end her life.

"I'm leaving you," she said through chattering teeth. He'd never hurt her in public before. But then again, she'd never tried leaving him before.

"I warned you!" It was a shout of rage that carried across the parking lot.

Benevolence was a town of good people who worked hard and cared about their neighbors. He was a stain on them all and proud of it. But there was no one here to help her. It was her against him. Until the police that Sophie probably—dear God, please—called. She just needed to hang in there for a few minutes.

"I fucking told you, didn't I?" Glenn shook her again, even harder this time.

Gloria shoved against his chest with all her strength, but his meaty fists closed around her arms, shaking her until the back of her head hit the truck window. With a bleak realization, she knew she didn't have minutes.

"Hey!" She heard a voice snap through the air. A woman. Blond hair.

But Glenn was obstructing her view. "Mind your own business, nosy whore."

"Glenn—" Gloria gasped.

"I'm sick of hearing it!" he said. His face was fire-engine-red with rage. He gripped her by the throat, lifting her off her feet.

Her air was cut off. She felt the pressure build in her head, watched the black creep in on the edges of her vision. Her feet swung uselessly, inches from the ground. It couldn't end this way. Her life couldn't stop at his brutish hands. She wouldn't be just another sad statistic.

Weakly, she reached for the hand around her throat. Everything was starting to go gray as her lungs screamed for oxygen.

With the last of her strength, she lashed her foot out and connected with his bad knee. At the same time, she saw a flash of blond, and Glenn was dropping her to the ground. She landed in a crumpled heap. The gravel bit into her legs, her side, but she was too busy sucking in broken breaths to notice.

There was a commotion behind her—shouts and curses—but it sounded so far away. She rolled over onto her back and stared up at the spring sunset coating the sky in pinks and oranges.

Never again.

CHAPTER 2

The stiff paper covering the exam table crinkled under her legs. She was cold in the anonymous gown designed to make examining bodies easy, impersonal. The curtain dividing the bed from the door was made out of the same threadbare blue material. There was a poster of a basket of golden retriever puppies on the wall, innocent and happy, tongues lolling.

In that moment, Gloria felt as though she were a stranger to innocence and happiness.

She thought about her alter ego, the Gloria Who-Left-Glenn-After-the-First-Time. At this very minute, that girl would be meeting friends for beers—no, martinis—in some swanky bar that no one had ever heard of in a city that everyone wanted to live in. She'd proudly walk inside in shoes that would make other women whisper, "I don't know how she does it." Pay for a round of drinks with her own money. Spend the rest of the night laughing and dancing.

But this Gloria? Was someplace else entirely.

Her body ached, but the pain felt dull, far away, as if it belonged to someone else. She was empty, cold. There was no sense of the victory, the pride she'd expected to feel. She'd done it. Almost died in the process. But she'd left Glenn Diller. And others had paid the price. The blond woman from the parking lot had been knocked unconscious. Luke Garrison had stepped into the fight. And now the town doctor had kindly canceled her evening plans to examine Gloria's bruised and battered body, saving her an expensive trip to the emergency room. She wondered if her freedom was already a bigger inconvenience than her abuse had ever been.

Why couldn't she feel anything?

The door to the little room opened, and Dr. Dunnigan poked her head around the curtain, her frizzy, strawberry-blond curls rioting above her ivory skin.

"I hope this means you finally left the bastard."

Sturdy and brisk, Trish Dunnigan suffered no fools except for the perennially foolish Gloria Parker. The woman had given Gloria her booster shots in elementary school and for the past few years had met her in the grocery store parking lot—one of the only places Gloria was allowed to go—to examine and treat her injuries.

Dr. Dunnigan had been the voice of judgment-free reason when everyone else had given up or been chased off.

He will kill you. He's escalating. It's a textbook abuse cycle. He's going to kill you, Gloria. Soon.

She'd told Gloria that a week ago while fixing her dislocated shoulder. Still she'd stayed. It hurt too much to think about leaving. About doing anything different.

And then last night, it had all changed.

It was just a kid and his friends playing music a little too loud in his first car two trailers down. But to Glenn, it was a reason to posture. He'd ripped him out of his car, thrown him on the ground, and screamed in his face about trying to sleep and peace and quiet and respect.

Humiliation. He dealt in it. Gloria. His coworkers. His

mother. Strangers who served him food or expected to be paid for services. There were people in this world who couldn't feel big unless they were making someone else feel small.

He'd dehumanized her, made her so small she'd all but disappeared. And when she'd tried to stop him last night, he'd thrown her to the ground next to the boy and spat on them both. Stripping them both of their power, their humanity, their worth.

He'd waited until she'd followed him back to the trailer before he slapped her and pushed her down, kicking her once. But he'd spent most of his anger on the boy and, deeming her of no consequence, sat back down to finish watching TV.

And then today, she'd packed her things, retrieved her small stash of cash she'd hidden behind the trailer's broken skirting, and left the bastard.

"It's over," Gloria returned numbly.

All business, Dr. Dunnigan checked her pulse, the dilation of her pupils. She pulled out her stethoscope, cool green eyes skimming what Gloria knew was a necklace of bruises forming around her throat.

The door flew open and bounced off the wall, temporarily obscuring the basket of puppies. Sara Parker, still in her hairstylist apron, burst into the room. For a woman never prone to dramatics, it was quite the entrance.

"Oh, God. Gloria. *Mija!*"

Gloria didn't want to see the pity in her mother's eyes. Didn't want to acknowledge that her pain hurt her mother as viciously as if it were her own.

"When I got that phone call, I thought he'd killed you."

The words broke down the walls of Gloria's shock, and hot tears spilled over onto her cold, pale cheeks. "I'm sorry," Gloria whispered as the thin, strong bands of her mother's arms welcomed her.

"My sweet girl. Are you done? Is this the end?" Sara asked. Gloria nodded. "It's over. He's in jail."

"Good." Sara swore colorfully in Spanish and then promptly closed the book on her anger. "You'll stay with me. I'll make chicken noodle soup."

"My bags are already at your house," Gloria confessed with a ghost of a smile. Even after all these years of estrangement, Gloria had known she could go home. With Glenn gone, her mother would be safe.

"Mm-hmm," Dr. Dunnigan harrumphed. "Now, if you don't mind, Mrs. Parker, I'd like to continue examining my patient."

Sara cupped Gloria's face in her hands. "Welcome home, *mjia*. I'll wait for you outside."

"Thank you, Mama."

A little of the cold in her soul faded. The sliver of fear dulled just a bit.

"Ooof," the doctor tut-tutted when she looked at Gloria's side where the gravel had abraded her skin. "It hurts now. But you'll heal," she predicted.

Gloria hoped the woman meant inside and out. Because right now, she wasn't sure if she'd ever feel normal again. Hell, she didn't even remember what normal was. What did her future look like? A girl who had barely graduated high school, never worked, and handed over any sense of self-respect to a monster. What kind of a place was there for her in this world?

In silence, she bore the humiliation of the exam, so familiar, somehow again dehumanizing—being reduced to injuries that she wished she'd been strong enough to prevent.

Dr. Dunnigan's fingers clicked away officially on her laptop, updating her records. "Pictures," she said, peering over her reading glasses.

Gloria had always refused the doctor's offer to document her injuries before. She'd never told Dr. Dunnigan that she had her own documentation, hidden away. Every bruise, every sprain, every broken bone. There had been days when she thought she'd never use it, never leave.

But she had.

"What am I going to do?" Her voice was hoarse as much from emotion as Glenn's brutish hands.

"You're not going to worry about making decisions today and for a while," Dr. Dunnigan said briskly. She shut her laptop and opened a drawer to pull out a small digital camera. "You made the hardest decision today. Now it's time to heal, rest, remember who you are without him."

Was she anyone without him? Was poor little Gloria Parker anybody without the stigma of abuse? Did she even exist in this world anymore?

"I feel like a ghost," she confessed softly.

Dr. Dunnigan helped her to her feet. "Feel real enough to me. Give yourself some time to heal, kiddo. Inside takes a lot longer than outside."

Gloria lifted her chin so the doctor could record the garish handprints around her neck and closed her eyes when the motion made her dizzy.

The camera shutter clicked quietly.

"Today you're not a victim. Today you're a survivor."

CHAPTER 3

He felt his legs warm as the pavement blurred beneath his feet. His muscles hummed as he pushed harder. Benevolence, Maryland, his town since birth, clipped past as he outran his demons. Cozy houses sat on pretty green lawns that butted up against tree-lined streets.

It was April, and the rain that had plagued them for a week straight had abated, giving way to one perfect day of sunshine and eighty-degree weather. Aldo Moretta had ducked out of the office an hour early to take advantage of it with a run.

He raised a hand to the hugely pregnant Carol Ann who sat in her driveway in a lawn chair while her husband, Carl, a stick figure of a man, weeded the front flower bed. Carol Ann wiggled her fingers at him.

There were a lot of things Aldo couldn't control, which was why he took very good care of the things he could. Like his body. He'd fine-tuned himself into an athletic machine with a six-minute mile and a three-hundred-and-fifteen-pound overhead squat. He made himself strong and quick and ready. In a few weeks' time, he'd be calling on it all. His National Guard unit was deploying—his fourth time.

He turned the corner and fished the biscuit out of his pocket at the excited yaps coming from behind Peggy Ann Marsico's three-foot-tall picket fence. Smeagol the beagle wagged his white-tipped tail in a blur. He tossed the treat and watched Smeagol catch it midair in a super-dog, ears-out dive. He grinned as the dog pranced proudly through the ferns, prize between his teeth.

Next door to Peggy Ann's beige and blue ranch was Lincoln Reed's place. Once an old gas station, the fire chief had transformed it into a killer bachelor pad. Linc made it his mission in life to bachelor the hell out of every eligible woman in the tricounty area. He was a charming, friendly commitment-phobe.

Linc was a blast to hang out with. It was too bad that he and Aldo's best friend, Luke, could barely tolerate the sight of each other.

"What's up, Moretta?" Linc called out, raising a beer while spraying down his truck with the hose. "Want a beer?"

"Maybe after a few more miles," Aldo called back.

"Swing back," Linc said, turning the hose on a grateful Aldo before switching back to the gleaming pickup.

With a wave, he was off again. He tuned in to his footfalls as he skirted the cemetery. He didn't look at the grave. Didn't have to. Every time he passed this stretch of gently rolling green dotted with white headstones, he remembered.

The years that separated him from the moment he found Luke curled around his wife's headstone, an empty six-pack next to him, disappeared. He'd held his friend while sobs racked the man's body as the grief he'd bottled burst through his cracks. They never spoke of that moment. They didn't have to. They were brothers without the blood. They'd traded life saves back and forth like kids traded baseball cards or Pokémon shit.

"Hey there, handsome!" Valerie Washington was seventy-three years old, looked like she was fifty, and acted like she was eighteen. She waved a margarita glass from her front porch where she was perched with a stack of romance novels and biographies, her fresh haul from the library.

"When are you going to divorce Mr. Washington and marry me?" Aldo demanded, jogging in place and flexing for her.

She slid her oversize prescription sunglasses down her nose and gave him a wink.

"When he stops being excellent in bed," she shot back.

Aldo blew her a kiss and pressed on, finally winding his way onto the lake trail. Benevolence was slowly waking up to spring. Green buds sprouted in the canopy above him while his feet raced over last year's leaves. Beginnings and endings.

And just like that, his thoughts turned to Gloria Parker. It had been a week since everything changed. A week of torture. Wanting something so badly. Knowing that he couldn't have it, try for it. Not yet. He'd left town last weekend under the guise of a fishing trip so he wouldn't show up on her mother's front porch begging to see her. Instead, he'd paced a cabin in West Virginia for forty-eight hours straight and ran himself into the ground on the mountain trails until he was too exhausted to even think about inserting himself into her life.

No. She needed time. Time to herself, to heal. He'd be patient. Just as he'd been since high school. Besides, Glenn could slide right through again. Could end up winning her back again. If that happened, Aldo knew he wouldn't be able to stay out of it.

He felt the afternoon sun on his face, the sweat as it rolled down his back and, for the first time in a long time, felt hopeful about being patient.

"You keep runnin' like that, you'll puke." Deputy Ty Adler, the man who had the distinct pleasure of placing Glenn Diller under arrest, joined him at the Y in the trail. He was wearing a Benevolence PD ball cap and a Not-So-Polar Plunge T-shirt.

"How's it going, Deputy?"

"Just fine. Just fine," Ty drawled.

Ty had moved to Benevolence in high school, laid eyes on teenage Sophie Garrison, and fallen flat on his face in love. It had taken him a couple of years to drag a commitment out of her, but they were happy, their little family of three.

Aldo was ready for his own happy.

"Heard you had some excitement last week," Aldo pressed, slowing his pace a touch to conversational speed.

Ty was in good shape, just not quite Moretta good shape.

"Finally got to put that asshole behind bars," Ty said cheerfully. "Must have been good news to you."

Aldo didn't have to see beneath his friend's sunglasses to know the man was looking at him. "About damn time."

"Seems I recall you and Diller going head-to-head a time or two right after high school," Ty mused. Folks in Benevolence called it fishing.

Aldo's hands closed into fists at the memory. "We were just kids then," he answered vaguely.

"And I seem to recall you getting piss-faced drunk after one shoving match," Ty reminded him.

"Nothing wrong with your memory," Aldo quipped, picking up the pace. He hid a grin as Ty's wheezing instantly increased while he fought to keep up.

"Come on, man. Don't turn on the afterburners."

"Give me one good reason."

"He's not gettin' out."

Aldo stopped, and Ty smacked right into him.

"Jesus, how do you do this without water?" Ty gasped, twisting open the mangled water bottle he carried. He guzzled deeply and handed it over to Aldo.

Aldo drank and waited for Ty to get to the fucking point.

"Anyway, as I was saying. Diller's not sliding on this. He attacked another woman, and she's fired up enough to press charges. Doc's testifying. Our boy Luke's a witness."

Aldo swallowed hard and forced his fingers to relax on the bottle.

"Gloria's charging him too," Ty continued. "Turns out she's got photos of every beating for the past few years."

The water bottle didn't stand a chance. Water gushed over Aldo's fingers, cramped in a death grip on the plastic. *Every beating for the past few years...*

Where the fuck had he been? Why hadn't he stopped it?

"Aw, man. No need to be wasteful," thirsty Ty mourned.

"How is she?" Aldo asked, his voice ragged.

Ty clapped a hand on his shoulder. They'd never talked about Aldo's feelings for Gloria. Hell, no one really knew there were any feelings. But Ty was sharper than his southern drawl let on. "She's good. Real good. Stopped in to see her yesterday. Glenn won't make bail. His mama's got nothing to put up for him, and the judge wasn't feeling very friendly toward him on account of him calling her a stupid bitch at his arraignment. So unless he can cough up two hundred thousand dollars, he's gonna rot in a cell until his trial."

"Fucker," Aldo swore quietly.

"Gloria's good though. This time is different," Ty predicted.

Aldo hoped to all that was fucking good and right in this world that his friend was correct. Neither he nor Gloria could survive another round.

Aldo jogged up the stone steps to the front porch of his Craftsman bungalow and pulled open the screen door. Sweaty, thirsty, and now more hopeful than he had been, he loped down the hallway to the kitchen in the back. He filled a glass straight from the tap, grabbed a beer from the fridge, and returned to the porch. Dropping down onto a chair that wouldn't disintegrate under his sweat, he propped his feet up on the railing.

He thought of Luke and the rumors that his recluse of an almost brother was shacking up with a stranger. The stranger who played a role in taking down Gloria's abusive asshole. He needed to touch base, catch up. Find out if Luke had suffered a head trauma and invited a psychotic woman into his home. Or if some miracle had occurred and his friend was finally loosening his grip on grief.

He had let his own life shit take the lead this week. It was time to check back in.

The neighborhood noise buzzed quietly around him. Pauletta's lawn mower coughing to life. Roberta Shawn's kids begging for popsicles.

He'd bought the house two years ago and, unlike his frozen-in-time friend Luke, had immediately started renovating. He had tweaked and painted and reconfigured until the four-bedroom house was ready. He believed. Aldo Moretta was putting it out there to the universe. He believed.

He was ready for the rest of his life to begin. He wanted the wife, the family, the backyard barbecues. He wanted neighbor kids playing capture the flag in his backyard. And he wanted every last one of those things with Gloria Parker.

CHAPTER 4

"Mama, I'm going...out." Gloria called, studying herself in the reflection of the mirror propped against the wall in her childhood bedroom. The walls were still the same aqua that she'd enthusiastically slathered all over the room for her fourteenth birthday. Her bold fuchsia and raspberry accessories were still scattered about. Echoes of a different girl. Brave, vibrant, goofy, unbelievably naïve.

She didn't recognize any traces of that girl inside or out as she adjusted the cheery floral scarf around her neck. It added a little something to her plain T-shirt and jeans while camouflaging the gruesome bruises that had faded to a lovely jaundice color around her neck. "I shouldn't be gone longer than an hour."

Her mother, slim and sad, appeared in her open doorway.

"You know you don't have to report to me," Sara reminded her.

Gloria dropped her gaze to the pink toenails on display in her flip-flops. Her mother had treated her to a pedicure—and a cell phone—as soon as she was well enough to leave the house. Gloria had spent the entire time shoving away the feelings of guilt and fear that swept over her.

"I know," she said sadly. "It's going to take some time."

Her mother came up behind her, slipping an affection-ate arm around her waist. Sara had the beautiful coloring and luxurious dark hair of her Mexican mama. Today, Sara looked younger than her own daughter.

"No one is going to push you to do anything you're not ready to."

"I know, Mama." Gloria did know. But knowing it and feeling it were two different things. Part of her felt like she was still trapped in that dingy trailer with the man who'd turned monster.

"Good," Sara approved. "I'll continue to remind you until you don't need reminding."

Gloria gave her mother a small smile. When the situation called for it, Sara could be tenacious, pushy even. "Let's promise to be honest with each other," Gloria begged. She didn't want things sugarcoated for her protection. She didn't want to be the weak one anymore. She could face the truth and probably survive it.

"Okay." Sara nodded. "I'll go first. You're too skinny. Too tired. You need good food and rest and time. Ten years isn't going to be easy to overcome. But now that I have you back, I'm never letting go. Not even if you try to slip away again. I will fight for you this time."

For a second, Gloria saw the whole mess through her mother's eyes. The alienation. The distance. The pain of watch-ing her only child lose herself to a man who was incapable of taking care. *A daughter too weak to stand up for herself,* Gloria thought wryly. "I'm so sorry, Mama."

"For what, love?"

"For hurting you. For disappointing you."

Her mother tsked. "You know what I see there?" she asked, studying their reflection.

"What?"

"Two very beautiful women who are going to have a very good life."

Gloria felt her lips quirk at the corners. "I hope you're right."

Sara turned Gloria to face her. "Have faith, *mija*. You're here now. That's a start."

Gloria felt the burn of tears. "Thank you for taking me back, Mama." This was her second chance. She wasn't going to need a third.

Sara rolled her eyes at the thanks that weren't necessary. "Go do your thing. Then come back. We'll drink wine, and I'll make salsa."

It was a real smile now. "I'll pick up the tortilla chips," Gloria promised.

———

Gloria straightened her shoulders and reached up to adjust the scarf again. She was more nervous standing here in the street, staring at the rambling three-story brick home, than she had been at Remo's the night she left Glenn.

"Shit," she muttered, losing her gumption and hurrying down the sidewalk. She'd take a stroll around the block, talk herself into it. "Get it together, Gloria," she told herself as her feet carefully avoided each sidewalk crack. "She's not going to break your arm or strangle you." Morbid pep talk out of the way, she rounded the block and took slow, deep breaths. By the time she found herself in front of the house again, she felt calmer...or at least slightly less crazy.

The woman was there on the porch, sweeping a winter's worth of debris off the wide planks. Harper Wilde, Deputy Adler—Ty, as he'd insisted—had told her. Harper, the stranger who had stepped in and saved her life in that parking lot, was now living with the reclusive Luke Garrison. There was a story there, but Gloria wasn't sure if she could ask for it.

She cleared her throat. "I'm sorry to bother you, but Ty told me where I could find you," Gloria called.

Harper leaned the broom against the railing and wiped her hands on the seat of her jeans. "Gloria, right?" she asked with a quick smile.

Gloria nodded. "I wasn't sure you'd recognize me. We weren't..."

"Formally introduced?" Harper supplied with a friendly wiggle of her eyebrows.

Gloria felt herself relax muscle by muscle. "Exactly. I hope you don't mind me stopping by."

"Not at all! You're giving me the perfect excuse to quit cleaning," Harper said, stepping off the porch. "Do you have time to come inside?"

Gloria hadn't expected an invitation inside. Hell, she'd expected a curt reaction from a battered woman who blamed her for the bruises. But Harper was moving around like she was used to a good ol' physical assault. "Um, sure. If you're sure you don't mind?"

"I would love some company," Harper insisted. "Especially if you tell me you haven't had lunch yet, because I'm starving."

On cue, Gloria's stomach growled. "Oh, um. I don't know if I should..." It was a knee-jerk reaction. There were no spontaneous invitations accepted when Glenn was waiting for her, timing her at the grocery store, or worse, tracking her down in public and dragging her home.

But this was her second chance. And damn it, she was taking it. Even if her heart was in her throat and the idea of walking into that house made her want to barf all over the sidewalk. She was used to fear. It had been her constant companion this last decade. Now was her chance, her *choice*.

"Please?" Harper cocked her head to the side. "I'd love to have some company."

Gloria nodded, unable to speak. What the hell kind of company would she be? Was she even capable of making small talk? She should have just written a nice apology/thank-you letter to Harper instead of trying to do this face-to-face.

Harper grinned. "Come on in."

Gloria's body still sang with minor aches and pains as she climbed the steps, but she was getting better. She was healing. This visit was part of the healing. Thanking and apologizing to the woman who'd been marred by her own personal violent nightmare.

Still, a letter would have done the job.

The front door opened into an empty foyer. The rooms on either side were bare except for a flat-screen TV and an antique sofa that looked about as comfortable as a cinder block. It felt like an abandoned house. No pictures on the wall, no furniture to speak of. There was a story here too. Gloria was sure of it. But they were a long way away from story-swapping friends.

She followed Harper down the hallway on lovely, worn hardwood floors to the pretty and—again—bare kitchen. Harper grabbed two plates from a cabinet and stacked them on the island. "Can you grab the bread for me?" she asked, unpacking sandwich ingredients from the refrigerator.

Gloria blinked and reached for the loaf of bread on the counter. She'd expected to come here and apologize, taking her lumps and the blame. Not make herself at home in a virtual stranger's house and make herself a sandwich.

Harper pushed a cutting board and ripe tomato into Gloria's hands. "Would you mind slicing this?"

"Sure," Gloria said, staring at the glossy red skin of the tomato, wondering what alternate dimension she'd walked into.

Gloria sliced, and Harper buzzed around the kitchen. "Roast beef okay with you?"

"Sure." Gloria said again, kicking herself for her limited conversational abilities. *For the love of God, come up with a different word!* "But you really don't have to go to all this trouble." *Good. A whole sentence. Nice work.*

"Well, you're helping," Harper insisted with a wink. She dropped dollops of mayonnaise on two slices of bread. "So what brings you to Luke's unfurnished abode?"

Gloria laughed softly. "It *is* kind of Spartan," she observed.

"I don't know if he's a minimalist or what," Harper confessed.

"Commitment phobic?" Gloria suggested.

"Even when it comes to furniture, it seems," Harper agreed. She handed Gloria a plated sandwich. "Water or soda?"

"Water, please," Gloria answered automatically. *There. She remembered her manners.*

They ate side by side on barstools at the island, the only seats available.

Gloria tried to focus on the sandwich, but the words she needed to say were bubbling up in her throat. "Harper, I just wanted to thank you," she said, breaking the silence.

Harper swiped bread crumbs off of her lower lip. "You're welcome. But it's just a sandwich."

Gloria laughed. "Not just for the sandwich, which is really good, by the way. For helping me with Glenn at Remo's. It's been going on for so long, or at least I've let it go on so long, that I felt like everyone had stopped seeing me." She paused, took a breath. "It took me seeing the situation I helped create hurt someone else to realize that it had to stop. And I'm sorry for that."

Yes, she had planned to leave Glenn. But Gloria wasn't sure she would have had the guts to press charges, to turn over all those humiliating photos to the police, if the man she'd once loved hadn't hurt someone else. That made her even more disappointed in herself.

Harper shrugged off the apology. "It was worth it if it helps you build a life you want. How are you?"

"I'm okay," Gloria said, pushing the pickle spear around her plate. "I'm staying with my mother for now. And I pressed charges." Feeling an unexpected lightness in saying the words, Gloria picked up her sandwich and took another bite.

There was so much silence in shame. Maybe getting the words out would ease a small bit of her burden?

"That's very brave of you," Harper said.

Gloria shook her head. "It would have been braver had I done it years ago."

Harper patted her hand lightly. "Life moves pretty fast. There's not a lot of room for coulda, shoulda, woulda."

"Sometimes that's all I can think about. How different my life would be if I had gone to college or never started dating him." *Whoa, Nelly.* First, she couldn't form a coherent sentence and now she was spilling her guts?

Harper's big gray eyes widened with understanding. "Maybe now you have that chance. To see what your life would be without him in it."

Gloria didn't know why she was blurting out her secret shame to a complete stranger. It must have been the roast beef. But she couldn't stop the flood of words. "It's hard. I don't really have any friends left. I guess it's not easy to be friends with someone who keeps making the wrong decision over and over again. Eventually, everyone has to decide whether it's worth it to keep trying."

And the old Gloria Parker hadn't been worth it.

"So what are you going to do now?" Harper asked as Gloria contemplated sinking into the downward spiral that beckoned.

She sat straighter. "I'm going to get a job, find a place to live, and be worth it." Gloria felt the words vibrate inside her. This was *her life. Her choice.*

Harper nodded her approval and bit enthusiastically into her pickle spear. "Sounds like a good plan to me. Is there anything I can do to help?"

"Wanna be friends?" Gloria offered. "I'll understand if your answer's no. Considering I got you punched in the face." A joke. A very small, not very funny joke. Maybe she really was going to be okay.

Harper gave her a long, slow wink. "I got myself punched in the face. And it got me waking up staring into the beautiful eyes of Luke Garrison. I think I owe you a lifetime of friendship."

Gloria's mouth stretched into an honest-to-goodness grin. It felt strange on her face. "I went to school with Sophie and Luke. He's a good man."

"Yes, he is." Harper nodded.

A memory of Luke and his best friend, Aldo, surfaced. It was a Friday night football game, and the two were strutting victoriously off the field. While Luke's then-girlfriend Karen jogged up to him for a kiss, for one shining moment, Aldo's dark gaze had met and held Gloria's. Just like that, late-blooming sophomore Gloria had developed her very first crush.

Gloria insisted on washing the plates while Harper put the sandwich fixings away.

"So how do you feel?" Gloria asked. "You got knocked around pretty hard."

She saw it in the way Harper's gaze skated left, in the tiny lift of her shoulders. *Secrets.* Violence left its dirty fingerprints on a person's soul.

"It wasn't so bad. And may I repeat: Luke Garrison."

"Well, there is that," Gloria said, letting it drop. She glanced at the clock on the microwave. "I'd better be getting back."

"I'm so glad you came," Harper said, walking her down the hallway to the front door.

"It was really nice officially meeting you," Gloria told her. "And one more time for the record, thank you, and I'm sorry."

Harper rolled her eyes on a bubbly laugh. "And again, no thanks or apologies necessary. I fully plan to be BFFs with you, and we should have dinner sometime soon."

Friends. Gloria wanted to cry with hope, with gratitude, with relief. Was there a possibility that she wasn't permanently damaged?

Harper opened the front door, and Gloria froze to the spot, staring at the shirtless, tattooed, sweaty man in front of her.

CHAPTER 5

His heart was lodged somewhere between chest and throat. The last person Aldo expected to find at his best friend's door was Gloria Parker. She stared at him with wide dark eyes full of shadows and questions.

"Did someone say dinner?" Aldo asked with what he hoped to God was a charming grin and not a fish gape. He was vaguely aware of the fact that he was shirtless and sweating profusely. Fortunately, that was one of his best looks.

"Hi, Aldo," Gloria said shyly.

He whipped off his sunglasses to see her better. Thickly lashed eyes, a smooth, tawny complexion that hinted at her heritage. The bone structure of a fucking model wrapped up in the body of a tiny pixie.

That was how he had always thought of her. Fragile, too pretty to touch.

He saw a hint of the bruising edging out of the top of her scarf, and he clenched his hands into fists on his hips. He was used to the rage, used to pushing it down.

"Hi, Gloria. How's it going?" *How's it going? She's recovering from a public physical assault, dumbass. How do you think it's going?*

She glanced down at her pink toenails and then back up at him. Aldo could have stood there all day taking her in. But the blond next to her cleared her throat.

"You must be Aldo because Gloria called you that," she said, extending her hand.

With great determination, Aldo dragged his gaze from Gloria's pretty face. "And you must be the famous Harper." He shook her hand. "I thought I'd stop by while my best friend is out of town to see why he forgot to mention that he has a live-in girlfriend."

"And make sure I'm not some kind of psychopath?"

Aldo blinked. *Touché, potential psychopath. Touché.*

Aldo hefted a shoulder. "You know the saying. Bros don't let other bros date psychos."

Gloria gave a soft laugh, and Aldo felt himself grow ten feet tall.

"I'm actually not familiar with that one. Is there some kind of test I have to take?" Harper joked.

But Aldo couldn't stop staring at Gloria. His gaze roamed her face, memorizing every detail. He hadn't been this close to her—close enough to touch her—in years. And the reason for that was behind bars.

With Herculean effort, he returned his attention to Harper. "Why don't I give you the test at dinner? Monday. Here. I'll grill burgers and dogs," he suggested, already plotting.

"Gloria, I feel like I should confirm that this gentleman actually is a friend of Luke's before I agree to let him cook dinner in Luke's house," Harper said gamely.

Gloria nodded, her dark hair falling over her forehead. "He is."

"Since elementary school," Aldo supplied, still looking at Gloria.

"Good enough for me. Seven here okay for you, Gloria?"

Aldo would have kissed Harper on the mouth if it wouldn't have messed up his long game with Gloria.

He saw Gloria hesitate, saw her questioning herself, and he moved an inch closer to her, slapping on his most flirtatious smile. "Please tell me you'll bring your apple pie."

He took a breath and went for it, taking one of Gloria's slim hands in his. He was touching her. *Finally.* He stared down at her long fingers and ran his thumb over the ridges of her knuckles. Goose bumps sprang up on her bare arms. He didn't know what was more powerful, her reaction to him or the thrum of his blood in his veins. "I'll be your slave for life," he promised.

Gloria's lower lip trembled before she bit it. She was staring down at their joined hands, and he could have died happy on the spot.

"I'll bring apple pie," she said softly. Slowly, she turned back to Harper. "I'll see you Monday, Harper."

She pulled her hand free in slow motion, and Aldo enjoyed the feel of her palm and fingers sliding over his. "See you, Gloria," he said, leaning against the doorframe in case she smiled at him and took him out at the knees.

The upward curve of her lips hit him squarely in the chest. He watched her leave, stepping carefully down the stairs. Probably still healing, he noted and once again swallowed the emotions that clogged his throat. There was a special place in hell for people who abused the innocents of the world. And Glenn Diller would be there. He would see to it.

"It's nice to see her smile," he said quietly. Belatedly, he remembered his audience. "So, Harper—if that is your real name—tell me about yourself."

She cocked her head. "Want to come in?"

"Normally, not until I know whether you can be trusted. But I'm four miles into my eight, and I could use some water."

He was used to the barren state of Luke's house, he thought, following Harper back to the kitchen. Without a push from someone, his friend would live like a squatter for the rest of his life. Maybe that "someone" was Harper. If she wasn't a psycho.

She handed him a water bottle, and they returned to the living room to perch on the homely sofa.

"So tell me about growing up with Luke," she said, all sunshine in her smile.

"He was always tagging after me, shadowing me, worshiping me," Aldo began.

Harper laughed. He fed her a few stories about summers and football and high school, all the while attempting to pry information out of her. But she wasn't forthcoming, parrying his questions about family and jobs and education with more questions of her own. He didn't get the psycho vibe from her. But the woman had secrets, and he hoped those secrets wouldn't hurt his friend.

"So do you know Gloria?" he asked, finally deeming it appropriate to steer Harper in the direction he most wanted to go.

"I actually just met her officially when she stopped by."

He rubbed a hand over his jaw and realized he'd forgotten to shave again. He'd have to get back in the habit if he was going to make a good impression. "Rumor has it she moved out and is pressing charges."

"Rumor has it," Harper agreed. Her smile was sneaky. "How long have you known Gloria?"

He didn't really want to spill his guts when his conversation partner was a vault in need of prying open. But it felt so fucking good to say Gloria's name out loud. "Since forever. She was a sophomore when we were seniors. Glenn was bad news back then too."

Harper rubbed her ribs. "Yeah, the years don't seem to have mellowed him."

"Heard you had quite the shiner." Either she was skilled with makeup or was a fast healer because the greenish-yellow bruising was barely visible.

"Please," she snorted. "You should have seen the other guy."

"Wish I would have been there." He said it lightly, but that thought had kept him awake every night since. He'd wanted his shot at Glenn Diller. Wanted it more than anything. A vision of Gloria smiling shyly up at him crowded into his mind. Almost anything.

Diller deserved to burn for what he'd put that girl through. If the legal system wasn't up to the task, he was.

"So how long have you been into Gloria?" she asked, bringing him out of the dark thoughts.

Aldo blinked. *Shit.* "Since I heard her sing in the high school musical."

Harper grinned, and he stared down at his water bottle.

"How did handsome football star Aldo not win the girl?" Harper asked.

His life's regret. "I never took the shot," he said with a sad shake of his head.

"Maybe now you can pull the trigger," Harper said, elbowing him.

"I like the way you think, Harper."

"Better bring you're a game to dinner Monday, sport," she teased.

"Sport? Are you serious?" Aldo scoffed, already planning all the ways he could sweep Gloria off her feet.

"Let the lousy nickname contest begin," she crowed.

CHAPTER 6

Sara Parker's kitchen was Gloria's favorite place in the world. Pretty white cabinets that they'd spent a week painting together when she was nine formed a tidy L. The countertops were covered in cobalt tiles, mirrored in the pretty blue glasses and colorful dinner plates in the cabinets above.

The room was friendly and colorful, speaking to the character of her mother.

Gloria dipped a tortilla chip into the bowl of fresh salsa and moaned with pleasure as the notes of lime and cilantro melted on her tongue. It had been years since she'd last sampled her mother's salsa. Glenn didn't like anything with spice…or flavor really.

"Good?" Sara asked, producing a bottle of tequila from a cabinet.

"The best."

"How did your secret errand go?" Her mother magically produced the ingredients for her infamous grapefruit margaritas, placing them neatly next to her industrial blender.

Sara Parker was a frugal woman, splurging on only what she deemed necessities—like a margarita blender. She lived below her means in a two-bedroom brick ranch that she had taken a decade to DIY into her own personal paradise. The living room was a shocking turquoise with comfortable white couches and walls cluttered with family photos. The only bathroom was a cheery canary with a frilly lace shower curtain and teal-framed mirrors. Sara's bedroom was a moody dark purple.

"It went…well," Gloria decided, remembering Aldo's quick grin and how it worked its way through her ribs to glow away in her chest.

"You like this Harper?" Sara asked, juicing half a grapefruit with vigor.

Of course her mother had known where she'd gone. Sara claimed to have mystical powers of sight passed down through her great-great-grandmother, a desert canyon shawoman. Growing up, Gloria had preferred to believe her mother had hidden video surveillance equipment around the house.

"I like her very much. She's happy, friendly."

"Good." Sara nodded briskly. The blender whirred to life.

Gloria made herself useful and pulled two margarita glasses from the shelf next to the sink. Candytuft and begonias bloomed in a riot of color on the other side of the window. Her mother had scrimped and saved for this house for two years after her husband, Gloria's father, had walked out on them. Sara had filled her life with work and pretty things. But without the man she'd called Daddy, Gloria had been hungry to fill the void of male attention. When Glenn Diller had taken her hand at a summer bonfire and kissed her in the shadows, tasting of beer and tobacco, well, she'd thought that void would finally be filled.

Her mother, on the other hand, had used the abandonment to build a life exactly the way she wanted it. She was a hairstylist, and had they lived in a more metropolitan area, Gloria knew her mother would have been a wealthy business owner. But Sara was content in Benevolence, running her own shop, giving Manhattan-worthy cuts at rural Maryland prices. She worked six days a week and had two part-time employees. She dated when she found a man worthy and otherwise filled her time with books and friends and wine.

Sara plopped a frothy pink margarita in front of Gloria. "Take your medicine, Gloria."

The Gloria Who-Left-Glenn-After-the-First-Time would have treated her mother to a spa day and lunch at a restaurant where waiters pulled out the chairs for you. They would have giggled through facials and shopped and enjoyed a whole day of pampering.

This Gloria, the broken one, reached for her mother's hand and squeezed it. "I want to be you when I grow up, Mama."

The iron-spined Sara bit her lip, her brown eyes welling with tears.

"*Mija*," she whispered. "Don't be me. Be you. And be happy."

"I'm not sure how," Gloria confessed, her own eyes filling. She'd cried more this last week or two than she had in the last decade, as if something had thawed inside her, letting loose a stoppered flood of tears.

"You listen to me, Gloria Rosemarie. Backbone runs in our family. It did not skip a generation," Sara insisted, her voice stern.

Gloria was the last in a long line of independent, steely, sometimes terrifying women. The last ten years had stripped her of any resemblance to her ancestors. She knew it had to be a terrible blow to her mother. To see her daughter lose herself to an unworthy man.

Bone-weary in this bright, cheerful kitchen, disappointment weighed heavily on her shoulders.

Who would ever want her like this? Why would someone big and beautiful and vibrant like Aldo Moretta want a crushed and damaged flower petal?

"Tsk-tsk," her mother clucked. "Enough of this pity party." She threaded her fingers through Gloria's long, unstyled hair. "I think it's time we make a change. Yes?" Sara was studying her with the critical eye of a professional.

Gloria patted her thick, shapeless mane. "Just like old times?"

"Yes, but with margaritas."

"Then absolutely yes," Gloria decided.

Her mother danced from the room. Music, bright and Latin, sounded from a wireless speaker near the refrigerator. It was a ritual they'd enjoyed a long time ago. Kitchen makeovers. Bonding. Music and laughter.

For the first time, Gloria felt like she'd really come home.

———

"Your good taste hasn't been damaged," Sara decided as she snipped and fluffed.

Gloria studied the picture on the incredible Pinterest board and swallowed hard. She'd begged her mother to choose a style for her, but Sara had refused. "You must get used to making your own decisions again," she'd said wisely.

Fortified by tequila, Gloria bypassed the safe shoulder-length styles and took her first big risk. She winced as inches of her dark hair fell to the warm tile floor. "It'll grow back," she reminded herself.

"You're not going to want it to," Sara predicted, rubbing a serum between her palms. "You will love this." Her mother worked the product through what felt like very, very short hair.

"Oh, God. What have I done?" Gloria groaned and reached for her margarita.

Her mother smirked without sympathy and drained the rest of her drink.

"Should you be cutting hair while under the influence?"

Sara snorted. "I do my best work with tequila."

Gloria laughed despite herself and gave herself over to her mother's ministrations.

"Okay. Time for the reveal." Sara handed Gloria the mirror handle. "New beginnings call for new hair."

The deep breath did little to settle her stomach. Her hair had been largely untouched over the last several years. Ever since Glenn had thrown a dinner plate at her for spontaneously cutting six inches off of her hair. *Women should have long hair. You look like an ugly little boy.*

She opened her eyes and took the first look at the new Gloria.

Her dark hair had lost its heavy length. Instead, it was styled around her face in a cloud of natural curl and volume.

"You look like Sophia Loren," her mother said with satisfaction.

Gloria reached up to touch it. "I don't look like me."

"You didn't look like you before," Sara countered, pouring more frozen goodness into their glasses.

Turning her head from side to side, Gloria admired the reflection. It was...perfect.

"I love it," she said, staring in the mirror longer than she had in years and *liking* what she saw.

"How do you feel about some makeup?" Sara tempted.

Makeup. Gloria had once loved all things cosmetic. She loved experimenting, making pretty. She'd done her friends' makeup for homecoming her junior year. Glenn didn't approve. She'd managed to hide a small stash of guilty pleasures from him for over a year before he'd found it and called her a whore for painting her face.

"Yes," she said, enjoying the spark she saw in her reflection. "And then let's go out to dinner."

Sara pushed the glass toward her. "We will Uber."

"Cheers." Gloria raised her glass, the smile stretching her face in unfamiliar and wonderful ways.

CHAPTER 7

She'd picked up her new phone to cancel at least a dozen times. It was a pity invite, she decided as she rolled out the pie crust with a panicked violence. "Harper felt sorry for me," Gloria told herself. Besides, her car was in the garage getting some of its rust removed and its brakes changed—thanks to her saint of a mother.

It was the perfect excuse to cancel. Of course, she could walk. It was only a couple of blocks.

"Gah!" Gloria swiped the back of her hand over her forehead in frustration, leaving a streak of flour behind.

Her mother was at work, queening around her salon, and she had the house to her self-conscious, terrified self. They'd gone to dinner in town that weekend, and it had been a mistake.

"Poor little Gloria Parker" had been on the lips of every patron as they smiled sadly at her. By the end of dinner, she'd felt like a zoo animal rescued from the wild where she was too weak to survive.

"Why am I even making a damn pie?" She wasn't going. She didn't know how to socialize. For all intents and purposes, high school sleepovers were her last real social experience, and she was quite certain none of that etiquette applied to a casual backyard barbecue. Though she couldn't help but wonder what Aldo Moretta's reaction would be if she hit him with a pillow.

She was definitely *not* going. The man left her tongue-tied, shy, and painfully nervous. The absolute last thing she needed right now was a crush on a man like that. Aldo's personality was as big as his barrel-like chest. Next to him, she'd fade away as she had with Glenn.

And she was good and tired of fading.

She draped the crust over the pie plate and spooned the filling into it, ignoring the way her hands shook.

The dream last night was still with her. Glenn, bursting into her room, murder in his eyes. He'd kill her in her mother's house. She knew it even when she'd woken up, sobbing and covering her face.

Too many times, it hadn't been a dream. The abuse—and worse, the fear—was engraved in her bones, woven into her DNA. She was a different person from the teenager Glenn Diller had claimed as his own.

Where was the girl who shoved Bobby Leinhart off Jamal Nguyen on the playground? The girl who'd argued with her English teacher for a full letter grade higher on her *To Kill a Mockingbird* essay? The girl who'd laughed and awkwardly flirted and sang?

Was she still in there? Or was she already dead?

In her head, she could still hear Glenn's hateful laugh.

She grabbed the wooden spoon out of the bowl and hurled it across the room. "Get out of my head!"

———

"I'm in love with your hair," Harper announced, opening the door before Gloria made it to the top step of the porch.

Self-consciously, she patted it with her free hand. "Really?"

She'd taken her time with the styling and with her makeup, and when she looked in the mirror, it wasn't the old Gloria she saw or the teenage, pre-Glenn Gloria. It was someone new.

"You look amazing," Harper insisted.

"Thanks," Gloria said, unaccustomed to compliments. "You look great too." It was the truth. There was an energy, bright and vivacious, that bubbled out of Harper even more so tonight than before. Gloria wondered if it was because Luke was home.

She followed her new friend inside and paused inside the door.

"Wait. Am I hallucinating?" she asked Harper, handing over the pie. Luke's living room and dining room were full of actual furniture.

"I don't know what happened, but I owe you big time." Harper's eyes twinkled. "The threat of having people over pushed him over the edge, and Luke went insane and bought out most of the inventory at Bob's Fine Furnishings."

Gloria followed Harper back down the hallway to the kitchen, which was now home to a new breakfast table and chairs. Luke Garrison himself was juggling side dishes from the fridge to the island.

"Apple pie and Gloria are here," Harper announced cheerfully.

Luke dumped his load and wiped his hands on his jeans before offering Gloria his hand. "Hey, Gloria. It's good to see you," he said. He was tall with military-short dark hair and hard hazel eyes. The ink on his forearm gave him the look of a badass, but it was the eyes hooded with a hurt that ran deep that made him irresistible. The long-term effects of grief, Gloria guessed.

She'd been cut off from the outside world but still knew the basics of his situation. No one would blame him for never

41

getting over it. But she hoped for his sake that Harper's presence was a sign that he was finally thawing.

"Where's my water?" A good-natured bellow sounded from the backyard.

"Where's my please and thank you?" Luke hollered back.

"Aldo." Harper grinned by way of explanation. "He's manning the grill. Claims Luke only makes charcoal burgers and blackened chicken."

Luke slung his arm around Harper's shoulder, and Gloria thought her new friend might split in two with happiness. This was not the same Luke Garrison who had mourned his way through life for the past few years. And it was beautiful to see.

If there was hope for him, maybe there was the tiniest scrap of hope for her.

"Water!"

"How about I take it out to him?" Gloria suggested. The way Luke and Harper were looking at each other, she was about to witness some NC-17 action.

Luke handed her two bottles and was making a beeline for Harper by the time the screen door closed behind her.

Aldo was behind the grill in shorts and a polo shirt stretched to capacity over that broad chest. His hair was still on the long side, curling at the ends. He stood with his feet braced apart as if ready to do battle with the meat on the grill. Everything about him from the muscled calves to the tattoos down his arms spoke of strength, power. A different kind than what Glenn had wielded against her.

"Did someone order a water?" she asked, praying that she sounded casual.

He tensed at the sound of her voice, and then a slow smile spread across his face as if he'd been waiting for this exact moment.

She brought it to him, every step that carried her closer to him feeling slower, heavier. The spring air between them thickened and blurred until she was standing in front of him and the rest of the backyard disappeared.

"Hi," he said softly. Then he leaned in, and instead of shaking her hand firmly like Luke had, Aldo brushed a kiss against her cheek.

"Hi," she croaked. She was lucky she didn't stutter and freeze to the space. But the spot where his lips had touched flared with the heat of the sun, guaranteeing that nothing would freeze inside her for a long, long time.

"You look great," he said.

"I…what?" She'd taken time choosing an outfit. Skinny jeans and a loose blue tank tucked into the front of her jeans and left long in the back. There were no more bruises to hide, and the leather wrap bracelets she'd added to her wrists, the heavy chandelier earrings she'd chosen, felt like a celebration of that.

"Your hair," he said. He took her chin, his touch achingly gentle, and turned her head from side to side.

Her heart rate kicked up at his touch. He hated it. He'd tell her she looked ugly. Or he'd lie to her, tell her she was pretty and not mean it. He wouldn't smile at her like that again. And she would wither up and die. *Okay, drama queen, slow your roll.*

"Brave choice. It works," he said simply.

Gloria felt her cheeks heat. It shouldn't matter what he said. But damn if his approval didn't feel really good.

"Thanks. My mom did it," she said lamely. God, how sad was it that she wasn't used to people being nice?

"So what do you think?" Aldo asked, pointing the tongs he wielded toward the house. "Luke's nesting, right?"

Gloria laughed, and it loosened her chest, allowing her to draw a free breath. "Definitely nesting."

43

"Harp seems good for him," Aldo predicted. "Maybe he's finally going to see that happily ever after."

"Let's hope there's one for all of us," Gloria said wistfully.

"Sweetheart, I can guarantee it," Aldo told her. He wasn't smiling, but the look in those warm brown eyes tickled her belly. This wasn't fear she was feeling. This was something entirely different.

CHAPTER 8

S o you're nesting now that you finally found a woman to tolerate you?" Aldo demanded, eyeing the apple pie that Gloria was cutting into neat slices.

Luke rolled his eyes and muttered "smart-ass" under his breath.

"Gloria, I think we're witnessing a real-life bromance," Harper said in a stage whisper across the picnic table. Night had fallen, casting the backyard into shadow. But to Gloria, the darkness felt like comfort, delivering with it a quiet kind of intimacy between them. There were no monsters lurking here.

Aldo shared the bench with her, and even though they weren't touching, she was very aware of his heat, his presence.

Luke's and Harper's joined hands rested in Harper's lap. Gloria felt a twinge of envy at the way they looked at each other. So much passed between them, not the least of which was longing, and she imagined the night would be an early one for their little party.

Would she ever find a relationship like the one across the table? Did she even believe in love?

"How's work going?" Aldo asked Luke. "You know, since you hired that horrible office manager."

Harper feigned a gasp of dismay and threw a piece of hamburger bun at him. Luke had hired Harper to manage the office of his contractor business.

"Work is going exceedingly well, and I hear the new office manager is a dream come true. A real hero," she insisted.

Gloria admired how relaxed and natural they all were, bickering back and forth. Meanwhile, she was tying herself up in knots about whether she should serve the pie. Was it her responsibility to offer it up since she brought it? Nerves. She was being ridiculous. It was a damn pie. Not a bomb to defuse.

"Anyone want a piece of pie?" she piped up.

"Yes!" came the unanimous response.

She served while Aldo shared a story about work. He was a structural engineer in a small firm in town. Gloria wasn't quite sure what a structural engineer did and made a note to look it up now that she had unlimited internet access. So much to catch up on. So many things missed out on.

Pie plated, Harper grandly suggested they adjourn to the firepit.

"Indubitably," Aldo agreed, pretending to adjust his invisible monocle. He carried his plate and Gloria's over to the fire. Was he doing it on purpose, being attentive? Was this interest or just being kind? Her mind was a whirl. Flirting, relationships. Gloria was so far removed from healthy social interactions that she couldn't tell if he was only being polite with his attentiveness.

"Oh my God," Harper moaned next to Gloria. "Heaven just exploded in my mouth. Will you teach me to make pie?"

"Yes, please, Gloria. Teach Harper to make pie," Luke insisted.

"I'd die a happy man if you would make me a pie a week," Aldo sighed from across the cozy fire.

There was that skitter of nerves again. Gloria wondered if she'd ever have a social interaction that didn't scare her out of her skin or turn her into an overanalyzing fool.

After pie came marshmallows, and Gloria basked in the praise at her perfectly toasted delicacies. Her father had taught her on a camping trip the summer before he left. At least she had that small piece of him.

"Hey, lover boy," Aldo called to Luke, holding his bottle aloft. "If you're done staring dreamily at your girl, I'm empty, and it's your turn to play host."

Gloria had watched Aldo throughout the night. He'd stuck with water until after dinner. This would be his second beer. Aldo Moretta didn't seem like the kind of man to overindulge in anything.

"Sure. No problem." Luke rose from his chair and reached for Aldo's empty. He tipped his friend's chair sideways and dumped Aldo onto the ground.

Gloria winced, waiting for his reaction, waiting for the quick rush of anger, the escalating retaliation.

But Aldo sat on the grass and laughed.

"Ladies, can I get you anything?" Luke offered.

Harper jumped to her feet. "I'll help you," she offered brightly. They hurried toward the house.

Aldo climbed gracefully to his feet, brushing the dirt from his shorts. He took the seat that Harper had vacated next to Gloria. "I give it ten minutes before they kick us out," he predicted.

"Well, it *is* a work night," Gloria said.

"I don't think they're worried about getting a good night's sleep," he said with a wink. "So how are things?"

"Things?" she repeated. Gloria ran a hand through her hair, still surprised at the length. She was suffering from nightmares of a reality she'd only just exited. She had no concrete plans, no confidence, and she wanted another piece of pie. But she was spending a spring evening under the stars with the boy from high school who gave her butterflies. "Things are pretty good."

"What's next for you?" he asked.

Stop the dreams. Remember what it's like to be a person. "I'm looking for a job," she blurted out.

"Yeah?" Aldo asked, looking interested. "What kind of a job?"

Gloria chewed on her lip. "I don't know. Something that makes me feel good. Something that lets me do something… nice." She laughed. "How's that for vague?"

"I'd offer you a job at my office, but I have a feeling designing bridge restorations and expense reports wouldn't be good or nice."

She wrinkled her nose. "Probably not." She'd once wanted to be in fashion or marketing. Something with color and beauty and fun. Though getting to stare at Aldo Moretta all day would be its own perk.

But she didn't want to be beholden to anyone. She wanted to earn a spot somewhere.

"You're staying around here, aren't you?" Aldo pressed. His tone and his warm brown eyes were serious.

She nodded, her earrings swinging against her neck. "Yeah. I'm staying."

That was one thing she wasn't going to let Glenn Diller take from her. Home.

CHAPTER 9

"Geez, don't let the door hit you," Aldo quipped as Luke slammed the front door behind them the second their feet hit the front porch. The look of love passing between the happy couple was hot enough to start a house fire, and Aldo didn't want to accidentally catch a glimpse of Luke's junk... again. They were close, but not *that* close.

"Where's your car?" he asked Gloria. "I'll walk you to it."

"It's in the shop. I walked."

"I'll drive you home," he offered. No way was he letting the woman who'd just walked out of a nightmare find her way home in the dark.

"Oh, I can walk," Gloria insisted.

"I know you *can* walk," Aldo teased, guiding her down the walkway to the street where he'd parked. "But if I drive you home, you're going to feel obliged to give me that last piece of pie, and, Gloria, there's something you need to know about me." He paused by the passenger door of his truck.

"What?" she breathed.

He wasn't imagining it—the air between them was charged. There was a connection being made. Whether it was natural or a side effect of the decade-long crush he'd had on her, Aldo didn't care. He reveled in it.

"I love apple pie for breakfast," he whispered.

She rolled her eyes. "You're ridiculous," she told him, but there was a smile behind her words.

"I'm ridiculous, and I'm taking you home." He opened the door for her and gave her his most charming smile. Legions of women had fallen for this. Well, maybe not legions, but a respectable number. They'd all been practice for the real thing. He'd been honing his weaponry, his skills, for this woman, this night. And he wasn't going to lose.

She took a step forward and hedged, second-guessing herself.

"Gloria, it's okay if you don't want a ride home. I'll walk you home, tell you you're the prettiest woman I've seen in my life, and make sure you get inside safely. We can drive or walk. The choice is yours."

She sighed. "Drive."

He ushered her into the truck and closed the door. *Aldo for the win.* Sliding behind the wheel, he started the engine. There was a part of him that didn't quite believe he had Gloria Parker sitting next to him. She'd been a pretty little thing in high school. All sweetness and sunshine. He'd looked more than twice. But the age difference meant a lot more back then. He was a senior, and she barely had a driver's license. By the time he'd decided it didn't matter, Glenn "Fuckhead" Diller had stepped into his place.

He'd thought about throwing his hat in the ring, but the one time he'd come close, Gloria had paid the price. Aldo never forgot that.

"So tell me what a structural engineer does," Gloria said, piping up over the low crooning of Blake Shelton.

Aldo grinned at her and made a left turn. "A structural

engineer designs structures like bridges and tunnels and buildings. We do inspections, some demo. We work a lot with contractors and architects to make sure what they're building isn't only pretty but sound."

"Wow. And you're in the National Guard too?" she asked.

He nodded. "We're deploying soon." In two weeks. Which was why he needed Gloria to know where he stood. He wasn't letting another decade go by without telling her how he felt. But tonight wasn't the time. She was still brittle, fragile. He'd watched her disappear into her head a half-dozen times tonight only to fight her way back. He admired the hell out of her for it. Enduring what she had and then making small talk around a picnic table was something a lot of soldiers couldn't handle when they came home.

"Oh," she said softly. "When?"

"Just over two weeks." He felt the twist in his gut when he said it. Before, picking up and hauling out had been inconvenient. But there wasn't much difference to him whether he was working his ass off at the office or in a godforsaken desert. He still had no one to come home to. That, to Aldo, made all the difference.

"Wow," Gloria breathed. "Where are you going? Are you nervous? When will you be back?"

He did the thing that felt most natural. He reached over the console and took her hand in his. "Afghanistan. I'm already anxious to come home. It's a six-month deployment."

"Six months?" she sounded upset, and it did something wonderful to his ego.

"Six months." He nodded. "Imagine where you'll be when I come home."

She sat quietly in the dark of his cab, eyes straight ahead. But she held his hand tightly as if she were afraid he'd pull away.

"Did you always want to be an engineer?" she asked, finally changing the subject.

"No. I wanted to be a ninja for a while. Then I moved on to a superhero. Then in kindergarten, I decided I wanted to be a dinosaur until my mom told me dinosaurs were extinct and I was a dumbass."

"No, she didn't!"

"Ina Moretta is a loud, mean woman," Aldo told her. "One time when Luke and I were kids—stupid kids—we were playing on the lake when it froze. Without adult supervision of course."

"Oh no," Gloria said, covering her eyes with her free hand.

"Oh yes. The ice broke, and I sank like a lard ass until Luke fished me out. But when Ma heard about it, she made me take ice baths for a week as punishment."

"She did not!" Gloria laughed.

"Okay, so maybe they were lukewarm baths, but still. The woman is a mercenary."

"I'd like to meet her someday," Gloria mused.

Aldo brushed his thumb over hers. "Say the word. I promise to stand valiantly between the two of you."

She laughed, the brightness of it filling up his truck, his chest. *Yeah, this is worth coming home to and not leaving again.*

He eased up to the curb in front of Gloria's mother's house. If she wondered how he knew where she lived, Gloria didn't ask. She slipped her hand out of his and fished the pie plate off the floor. "I believe this is your payment for chauffeuring me," she said.

He caught a whiff of the cinnamony goodness under the foil. "I think we should get married," he decided.

Gloria's jaw dropped, and then she laughed again.

"I'm serious," he insisted. "Just, maybe spend the next six months thinking about it, okay?"

"Yeah, I'll do that," she said, still laughing when she released her seat belt.

"Hang on," he said, sliding out from behind the wheel. He hurried around to her door and opened it. "You're engaged to a gentleman."

She stepped down onto the sidewalk. "I am?" There was a lightness in her words and in her eyes that sparkled under the streetlights, and Aldo couldn't think of anything he wanted more than to kiss her right then and there.

There was a low rumble behind them, and Gloria flinched. The light fading from her face was replaced with a flash of fear. Aldo turned, putting her behind him, and spotted a neighbor two houses down wheeling their trash bin to the curb.

He turned back, intending to rub the goose bumps off her arms with his big, warm hands. But when he reached for her, she took a nervous step back. "Sorry," she whispered, hunching her shoulders.

"Gloria." He said her name softly. "It's okay."

She gave a jerky shrug of her thin shoulders that broke his heart a little bit more. "No. It's not. And I don't know if it ever will be." Her whispered confession destroyed him.

"Sweetheart," he tried again. But when he saw her nervously swipe her slim fingers under her eye, he couldn't stop himself. She couldn't cry in front of him. He'd never give her a reason to, he vowed.

Slowly, carefully, he wrapped his arms around her and held her against his chest. She tensed against him for a second, and with a sigh too big for her body, she let go and relaxed into him.

"Have you thought about talking to someone?" he asked gently.

"I'm talking to you, aren't I?" Her muffled voice carried just enough annoyance that it made him smile.

"I meant a professional. Like a counselor, a therapist. Someone who knows what you're going through."

She was quiet for a long moment. "I don't have health insurance. And I'm not sure if I even have the words to talk about anything with anyone."

He wanted to fix it for her. Wanted to step in and solve every problem she faced. But that wasn't what she needed. Gloria needed to find out that her own two feet were steady, dependable.

"Everything is going to be just fine, Gloria Parker. You wait and see." They stood there under the night sky, and Aldo stroked his big hand over her back until her shivers went away.

CHAPTER 10

About time," Aldo said, tossing his duffel in the back and climbing into the passenger seat of Luke's truck. They were needed on base for the usual predeployment medical exam and a handful of briefings. The perpetually early Luke—Captain Garrison for the next day or two—was running twenty minutes behind and had a shit-eating grin that wouldn't quit on his face.

"I'm not that late," Luke argued, pulling away from the curb.

"No explanations needed. I can see from the stupid look on your face why you're late." Luke Garrison was getting some. While Aldo would, of course, rub it in his friend's face, he was happy to see Luke finally moving on with his life.

"You're full of shit," Luke shot back.

Aldo snorted and changed the radio station. "I've known you since I saved your ass from that beatdown in first grade. I know your stupid looks."

"And I still maintain that I could have taken those guys on my own."

"There were three of them, and they were in fourth grade," Aldo said dryly.

"Well, if you did *assist* me in that situation, I saved your ass from drowning in the lake when we were twelve."

Aldo shrugged. "I thought the ice would hold."

"We were grounded for all of January for that one," Luke recalled.

They chuckled. "Our moms were so pissed. So what does Claire think of Harper?" Aldo fished. Luke was a fucking underground bunker. He didn't open up easily. Or ever. Every once in a while, Aldo took a crowbar to his friend. Mostly to test the man's mental state. And partly just to screw with him. It was what guys did.

After a brief, stony silence, Luke crumbled like an origami crane. "She loves her. Thinks she's just what I need." That shit-eating grin was gone.

"Is she?" Aldo prodded.

"What I *need* is peace and quiet. Harper is anything but that."

Aldo laughed. It was Luke's fatal flaw, believing that what he needed most was to be left alone with his grief and regrets. If anyone could convince him otherwise, Aldo hoped it was Harper Wilde. "So why is she here?"

Luke shrugged, taking the ramp for the highway. "It started as a favor. The girl had no place to go and no way to get there."

Aldo knew the story. After a very bad day, Harper had coasted into Remo's parking lot on fumes and spotted Glenn Diller attacking Gloria. When Glenn had turned his fury on Harper, Luke had appeared and smashed the monster in his fucking face. Aldo's hand balled into a fist in his lap.

What he wouldn't give to have been the one to finally stop him.

"And then?" Aldo asked, keeping the conversation moving.

Luke cleared his throat. "Well, you've met her."

"I have." Aldo nodded. "Think she'll stay?"

Luke shook his head, his jaw tightening. "Nah. She's got things to do, places to go. Six months is a long time to ask someone you just met to wait."

"It's a long time to ask anyone to wait," Aldo reminded him. "She would, you know." Harper would. The way she looked at Luke, like that grumpy son of a bitch had invented vibrators, screamed the big L-O-V-E.

Luke scrubbed a hand over his chin. "I don't know if I'd want her to."

"Bullshit," Aldo argued cheerfully. It was fear that had Luke by the throat. Fear that feeling something for another woman would somehow lessen what he'd once felt for his wife.

"Kiss your mother with that mouth?"

"Where do you think I learned it?" Ina Moretta's vocabulary would make a trash-talking UFC fighter at weigh-in blush. Her mastery of four-letter words was legendary.

"Speaking of women," Luke said, suddenly chipper. "Harper seems to think you have a thing for Gloria."

Aldo let out a sigh through his teeth. "She's not wrong."

"You've always had a thing for anything with a nice pair of legs and big brown eyes," Luke pointed out.

"Where do you think I got my type?" It was true. Aldo had sowed his wild oats, expecting that high school crush to fade away into nostalgia. He'd dated. He'd fucked. He'd enjoyed the hell out of himself, all the while wondering where the connection was.

He'd found it, finally. Monday night with Gloria wrapped up in his arms under that lonely streetlight.

"So if you've been carrying this torch since high school, how is Glenn still alive?" Luke asked, knowing his friend so well.

Aldo automatically tamped back the reflexive burst of fury. It hadn't been his business. When she stayed, he accepted her choice. She wasn't his to defend and protect. "I ask myself that every day. The deployments made it easier to think about something else. Gave me something to focus on."

They'd also given him an escape from what happened the first and only time he'd done something about Diller. The price paid hadn't been his. And that haunted him to this day.

Aldo drummed his fingers on the roof of the truck. "I gotta say," he said, changing the subject. "I'm thinking about retiring. This is number four, and I want to make it my last."

"Really?" Luke asked, sounding surprised. To Luke, the guard and the deployments were what kept him going, kept him trudging one foot in front of the other.

"We've been doing this since high school. That's twelve years of packing up and moving out and hoping we come back after the job's done. I'm ready to stay put. I want to put more time into some engineering projects. And then I want to make a nice girl the next Mrs. Moretta."

"Jesus, Aldo." Luke sounded shocked...and a little sick. "When the hell did you decide all this?"

They'd enlisted together, trained together, deployed together. This was the first time Aldo's course had diverged from Luke's.

"About ten seconds after I found out Gloria moved out." It was the truth. It was time. Aldo felt it in his bones. He was ready to be a full-time civilian, a husband, maybe a father. It was time for the rest of his life to start. "Don't tell me you're not ready to hang it up."

"It's all I've got," Luke said quietly. "The guard and my business."

"You've got your family, and you could have Harper too if

you wanted. Come home to that sweet face every day and find out what trouble she got herself into? There's something to look forward to."

Luke's lips quirked. "She is trouble. I'm concerned about releasing her into the wild."

"She needs you." And that was what Luke needed most, someone who needed him.

"She needs her fucking parents, but they're dead. She's got no family. Just scars from all those years in foster care."

Aldo swore. He knew Luke well enough to know the man wasn't talking metaphorical scars. What was it with fuckers hurting women? "And you'd do anything to make it better, but you just don't know how to help," he surmised. Aldo was well acquainted with that brand of helplessness.

"Exactly." Luke gripped the steering wheel until his knuckles went white. "Fact is, I just don't have room in my life for her."

"You've got the room. You're just too chickenshit to make it." Checkmate.

Aldo had lived the last ten years in fear of doing something that would get Gloria hurt…again. And he planned to spend the rest of his life making sure no one ever hurt her again.

CHAPTER 11

I'm here because someone—a friend—suggested I should talk about…it. I've never been to therapy before. Am I doing it right? Ha.

I don't really know where to start. I mean, I know what happened. I know why it happened. But I really don't know if talking about it is going to help anything… It was ten years. How can I summarize ten years?

I'm living with my mom. It's temporary until I can find a job, a place to live. She bought all these books over the years about abusive relationships, the psychology of them, how to help, what not to do. She was studying up on how to help me when the time came.

My dad abandoned us. I get that I was hungry for strong male attention. I really get how slow and subversive the pattern of abuse can be. I was the lobster in the pot. I didn't know it was boiling until all my options were gone.

He was my first real boyfriend, and things were so…intense. I was a sophomore dating a senior. I was suddenly someone. He made me feel like I was the center of his world. And he was everything I needed. He slowly, systematically took the place of my friends, my family. He was so possessive and jealous, and I'm ashamed to say that, at first, I liked it.

I thought it meant he really cared.

He told me he loved me on our second date. God. Neither one of us knew what that word even meant. I still don't know what that word means. But now I know what it doesn't mean.

He hit me for the first time a few months into our relationship. It was the summer after he graduated. I don't know what set him off. Though I eventually became quite adept at predicting what would set him off.

He was so apologetic after it happened. He cried, said it was an accident. Promised it would never happen again. I could make him feel better by forgiving him. I had the power.

I didn't have the right lines or boundaries. I didn't know that hitting shouldn't be the line. Restraining, pushing, controlling, being disrespectful should be the line. But by the time he hit me, I was already so isolated. My mother and I were barely speaking. She couldn't stand watching me lose myself to this person. She woke me up the morning after Glenn hit me, put me in the car, and drove me to my grandparents' house for a "spontaneous visit."

I was terrified Glenn would think I left him. I called him as soon as we got there, apologizing. Telling him we were still good. I was so scared. I didn't know what he'd do.

He came after me. He brought me flowers. He picked me up and drove me home. My mother watched us pull away… It was like we were saying goodbye.

He didn't hit me again for two years. I thought we were in love. I believed that it was a one-time thing. He wanted me to drop out of school, said he couldn't stand me being around all those other people. He wanted me to spend all my time with him.

We were having sex, and it was getting rougher. Less…romantic. He would put up a fuss every time I said I was going to a football game or hanging out with friends. It got easier to give in. We'd fight. He'd grab me, leave fingerprints. Once he tripped me in front of his friends because he saw me talking to one of them. But it was always easier to accommodate him. I needed him. He made me feel special, important.

I'd never been everything to someone before, not even my mom...

She's so strong. So brave. Being just a mom wasn't enough. She wanted a whole, colorful life. That's not a statement on how she felt about me or my worth. I get that now. Being a mom wasn't enough for her, but I made being Glenn's girlfriend everything that I needed.

Things got worse after I graduated. All those old plans for college or fashion school or traveling? They were all gone. I remember everyone else in my class was talking about college applications and financial aid, and I was trying to perfect a fucking meatloaf recipe—sorry—because it was his favorite.

He got a job in the kitchen cabinet factory right out of high school. I moved in with him when I graduated. He made me miss the graduation party my mom threw for me. I was too busy unpacking my stuff in his trailer to see my grandparents and what few friends I had left.

It was around that time that I stopped being special. He had me at his beck and call twenty-four seven. He didn't need to pursue me anymore. He just needed to keep me locked away.

He timed me when I went to the grocery store or the bank, and if I was a minute later than I had been the last time, he demanded to know why. Who did I talk to? Who was I cheating on him with? Did I want to screw the guy behind the register? He broke my cell phone so I couldn't talk to anyone. He'd hide my car keys unless I was going somewhere I had permission.

He hit me again. Apologized again. Always apologizing.

His dad drank and beat his wife, so that was what Glenn did. He drank more, and things got worse. I couldn't anticipate his moods anymore. He liked that. Liked having me constantly tiptoeing on eggshells. One day, he didn't want to hear me speak.

The next day, he'd hold me down and choke me if I didn't say "good morning." He was in control over another human being.

He raped me once.

I left.

I went to my mother's and lied. I told her we had a fight. She didn't believe me. Mothers can see that kind of spiritual damage on their daughter's souls.

When he showed up at her house, I went home with him. I knew he would hurt her. He wouldn't just use that pain and intimidation on me. He would use it on my mother. And you know what? She would have fought back. She would have called the cops, pressed charges, and gouged that asshole's eyes out.

And that's why I went home with him. Because I wasn't her. I couldn't do those things. I deserved to be beaten and broken.

But I pictured it. I pictured what would happen if he spread his violence. And I started plotting. I started saving what little money I could. I stashed it in a tampon box. And I started envisioning a life without him. He cheated on me when he wasn't too drunk to get it up. I knew every time he came home smelling like sex.

He called me names, threw food at me, hit me when he remembered I existed. I started fighting back, pathetically. It made him laugh.

I was nothing. Less than nothing.

And I let it all eat at me until I would rather die than spend another night with him.

It took me years. Years. Life wasted. I'm twenty-seven years old, and I've never had a job or lived on my own. Hell, I've never paid taxes or had health insurance. I don't know what to do, where to go, who to be.

When I was sixteen, I had a plan, I had dreams. I knew what I wanted.

I can't even remember those dreams. What does someone do without dreams? The only ones I have now are nightmares.

CHAPTER 12

Aldo: How do you feel about lunch with your fiancé?

Gloria stared down at her phone and tapped her fingers on the keyboard of her mother's elderly laptop. It had been a week since she'd had dinner with Luke and Harper. A week since Aldo had driven her home. A week since he held her in the dark as she unloaded a decade's worth of tearful regret.

She'd convinced herself that Aldo Moretta wasn't in the market for a fixer-upper like her. He was just being kind. The man had a giant heart shoved into the confines of his expansive chest.

And now he was asking her to lunch. A pity invite?

"It's better than writing a résumé for a loser with absolutely no experience at anything besides baking pies and washing dishes," she muttered. Her résumé had her name at the top, her mother's address underneath, and nothing but a high school degree on it. She was rotating between shame and frustration.

Gloria: Lunch would be great. Where? When?

The response was instantaneous, and she wondered if he was sitting there waiting for her response.

Aldo: Meet me at my office in half an hour?

Half an hour? What was she going to wear? She hadn't even showered yet. Where was her deodorant?

"Shit. Shit. Shit," she muttered under her breath, and she dashed down the hallway to her bedroom.

———

Lewiscki and Moretta Associates—of course he was a partner—was housed in a yellow brick building on the far end of Main Street. It was a quick four blocks from her mother's house, and once Gloria had given up trying to dress to impress, she made it with a minute to spare.

She parked on the street and got out, looking at the glass front door and debating whether she should go inside. Her phone buzzed.

Aldo: Come inside. I'll show you my fancy corner office.

Gloria looked up and saw him grinning at her from the second-floor window. He waved. She waved back mechanically. *Just a pity invite. Don't get your panties in a twist*, she reminded herself.

She took the stairs to the second floor and hesitated for only a second or ten outside the Lewiscki and Moretta Associates door. "Oh my God. Just open the damn door, Gloria."

She did as she told herself, the metal handle cool to the touch, and walked into chaos.

It was an open workspace with desks and flat surfaces crammed everywhere. There were blueprint-draped work tables, desks buckling under computer equipment and files. Even the industrial gray carpet was camouflaged beneath ignored paperwork. Phones rang. Faxes beeped. And a dread-locked IT person dismantled a copy machine in the corner.

A woman with short, jet-black hair cropped close to her scalp swore at a huge computer monitor while an early twenty-something associate ran from the conference room lugging a laptop, tablet, and stack of files thicker than the entire Harry Potter series.

Aldo, the calm in the storm, approached.

Oh, God. He was wearing a tie. The sleeves of his sexy as hell button-down were rolled up to his elbows. She really liked that look. A lot. Attraction was a vague memory to her, but the biology of it was waking the hell up inside her, setting her sensible underwear on fire.

"Hey," he said, giving her that dimpled grin, his brown eyes warm on her face.

"Is this a bad time?" Always apologetic. Always worried about being an inconvenience.

"Son of a motherfucking shit-ass mess!" The Halle Berry look-alike slammed a palm down on her table. Gloria jumped.

"You fix it?" Aldo asked pleasantly.

"I fixed it," the woman said, rolling her shoulders, showing off toned arms that spoke of hours spent in the gym.

"Gloria, this is my partner Jamilah Lewiscki. She's a struc-tural engineer by trade and a database engineer for funsies," Aldo said, making the introductions. "Jamilah, this is Gloria, my lunch date."

Jamilah, unburdened from whatever thing she'd fixed, threw up a friendly wave. "Gloria, do me a favor and get this guy out of my space so I can get something done."

Infinitely mature, Aldo stuck his tongue out at her. "You're gonna miss me when I'm gone."

"Probably won't even notice," Jamilah sniffed. She snuck Gloria a wink that said otherwise.

"Come on," Aldo said in Gloria's ear. "I'm starving."

"What about your corner office?" Gloria asked.

Jamilah snorted. "That's what he's telling his lunch dates these days?"

Aldo grinned and waved grandly toward the U-shaped command center in the back, wedged in between a restroom and the water cooler. It was the only spot in the entire office that maintained any semblance of organization.

"Fancy," Gloria said.

"Yeah, only the best of the best for us managing partners," Aldo said, flashing her that devastating smile.

"Don't forget you've got a three o'clock," Jamilah said without looking up from her screen.

"Yeah, yeah," Aldo said as he guided Gloria toward the door. "Let's go before they decide they can't live without me."

It was the quintessential kind of spring day that had bodies waking up after a long winter and feeling that burst of energy that came from the yellow sun warming too-long-cold skin. Gloria fell into step with Aldo, and together they walked down the block. She was careful to keep her distance. She'd cried on the man only days ago and was nervous that his inherent goodness would have the same effect on her again.

There was a café here. New and wheatgrass-y from the looks of it. Gloria had never been there before. But there were a lot of places she'd never been before.

Aldo held the door for her. "Quick pit stop," he promised.

Gloria stepped inside and clasped her hands in front of her while Aldo bulldozed his way to the cashier. "To go for Moretta," he called out.

The older woman behind the register patted her silver

bun. "As if I didn't know who you were," she purred under huge red Sally Jessy Raphael glasses. "Your man friend here comes in for lunch three times a week, honey," she told Gloria.

Her man friend? Adorable.

Gloria pressed her lips together to keep from laughing.

Sally Jessy hefted a huge paper bag with handles over the counter. "Threw in a few of those gluten-free Danishes you're so fond of," she said in a stage whisper.

"Estelle, I'm in love with you," Aldo professed, doling out cash.

Sally Jessy Estelle sighed dramatically. "That's what you tell all the seventy-somethings. Enjoy your date," she said to Gloria, wriggling her painted eyebrows.

He put his hand at the small of Gloria's back and led the way back outside and to his truck. She breathed a sigh of relief when she didn't spontaneously burst into tears of self-loathing and hopelessness at his touch.

"I hope you don't mind that I ordered for you. I got a few sandwiches and soups that you can choose from."

Thoughtful, not pushy, she decided.

"That's great. Thanks," she said.

Aldo popped the bag into the back seat of his pickup. "Do you have enough time for a picnic at the lake?"

Jobless, homeless, prospectless, she had all the time in the world.

"I do if you do," she said.

"You just made my day." He skirted the truck and opened the passenger door for her.

A five-minute drive later, Aldo pulled into the recreational area parking lot at the lake. He led the way down to the lakefront and, ignoring the picnic tables, steered her toward a small copse of trees. He unfurled the lightweight blanket under his arm and gestured for her to sit.

Gloria was glad she hadn't gone for a skirt or sundress. The red capris—another gift from her mother, whose horror at her pathetic wardrobe was justified—were just right for picnicking. Aldo plopped down next to her, energy in every movement.

She liked being around him, liked the level of enthusiasm he had for everything. It was like being close to that spring sun. Energizing.

He unpacked the bag. A huge salad with grilled chicken for Aldo "My Body Is a Temple" Moretta. Two sandwiches, a cup of split pea soup, and a small Caesar salad for Gloria to have her way with. The Danish, a cherry and a cheese, looked delectable.

He unscrewed the lid of a water bottle and handed it to her. "Did I do okay?"

There was no planet on which Aldo would need encouragement. But today, nerves shimmered over his sexy surface.

"You did great," she told him. Gloria shoved aside the need to wait for permission and helped herself to half of a chicken salad sandwich and the soup.

They settled into a companionable silence, enjoying the food, the sun, the glitter of the water in front of them.

"Did you go to the Plunge?" Aldo asked her, referring to Benevolence's annual fundraiser. The Not-So-Polar Plunge happened in April every year because the water was still damn cold by that time.

She shook her head and covered her mouth, suddenly not sure how to eat around other human beings. Most of her meals the last few years had been alone. "No, I didn't."

"Heard Luke almost got into it with Linc Reed," he said conversationally.

"Do they still have that rivalry thing going?" Gloria asked, taking a sip of water. She remembered vaguely the year that Luke and his then-girlfriend, Karen, had broken up. It had been the talk of the halls at Benevolence High. Linc had moved in quickly, and Luke had taken exception.

They talked in fits and spurts about Aldo's job, the college time he'd squeezed in between deployments, about Benevolence in general. He was a charming gossip, never salacious, only entertaining. Gloria couldn't help but admire how utterly confident, how comfortable, he was.

Aldo finished his half-gallon of vegetables and leaned back on the heels of his hands, his legs crossed at the ankles, the picture of relaxation.

"I had an ulterior motive for asking you here," he confessed.

Gloria stopped midchew on the respectable, gluten-free baked good. "You did?"

Did he want her to water his plants while he deployed?

For fuck's sake. Could she maybe attempt to stop being a doormat in her own mind? Maybe the man wanted to make out with her. Damn it. She should have shaved her legs.

He was watching her, eyes squinting in the sun. She liked the crinkles by his eyes.

"I'm leaving in a week," he began.

Gloria felt her face fall. It was stupid to be attached to him. They'd spent a handful of hours together. They weren't even friends. But that didn't change the fact that she was bitterly disappointed that he was leaving.

"Do you need someone to water your plants?" she offered lamely.

"I don't—Actually that would be really great. If you wouldn't mind."

Great. Something to add to her résumé. Plant sitter. Awesome. Oh, God. What if she killed all his plants?

"Sure." There was more enthusiasm in summer school attendees than she put in that one word.

"But that's not what I was going to talk to you about. I'd like to date you, Gloria."

The glug of water she'd just taken to wash down the bitterness of disappointment came back out on a cough and ran down her chin. Gently, he mopped her face with a napkin.

She swallowed what was left in her mouth. "I'm sorry. I don't think I heard you correctly."

He grinned. "That's not the reaction I was expecting. It'll be a fun story to tell our grandkids though."

Gloria's head was spinning. "Back up a minute?"

He nodded amiably. "Sure. See, I've had a crush on you for a touch over a decade. And I didn't make my move for a variety of reasons. But I've never stopped crushing on you. So when I get back in six months, I'd like to take you out."

"You want to go on a date with me in six months?" She couldn't date someone! She couldn't date Aldo. She didn't even know how to be attracted to a man, let alone date, be in a relationship.

"I can see I've swept you off your feet." He reached for her hand and gave it a reassuring squeeze. "The choice is yours. If you think I'm a hideous beast with no redeeming qualities, say the word, and I promise to go back to admiring you from afar."

What was there to admire? Was there some kind of victim fetish that existed out there in the dark corners of the internet? Gloria made a mental note to check.

"I don't think you're a hideous beast," she assured him. "But I'm not sure why you'd want to date damaged goods."

He squeezed her hand tighter. Not so that it hurt or made her give in but so that she could feel his strength and take comfort in it. It was nice. "I know *why* you think that, sweetheart, but I hope you know I could never think of you that way," he said softly. The gentleness in his tone, his touch, brought the burn of tears to the backs of her eyes. "That's why I'm not begging for a date now. You just got your freedom back. You need to build a life that works for you. And when I come home—if you'll have me—I'm going to fit myself into that life."

"Did you forget to take some kind of medication today? Maybe hit your head?"

With his free hand, Aldo cupped her cheek. The touch was so tender, so sweet, that Gloria felt her heart do a belly flop right into her stomach. "Here's the thing. I don't want to terrify you, but you're stronger than you think, Glo. You can handle the truth. I think you might be the girl I've been waiting my whole life for. But I want you to see who I see. I want you to remember what it's like to be you."

She closed her eyes and leaned into that big, warm palm. "I don't know if I can," she confessed.

"I believe in you, Gloria."

"What if I'm different than you think?" she whispered.

He shifted closer to her. "Then be different. Be you. There's so much good inside you. No one can take that away from you."

"I can't just fall into another relationship, Aldo," she breathed. "I can't get carried away and lose myself again."

"I know. I also know you don't believe me when I say I know you won't. But it's the truth. You're never going back there, Gloria. You're stronger than that."

He believed that. He honestly believed she wouldn't make another mistake that had already cost her so much of her life. She could see it in his eyes, so earnest. He was so careful with her. But that didn't mean he would always be. And it didn't mean that she was as strong as he thought she was.

"One date when I come home," he pressed. "I couldn't

leave next week without telling you how I feel. Without asking you."

He was pressuring her, but in a way so different from Glenn.

"What do you want me to do while you're gone?" she asked.

He shook his head. It was the wrong question. It was the question of someone accustomed to not mattering.

"Do what you want. Whatever you need. Find a job. Go to school. Travel. Date. I'm coming back, and I'm coming back to ask you out. But you need that time to yourself. Take it. Find yourself. Be yourself."

She nodded, wondering how he could be so sure, why he wasn't demanding a promise to him right here and now. Because he was Aldo. He had faith.

"One date?" she repeated.

"It's all your decision, Gloria. Your choice. I won't pressure you. I don't want you like that. I'm not going to step on you making a life for yourself. I want to be a part of what you build. Okay?"

She nodded tentatively. In six months, she would have a first date with Aldo Moretta. She would be different than she was today.

"Okay. And I'll still water your plants."

CHAPTER 13

"Y ou look great," Harper said with enthusiasm.

"Thanks," Gloria replied automatically. Her friend had reported that same fact four times now, and she wondered if Harper were even more nervous than she was. She'd dipped into her slim stash of cash for the outfit. Red espadrilles, navy cropped pants with white blooms everywhere, and a white short-sleeved sweater. An investment in her future. If she had one.

Harper chattered on about floral designs and the industry, waving her hands in excitement.

Gloria thought about the Gloria Who-Left-Glenn-After-the-First-Time. Where would she work? She wouldn't be terrified of job interviews. She'd sweep into them, utterly fashionable and perfectly poised, with a confidence that convinced everyone she was the best fit for the job. That Gloria would be important. She'd fill an essential role. Indispensable, her annual reviews would say when they were delivered with a hefty bonus.

"Claire says that Della and Fred are the nicest people in the world, and they're not necessarily looking for experience but someone with enthusiasm," Harper continued, bringing Gloria back to her current reality.

"Enthusiasm," Gloria repeated. Her thoughts had been a blur set on repeat since lunch with Aldo two days before. The man wanted to date her. But not the present her. The six-months-into-the-future her. What if six-months-into-the-future Gloria was no different from the current "poor little Gloria Parker"? What if she were a cabaret singer in Reno? What if—

"I have a good feeling about this," Harper insisted, drawing her from her thoughts.

The owners at Blooms had reached out to Gloria at the behest of Luke Garrison's mother, a part-time florist, about a job managing the flower shop. Both Fred and Della were looking to free up more of their time to start traveling. The RV was waxed and gassed up, ready to go for the summer. But they needed someone who could handle the day-to-day of the business.

"Do you really think I can manage a business?" Gloria asked. There was no way she was getting this job. They would have to be insane to hire her.

"Do I look like an office manager to you?" Harper teased. "Every job is the same. You learn the people, and you learn one task at a time. Boom. You're a vital, contributing employee."

Gloria wasn't quite as confident as Harper.

The interview request had come when she was minutes away from applying for a job at a fast-food drive-thru. To be fair, Gloria didn't have any experience there either. She would rather surround herself with flowers than hurried people throwing orders and money at her through a greasy window. But she'd do either and be damned grateful.

Physically, she was healed. And she wasn't going to get anywhere emotionally until she could become a productive member of society.

Blooms was housed in a cheery glass and wood-shingled building on the outskirts of town. A riot of colorful flowers crowded the front windows, giving the place the look of an exotic forest. It even *smelled* beautiful.

Gloria's espadrilles froze on the sidewalk. "I don't think I can do this." It was too pretty, too busy, too much. She had no experience. Two weeks ago, her goal in life had been not to take another punch. What the hell did she know about lilies and… hell. She couldn't even name another flower off the top of her head. She was going to vomit on the sidewalk. That would be a stellar first impression.

Harper snapped her fingers in front of Gloria's face. "Hey! You tell that voice to shut the hell up."

"What voice?" Gloria asked, turning her back on Blooms, not able to bear the disappointment.

"The voice that is telling you you're worthless, you're nothing, you'll never make anything of yourself. Blah blah blah."

"How did you know?" Gloria asked. She'd started talking to herself a while ago for company. Pathetic. She knew it. But if she'd suddenly lost the ability to keep her thoughts to herself in the company of others, she needed more than one appointment with a therapist.

"I've had those voices," Harper said simply. "Spoiler alert: they only tell lies."

Gloria clenched her hands into fists and crossed her arms. "How do you get them to stop?"

"What would you do if someone came up to me right now and told me I had a stupid, ugly face?" Harper asked.

Gloria couldn't imagine anyone telling Harper that…and living to tell the tale.

"You'd defend me or tell me it wasn't true," Harper steamrolled on. "Talk to yourself like you're your own best friend, and those other voices will leave you alone."

Huh. Easier said than done.

"Just try it," Harper insisted, sensing her reluctance.

"Do you really think I can do this?" Gloria asked, watching a man in jeans and flannel struggle through the door under a massive pink and ivory bouquet.

"We're having a baby girl," he announced to them and practically skipped to his car in the parking lot.

"Congratulations," Gloria called after him.

Harper laid a hand on Gloria's shoulder. "You're asking the wrong question. Do you *want* this? Do you want to know who's having a baby girl and who got in trouble for forgetting a birthday? Do you want to be part of every graduation, anniversary, and funeral in this town? Do you want to make beautiful things and help people give beautiful gifts?"

She didn't have to think about it. "Yes."

"Then get your tiny ass in there." Harper steered her toward the door. "I'll wait for you out here, and we'll go to lunch to celebrate."

"What if I don't get it?"

"Then you had your first job interview of your life, and the second one will go even better."

With a small nod, Gloria straightened her shoulders and marched up to the front door. "I'm getting a milkshake," she told Harper.

"That's my girl!"

Inside it was cool and fragrant. There was music, soft and spa-like, filtering through speakers tucked away in corners. Natural wood shelves lined one wall, filled to the brim with greenery, vases, and knickknacks. There were ready-made wildflower bouquets in buckets next to the register, the perfect impulse purchase. Larger, more impressive arrangements were on display in a cooler against the wall. Tall houseplants made up a jungle of sorts in the middle of the tile floor.

A buxom woman wearing reading glasses on a chain tottered out of the back with a clipboard in one hand and an iPad in the other. Her blond hair was streaked gray, and she wore chunky silver earrings.

"Gloria! So great to meet you officially. I'm Della."

Gloria recognized her in the way that one small town resident recognizes another resident they've never actually met.

Mechanically, Gloria extended her hand. "Thank you for having me, Della."

"Let me show you around," Della said. "This is the sales floor," she said, waving her arm grandly at the colorful chaos around them. "We do a lot of spontaneous foot traffic business with the ready-made bouquets. But most of our business is special orders, birthdays, funerals, weddings, apologies, etc." She waved to the register. "You'd be responsible for answering the phone, ringing up sales, updating SKU information in the POS. How are you at social media?"

"Oh. Um. I have Pinterest."

"You'd need to learn Facebook and Instagram. Screw Twitter. Buncha whiners. My nephew told me I can run ads based on geographical location through Facebook, so I want that to start ASAP."

Ads? Geographical location? Instagram? Gloria was starting to hyperventilate.

Della led the way past the register and into the back room. If it was chaotic in the front, it was tornado aftermath back here. Work surfaces were littered with cut stems, chunks of green Styrofoam, pieces of ribbon. Bruised petals were carelessly strewn in and around the two trash cans. Shelves held a clutter of supplies, shears, and greeting cards.

"This is where we assemble most of our arrangements," Della explained. "We had a wedding this weekend, and we're still cleaning up. In there"—she gestured toward a big metal door—"is our cooler where all the fresh blooms are kept. Deliveries come in the back and go straight into the cooler. Sometimes you might need to whip up an arrangement if none of our floral designers are available."

Gloria nodded, not sure if she should be taking notes.

"For this position, you'd be doing a little bit of everything. We need someone who will coordinate deliveries, handle orders, potentially yell at suppliers when the orders come in wrong." Della led the way into a narrow hallway off of which were a small bathroom, an equally sparse kitchen, and an office in the midst of what looked like a purge. "We use QuickBooks. Willing to train, of course."

Gloria wasn't one hundred percent sure what QuickBooks was. And she was pretty sure the only thing she was qualified for was sweeping the floors here.

"Let's grab some coffee," Della decided, leading the way back to the kitchen. She poured from the pot into floral mugs and gestured at the rickety table in the corner.

Gloria hesitated and then grabbed two sugars. She was more of a tea person, but she could manage a coffee if it made a better first impression. She took the seat opposite Della. The woman measured her with cool green eyes. Gloria sipped. Della nodded as if she'd decided.

"So the job is yours if you want it."

Gloria blinked. "But you haven't even asked me any questions."

"Look, I don't like the whole 'show me your résumé' song and dance. None of our employees came from a flower background. I hire people, not experience."

Score one for Gloria.

"I've never had a job, and I don't know what QuickBooks

is," Gloria said. It was suddenly imperative that she be completely honest.

"Let me tell you a story, Gloria. I was married before. Twenty-two. An idiot. Married the first guy who made eyes at me. That guy turned out to be an ass. Took me two years to get out with a black eye, a broken arm, and a baby on my hip. I drove all night, heading east, and I landed in this Podunk town in Indiana. I dug out change from the floormats of my third-hand car just to get a cup of coffee at a diner."

Della paused, staring down at her mug fondly.

"Mabel, the blue-haired, pack-a-day smoking owner, took one look at me and gave me a job on the spot and a room to rent. She changed my life. And I promised myself that someday I'd be in the same position to do something for someone."

Gloria looked down at the worn tabletop. Shame flushed her cheeks. "I don't want charity," she said quietly.

"Good. You shouldn't." Della nodded briskly. "This is a chance to learn, to work really damn hard, to earn your way. So if you're not up for that, then no hard feelings. But if you do say yes, you'll start tomorrow, and I promise you we'll teach you everything you need to know and someday you'll be in the position to give someone else a chance."

Gloria pursed her lips, feeling emotion tighten her throat.

"Are you ready to work your ass off? Be proud of yourself? Learn a daisy from a daylily?"

Gloria nodded. "Yes. Yes, I am."

Della cracked a smile that lit up her whole face. "Good. I'll see you at seven tomorrow morning."

"Really? Are you sure? I mean I don't know half the things you want me to know."

"You can learn them, can't you? And I can be patient until you get your feet wet."

Gloria was out of her chair and hugging Della in a show of spontaneous affection. "Thank you! Thank you! I'm going to try really hard to make sure you never regret this," she promised.

Della chuckled. "Don't be late. Oh, and wear comfortable shoes."

Harper was sunning herself on a stack of mulch bags in the parking lot when Gloria skipped over to her.

Gloria nudged her friend's foot, and Harper peered lazily over her sunglasses. "Well?"

"Let's get lunch. My treat!"

She'd worry about how the hell she was going to learn it all and make sure Della never regretted her decision later. For now, she was going to drink a milkshake and figure out what to wear to work tomorrow.

CHAPTER 14

Gloria: Who's got two thumbs and a job at Blooms? This girl!

Aldo reread the text for the seven hundredth time and clicked on the picture she sent with it. She was grinning and pointing at herself with both thumbs. He doubted Gloria saw anything special in the picture, but it was there. That joy radiating out of her reached out and grabbed him by the throat every time he looked at it.

He'd wanted to get her a job, wanted to help her on her path, but the confidence she built by doing things on her own was even more gratifying.

"Get off your phone! You're surrounded by loved ones, dumbass!" His mother's shout, fortified by the better part of a bottle of wine, dragged Aldo back to the present. He was at his and Luke's going-away dinner, a two-family tradition since their first deployment.

Aldo tucked his phone back into his pocket. "Sorry, Ma."

"You're a *Candy Crush* addict," Ina complained, shifting into pot-and-kettle mode. His mother spent more time playing games on her phone than she did gardening, drinking, and sleeping combined.

He'd beaten her once at *Words with Friends*, and she'd thrown her phone out of the car window in a bad loser rage, earning a $200 fine for littering from Deputy Ty.

Claire, Luke's mother, joined them at the table. Her eyes were red-rimmed.

It was due only in part to their deployment. Luke had just announced that Harper, the woman Claire hung all her hopes on, was leaving town for a new job. Their relationship was ending when Luke and Aldo got on that bus in the morning. Disappointed in his friend, Aldo had whispered "chickenshit" under his breath at the announcement, and his mother had kicked him in the shin.

He hated that Luke was too scared to make a commitment. Hell, Luke had already made a commitment. He was too much of a wuss to see it through. He and Harper were living together, were working together, and between the two of them had accidentally adopted two shelter dogs. They were *in* a damn relationship.

It was strange, thinking that as they boarded the bus tomorrow, Luke's chance at happiness was ending while Aldo's was just beginning.

"Well, I guess this is another goodbye," Claire sighed. She reached for Aldo's hand, squeezed. "You come home safe to us." It was her traditional send-off. Claire and Ina had divided the mothering all through childhood and the teenage years and had never gotten out of the habit even though their boys were now men.

"I promise," he said. And he meant it. Aldo wasn't just coming home to work and family. He would be coming home to Gloria. If she'd have him. That alone was making him anxious about leaving. Deployments were difficult, generally boring, and sometimes terrifying. Knowing that there was someone waiting for him this time? Well, he was wishing it was all over already.

He could see himself coming home to her. Climbing off the bus and finding her in his arms, a flash of color and sweetness.

Aldo shifted in his seat. He wished Gloria was here tonight. He needed to see her one last time.

"Ladies, I think I'm going to call it an early night."

————

The second pebble hit its target and the third. He didn't have to toss the fourth because the light in the room came on. A soft glow behind white lacy curtains.

"Aldo?" Gloria's voice was sleepy.

"Shit. I'm sorry. Did I wake you?" He was standing in the middle of her mother's azaleas at 11:00 p.m. like a crazy person.

"A little," she yawned. "How was your dinner?"

Harper or Claire would have told her.

"You weren't there," he said.

She gave him a sleepy smile and settled her chin on her hand. "I wasn't invited."

"You should have been. I mean, I should have invited you." Aldo scrubbed his hand through his hair. He wasn't doing this well. He was usually more suave, less desperate.

"Do you want to come in?" Gloria offered.

"Uh, can you come out?" Aldo alone with Gloria in her bedroom was probably not the best way to give her space to build her own life. Resisting those sleepy smiles and whatever flimsy pajamas she had on would be easier outside than next to an inviting bed.

She gave him a grin and slid her ass onto the windowsill. He moved forward, crushing plants under his feet, and caught her against him as she slid out.

Dear God in heaven. She was wearing tiny cotton shorts and a camisole thing. Her hair was tousled around her face, and in the moonlight, he could see she didn't have a stitch of makeup on. He'd never seen anything more beautiful in his life.

Grimly, he set her down half a step away from him. They were not at the point in their relationship where he was comfortable sporting wood around her. Not yet at least.

"I expected you to use the door," he teased.

"I expected you to use the phone," she shot back. Sleepy Gloria was spunkier. As if the veils between who she was and who she'd been told to be were thinner.

"Sorry." He grinned without a hint of real apology. "I came to…give you my house key." He wrestled his key ring out of his pocket. He'd bought a dozen houseplants this week for the express purpose of having Gloria in his house weekly while he was gone. He loved the idea of her being there, surrounded by his things while he was half a world away.

"I kind of thought you were kidding about the plants," Gloria told him, accepting the key.

"I'm totally into plants. Plants make oxygen." *For the love of God, stop talking, Moretta*, he told himself.

"How often do you want me there?" she asked.

Every damn day. "Once a week should be good." At least he hoped. He was pretty new to this "having plants" thing.

She shivered and crossed her arms over her chest. Aldo couldn't help himself. He closed his hands over her upper arms and rubbed warmth into them. "Is this okay?" he asked softly. He needed her to know that everything regarding her body was her choice.

"Yes." Her response was breathless, and even in the dark, he could see the look of wonder in her brown eyes. He wanted every touch to be beautiful for her. To erase one by one the hurts, the scars, the fears.

Any other girl he'd be reading the signals as pro kiss. He'd feel confident about making his move, smoothly of course. But Gloria Parker wasn't just any other girl.

"I should probably go," he said, continuing to rub her arms. Everything about her was so small, delicate. He wished to God that he could be here to watch out for her. To witness her transformation back to who she was.

"You know, I was thinking," Gloria began, taking a step closer. She was looking up at him with mischief in her eyes.

If he didn't get out of this flower bed in the next ten seconds, he was going to do something stupid that he promised himself he wouldn't.

"What were you thinking?" he prodded. Promises be damned.

"If we're going to go out on a date when you come back, shouldn't we make sure that we're…you know"—she gave a little shrug, a tilt of her head—"compatible."

"Compatible?" he parroted the word back to her.

"Imagine a six-month buildup and then we have our first kiss."

He nodded, imagining exactly that.

"And it sucks."

He blinked. "Excuse me. Aldo Moretta doesn't suck at kissing."

"Well, I wouldn't know that, now, would I?" Gloria teased. She looped her arms around his neck, bringing them body to body. His arms went around her reflexively as if they knew exactly where she belonged.

"I can't have you worrying about a kiss for six months."

"I was hoping you'd say that."

She met him halfway, on her toes in the middle of a bed of spring flowers. And when those soft, soft lips found his, he heard music.

His body revved to life like it had been waiting for this exact moment, this exact kiss, to finally, finally live.

He brought his hands to her face, cupping her cheeks while he savored, sampled. When her fingers tightened on his collar, when she shivered closer to him, he fought the urge to press her against the house and take.

She'd had enough taking. It was his job to give. She opened her mouth beneath his, and he tasted her, gently, thoroughly. Her knees buckled, and damned if his own legs were a little unsteady. The innocence, the eagerness, of her mouth nearly drove him to his knees. He wanted to touch her, to love her, to worship her.

"Are you cold?" he asked, pulling back a breath.

There were goose bumps on every inch of her skin.

She shook her head, all heavy eyes and soft smile. "What's the opposite of cold? My vocabulary seems to have deserted me."

"Hot. Very, very hot." He kissed her again. A little harder, a little more breathlessly. It was just a kiss, but his cock acted like she'd stripped naked and begged him to take her. He wanted her so badly it hurt. Aldo knew he'd spend the next six months taking this memory out and admiring it every five seconds or so.

"Yes. That's what I am," Gloria decided, settling back on her heels.

He wouldn't push her any further. She'd given him too much already. And he was grateful, humbled, fucking leveled.

"So do you think there's some chemistry there?" he asked. There was more chemistry between them than a Mentos and a Diet Coke.

She grinned, flashing him that white-toothed smile. "I think I might need to dust off my biochem books and study up on what we have here."

He wrapped her in his thick arms and pulled her close.

"I can't wait to come back to you, Glo."

She rested her cheek on his chest. "Come home safe, okay?"

"Promise."

"You should get some sleep," she insisted, stroking her hands over his chest.

He'd rather stand here all night doing this. Slowly, reluctantly, he released her. She looked thoroughly kissed, with mussed hair and swollen lips. "Should I tuck you in?" he suggested wolfishly.

"We'll see how our first date goes."

Aldo shoved his hand through his hair. "Uh, I just realized. I don't have a spare key…"

Gloria's laugh sounded like a fucking choir of angels to his ears.

She handed him the key back. "Why, Mr. Moretta, did you make up an excuse to see me?"

"Six months is a long time," Aldo told her, thumbing over her lower lip. "I needed to see you one more time."

"Hmm."

"I'll leave the key under the mat on the front porch for you."

"Okay. Thanks for…stopping by." She grinned at him, and all was right with the world.

He took a step back to prevent himself from grabbing her again and tripped over a pink flamingo. It crunched under his foot.

"I'll buy your mom a new one," he promised.

She was laughing now.

"Hey, one more thing," he said, picking his way carefully out of the flower bed.

"What's that?"

"If you date…"

She cocked her head, listening.

"Just try not to fall in love."

CHAPTER 15

I got a job, and I kissed a man.

I know. I know. Before you say it, I can't jump into another relationship. I read the books, remember?

I got the job through my membership with the Domestic Violence Survivors Club. I know I should feel grateful. But I'm tired of being "poor little Gloria Parker." I want to be more...or less. Just Gloria Parker.

Will that ever happen? Will people ever look at me and not think about Glenn Diller?

I'm working my ass off, and it feels good to be needed and to exercise my brain. But it feels...surreal. Like at any moment, I'm going to wake up on that ratty mattress in that stinking trailer. I'm still having the dreams. I don't know if they'll ever go away.

Glenn's gone. Hopefully for a long time. He never made bail, likely won't get out for years. But I still feel like his shadow is following me everywhere. Why can't the Gloria I was with him disappear too?

I know I should be patient. But I have so much time to make up for. How much more time am I going to lose to him? Why can't I just snap my fingers and be better?

Why couldn't I drag Aldo Moretta through my bedroom

window that night? He's gone. Six months. I need those six months to decide if I want to have a relationship with him. I already know I do. But which Gloria is that? The battered victim? Poor little Gloria Parker who needs to be protected from life? Or a me I haven't met yet? Who's calling the shots?

I see the way everyone looks at me. I haven't done anything to change their minds about me yet. I can't be defined by Glenn anymore. I can't define myself by Aldo either. There. Happy?

I have a beautiful, kind, sexy man who wants me. And I'm not allowed to want him back. Glenn keeps ruining everything...or I keep letting him.

The abuse wasn't the problem, not the big one. It's the echo of it. In the moment, I felt like I won when he hit me. I pushed him. I made him lose control. Afterward, he was sorry, so sorry. For a while anyway. I had the power. But there's nothing healthy about a violent power struggle. And now there's this echo of that cycle in me. Like it's all I know.

A delivery driver was yelling at someone on the phone this morning, and I flinched like it was me. I flinched like I was going to take a hit. Della saw it. She looked...not disappointed but sad. Like maybe I'm stirring up her own echoes.

Glenn had me convinced that I was responsible for his every mood. Is that true? Can that be real? Isn't it narcissistic to believe I was the reason behind everything he ever said or did? Am I responsible for how other people feel?

I hate that I don't know who I am without him.

I think "poor little Gloria Parker" bothers me because that's how I see me. And I don't know how to see me without someone else in the picture...

Work is good. Hard. Terrifying. I don't want to disappoint anyone. I'm still half convinced I'll fail. My friend told me to talk to myself like I'm my own best friend. Which is ironic, considering I started talking to myself for company years ago. But I didn't realize Glenn's voice in my head is me too. That I can change those words.

I can change that voice. When I remember. When I can take a step back and remember that it's not the truth whispering around my brain.

I guess what I'm saying is I'm still lost. Still scared most of the time. Still lonely. I don't know how to be a part of anything. Aldo's gone, and I worry about him. National Guard. Afghanistan. Bad things happen to soldiers every day. I know we're not together, and I know I can't hang my happily ever after on him, but can I handle it if something happens to him? Can I handle anything? Everyone's working really hard to build this safe, happy bubble for me. My mom, Harper, Della.

But I can't help but wonder if I can survive without the bubble.

So that's where I am. Grumpy, confused bubble girl.

CHAPTER 16

The two dozen white lilies seemed funereal to Gloria, but that was exactly what Mrs. Nicklebee ordered for her fancy annual sorority reunion tea and pastry party centerpiece. Claire Garrison had done a lovely job making the arrangement pretty and fun with twists of greenery and baby's breath. But as a whole, it still said RIP to Gloria's thinking.

The customer in question bustled through the front door, chatting animatedly on her phone, her synthetic auburn wig clinging lifelessly to her shoulders. Cursed with low thyroid numbers, she had a different snazzy wig for every day of the week. Some were better than others.

"Of *course* I'm making mojitos," she said in a huff.

A lifetime ago, Mrs. Nicklebee had taught Gloria's Sunday school class. But it was likely she had no recollection of Gloria as she'd faded from existence, a shadow of her former self.

"Oh!" The woman's eyes widened when she spotted Gloria behind the register. "I have to call you back, Flo." Unceremoniously, she disconnected and dumped the phone in her purse. "Hello there, Gloria!"

Okay, maybe Mrs. Nicklebee *did* remember her. Perhaps it

had been her stirring performance as donkey number two one Christmas Eve?

Mrs. Nicklebee cocked her head. "How *are* you, dear?" she asked, her tone dripping with sympathy.

Or perhaps it was that everyone in all of Benevolence knew that Gloria had spent the last decade getting knocked around.

Gloria forced a cheery smile. "I'm just fine, Mrs. Nicklebee. Aren't your flowers lovely?" She slid the vase closer and stuffed her hands in the pockets of her bright green apron.

"Of *course* they are," Mrs. Nicklebee crooned. She whipped out her husband's credit card with long-practiced skill. Mrs. Nicklebee had never had a job in her life either. She claimed running a childless, petless household with a part-time house-keeper was work enough. Mr. Nicklebee either enjoyed having his wife home or was too terrified to voice his opinion. Either way, he spent his free time "yes, dearing" her.

"I hope you know we're all rooting for you." Mrs. Nicklebee beamed at her. "It's never too late to turn things around."

"Thank you," Gloria said, feeling both humbled and humiliated. She swiped the card forcefully.

"Have you heard from that unfortunate Glenn since his arrest?" Mrs. Nicklebee prodded.

Gossip was a second language in Benevolence, and everyone spoke it fluently. With shaking hands, Gloria tucked a shallow cardboard box under the vase for Mrs. Nicklebee's short drive home and wondered if she could sink behind the counter and lie on the floor until the woman left.

"Mrs. Nicklebee! I hope you like your lilies!" Claire, angel disguised as a part-time floral designer, appeared at Gloria's elbow. "Are you using your ivory tablecloth?"

Gloria took the opportunity to duck into the back room, her cheeks warm with shame.

Of course, it wasn't any protection from Mrs. Nicklebee's stage whisper. "I think it's lovely what Della did, giving poor little Gloria Parker a job."

The stool next to the work table protested when she dropped down on it in a huff. Impatience niggled at her. How was anyone ever going to see her as anything else but "poor little Gloria Parker"?

She heard the chimes of the front door and breathed a sigh of relief knowing that Mrs. Nicklebee had fluttered away to wreak havoc on someone else's life.

Claire poked her head into the room. "You okay?"

She was tall and lean with work-roughened hands and a soft smile. Her salt-and-pepper hair was worn in a dramatic pixie cut that suited her to a T. She was also incredibly kind without being condescending.

"Thanks for stepping in," Gloria said, studying her fingernails and wondering if she should take up chewing them to help cope with the feelings that bubbled up within her and threatened to overwhelm.

Claire pulled up a stool next to her and stretched her long, denim-clad legs. "I didn't want you knocking Mrs. Nicklebee's wig off her head."

Gloria's eyebrows lifted. Claire's assumption that she'd turn to violence instead of bursting into tears cheered her considerably. "You weren't worried that I'd curl into the fetal position behind the register?"

"It took backbone to leave. It took backbone and more than a bit of recklessness to want to confront him." Claire picked up a thick-stemmed peony. "You're not some dainty blossom waiting to be crushed, honey. And eventually people will see that. Be patient with them…and yourself."

"I hate being a victim." The confession took Gloria by

surprise. Apparently opening up to a therapist meant she'd be releasing the kraken to unlicensed listeners too.

"Then don't be," Claire said lightly, jabbing her with the stem. "Be beautiful. Be fun. Be busy. Be excited. Be you. Everyone else will eventually catch up. You just have to give them something else to see."

"You're a pretty smart advice giver, Claire."

Claire rolled her eyes heavenward. "Would you *please* tell my children that? They insist on learning everything the hard way."

———

Gloria decided to take Claire's advice and get busy. She tackled the back room, determined to restore order to the supplies and tools. With every shelf righted, every cubby organized, she felt calmer. The stainless-steel work tables were next, doused with spray and polished until they gleamed. The half-dozen pairs of shears were collected and hung neatly on the pegboard that appeared to have been abandoned some months before.

She gathered up discarded blooms—peonies and spray roses—scattered about from the centerpieces Della and Claire had worked on that morning and she made her first official bouquet. It was chaotic and ever so slightly misshapen, but she liked it. Things didn't have to be perfect to be attractive or interesting. She tied it with a shiny ribbon and, after the slightest hesitation, added it to the ready-made arrangement trough without asking for permission first.

Her phone buzzed in her apron pocket, and she fished it out.

Harper: Lunch with me and Soph at the diner?

Gloria considered.

Gloria: Can you guarantee no one will refer to me as "poor little Gloria Parker" within earshot?

Harper: Solution: Sophie and I will talk really loudly so you can't hear anything else.

Gloria: Good enough for me.

She let Claire know she was taking her lunch and made the two-minute drive to the diner. "Give them something else to see," she reminded herself before walking in the front door. It smelled of hot roast beef sandwiches and french fries. The floor was the required black-and-white checker pattern, the booths requisite red vinyl. It was packed. Tables were hard to come by during the lunch rush.

Sophie, with her dark hair tied in a high ponytail, waved to her from the back booth. Gloria slid into the red vinyl next to Harper.

"Gloria, I don't know if you've noticed," Sophie began. "But our lovely friend Harper is still here."

Gloria looked from woman to woman. "What am I missing?"

"She was going to leave town when Luke deployed," Sophie said. "Didn't she tell you?"

At the mention of the deployment, Gloria found herself back in her mother's flower bed, reliving the most amazing kiss of her life. God, she missed Aldo, and she wasn't even sure she had the right to.

Harper grimaced. "I'm not used to having actual friends, so I'm not great with the communication."

That made two of them.

Sophie dropped her head back and released a dramatic sigh. "Okay, so Harper and Luke got together because I, a genius, manipulated them into pretending to have a relationship. Of course, per the aforementioned genius, *I* knew full well that Luke wouldn't be able to resist a hot blond who cruises the kitchen naked—"

"Not true. I was wearing underwear," Harper cut in.

"Mostly naked," Sophie corrected. "Fake relationship became real. But these two yahoos thought that the best thing to do would be to part ways when Luke left with his unit. I know, so stupid."

"You're a jerk," Harper laughed, clearly unfazed.

"Fortunately, my mule-stubborn brother—Luke, not James, since there are two—came to his senses and demanded—"

"Asked," Harper corrected.

"Whatever. Begged Harper to stay." Sophie stretched both arms over the back of the booth and looked smug. "The bottom line is, I'm a genius, and Harper and Luke are in a relationship."

"I feel like a slow clap is called for," Gloria said.

Sophie pointed at her. "You're funny. I like that about you."

Well, at least there was *some* part of her she hadn't allowed Glenn to destroy.

"Now that we're all caught up on my love life," Harper said dryly. "How's work going?"

Gloria realized Harper was talking to her. She, Gloria Rosemarie Parker, had a j-o-b. The rush of pleasure at the realization was swift, potent.

"It's going well. Claire and Della have been very patient with me." She had a lot to learn, enough that it was still overwhelming. But Gloria had a glimmer of hope that she'd be able to hold her own…in a year or two.

They ordered—an iced tea and tuna melt for her—from Sandra, the redheaded waitress/proprietress, who only gave Gloria the "aw, poor girl" look for a second. Once the food arrived, they slid into a comfortable banter about work, kids, and town gossip.

"Heard Mrs. Nicklebee was excited to make a purchase from you," Sophie said, snagging a french fry off Harper's plate.

Gloria resisted the urge to make a face. "She seemed to like her flowers," she said, taking a bite of tuna to prevent herself from having to comment further.

"You grew up here," Sophie said after a gulp of her diet soda. "You know everyone feels entitled to everyone else's business."

"I'm hoping that someone else's business will interest them soon," Gloria sighed. She wondered how interested people would be to know that she'd kissed Aldo, that she had a tentative date with him when he came back. Would they think she was crazy? He was crazy?

A threesome, two men in business casual khakis and polo shirts and a woman in a flowing maxi dress, took stools at the counter. Gloria recognized the woman as Kate Marshall from the town council and owner of a mortgage company.

The man in the pale pink polo that hugged his beer belly hung up his phone and tossed it on the counter in disgust. "Well, Merle's hip is officially broken."

"This is a disaster," Kate grumbled. "The man's been chairing the Fourth of freaking July festival for thirty years. Who the hell are we going to find this late in the game?"

Gloria perked up, openly eavesdropping now. Harper opened her mouth to say something, but Gloria shushed her. She had been an organizer in school. She'd once loved the neat and tidy coordination of tiny details into one big, cohesive picture.

She'd once clearly been a nerd, Gloria realized.

"I sure as hell don't have time," Combover announced.

"We don't even have three months," Kate lamented. "Who's going to volunteer to step into this mess? The 5K, the parade, the carnival, the fireworks. We're screwed."

The Gloria Who-Left-Glenn-After-the-First-Time would be involved. She'd be a volunteer, a doer, an organizer. She'd champion causes and lend her resources to support the community at large. She'd be on boards and hosting functions, making a difference.

Gloria rose as if pulled by puppet strings. "I'll do it," she announced loudly.

Conversation in the diner came to a screeching halt.

Sophie's bite of sandwich fell out of her mouth and onto her plate.

CHAPTER 17

He had sand in every fucking crevice. To top it off, the sand was mingling with the sweat that flowed from a bottomless, salty well, creating a kind of exfoliating slurry that Aldo knew from experience would take more than a week's worth of showers to get rid of.

Afghanistan. Seven thousand miles from Benevolence. From his house. From his mother—that part wasn't so bad. His job and his friends. The rocky landscape bounced heat back off the ground like a convection oven, cooking everything on its surface. He'd get used to it—mostly. He always did. But as a first lieutenant, part of his duty was to help his unit acclimate.

This stony slab of desert was about as far as you could get from the comforts of the United States. Not only was it a combat theater with swarms of insurgents hoping to at least get a shot at any foreign "interloper," it was also hot as balls and riddled with opium, and the education level peaked around first grade. But over the years, he'd learned to embrace the discomfort. It made going home all the sweeter.

He pushed through the tent flap and angled himself toward his cot. It was a cozy setup with fourteen other soldiers crammed under the musty canvas.

"Hey, LT," Private First Class Scotty Kettle greeted him, opening one eye on the cot next to Aldo's. He was stripped down to briefs with a battery-operated fan blowing on his head. At nineteen, fresh out of high school, it was the kid's first deployment.

Aldo grunted a greeting and toed off his boots. He yanked the blanket back on his own cot. He always checked for spiders. After his first encounter with a camel spider the size of a dinner plate, well, he never took any chances.

He stripped off his shirt and pants and flopped facedown on his spider-free bed.

He'd been up for thirty hours straight, starting with a stint in the southern guard tower, flowing into a briefing with the base's Afghan interpreters, and ending with a briefing and firearms training with the Afghan National Security Forces.

That was their primary mission. Training and advising the local security forces to be able to handle whatever the insurgents threw at them. Glorified babysitting. But he was proud to see the strides made since his last tour.

Luke—Captain Garrison here—had different responsibilities. Personnel. Briefings out the ass. Dealing with the higher-ups.

Aldo preferred his own. He liked getting dirty, liked getting to know the locals. He was a buddy and a shoulder when needed and the man screaming in your face to push harder when the chips were down. More babysitting.

"Rough day?" Aldo asked Scotty.

"It's fucking hot, sir."

"Wait until August," Aldo said cheerfully. Sympathy never accomplished what preparation and white-knuckled determination did. "Missing home?"

Deployment could be boiled down to this: mind-numbing

tedium punctuated with a fear for your life that you could taste. It took homesickness and magnified it into an obsession that some never recovered from.

He could hear the hard swallow. "Little bit."

"You'll be back before you know it. Swimming in pools, kissing pretty girls, smokin' ribs."

"Weird to think that it doesn't all stop just because we're here," Scotty said.

Aldo thought about his mother heading to bingo. About Jamilah kicking ass on job sites and in conference rooms. About the butts on the stools at the diner and the cold beers poured at Remo's.

While he worked his ass off and wrestled with spiders and boredom here, his mother's cholesterol went up another five points, and Gloria was smiling smiles that he'd never see.

"You got a girl at home?" Aldo asked, already knowing the answer.

"Yes, sir. Mandy. We're engaged."

Nineteen and engaged. Nineteen and spending six months avoiding indirect fire. Nineteen and responsible for keeping his unit alive. *They just kept getting younger.*

"Congratulations. What's the first thing you're going to do when you get home?"

He listened to Scotty wax poetic on his mama's potato salad and Mandy's pretty smile.

The first deployment changed things. Not just in the man—or woman—but in every relationship they had back home. Seeing the slice of the world that most Americans were lucky enough to never know existed changed the DNA of a person.

Scotty would go home, God willing. But he'd be different from the kid who got on that bus. Aldo hoped Mandy was the accommodating type.

"She'll be waiting for you when you get back. Probably already has a wedding dress picked out," Aldo predicted. He didn't know Mandy from Eve. But what Scotty needed right now was hope. And maybe Aldo could use a dose of it too.

Aldo closed his eyes and thought of Gloria. She'd be at his house this week in his inner sanctum. He could picture her in his bedroom. Hell, he'd put two of his new plants on his dresser just so he knew she'd have to go inside. He wanted her there, more than he could say. It was purely selfish.

He could see her. That short, sassy hair, her bright smile, letting herself into his house with a key.

He purposely hadn't given her a way to contact him. She had so much living that she was entitled to. He didn't want to get in her way, roping her into some weird long-distance relationship. No, he wanted her. He wanted her strong and confident with six months of decisions she made herself between them. He'd fit himself into her life any way she'd let him. But after that kiss in the dark...well, he was feeling real hopeful that she'd be willing to make some serious room for him. Like dresser-drawer, key-to-the-house room.

He dropped off to sleep, thinking about Gloria sitting on the chair on his front porch, smiling and waiting.

CHAPTER 18

The key was hot in her hand, its ridges digging into her palm. Gloria clung to it, running her thumb over the cuts, using the sensation to tear her focus away from the envelope in her bag.

Lord only knew why she'd brought it here, to this tidy bungalow with its welcoming front porch, its neat trim work, its subtle hints of masculinity.

Aldo's house. She'd be safe here, Gloria thought, mounting the steps one at a time as if approaching the altar of a church. With reverence, with hope, and the slightest taste of fear.

She opened the screen door and slid the key into the lock, not wanting to be observed skulking about his front porch. There was enough talk around town about her. Maybe she'd gone a little far in giving Benevolence something else to see besides a broken, battered woman. But there was no turning back now.

She was officially coordinating the town's Fourth of July celebration.

And in small-town America that served up a large percentage of its populace to the nearby National Guard unit, well, she couldn't afford to screw it all up. There was nothing bigger in Benevolence than its homage to the country and its patriots.

Gloria had been feeling fairly confident—or was that delusional?—in her ability to coordinate it all.

And then the letter arrived.

The envelope stamped with the telltale *Mailed from a state correctional institution* mark. She turned the knob and pushed open the heavy wood-and-glass door.

He'd gone for light hardwood throughout. Original, Gloria guessed by the scarring. Battered but beautiful. The walls were a pristine white that, if given the chance, she would change to hunter green or a slate blue. The living and dining spaces were open to each other, bisected by the staircase. There were plants crowded on end tables, perched on the fireplace mantel, and crammed onto the built-in shelves.

Gloria didn't know a ton about taking care of living things, but she assumed that plants needed light more than books and magazines. She stepped up to the aloe plant on the mantel. It was still in its brown retail pot, a dinner plate shoved underneath to catch excess water. A quick spin of the pot revealed the price tag.

The plant next to it, a small Boston fern, still bore its identification marker in the soil.

She examined the other plants in the room. Had Aldo purchased an entire garden center's worth of plants just to give her something to water?

The thought made her smile. It wasn't so much underhanded as opportunistic. And dare she think it? A little romantic. She'd offered to water his plants after all. Had he really wanted her in his house that much?

Considering the possibility gave her a dark thrill that propelled her up the L-shaped staircase in search of his bedroom. There were three bedrooms on this level. A lot of room for a bachelor. Gloria found the master at the back of the house with a wall of windows overlooking the backyard. The furniture—a bed, a dresser, and an oversize chair—was Aldo-esque. Sturdy, masculine, but still friendly, she decided, perching on the soft mattress. Eyeing the pillows, she thought about Aldo Moretta, her past crush and potential future boyfriend, laying his head there.

He'd hung photos on the walls in here. His mother, him and the Garrisons. One of him and Luke shirtless and laughing in some desert. Both men were excellent physical specimens. Both were mugging for the camera. But only one of them had her pulse kicking into gear. Gloria wasn't sure if her libido was coming back to life or if it was rusty and confused from disuse. She shouldn't be having these feelings, that quickening, that honeyed slide into attraction. It was too soon. She didn't *really* know him. Hadn't she vowed that she'd never make that mistake of falling too fast again?

With reluctance, she turned away from the photo. There were more plants here, stacked like mismatched socks on his otherwise orderly dresser. Aldo had wanted her in here. Wanted this connection to her. Whatever his reasons, Gloria needed it too.

She slipped off her shoes, pulled the offending letter from her back pocket, and settled back against Aldo's pillows, his scent rising up around her. A protective shield between herself and what waited for her inside the envelope. She didn't want to open this in her mother's house. Not in that sweet sanctuary. Gloria wouldn't invite Glenn and his evil into that space. Here, she was protected.

She slid her thumb under the tab and ripped the envelope open like the tearing off of a bandage. The handwriting, so terrifyingly familiar, leapt off the page with its intended message: hate.

You owe me and you will pay.

When I get home, you'll never forget your place again.

She swallowed hard against the fear and bile that rose in her throat. "He can't touch me," she reminded herself, pressing her face into Aldo's pillow. "He can't ever touch me again." But the words didn't ring true. There were too many ways for the system to fail her. Too many ways for Gloria to fail herself.

"Get a grip," Gloria muttered. She forced herself to sit up and look at the letter. She was here, and he was miles away, behind bars. Nothing was wrong in this moment besides the fact that he could still touch her with his poison. Venom through ink. She could feel him in the room with her.

"Read it again," she told herself.

Steeling her spine, she read the words again. Reminded herself where she was, where *he* was.

Sobriety hadn't done Glenn any favors. He was still a warped, miserable monster. And he blamed her for it all. But he was wrong. She had already paid for her mistakes. It was his turn.

Glancing around the room, feeling Aldo's presence, Gloria breathed deeply. She couldn't put another man between her and Glenn. No. It wasn't healthy. But maybe she could put the spirit, the essence of Aldo Moretta's faith in her, in that craggy, terrifying void.

She swiped at the tears that had slipped unnoticed from the corners of her eyes and reached for her phone. "Hi, it's Gloria Parker. Do you have a minute to talk today?"

———

Ty and Sophie Adler's house was bursting at the seams with a barking dog and laughing toddler. Ty, in a T-shirt and gym shorts, met Gloria on the front stoop.

"I'm sorry." Gloria apologized on automatic. "I didn't realize it was your day off. We can talk later." She made a move to back away, to stop inconveniencing him.

"If I didn't have time to talk, I wouldn't have told you to come on over," Ty argued good-naturedly. "Now, come on inside so my wife and I have to pretend to be human beings in front of company."

He held the door for her and waited until she tentatively stepped across the threshold. This wasn't a matter she wanted to bring into the man's home. It wasn't something she felt like she could or should share with Sophie. They were new friends. New friends didn't dump abusive letters from psychotic exes on each other in the early phases of friendship. They talked about nail polish colors and buy-one-get-one deals at the grocery store.

"Hey, Gloria," Sophie called from the kitchen over the shrill of toddler. "I made some lemonade. Want a glass?"

Cold lemonade on a throat scorched from bitter emotion. "That would be great, thanks," Gloria called back.

The source of the giggles rocketed out of the kitchen and threw himself at his father's knees.

"Daaaaaaaad!" Josh Adler was five hundred pounds of energy packed into the wiry build of a three-year-old. He favored his father with dirty-blond hair and a dimpled chin. But it was all his mother's mischief that danced in his bright eyes.

Ty hefted his son high, expertly missing the turning ceiling fan by inches. Sophie breezed into the living room, pretty in leggings and an off-the-shoulder top. She handed Gloria a tall glass of lemonade garnished with a wedge of lemon and sprig of lavender and pressed a borderline indecent kiss to her husband's mouth.

The irony of wild child Sophie Garrison settling down with ultimate good-guy-with-a-badge Ty was amusing enough to bring a smile to Gloria's face. Love could heal, Gloria decided, watching the three of them glow together as a unit.

The pang of longing hit her hard, square in the heart. Would she ever have an ounce of that happiness? That belonging? Would she ever have a family? A man who looked at her the way Ty looked at Sophie?

Embarrassed, Gloria looked away. One of the throw pillows on the couch moved, then barked. And she realized it was a tiny dog…with couch stuffing hanging out of her mouth.

"Damn it, Bitsy," Sophie yelled.

"Damn it, Bitsy," Josh repeated.

"Nice goin', Soph," Ty said, juggling Josh into his mother's arms. "Why don't you take our future felon here and make yourselves scarce?"

"Come on, Mr. Parrot," Sophie sighed, toting Josh up the tidy little staircase. Bitsy followed on Sophie's bare heels.

"Step into my office," Ty said, opening his arm toward the couch. "I assume this has something to do with Glenn Diller?"

Gloria nodded and sat on the cushion that hadn't yet been eaten by the dog. She pulled the letter from her purse and held it for a moment. She was so used to hanging on to her shame, her secrets. It was hard to turn that off. Hard to break open and share that shame.

"I got this in the mail last night." She handed the envelope, the shame, over to him.

Ty read it, his eyes going cop cold.

"There's nothing you can do about it, is there?" Gloria sighed. She'd known. But that didn't mean she wasn't pissed.

"There's no specific threat," Ty said diplomatically.

"He tried to kill me. He spent the last decade beating the life out of me." Gloria couldn't quell the red rush of fury that swept through her body.

"The law's the law," Ty said, bravely stepping into her anger. "I'm not saying it's right. And I'm definitely not saying that he has the right to keep on torturing you. You need a personal protection order. We can turn letters like this into a crime."

"And the law will do what the next time he threatens my life?" Gloria demanded. *Nothing. They would do nothing.*

"Not much," Ty admitted. "But every brick you add to this case, every piece of evidence keeps him away from you."

"Why is it my job to prove that he's a monster?" She collapsed back against the cushion. "Why does it fall on me to fight to be safe?"

"I'm fighting with you, Gloria." Ty's eyes were serious. "I'm not going to let him anywhere near you ever again. But I have to operate within the law. So why don't you come on down to the station tomorrow, and we'll start the paperwork. I'll do what I can, I promise you that."

Gloria nodded numbly. It wasn't enough. She wondered if anything would ever be enough as long as Glenn Diller was still alive. Would she ever feel confident in her safety?

"Mind if I hang on to this?" Ty asked, tapping the letter against his palm.

"Knock yourself out."

CHAPTER 19

"Move that ass, Private," Aldo bellowed as a freckled white guy from Omaha, Nebraska, chased fruitlessly after Corporal Talia Williams, a woman with seven inches of leg and two deployments on him. "Move! Move! Move!"

He cracked a grin from his vantage point—a cobbled-together lifeguard chair made by a bored maintenance crew—as the private took a nose dive into a muddy trench that Williams vaulted like a gazelle.

The cheering from the tire flip zone caught his attention, and he pulled out his field glasses to watch Luke hefting a truck tire that came to chest height. "Nice job, Captain," Aldo announced through his bullhorn.

All around him, men and women challenged themselves with physical feats of strength. Gritted teeth, dirt and sweat mingled on skin of every color. Accented "fucks" and "son of a bitches" rose up from the desert floor.

Shared suffering, he thought with satisfaction. It cemented relationships, built teams. These soldiers had one another's backs by the nature of their deployment. But sweating through the dusty desert duty, the physical discomfort of deployment, missing everyone and everything that was important "back home" forged a different, deeper bond. They were brothers and sisters in a camo-colored, duct-taped family that battled both boredom and life-and-death situations.

Aldo took this connection as seriously as he did the rigorous National Guard training. To him, a good soldier didn't only know how to tear down and rebuild their M-4. A good soldier loved the unit, thrived on the discomfort, and pushed all the harder because of it.

He set the example that he needed his team to live up to. Strength, positivity, loyalty. A whistle blew, and a cheer roared through the ragtag crowd gathered at the finish line. O'Connell, a long-legged, battle-tested Irishman whose credits included amateur mixed martial arts titles, crossed the finish line six feet in front of the next closest competitor as he'd been favored to do.

Toward the end of the requisite thirty minutes of rest for the winner, the chant began.

"Mor-et-ta. Mor-et-ta." The crowd increased and the chanting grew louder. This was their version of fun. A half-mile obstacle sprint in eight-million-degree heat under the unrelenting sun.

Aldo had a title to defend. Once every month or so during deployment, he organized the course, and he challenged the winner to a rematch. And he won. Always. Not because he was the fastest or the strongest. But he never let the possibility of losing enter his stubborn mind. He believed in victory.

His athleticism was well-honed, his body toned and trained for performance. It was as much a part of him as his loyalty. He was fast, strong, and ruthless. Characteristics, capabilities that served him well in all areas of his life.

It was his job to be the best, to set the example.

He crossed the hundred yards of dust and rocks, rolling his

shoulders, stretching his chest as he went. O'Connell met him with a grim handshake. There were no trophies at stake. Just pride, which, to Aldo, was worth more than any award.

Second Lieutenant Steph Oluo gave them both a nod. "Gentleman," she began grandly into the megaphone. "Once through the course. First one to cross the finish line wins. Any questions?"

There were none. Neither competitor wanted to waste their oxygen on words.

The crowd, half exhausted from twelve-hour shifts and the other half just getting ready to begin another monotonous day, picked their favorites, alternating between cheers and trash talk.

He wouldn't change a damn thing.

Aldo went through the course once more in his head. It was a circle, ending where it began, but between start and finish was a half mile and six obstacles. Aldo gave his quads one final stretch, feeling the muscle fire up under the strain.

He toed the dirt line with his boot next to O'Connell and let the crowd noise fall away. He could hear his breath, his heartbeat steady in his head. Instead of a pistol start, they went for drama, and two NCOs chucked lit flares into the dirt. Aldo shot off the line like a bullet. He was a big guy. Speed didn't come naturally. It came through constant hard-fought battle.

O'Connell was snapping at his heels as they rounded the first turn. Aldo's body warmed and sang with the pace. His hands carved a knife-edge swale through the sweltering desert air, his arms pumping like a metronome. The Jeep tires were first. Two sets of tires, two by two. Aldo lifted his knees and jogged through them, fueled by his competitor in his peripheral vision.

They cleared the tires at the same time, taking off into dead sprints toward the over under over, a pair of five-foot walls sandwiching a low crawl. He easily cleared the first wall, but the rocky desert floor was murder on his knees in the crawl. The pain motivated him.

Taking a sharp stone to the palm, Aldo pulled himself out from under the netting a second after O'Connell.

He made up time scrambling over the second wall and let his legs eat up the distance between them.

They hung together, neck and neck, swapping for the lead, never more than arm's length from each other. O'Connell's high school athleticism was showing, but so was his youth. His breath was coming in sharp heaves as he pushed himself into the red zone. Aldo would wait him out, make his move at the end when the twentysomething was gassed.

"You gonna puke?" O'Connell groaned as he heaved himself over the first sawhorse.

Aldo jumped it and the second one with gazelle-like grace. "Nope. You?" He took great pride in the fact that he didn't sound winded.

"You're playing with me, aren't you, LT?" O'Connell gasped. He landed hard and came up running.

"I want you to feel that you're doing well," Aldo said conversationally.

"I really hate you, LT."

Aldo laughed and launched himself at the last obstacle between them and the finish line: a ten-foot wall with ropes. He ignored his rope, running straight up the wall, and just when gravity kicked in, his fingers closed over the top. He pulled himself up and over and dropped into a crouch, waiting until he heard O'Connell hit the ground next to him before taking off.

One hundred yards to the finish. His legs churned, arms pumped, every cell in his body fired to do its job and carry him across the finish line.

He was fucking alive and strong. And a winner.

An hour later, rehydrated, stretched, and congratulated, Aldo flopped down on his cot. He slipped the photo, protected by a sandwich bag, out of his chest pocket. Gloria grinned up at him from the side of the lake, hair touched by the wind. He loved that glimpse of lightness in her eyes, around her soft mouth, that he hoped would be there permanently. He longed to see her without the pinch of pain and shame.

He'd snapped the shot of her during their little lake picnic. Aldo had wanted a picture of the two of them, needed it. But it would be too easy for him to write a story from a picture. Too easy to build up a relationship that didn't yet exist. Couldn't yet exist. She needed this time and distance. Putting restraints on her, demanding exclusivity, wasn't fair. It was the same reason he'd resisted the urge to give her his contact info. She needed the time.

He hoped he'd survive the wait.

"Mail call," Luke announced, shoving through the tent flap. He had twin packages under his arm.

Casually, Aldo slid the picture back into his pocket. "Whatcha got there, Cap?" he asked.

"Looks like we both got something from Harper," Luke said, tossing a box into Aldo's lap. Aldo wondered if his oldest friend realized he was grinning like a kid on Christmas morning.

"That Harp is something." Aldo held up the dirty mad libs notebook and the six-pack of socks she'd packed for him.

Luke was studying the bag of cookies as if it were an ice-cold six-pack, love written all over the dumb bastard's face.

"Miss her?" Aldo prodded.

"Huh?" Luke tore his eyes away from whatever shenanigans Harper had packed for him. "Yeah. Sure."

Aldo sighed. His friend was one of the smartest, most loyal men in the world. And he could be a real dumbass.

"You're not a terrible asshole for having feelings for her, you know," he told Luke.

Luke swallowed, and for a second Aldo thought he'd blow it off. "I feel like I am," Luke admitted.

"She wouldn't want you to be alone forever, man," Aldo said, careful not to mention the name that still hit Luke like a knife to the heart. "Besides, you'd have to be a complete fucking moron not to have some kind of big feelings for Harpoon. I'm half in love with her."

Luke gave a rusty laugh. "She's something."

"What'd she send you?" Aldo asked, making a reach for Luke's box. He didn't like to push Luke too hard when it came to the woman he'd loved and lost.

Luke held the box out of his reach. "I'll show you if you come clean about that picture in your pocket."

"Asshole," Aldo grumbled playfully.

"That's Captain Asshole to you," Luke teased. With a ninja-like move, he feinted left and snatched the picture from Aldo's shirt pocket. "Aha!"

"Please," Aldo scoffed. "Like you didn't know who it was."

"What's going on there?" Luke asked, dumping his box in Aldo's lap.

Aldo pawed through it on principle and stopped when he got to the small stack of pictures. Harper and the dogs. Harper in the office with Beth and an even grumpier than usual Angry Frank. Harper and Gloria… A fist closed around his heart and squeezed. They had face masks on and were making fish faces for the camera, and Aldo had never seen anything so damn beautiful in his life.

"Shit." He'd been doing well. Not thinking of her every ten seconds. Staying focused on what needed to be done. "You think she's doing okay?" he asked.

116

"Yeah, I think so. Harper wouldn't let her not be okay," Luke told him, rubbing a hand absently over his chest. "I could really go for a beer or ten right now."

"How about a run instead?" Aldo offered. "Nothing like a few miles choking on dust in heat that feels like you're wearing a parka to get your head right."

"Let me change."

CHAPTER 20

One month into deployment…

It was weird being back here. Back in the same gravel lot where she'd nearly lost her life a few short months ago.

But so much had happened since then. *A lifetime in some ways*, Gloria thought, deliberately turning away from the spot where she'd taken what she thought was her last gasping breath. She focused on the neon signs in the skinny windows and the music that was leaking out of Remo's front door.

Different circumstances. Different life. She was an independent woman. Okay, so she was living with her mother, but she was working a full-time job and ready to buy herself a glass of wine with her first official paycheck, damn it.

Her ballet flats hit the planks of the front porch with conviction, and when she opened the door, it was to a jovial Benevolence happy hour, not a murderous monster.

Fortified, Gloria stepped into the Friday night party and made a beeline for the bar. She smiled at the whispers. She was giving them something else to think about. "Poor little Gloria Parker" was slowly being replaced with "that Parker girl who took over the Fourth of July." She'd yet to do anything grand with the planning, but just volunteering was enough to get tongues wagging.

"Well, if it isn't 'I Volunteer as Tribute,'" Sophie said with a wink when Gloria slid onto a barstool. "What'll it be?"

Sophie was pink-cheeked and hustling behind the bar, as much a Friday night staple in Benevolence as the band that crowded onto the tiny scrap of stage.

The twenty dollars Gloria had allotted herself for frivolous spending was burning a hole in the back pocket of her thrift-store-find jeans. "A glass of house chardonnay," she decided. God, these tiny daily decisions that she was now free to make, *responsible* to make, both thrilled and overwhelmed her.

"Coming right up," Sophie said, expertly pulling two pints simultaneously while nudging the bar fridge shut with her hip.

Moments later, a stemmed glass appeared in front of Gloria on a paper napkin.

"Hey, Gloria. It's nice to see you out and about!" Harper floated up to the bar with an empty tray. Harper had taken on a Friday night shift at the bar to keep herself occupied and out of trouble while Luke was deployed. Rumor had it Luke wasn't a fan of both his sister and girlfriend closing down the bar every Friday, but no one told Harper Wilde and Sophie Adler how to live their lives.

Gloria loved that about them.

"I'm celebrating my first full paycheck from Blooms," Gloria confessed.

"Good for you!" Harper said, traying up a round of drinks as fast as Sophie poured them. "Claire says you're doing a great job."

"Thanks." Gloria felt her blush deepen. "I really like it there. Um, have you heard from Luke?" She was going on a bit of a fishing expedition. If Harper had heard from Luke, she probably had news on Aldo.

The dreamy grin nearly split Harper's face in two. "I had an email from him Wednesday, and I talked to him last week." A love like the one that lit Harper's gray eyes could survive the long distance. Gloria was sure of it.

She twirled the stem of her glass between her fingers. "Did he say how Aldo's doing?"

"Ooooooooh," Sophie cooed behind the bar. "Someone has a crush!"

Gloria felt herself turning an even brighter shade of pink. Was it only a crush, she wondered. Or did the potential of a future with the man make it something more? These were questions she'd like to ask the man in question, who'd given her no way to contact him during his deployment. Whether that was Aldo being chivalrous and heroic or disinterested, she wasn't certain.

"Stop picking on her," Harper ordered. "Don't mind Sophie. She thinks she's Cupid."

"By the way, you're welcome," Sophie said pointedly at Harper, winking.

"Anyway." Harper rolled her eyes at Sophie. "Luke did mention that Aldo's organizing some crazy boot camp workout competition with a bunch of the people from their unit. Tire flipping, rope climbing. He promised to email pictures."

Gloria nodded and worried about how to beg for an email address without sounding desperate.

"I could give you his email address, you know," Harper offered, reading her mind.

"Don't you think that would be…weird?" Gloria asked even while her insides were screaming *Get the email address!*

Harper hefted her tray. "I think you guys waited long enough. Don't you?" She headed into the crowd and called over her shoulder. "I'll send you his email address."

Gloria couldn't stop the smile that overtook her face. Aldo

may have wanted to protect her, but she needed to get used to making her own decisions. And she *decided* that she and Aldo should keep in touch.

"Ah, excuse me, Gloria?" Bob of Bob's Fine Furnishings fame stood before her. "Rumor has it you're handling the Fourth festivities."

Gloria blinked, realizing this was the first time in her entire life that a man had approached her in a bar. He was, of course, married to Becky, twenty years his junior. But she was still counting it.

"Yes. Yes, I am," she said with more confidence than she felt.

Bob bobbed his head. "Great. I have a question about the vendor fees for the festival. As a sponsor of the 5K, am I getting the same discount on my hot dog stand that I got last year or have the discounts changed?"

Gloria was only about one-third of the way through the two dented cardboard boxes filled with papers that Merle's granddaughter had dropped off about an hour after her ill-conceived volunteering.

"I'm going to have to get back to you on that," she said. "Can I have your email address?"

While Bob rummaged for paper and a pen, Ms. Valencio from the grocery store bellied up with her empty cigarette holder and raspberry-red hair. "Got a question for you on parking and the parade." She launched into a recounting of the last seven years of Fourth of Julys and their inconveniences.

Gloria felt her eyes glazing over. All of Benevolence seemed to have appeared in front of her with questions.

Sophie shot her a quick grin and topped off Gloria's glass.

———

An hour later, Gloria had a list of twenty-two email addresses, fifty-odd questions that she'd "get back to them on," and a splitting headache. She chugged the ice water Sophie had thoughtfully left next to her empty wineglass.

"How's my favorite bartender?"

Gloria lifted her head from the bar at the rich baritone.

Sophie rolled her eyes good-naturedly. "I bet you say that to all the bartenders, Linc, including Titus."

Lincoln Reed, fire chief, ladies' man, all-American hunk of man candy, gave Gloria an assessing look.

"Well, well, well," he said.

Sophie raised a perfectly arched eyebrow in his direction. "Down, boy. She's new to the single life."

"I'd be happy to ease you into it." Linc winked. He was a shameless flirt but in a friendly, habitual way that had Gloria smiling shyly.

"That's very generous," she said, looking down at her hands clasped in her lap.

The band kicked into a ballad. Linc held out his hand and gave a mock bow. "Care to dance, Ms. Parker?"

Sophie gave her the "get your ass out on the floor" shoulder shimmy.

Exhausted, confused, and maybe the tiniest bit curious, Gloria took a subtle breath and put her hand in his. He led her toward the edge of the dance floor, his back muscles making a hypnotizing show under his tight gray T-shirt.

He was taller than Aldo but not as broad. And when he coaxed her into his arms—with a respectable distance—when he smiled down at her like she was the only woman in the room, Gloria felt nothing.

A man was flirting with her in a bar. A gorgeous, confident, sexy man. And she felt like she was dancing with a first cousin.

What had Aldo Moretta done to her?

CHAPTER 21

L et me get this straight." Second Lieutenant Steph Oluo shot Aldo a look that told him he was a huge dumbass. "You didn't give her any way to get in touch with you?"

Aldo brought one hand to his temple, keeping the other firmly on the wheel of the big-ass truck. His eyes never left the skinny village road they were navigating. "The spirits are telling me you are not impressed," he said in his best psychic woo-woo voice.

Their small convoy was delivering food and supplies to Afghan forces outside the wire. Aldo had volunteered for the mission to keep the antsiness from eating him alive on base.

"Men are dumbasses," Oluo snorted, her cool gray eyes scanning the buildings around them. They were both familiar enough with missions like this that they could banter without stealing focus from the necessary constant vigilance.

What might look like a sleepy village was often a hole for insurgent forces with snipers. Villagers, in their loose linen dress, hurried about their days. Most pointedly ignored the six-vehicle convoy that was plowing its way through their streets with guns at the ready.

"She's been through a lot," Aldo argued. He hadn't shared Gloria's secrets, just that she'd gotten out of a bad relationship.

"You could have been using these six months to, I don't know, build up a rapport with her," Oluo pointed out. "You know, maybe be friends with the girl first before you try to jump her bones."

"I'm not trying to jump her bones," Aldo said defensively. He saw brake lights and rolled to a stop behind the truck in front of them.

They both scanned the buildings around them for signs of activity. A minute passed in tense silence. He could feel *something* out there on the horizon. That tingle at the base of his spine had been honed by countless near misses. The last one, a sniper on a rooftop, had lined up a shot on Luke. Aldo had bruised his friend's ribs in the rush tackle that had the bullet missing them both by inches.

"Seeing anything?" Aldo asked into the radio.

Static and squawking. "Nah. Just a goat herder with a livestock traffic jam."

Neither Aldo nor his passenger relaxed until the truck in front of them shifted into gear. "All clear," the radio squawked.

"You are too trying to jump her bones," Oluo accused, picking up the thread of conversation where it had dropped. It was something they all excelled at after a few weeks of having normal, mundane tasks interrupted by threats and adrenaline.

"Okay, so maybe *eventually*—"

"Aha!"

"I don't want to get in her way for a while. I want her to find the life she wants without building it around some—"

"Dumbass lieutenant?" Oluo supplied helpfully.

"I was going to say devastatingly handsome, romantic leading man."

Oluo grunted, not sounding particularly impressed.

"She deserves this chance to be on her own," Aldo pressed.

"Of course she does. But what if she meets some guy while you're rolling around the desert for six months?"

"Five," Aldo corrected her. He was counting not only the days but the hours. "And I just want her to be happy." He'd die of a smashed-to-pieces heart. Or he'd wallow in self-pity for a year or so before swearing off women permanently and becoming some kind of mountain-dwelling hermit.

At least that was the plan.

"I don't know," Oluo teased. "Good-looking girl like that isn't going to stay single for long." Oluo knew what she was talking about. She came out to her parents at age eleven, insisting that her feelings for Miley Cyrus were not merely friendly. She'd been with her girlfriend, a kindergarten teacher, for four years.

"Gloria deserves a man who is going to look at her like she is the best thing in his life for the rest of hers," Aldo said, gripping the wheel.

"Well, shit." Oluo laughed. "Never would have taken you for a softie. Maybe she'll wait around for your dumb ass."

She landed a punch on his shoulder.

And the world went to dust.

Pressure, a wave of it crushing his body against itself. Red and brown, swirling in front of him as his empty lungs begged for air. There was no sound, just a dull roar from far away. Nothing but pressure and dust.

He couldn't tell where his body ended and the desert dirt began.

Was that gunfire? Why couldn't he fucking move?

Move, Moretta! Move your fucking lard ass.

Was he dead? Fucking damn it all to hell! Had he died without getting another kiss from Gloria Parker?

"Gloria."

"Stay with me, man. You hear me?"

Gunfire. Screaming. So much dust. And there was red, red, red everywhere.

He was moving. At least he thought he was. And then there was pain. Worse than the crushing pressure. Tearing, shredding, stabbing. His lower body was on fire. He couldn't pinpoint a location as it raced through him, lighting up nerves.

"Medic! I need a fucking medic!"

He couldn't move. Couldn't open his eyes.

"If you die on me, buddy, I will never fucking forgive your ass!" Luke's face wavered in front of him. His jaw was tight, and there was blood on his face.

"You hit?" Aldo rasped, the words ripping his throat open.

"No, you stupid son of a bitch, and don't even think about dying."

"Oluo?"

"I don't know, man."

"Gloria."

Someone moved his hand over his chest pocket where he kept the picture of the woman he was pretty sure he loved.

If it was too late, he was pissed enough that he was coming back to haunt someone.

There were more hands moving over his body, more commands.

Stay down.

Hurry up.

It's bad.

IED.

His leg. Jesus, his leg.

Don't you fucking let him die.

Return fire.

I love you, man. You're my best friend…

But Aldo was separate from it all, drifting away in the dust that would never settle. It didn't hurt anymore.

CHAPTER 22

L ook who's awake," croaked a voice that sounded vaguely familiar in a world of strange. It was coming from far away and Aldo realized he was wearing a headset.

"Oluo?" It felt like razor blades slicing open his throat. Everything was too bright here as if they were on the surface of the sun.

"Yeah, man."

"Everyone else okay?" he rasped.

"Dunno," Oluo responded. She sounded weak.

With heroic effort, Aldo managed to open one eye. A chopper. They were in the air.

"Don't move, Lieutenant." A different voice. This one attached to a grim-looking woman in blood-stained camo scrubs and blue surgical gloves.

"FST?" he read on her uniform.

"Forward surgical team," she said briskly in his ears as she sank a needle the size of a canoe oar into his arm. "You and the second lieutenant are being airlifted to a combat support hospital."

"Bagram?" he coughed. Goddammit. He needed to stop talking. Every word was slicing his dust-packed throat to ribbons.

"You're saving me the trouble of asking you what day of the week it is," she said calmly. Everything about her was all business. The sleek bun, the set of her jaw, the line carved between her eyebrows. The woman was a professional. A stunningly beautiful one. "I can't give you any water because, as soon as we land, you're going straight into surgery."

Aldo felt a hand groping for his. Oluo. He squeezed it tight.

"How's my girl here, doc?" Aldo asked. She was awake and alive, but the fact that Steph "Balls of Steel" Oluo was clinging to his hand meant that one of them was probably on death's doorstep.

"Two GSWs. One to the shoulder, one in the gut. And a dump truck of desert grit in both," Dr. Dreamy said conversationally in that faraway voice. "She's gonna be fine."

He blew out a breath, and the doctor looked down at him. "Me?"

"Not great," the doctor said, still seeming largely unconcerned. She hung a bag of plasma over him and leaned in. Aldo looked into eyes so green they made him think of spring. She had a deep scar that curved under her left eye. It only added to the mystery of her appeal.

"You can tell me straight if I'm gonna die."

Her face softened, and she patted him on the chest. "I promise you're going to come through this. Might not be pretty, but you give off a tough guy vibe, so I believe in you."

"My leg…" He couldn't get more words out. But he could tell by the set of her jaw that it was bad.

"I'm being straight with you. There's a good chance we can't save it," she told him without looking down the stretcher. "But before you go all 'I'm a cripple,' 'I'm half a man' on me, I'll remind you that prosthetics have never been better, and if you're not a dumbass about it, you'll probably be able to do everything you did before."

Fuck. Fuck. Fuck. Fuck.

"Chicks dig amputees, right, Oluo?" he asked weakly.

She choked out a laugh. "Fuck yeah, they do." She squeezed his hand until it was the only thing he could feel.

Dr. Dreamy moved between her patients, stepping over their joined hands like a ballerina on stage instead of a combat surgeon midflight. "I predict you both will be having ice cream for dinner together in forty-eight hours," she told them, earning a snort from the lactose-intolerant Oluo.

"How'd it go down?" he asked, his brain scrambling over the events.

"IED, I think. Took out our truck. We started taking fire from both sides," Oluo told him.

"How'd you get out?"

"Did a damn belly flop into the dirt and crawled into a goat shit–splattered alley. O'Connell found me and carried me like a goddamn baby."

Aldo wanted to laugh but didn't think he'd survive it. The carrying would bother her more than the gunshot wounds.

"How did I get out?"

"Captain Garrison," she said simply.

So he and Luke had traded another round of lifesaving. Aldo closed his eyes and sent out a silent thank-you to his friend. This had better be the last fucking time unless one of them needed a kidney someday. They fell into a silence under the thrum of the copter blades.

"Anyone else hurt?"

"I don't know, man. It was chaos, and there was dust and blood freaking everywhere." Her voice cracked, and he gripped her hand hard.

Aldo tried to turn his head in the cradle it was strapped into. "Oluo?"

"Yeah, man?" she said through gritted teeth as Dr. Dreamy cut the shoulder of her uniform open.

"Chicks dig bullet scars too."

She laughed, her teeth chattering now, and Aldo felt a tear leak from the corner of his eye. He was so damn tired. He hurt so damn much. And this was only the beginning.

They clung together like that as the doctor, speaking quietly into her headset, danced over and around them, poking, prodding, taping, until landing. Aldo weakly tried to reach for Dr. Dreamy as the ground team swarmed his stretcher. "Will you call my mom, doc? Tell her what you told me. No bullshit. Give it to her straight."

Dr. Dreamy pulled her headset off. "Yeah. I can do that."

"She'll probably cuss you out," Aldo warned her. "Don't take it personally."

She gave him a smile. "I'll cuss her out right back."

"Thanks..." He drifted off as the stretcher was wheeled away from the helicopter.

CHAPTER 23

"T hanks for getting back to me, Sheriff," Gloria said into the phone. "I had some questions from people about security during the festival." It was embarrassingly great to talk to law enforcement about something besides her ex-boyfriend.

Sheriff Bodett waded through her questions and provided answers that she dutifully scrawled down in her notebook. She needed to learn to type faster, Gloria decided. It would save her a lot of transcription time. She eyed the stacks of paper taking up her mother's kitchen counter. Time and paper and kitchen real estate.

"Thanks again. I appreciate your time," Gloria said, wrapping it up. "And if there's anything you need from me, don't hesitate to call." She was getting a dozen calls a day about the festival that was still weeks away. It wasn't exactly a social life, but she'd take it.

"Anytime, Gloria," Sheriff Bodett said. She could hear him slurping up his soup lunch. "You're doing a fine job."

Gloria felt herself go pink at the praise. "Thank you, sir. I appreciate it."

They disconnected, and as Gloria dug into her emails, her phone rang again. It took her almost twenty minutes with the town manager's assistant to fix the issue with the parade permit. She spent another five minutes dodging pointed questions about what she'd been doing at Aldo Moretta's house this week from Georgia Rae, the mouth of Benevolence, who'd actually shown up on the doorstep with gossip muffins.

Closing the door on Georgia Rae's retreating figure, Gloria decided she'd earned a little break, on her day off no less, and flopped down at the counter with her mother's laptop.

Gloria opened up the photo gallery of the one-bedroom apartment again and clicked through. It was small but cute. And she still couldn't quite afford it. She was saving every penny for a security deposit and first and last month's rent. In a few weeks, a few paychecks, she'd be ready to find her own place.

She'd do a little dreaming on Craigslist and Pinterest, of course, for decor ideas. *Visualizing couldn't hurt, could it?*

Gloria rolled her shoulders and stretched. The kitchen still smelled like the cookies she'd baked earlier that morning. Baking had turned out to be surprisingly therapeutic. Every time she had a nightmare or someone gave her the "poor little" look or she started to panic about letting an entire town down, she erased it with sugar cookies and fruit cobblers.

She slipped a cookie off the tray and nibbled.

The doorbell rang, and she reluctantly closed her mother's laptop.

"Harper! This is a nice surprise," Gloria greeted the disheveled blond on her front step. She leaned down to rough up Lola's massive head. The pit bull was a charcoal-gray wrecking ball of muscle and love. Her tongue lolled out and swiped over Gloria's entire face.

Max, the little three-legged something or other, pranced in and out of her knees until she picked him up. "Yes, I see you too, Max! Can you come in, or are you just passing by?" she asked.

Harper pushed her sunglasses up on top of her head, and Gloria felt her heart trip up. Harper's gray eyes were red-rimmed and bloodshot. "I actually have some news about Aldo," she said, her voice tight.

Gloria felt the breath leave her body. No. Not Aldo.

"He's hurt, Gloria," Harper said, the words tumbling out of her. "He came through surgery, and the doctors are hopeful. They had to take part of his leg."

Gloria closed her eyes as her vision swam. He was alive. That was what mattered most. Aldo was alive. Max wriggled in her grasp and whimpered. She nuzzled him to her face.

"Aldo…" She couldn't get anything else out. Her throat was closing up around a lump that might never go away.

Harper grabbed her arm. "He's going to be okay. Luke emailed me this morning and said the surgery team's only concern right now is infection." She paused. "He hasn't woken up yet." Her voice broke a little bit, worry and fear in her eyes.

"But he will," Gloria said with a certainty she didn't know the origin of. But she was clinging to it. He would wake up, and he would come home.

"Yeah. He will," Harper agreed. Tears filled her eyes.

"I emailed him Friday night after you gave me his address," Gloria confessed on a shaky breath.

Harper bit her lip. "Then he'll have something to read when he wakes up," she decided. "So speaking of Aldo, would you mind giving me and my two stinky mutts a ride to Mrs. Moretta's house? I left my car there last night, and I wanted to check in on her."

Mrs. Moretta? Meet Aldo Moretta's mother? Gloria glanced down at her cutoffs and flour-spattered pink T-shirt. "Umm."

Harper's face brightened. "Are you nervous about meeting his mother?" She gasped in delight.

"It's Mrs. Moretta!" Gloria tried to defend herself. "She's terrifying. Who wouldn't be nervous about meeting her?"

Harper grinned.

Crap. Fine. Whatever.

"Oh, screw it!" The woman would take her as she was or not at all, Gloria decided. "Just let me brush my hair and bag up some of the cookies I baked this morning."

CHAPTER 24

Mrs. Moretta was even more terrifying in person. Gloria's potential future boyfriend's mother was a loud, opinionated grump.

She threw open the door before they had even crossed the porch. "He's awake, and he asked if everyone else was okay and then said he wanted a cheeseburger," Mrs. Moretta announced. "And now I have to pack to meet him 'somewhere' in the near future, which is a pain in my ass. I didn't ask my son to blow himself up. Who's gonna water my plants and get my mail and steam iron the draperies? Draperies don't just do that themselves."

"I'd be happy to help while you're gone," Gloria stupidly volunteered.

She really needed to stop doing that.

Mrs. Moretta harrumphed. "Who the hell are you?"

"Mrs. Moretta, this is my friend Gloria." Harper made the introductions.

"Ohhh. So *you're* the girl my son has his eye on," Mrs. Moretta said with a fierce frown, giving Gloria a withering once-over.

Gloria did her best not to wilt under the woman's stare.

"Sorry," Harper hissed under her breath. "It slipped out. There was wine and tears."

"You think I'm deaf just 'cause I'm old?"

Mrs. Moretta couldn't have been more than fifty-five. But she sure had the crotchety thing going for her.

"Well, come in then," Mrs. Moretta demanded, shuffling away from the door. She was round and soft in the body and hard and sharp in the tongue. She snatched the offered bag out of Gloria's hands.

"I thought you might like some cookies," Gloria began.

But Mrs. Moretta had already opened the bag and shoved a hand inside. "You're probably as hungover as I am," she said to Harper, offering her the bag.

"I wouldn't say no to a coffee as big as my face," Harper told her, helping herself to a cookie.

Harper had explained the emotional, boxed wine sit-in she, Claire, and Mrs. Moretta had shared last night. Hence the movie-star sunglasses Harper was rocking.

The dogs wandered into the kitchen and lay down on the cool tile.

"You make coffee." Mrs. Moretta pointed at Harper. "And *you* can help me pack."

"Me?" Gloria asked.

"How else am I supposed to tell if you're good enough for my son!" Mrs. Moretta shook her head like she was tired of explaining things to idiots and mounted the steps to the second floor.

"Good luck," Harper sang under her breath.

Numbly, Gloria plodded up the stairs to her doom.

Mrs. Moretta's bedroom had been hosed down in baby pink. The walls, the bedspread, the pillows, the carpet. There was a huge flat-screen TV hung on one wall and a white dresser with pink roses on the other. The dresser drawers and closet doors were flung open, and clothing was everywhere except for in the open suitcase on the foot of the bed. What looked like a floral muumuu was draped over the pink armchair in the corner.

"What do you pack for an open-ended hospital trip?" Mrs. Moretta demanded.

"Um. Underwear?" Gloria guessed.

"Never wear it!" The woman sounded like a foghorn proudly proclaiming her commando status.

She should have brought the cookies up with her. And wine. She could use some right about now. A gallon of it.

"Okay." Gloria took a deep breath and forced herself to focus on the task at hand rather than the absurdity. "Let's start with comfortable clothing. You don't want to be sitting in a hospital room in stilettos and leather pants."

Mrs. Moretta guffawed. "So you're funny then?"

Gloria gave a little shrug and pulled a cardigan sweater with a dozen cats embroidered on it. "I guess so. Let's do some layers in case the hospital is cold."

"Do you plan to have babies with my son?" Mrs. Moretta demanded when Gloria folded up a pink T-shirt with rhinestones inexplicably covering only the breast region.

"Babies aren't really on my radar right now," Gloria said slowly. And one kiss wasn't exactly a marriage proposal. One mind-melting, bone-warming, remember-for-a-lifetime kiss. But still.

Mrs. Moretta hurled a mud-brown turtleneck sweater at her.

"Huh," she harrumphed. "Well, I suppose in your situation—being new to relationships that aren't complete shitstorms and all—it's smart to take it slow."

Was that a compliment? Gloria couldn't tell. She folded the turtleneck and stuffed it in the suitcase.

"How about marriage?" Mrs. Moretta demanded. "You're not one of those broads who thinks she's too good to wear a ring, are you? Because I won't like that." She shook a metal clothes hanger at Gloria.

"No, I like marriage. At least the idea of it. It would have to be a very special man."

"You mean to deal with all your baggage?" Mrs. Moretta shouted.

"That, and he'd have to be special for me to deal with his baggage."

Still wielding the clothes hanger, Mrs. Moretta frowned for a moment. "That's smart. So you're funny and smart. And your cookies are okay. As long as you're not some kind of crazy bridezilla or an alcoholic asshole or some horny one-night-stand kinda gal, you have my blessing to date my Aldo."

Gloria gave up all pretense of being calm and collected. She flopped down on the pink satin bedspread, nearly sliding back off. "What makes you think Aldo would even be interested?" she asked. He'd shown some very definite interest before he left, but what if he came home different? What if everything was different?

"That weird, perky, sunshine-and-puppy-dogs, little blond downstairs says so," Mrs. Moretta announced as if Harper Wilde held the keys to all the secrets of the universe. Maybe she did. Gloria could hope, couldn't she?

"How is he?" Gloria blurted out. She'd had nothing but fourth-hand information. She needed something.

"I spoke to some combat surgeon. The mouth on that woman." Mrs. Moretta whistled. It sounded more like a compliment than a complaint. "She said he was more concerned with the rest of his guys and gals than he was himself. And he made her promise to call me." The woman's eyes watered up in the first show of real emotion. "I can't wait to talk to that stupid son of a bitch and find out how he got himself blown up."

Mrs. Moretta hiccupped. Gloria wanted to reach out, offer a comforting hand squeeze, but felt like Mrs. Moretta wasn't the affectionate type.

A pair of purple corduroy pants hit her in the face.

"Let's hurry it up." Mrs. Moretta sniffled. "They might want me to fly to Germany or Guam. I'll need you to water the plants, feed the birds, clean the curtains, do a little light weeding out front and in the garden. Oh, and maybe run the vacuum upstairs and down. The dusting polish is in the closet. You could start when I leave, or maybe you should come by to help out now since I'm so bereaved."

CHAPTER 25

To: Aldo Moretta
From: Gloria Parker
Subject: Just hi!

Hi Aldo!

I bumped into Harper at Remo's last night, and she gave me your email address. I thought I'd say hi. Okay, I'm lying. I don't feel right starting off our email relationship with a lie.

I went to Remo's with the sole purpose of forcing Harper to give me your email address. I hope you don't mind. I know you didn't want to have some long-distance thing going. But I missed you. Is that okay? I mean, I know it's weird to miss someone who I don't know well...

Anyway, if it's not okay, ignore this whole thing and pretend it's a spam message from an erectile dysfunction supplement company...wait, that's weird. Don't do that. Good news! I'm as awkward in email as I am in person! #consistency

Your plants are doing well, and wildlife has yet to

break into your house and claim it as their own. In other town news, I'm organizing this year's Fourth of July after Merle broke his hip. I'm not sure if it was my people-pleasing OCD or a genuine desire to shut Georgia Rae up about the parking space she's complained about for the last seven years.

I feel...good. Work is fun and challenging, and I think exactly what I need. You'll be happy to hear that I haven't broken down and sobbed on any near strangers lately, though I might be holding out for you to come back.

I hope all is well with you. I don't know if it's okay to ask questions like where are you, what are you doing, do you miss home?

Good luck. Be safe. I'm thinking about you.

Love,
Gloria

He reread the email for the four thousandth time. The email he'd never replied to. He'd gotten it two weeks after it was sent. After "the incident," three surgeries, a touch-and-go infection, and his first torturous rounds of physical therapy that left him weak and gasping.

"Put that thing away before you crash this plane," his mother bellowed from his elbow in her first-class seat. A retired couple on their way home from a three-week stay in Europe had given up their seats after spotting Aldo in uniform and on crutches. He'd refused the wheelchair.

He couldn't say why that pissed him off. But most things since arriving in Germany half a limb short had. As far as he could tell, the bastards who had tried to kill the better part of his team—and nearly succeeded with him—had planted their hatred inside him. It thrived in the pit of his stomach, a bright red rage curled around dark, wispy tendrils of something even worse. Fear.

"You don't need to scream at the whole plane," Aldo snapped back at his mother. They'd spent the last ten days together, and they were headed stateside for a short stint at Walter Reed and then home. And if he didn't get some alone time soon, one or both of them was going to end up dead.

"What? You think you deserve the wiffy just because you're a wounded soldier?"

Ina was both proud of his sacrifice and inconvenienced by it. She managed to roll compliment and jab into the same sentence while butchering the word *Wi-Fi*.

Aldo shut his laptop, stuffed it back in his bag, and stretched his legs out. Leg. Leg and prosthesis. Mentally, he was no more prepared to have one leg than when Dr. Dreamy had given him the heads-up.

He was nothing without his athletic prowess, his strength, his speed. War had taken it all from him. It had robbed him of his sleep, his body, his confidence. He felt like a shadowy monster returning to a place that might not even feel like home again.

"Are you sleeping?" Ina jabbed him hard in the ribs with her elbow, the only part of her body that was pointy. "What movie should I watch?"

"Jesus Christ, Ma."

———

Walter Reed was more of a formality, and Aldo found himself home within days. "Home" was his mother's house for the next few weeks. He was determined to whittle that timeline down to days. She had a spare room—practically a closet, and just as jammed full as one—and bathroom on the first floor, and he "required supervision."

Stubbornness had him insisting on carrying his duffel slung over his shoulder as he crutched his way impatiently up the porch steps.

Through his exhaustion, his constant roiling anger, he didn't notice the red, white, and blue hanging baskets on the porch. Inside, he blocked out his mother's incessant yammering about drapes and birdfeeders and hopped back through the kitchen and off the sun porch to the room he was sure he'd need to shovel pounds of shit out of before he could even enter.

He was wrong. The room was neat as a pin, the twin bed made with fresh linens instead of buried under every single issue of *Cosmo* that his mother had collected since 1974. Gone were the baskets of yard-sale-find Beanie Babies and porcelain bird figurines. Pawing through the neatly stacked clothing on the skinny table, he discovered several of his favorite T-shirts and shorts.

His iPad, chargers, and underwear all made the move.

His mother, bless her hollering heart, apparently had gone to great lengths to make his transition an easy one. Aldo felt a vague sense of guilt for doing nothing but griping at her for the past few weeks.

Conscience heavy, he crutched back into the kitchen and found his mother cutting into a pie.

"Ma, if that pie was here when you left, you could get food poisoning. I told you before not to eat moldy food."

"Leave me alone. This is welcome home pie," she grunted, shoveling a slab onto one of her tiny rose leaf tea plates. For a ham-fisted banshee, his mother sure appreciated fine, dainty things.

She shoved a card into his hands and watched him owlishly as she hefted the first bite to her mouth.

Welcome home, Morettas.

Gloria

"Why is she leaving pies in your house?" Aldo demanded, gripping the card. Reading her name, let alone saying it, was painful. A reminder of the life that he couldn't have now.

"Dunno." Ina shrugged her linebacker shoulders. Everyone always assumed Aldo got his build from his father, but his dad had been a slim-shouldered string bean with a toothy grin and a stratospheric stress level who'd keeled over from a heart attack when Aldo was thirteen. "She was supposed to do a few things around here for me while I was babysitting your ass. Does that bother you?"

His mother was like a bulldog with a chew toy when she was trying to pry information out of him.

"Nope," Aldo lied. "I'm going to sleep." Without another word, he headed back to his room, ignoring his mom's calls about his piece of pie.

He shut the door and leaned against it, letting the ache in his leg permeate everything. He could block it out for minutes at a time, could forget for moments what had happened, but it was always there lurking under the surface. The pain, the memories, the fear that he would never be normal again. His life would never be the same.

In all his deployments, he'd been prepared for the fact that he might not come home. Soldiers all faced it, dealt with it in their own way. But never in his wildest nightmares had he predicted this. The sheer magnitude of the loss.

Yes. He was home and alive. But he wasn't whole. And she deserved someone who could protect her. That man was no longer him.

CHAPTER 26

Gloria juggled the plastic container to her opposite hand and rested the flowers on her hip. Welcome-home accessories stabilized for the moment, she stabbed at the doorbell.

"Don't be nervous," she encouraged herself. "You're just a friend stopping by to see another friend and his super scary mother."

"Aldo, get the damn door!" Mrs. Moretta shouted from somewhere inside the house.

"You get the damn door! I'm on crutches, woman!"

A shouting match broke out on the other side of the front door, and Gloria immediately regretted her decision to pop by.

"Oh, God," she whispered. Maybe she could hustle down the sidewalk and sneak away—

The door was wrenched open, and Gloria's jaw dropped.

Aldo, looking thinner, almost gaunt, was glaring at her. His hair, longer and curlier than she'd ever seen it, was rumpled like he'd just gotten up. He had a scruffy beard that looked as though he'd paid it no attention. He was wearing gym shorts, and his left leg was bandaged where it ended just below the knee.

"Fuck," he swore softly and half closed the door, blocking her view of his leg.

"Who is it?" Mrs. Moretta screamed, like a wounded wildebeest trapped in quicksand.

"Come see for yourself," Aldo yelled back.

"Um, hi," Gloria said. "I brought you soup. And flowers." She'd spent an hour and a half pulling together the perfect bouquet under Claire's watchful eye. Black-eyed Susans for encouragement, chamomile for energy, jasmine for cheer, and ranunculus just because they were so pretty.

Aldo made no move to invite her in...or say anything at all. He simply continued to stare at her with what looked like a war of emotions behind those shadowed eyes.

Pain. She read it on him as if he'd tattooed the word on his forehead. And her heart hurt for him. She knew pain. Knew the fear that came with it.

"How are you?" she asked, her voice barely above a whisper.

"Fine," he snapped.

His mother bustled up behind him.

Aldo stepped back, letting Mrs. Moretta at the door. "You can answer your own fucking door from now on," he said in a low voice. But Gloria still heard him loud and clear. Both women watched him as he hurried away from the door as fast as his crutches would carry him.

"I didn't raise any assholes," Mrs. Moretta called after him.

"Apparently you did," Aldo answered bitterly before slamming a door in the back of the house.

Gloria didn't know what to do. She'd expected...well, she hadn't known what to expect. It certainly wasn't this rejection though.

"Sorry about him. He's been a dick and a half since getting blown to kingdom come," Mrs. Moretta said. "What's in the bowl?"

Gloria felt like she was doing the walk of shame when she walked back in the door at Blooms. She'd used her lunch break to make her delivery, and Claire was perched on a stool behind the register reading a paperback when she returned.

"Well? How did it go? How does he look? Did he like the flowers?" Claire peppered her with questions, excitement bright in her eyes.

"It was, uh, fine. He's fine, so he says. He looks…" Gloria was humiliated to find tears welling up in her eyes.

"Oh no. Oh, sweetie. What's wrong? Is it his leg?"

Gloria shook her head and snatched a tissue out of the box next to the computer before she could completely dissolve. "No. I've never seen a sexier amputee. But he's *different*." Her biggest fear. She blew her nose and stared up at the overhead lights, willing the tears to evaporate like the hopes and dreams she'd stupidly hung on a man she barely knew. "He's so angry. And hurt. I can tell he's hurting. But he's so…closed off. He didn't want to see me."

Claire shoved off the stool and grabbed another tissue. "I command you to stop right there. You're not to cry a single tear over whatever he said or didn't say. I'm so sorry that happened, and I'm going to kill Ina for not telling me Aldo was struggling. This has nothing to do with you and everything to do with him. Everyone heals differently."

"Sometimes people don't heal," Gloria said, jabbing crescents into her palm with her fingernails. She would not cry. She would not feel like her chest had caved in. When had she built all these dreams around him? When had she decided that Aldo Moretta was the one man for her? God, she was still a silly, stupid little girl.

"You can go ahead and stop whatever vicious dialogue that's

happening in your head right now, missy," Claire said sternly. "I can see that nasty little voice working its poison."

Gloria took a deep breath, breathing in the scents of eucalyptus and rose. They soothed her immediately. She checked in with her body. No pain anymore. No soreness. She didn't have injuries to tend to daily. She only had a small hole in her heart, and *that* she could survive.

"That's better," Claire said, observing the straightening of her shoulders. "Now, do you want to go home, or do you want to help me make a carnation blanket for Lou Turnbill's old-ass horse in honor of the Belmont Stakes?"

"I want to make a damn carnation horse blanket."

CHAPTER 27

I'm embarrassed. And hurt. And so stupid.

Why was I counting on this? I could see myself with him. I could see us making homemade ice cream on his porch or kissing in the rain. Going grocery shopping. Curling up on the couch with popcorn and a movie.

He kissed me before he left. He kissed me the way a man kisses a woman he won't forget.

And now he's back, and he looks at me like I'm a stranger.

Is it because of his injury? Is it post-traumatic stress? Or were his feelings just not strong enough?

I want to make him talk. I know what it's like keeping feelings, secrets, bottled up. It's poison. It eats at you from the inside out. But it's not my place. At least I don't think it is. Hell, I don't know what my place is. I've never had a place before.

I've never had permission to speak up or call someone out. And I'm still waiting for permission. That makes me angry with myself. Why can't I be strong? Why is it this constant battle of second-guessing myself and hoping someone will do right by me? Why can't I be like Harper or Sophie? They're so confident and real, and if someone tried to take something from them, they'd laugh in their faces.

Why can't I be like that?

Will I ever be like that?

And don't say "give it time." I'm tired of waiting. Why not now?

I'm tired of feeling stuck. I think I was waiting to begin my life until Aldo came home, which, by the way, is exactly what he asked me not to do. So now what's stopping me from finding a place to live? Or signing up for some online courses? Or dating?

Okay, maybe not dating. I danced with a gorgeous firefighter who flirted with me, and I felt nothing. So maybe that part of me is still…damaged.

I got another letter this week. And I'm more upset about Aldo rejecting me than Glenn threatening me? It's humiliating. Why am I letting either man affect me? One's behind bars, and the other has made it very clear that he wants nothing to do with me.

I want to be my own damn hero. It would be a nice change from being my own biggest problem.

When did I decide that my worth came from how someone else sees me? Does that happen when a girl grows up without a father to tell her she's smart and kind and pretty and worth so much more than the scraps of attention users will throw her way?

Or was I born hungry for someone else's opinions?

I don't even know what I think about myself. Am I smart? Am I organized? Am I a good person? Or am I just a collection of all the damage I've allowed someone to do to me?

And if so, how do I become my own hero? Because I'm ready. I'm done being damaged and fragile and careful and scared. I'm done.

CHAPTER 28

You're driving me fucking nuts!" Aldo yelled from the living room. If he ever learned to speak at normal volume again, it would be a miracle straight from the little baby Jesus.

"That's a fine way to talk to the woman who dropped everything to nurse you back to health because you couldn't swerve around a bomb," his mother snarled back from the kitchen.

"You played *Candy Crush* and yelled at me if I didn't turn on *The Price Is Right* every day," Aldo roared.

"You aren't driving yourself to PT. I don't care how big and tough you think you are. So you're welcome to walk. Go ahead and hitchhike. See if I care. I didn't raise you to be a grown man who shouts at his own mother."

"That is exactly who you raised me to be!" If he had to spend one more second listening to Ina Moretta grouse about the evening news or the price of cream-filled donuts or his lack of gratitude when she woke him from the only sound sleep he'd had since the fucking bomb to show him a funny dog video on her phone, he was going to murder her.

"Hey!" A third voice joined the fray from the area of the front door.

Aldo crutched into the foyer, and his mother poked her head out of the kitchen.

Harper stood in the doorway, legs braced as if for a fight. She had a bulging bag in one hand.

"Come right on in, bursting into my house like that. Didn't your parents teach you any manners?" Ina yelled.

"They must have died too soon, I guess," Harper said several decibels above conversational tone.

Aldo blindsided her with a bear hug, dropping his crutches on the floor. He didn't question this sudden rush of affection that welled up in him like hope. He didn't care if he was just relieved that there was now someone present who would keep him from going to jail for homicide or if he was happy to see a friend he hadn't let down.

Harper grabbed on to him and held tight. Aldo knew Luke would have given anything to trade places with him in that moment.

"Pick up your goddamn crutches! You know the doctors don't want you walking unassisted yet!" His mother continued on, sprinkling in some colorful Italian for variety.

"I'm glad you're home. And alive," Harper said into his chest.

"I will marry you and have your babies if you get me the hell out of this house. I have a PT appointment in thirty."

Harper looked him up and down, and he tried not to flinch when her gaze lingered on the gleaming titanium that was now part of him.

"Luke might have a problem with the first, but I'd pay money to see the second. So it's a deal. Besides, I want to see what you can do with that hardware."

"I can do anything. They just won't fucking let me." The frustration bubbled up again, bleeding into the happy.

"If you don't do what the doctors tell you, you'll end up screwing up your stump or breaking that thing," his mother warned, pointing at his prosthesis.

"Mrs. Moretta, I'm going to take Aldo to his appointment today," Harper said as a grin spread over her face. "Is there anything you need while we're out?"

Ina grumbled for a moment. "Well, I suppose I could use another box of chardonnay."

Aldo used the cursed crutches to get to Harper's VW Bug and then tossed them into the back seat before lowering himself gingerly into the passenger's seat. Everything still hurt. Everything still exhausted him, and he didn't like the whole "be patient" line about waiting for his strength and mobility to come back. What if the pain never went away? What if he missed his leg for the rest of his life?

Harper slid behind the wheel and started the ignition. The car purred to life, thanks to a complete overhauling Luke had surprised her with before deployment. His friend might be a scaredy-cat dumbass, but he was a thoughtful, generous one.

Aldo dropped his head against the seat. "I love that woman, but I swear to God, one of these days, one of us is going to murder the other."

Harper snickered and shifted into reverse. "That was World War III in there."

"That's what happens when you spend two fucking weeks straight with Ina Moretta. I think it was her goal to drive me crazy."

"I hear that's what moms are for," Harper said, backing down the driveway into the street. "Where are we going?"

Aldo gave her directions, and they cruised their way out of town.

"By the way, there's a bag of goodies in the back for you," she told him.

Aldo swiveled in his seat and grabbed at the gift bag. "Where's the candy?" he demanded. He treated his body like a temple ninety-nine percent of the time. That one percent was reserved for Skittles and Sour Patch Kids.

"It's in the bottom. I consulted with Luke on this, so a lot of it you can thank him for."

"New earbuds and an MP3 player?"

"It's full of get-pumped playlists for therapy, and you can also use it to drown out your mom."

He pulled out a tiny plastic egg next. "Earplugs."

"Luke said your mom snores."

"Like a fucking company of lumberjacks at a chainsaw convention. What's this? A bracelet?"

Harper rolled her eyes. "Yeah, I thought you could start accessorizing. No, it's one of those step counter heart-rate monitors. It's what normal people who don't run half marathons on the weekend use to measure their fitness. And since, for the next week or two, you probably won't be hitting a 10K, I thought you could use it with your physical therapy. It'll sync with your phone too."

He stared at it. *Since you won't be hitting a 10K…* He could barely hobble to the bathroom and back without breaking out in a cold fucking sweat. "This is cool, Harpoon. Thanks."

"Seriously? You're gonna go with Harpoon?" she teased.

He was too tired to play. "We'll see where the day takes us," he said, unwrapping a mini chocolate bar and popping it into his mouth.

CHAPTER 29

The clinic was a twenty-minute drive north of town. Aldo ate candy and stared pensively out the window, ignoring the sidelong looks Harper sent in his direction. He knew he wasn't his old self. He didn't need another reminder.

She called the office to tell them she would be back in later and made some murmurs that he could tell were dodges to questions about him. Everyone wanted the inside scoop on how Aldo Moretta was dealing with coming back in pieces.

"Beth wants me to hug you for her," Harper said, dropping her phone in the console where she'd probably forget it.

"I have a feeling I'll be getting a lot of that," Aldo said grimly. He didn't want anyone's pity. He didn't want their attention. All he wanted was to be left alone.

"I know there's a certain beautiful brunette who'd be willing to get in line to hug you," Harper said slyly, twisting the knife she didn't know he carried in his chest. Seeing Gloria had been a fist to the gut. She was bright and beautiful and happy and hopeful. And he couldn't be the man she needed. He'd missed his chance for the final time. When she'd looked down, he thought he'd die of shame. When he'd turned his back on her, well, he'd turned his back on the future he'd so desperately wanted.

It was for her own good. And he'd regret it to his dying day.

He grunted and prayed that Harper would drop it. Obviously, the friends hadn't spoken since his dickhead production at his mother's front door. But Aldo's luck had run out in Afghanistan, and it sure as hell hadn't come back since. The sooner everyone got used to it, the better.

"Have you talked to Gloria?" Harper asked.

"No."

"Care to expand on that? I feel like I'm talking to Luke here," Harper sighed.

"Turn here," Aldo said, relieved to see the white stone new construction on the right. The whole front of the building was handicap parking, and he swore he'd put his fist through his PT's face if he or she suggested a handicap sticker for him.

Harper pulled into the lot and eased to a stop at the doors. "I'll grab your crutches," she told him.

"I'll walk from the parking space," he said with enough snark to dent Harper's sunny disposition. He was an asshole, and he couldn't stop himself.

She shrugged. "Fine." And then proceeded to park in the very last space at the far end of the lot. She took the keys out of the ignition and dared him to say a word. Ignoring her, Aldo stepped out of the car, standing on his good leg. Harper wrestled his crutches out of her minuscule back seat.

"Get your ass in there," she said, handing over the crutches.

He wasn't sure what pissed him off more, that he was being an asshole or the fact that he didn't want to go in there alone.

"You can come in if you want," Aldo muttered and started for the entrance without looking back.

He worked to keep his face neutral even as moving from

the car to the door sapped him of what energy he had. He was already sweating, and he hadn't done a goddamn thing. It was as if his entire life had been all for nothing. Gone in a second, destroyed by one random explosion.

Harper caught up to him and pushed the button that swung the automatic door open. Together, they stepped into a waiting area that still smelled of new carpet and fresh paint. They waited for a few minutes. Not long enough for him to stop sweating before a nurse in annoying floral scrubs called for them.

"Lieutenant Moretta, welcome to PT. I'm Annalise." She extended her hand to him.

She was tall, slim, and utterly no-nonsense. And he didn't see any signs of pity or "poor baby" in her hazel eyes behind her glasses.

He shuffled his crutches and shook her hand. "Aldo," he said by way of introduction. He wasn't keen on his rank following him into what was his earlier-than-planned civilian life. The nurse turned to Harper, and before Aldo could cobble together a "best friend's girlfriend and woman I begged to drive me here" intro, Harper took over.

The two women exchanged names and shook hands.

"Thanks for coming," Annalise said, leading the way through the door into a space with padded tables and cardio machines. Exercise balls, wooden benches in varying sizes, and even a small trampoline were neatly organized on the beige carpet. The dreaded bridge of steps was sequestered in the corner next to a stack of exercise mats. It was half gym, half day care. "It's important for family to be involved in recovery."

"We're just friends," Aldo mumbled.

"Well, it always helps to have another pair of eyes and hands," Silver Lining Annalise told him. She pointed to a pair of chairs next to a set of parallel bars. "Let me get these set to your height, and the doctor will be here shortly."

God, he hated these bars. He'd fallen from them about a dozen times in Germany and once or twice at Walter Reed Medical Center, his arms too weak to hold his body weight. And when he wasn't falling, he was sweating and swearing and hating his own weakness.

Harper was silent for once next to him, and the look on her face told him she was worried about him.

"Lieutenant." A slim man in a white coat and thick-rimmed glasses approached with a clipboard and a half-drunk green smoothie. "I'm Dr. Steers. I've heard a lot about you."

The introductions were made while Aldo felt a surge of anxiety rush through his system. Part of the "healing" process apparently involved facing his own failings again and again and again. It would either break him, or he'd crawl through it half the man he'd been.

"Let's get started, shall we? Lieutenant, Walter Reed gave me your file, and you already have our staff impressed. To be where you are right now, barely a month from the injury, is almost superhuman."

Superhuman, huh? That sounded more like the old Aldo. He hoped to God the doc wasn't blowing smoke up his ass. This was the first scrap of hope he'd felt since… *Dust. Red. Silence.*

Since.

"He *is* pretty awesome, isn't he?" Harper insisted.

"We can understand the lieutenant's frustration with the pace of therapy, and we'll do our best to write a program that challenges him at his level. We just need to make sure we're not asking too much of your body while you're still so early in the recovery process. Okay?"

Aldo nodded. He'd heard the bullshit before. Rest. Slow.

Incremental progress. Blah blah blah. Never be who he used to be. That last one was part of his own internal monologue.

"So let's get you up." Dr. Steers pointed at the bars. "You know the drill."

Aldo stood and handed his crutches to Annalise. He gripped the ends of the bars and walked, one foot in front of the other, moving one trembling muscle at a time, toward Dr. Steers, who paced him backward on a wheeled stool.

Fuck. It hurt. Everything hurt. He was so sick of feeling like this. Weak, wrung out.

"Looks good," the doctor said, making notes. "Go ahead and go back to the top."

Aldo walked the bars, up and back, again and again, pausing here and there to make slight adjustments to the metal and plastic that were supposed to be part of his body now.

"Lieutenant, let's try it without the bars," Dr. Steers said, peering over the tops of his glasses.

Aldo dropped his hands to his sides and put a little saunter into his stride as he walked slowly toward Annalise. It took every ounce of effort to keep his face impassive. But beneath the surface anxiety, exhaustion, and a fleeting spark of hope all danced a two-step.

"That's perfect," the doctor said with an approving nod. "Your gait looks great."

Again and again, they put him through the paces without walking aids. But this was where he thrived, going up against the wall and finding those last pockets of energy or persever-ance. It was like finding a piece of the old Aldo. *And fucking hell, it felt good.*

His T-shirt was soaked fast to him with sweat, and his quads were trembling from walking. But he was pushing *hard*. And that was where he was most comfortable.

"Let's take a quick water break, and then we'll move on to some of the balance exercises," the doc suggested.

Aldo tried to play it cool but dropped into the chair next to Harper like a stone.

Annalise directed Harper to a refrigerator with water, and she returned with two. Aldo drained half of his with the desperation of a desert wanderer.

The doctor piped up again while Aldo wondered if he could talk Harper out of her water. "I know the energy expenditure is frustrating. Typically, mobility with a below-the-knee amputation consumes up to forty percent more energy than what you're used to. That's why you feel like you just finished a marathon. It might only seem like a few steps to you, but to your body, it feels like almost double that."

"I'm fine," Aldo insisted. "I can do more." At this point, he wasn't sure if it was a lie or sheer stubbornness.

"Lieutenant, you live up to the hype," Annalise said, readjusting the bar height, which thank the fucking gods meant he was definitely done with them. "You're a beast."

"When can I start running?" He dared them to tell him he couldn't. That he "might never." That was what the last two doctors said. Managing expectations.

Dr. Steers gave him a long look. "I'm going to make a promise that in most cases I don't get to make. Soon. In fact, I think you'd be a great candidate for a carbon fiber running blade."

Aldo gave a brisk nod, but his heart was busy climbing its way into his throat. He could run? And not just "might." He *would*. If he could run again, maybe…

No. Gloria deserved a man who could keep her safe, make her feel secure.

She was better off without him.

But it was her face that he saw through the rest of his appointment. Through the balance and strength exercises, the electrical stimulation, and finally the massage that soothed his screaming muscles.

CHAPTER 30

Y ou don't have to be my new therapy buddy," Aldo told Harper once they were back in the car. This time, it was physical exhaustion that had him acting like a bear. Annalise had dumped a stack of papers detailing at-home exercises on Harper on their way out.

"I don't mind," she said, slipping on her sunglasses. "But I'll understand if you'd rather have your mom take you."

He felt his lips lift in an involuntary smirk. "Very funny. Want to grab some lunch?" He hadn't been hungry in weeks, but now he felt like he could lay into a side of beef.

Harper's stomach gave an inhuman gurgle. "More than anything in the world."

She took them through a drive-thru and put the top of the VW down in a sunny, waterfront park. Aldo watched her chow down on her burger with gusto.

"Have you talked to Luke?" she asked with her mouth full.

"A couple of times. Not since I came home though," he told her. The conversations had been rushed. Aldo had gotten updates on Oluo, healing fast and raring to go back. But neither he nor Luke felt inclined to talk specifics about the incident.

Harper stared at him and chewed.

Aldo rolled his eyes. Maybe he was a little rusty on this conversation thing. "He sounds like he's doing okay," he told her.

"Does he?"

"He won't let me thank him." It had bothered him since that first call. Out of surgery, covered in bandages. He hadn't even seen his leg yet. Someone had managed to patch Luke through to his hospital room. It was a short conversation in which Luke's response to Aldo's heartfelt, drugged-up gratitude was a succinct "fuck off."

"For what?" Harper asked, the remains of her burger forgotten in her lap.

"He didn't tell you that he dragged my ass out of there under fire while ordering everyone else to pull back?"

"He *what*?"

"Shit," Aldo said. "It's all kind of a red blur to me. One second I'm driving down this stretch of road, the next I'm falling out of the truck. I couldn't hear or feel anything. All I knew was I couldn't move. I thought I was dead."

The breath he took didn't slow his racing heart. But at least he was talking about it, getting the poison out one drop, one word, at a time. He swiped at his brow.

"Then there's Luke hovering over me. looking like he's screaming. He dragged me behind a truck, used my belt as a tourniquet. I passed out, but they tell me he carried me under fire while the rest of the guys laid down cover."

Harper gripped her soda so hard Coke rolled down the sides. "Why the fuck didn't he tell me?" she demanded.

"Why the fuck won't he let me say thank you?" Aldo countered.

Harper leveled a look at him, and Aldo shook his head in perfect understanding.

"Because he's Luke," they both said.

"I'm going to type an email in all caps to him when I get home tonight," Harper told him.

"I'll mail him a thank-you card with all caps," Aldo decided.

"So why are you avoiding Gloria?" she shot back.

Aldo dropped his head against the seat back. "Anyone ever tell you you're tenacious, Harpoon?"

"Oh no, you don't. I live with Luke '*Jeopardy*' Garrison. I will not be put off by you trying to turn Q and A into Q and Q. Aren't you interested in her anymore? Did your feelings change?"

Frustration bubbled to the surface. "Harper, look at me." He pointed at his prosthesis. "I can barely fucking walk. How am I supposed to sweep her off her feet like she deserves?" *Let alone protect her from whatever nightmares lurk in the shadows.*

Besides, why would she even want him at this point? He couldn't be who she needed. He wasn't the same man who kissed her in the dark hours before deployment. He was something else now, inside and out.

Harper pinched the bridge of her nose and took a deep breath that sounded more like a hiss. "Okay, I don't even know where to start with your asininity."

"Not a word."

"Totally a word. First of all, you think you're somehow less of a man because you're sporting a new leg? That's the dumbest thing I've ever heard. And I've heard a lot of stupid shit. Your leg has nothing to do with the man you are. Your *attitude*, on the other hand, has everything to do with it." She poked him in the chest, hard, letting him know exactly what she thought of his piss-poor attitude. "This 'woe is me' disabled-cowboy crap act is not doing you any favors. Man up and be the rock star you've always been."

He thought she was done. Maybe she had a small, tiny,

practically invisible point. But before he could be magnanimous with his admission, Harper's mouth started again.

"And second, Gloria isn't some fragile flower. She's funny and smart, and she's clawing out a brand-new life for herself. One you could be a part of. You know what would be amazing for her? Some guy who is willing to be vulnerable in front of her. Someone who needs her. Do you know what that would do for her confidence? Finally being in the position to help someone else?" Harper was yelling at Ina Moretta volume now. She grabbed a handful of fries out of her burger box and wielded them at him. "She blushes every time someone says your name. And she survived the Mrs. Moretta inquisition."

Uh-oh.

"Inquisition? Oh shit."

Harper looked smug. "By the end of it, your mom was asking her for her jam thumbprint cookie recipe."

So that was how Gloria got roped into taking care of his mother's house. Hell. She'd been maintaining two Moretta homes by herself, and he hadn't even thanked her. He was such a pathetic asshole.

"This is too much to take in," he sighed.

"Eat your burger. You're weak with hunger and stupidity."

He reached into the bag, unwrapped his burger, and took a huge bite.

"Do you really think she'd want to be with me like this?" he asked, his mouth full.

"I'm going to pretend you weren't just that stupid right now." Harper threw a fistful of french fries at him, and for the first time in weeks, Aldo felt good.

CHAPTER 31

Gloria muscled the couch her mother swore was a second-hand bargain at a thrift shop into place along the long wall of her living room. Hers. The entire one-bedroom, one-bathroom, six-hundred-square-foot, third-floor walk-up was hers.

Her fingers brushed something on the soft cushion, and she choked out a laugh at the price tag. Her sneaky, lying, sweetheart of a mother.

Her eyes filled again. She'd already had her little cry this morning, happy tears as she lugged the first box of her meager belongings up the stairs. Right now, the space was a disaster of half-packed boxes and mismatched furniture and kitchen accessories cluttering the floor and every other flat surface. Oh, and there was the entire corner dedicated to her eight thousand pounds of Fourth of July paperwork, posters, and a few yards of red, white, and blue bunting that Estelle from the restaurant by Aldo's office gave her "in case someone needed it."

But she vowed that by the time she went to bed tonight, it would be perfect.

Home.

A grunt and groan from her open front door caught Gloria's attention. Harper, generous friend that she was, hauled the faux-leather tufted ottoman—a legitimate thrift store find—through the door and into the living room. She flopped down on top of it and heaved a sigh.

"You're going to be in amazing shape just from bringing groceries home," Harper gasped. "I can't believe we got the couch up here ourselves."

Gloria laughed as she unpacked the last dish of her brand-new dinner service for four. "I can't believe it's mine. I can put something on the counter, and it will still be there when I come back. I can watch anything I want on TV. I can lounge around naked all day if I want!" She ticked the items off on her fingers.

Her own place. She'd been frugal with her paychecks and had saved up for the first month's rent and security deposit with no one else's help. She'd done it, snagging the creaky-floored apartment two floors above Dawson's Pizza. Even now, the faint scents of basil and garlic could be detected on the breeze from the open windows.

She met Harper in the living room, and together they appreciated her view through the tall bow window. Main Street Benevolence bustled below. Across the street, the police station's glass windows gleamed, and the door to Common Grounds Café opened and closed.

It was part of what she loved about this particular apartment. She was in the middle of all that was Benevolence. She was a part of it, even if it was only by proximity. And she loved it so fiercely it made her chest burn with something that felt suspiciously like pride.

"This is pretty perfect," Harper said in approval.

Gloria couldn't have agreed more. "Want a drink?"

"For the love of God, yes! Please!" Sophie's voice was muffled by the box of kitchen miscellany that covered her face and chest. She dumped it unceremoniously in the middle of the kitchen floor, a characterless beige tile that Gloria had joyfully scrubbed clean ten minutes after she got the keys.

Sophie flopped down in a dining chair. "That's literally the last thing. You're all moved in."

Gloria grabbed the six-pack of soda she'd stashed in her fridge and squashed the urge to pirouette around the boxes and bags. She'd do that when she was alone.

Harper jogged to her bag. "Wait, Gloria! Put the can down! We can't let the first drink in your very own home be diet soda."

She revealed a bottle of champagne with a flourish.

Sophie clapped her hands. "Nothing happier than the sound of champagne being uncorked!"

Harper helped herself to the meager collection of coffee mugs that Gloria had put away in the cabinet and poured.

"I'd like to make a toast," Gloria told them, accepting a mug. "Thank you both so much. It means the world to me to be independent, but it's even better to have you two as friends that I can depend on if I need to." She'd never had that before. The fact that these two women had volunteered to lug her hodgepodge collection of belongings up three flights of stairs made Gloria feel like the luckiest woman in the world.

"Aw! Cheers!" Harper, then Sophie clinked their mugs to hers.

Sophie left shortly after to help Ty convince their son that he wasn't a dog and did indeed pee inside, unlike Bitsy. Harper stuck around to help with some of the unpacking.

"I really appreciate the help," Gloria called, stacking glasses neatly in the cabinet next to the sink.

"I'm happy to help," Harper said from the living room where she wrestled with the cords of Gloria's small TV and a new-to-her DVD player. Gloria was sharing Wi-Fi with her neighbor and hadn't sprung for cable. She didn't want to overextend herself her first month living on her own now that she had rent and insurance and utilities to pay. It was the first time in her life she was making money, and she was determined to manage it carefully. No shopping sprees or filet mignon for her.

Gloria joined Harper in the living room and sank down on the couch. It was welcoming, soft, and a vibrant purple that added the perfect pop of color against the white walls and light oak floors.

"So how's Aldo doing since he came home?" She hugged a yellow throw pillow to her chest to ward off the automatic ache.

Harper frowned at the back of her TV. "He's, uh, doing okay. I think the therapy is helping mentally. Physically, he's a beast."

"He always was," Gloria said wistfully.

Harper dropped the cord she was fighting with. "Listen, Gloria, I don't know exactly what his problem is, but I hope you know that that's what it is. *His* problem. It has nothing to do with you."

"I think I had got my hopes up a little too high that we could be something together. That I could be something to him," Gloria confessed, picking at the tufted button on the pillow.

"Whoa! Let's back that truck up real fast." Harper grabbed her champagne mug and flopped down next to Gloria. "You can't put your worth in someone else's hands like that. Whether those hands are stroking you or hurting you. It doesn't matter. Your value comes from inside. Whether you mean something to him or not has nothing to do with how inherently valuable you are."

Spoken like someone who's been through therapy, Gloria thought. Hmm.

"I get it," she told her friend. "And I think I'm starting to believe it. I know I'll be *okay* without Aldo Moretta, but I'd still like to at least give it a shot." Or she had before their last encounter.

"Now you're speaking my language," Harper said.

"Is that how you felt about Luke?"

Harper took a swallow of champagne. "That's how I still feel about Luke. I know that I'd be okay without him—after an exceptionally long mourning period, of course. But I want to be great with him."

"So now that I can cross off 'get an apartment' from my list, my next goal is to be great no matter who is in my life," Gloria guessed.

"Bingo."

"Men," Gloria snorted into her mug.

"Tell me about it," Harper sighed.

"Let's order some pizza," Gloria decided.

"That's the best idea you've ever had in this apartment."

———

That night, alone, tucked into clean sheets on her childhood bed in her very own place, Gloria grinned up at the ceiling of her very own home.

"I'm going to be great," she whispered to the shadows. Tonight, she was enjoying the wanton freedom of sleeping naked for the first time in her life.

CHAPTER 32

I want to learn to run." Harper bounced on her toes, dancing around him like an annoying, yappy dog.

Aldo growled from his hamstring stretch on the grass. She'd taken his PT homework seriously, and together they'd been working out in the park at the lake three days a week. He hated to admit it, but even *he* was proud of the progress he was making now. They'd walked two miles today. Two fucking miles on trails. He'd stumbled more than once. But he'd made it without feeling like he was going to keel over and die.

"What brought this on?" he asked, bowing forward over his extended leg and prosthesis. His hamstring argued with him.

"You and Luke run. I've seen him leave the house with his brain full of crap and come back from a run smiling. I want that. Plus, I've been eating a lot of pizza lately, and I helped Gloria move and couldn't walk for three days."

"Okay." Aldo shrugged, pretending not to be hung up on the *helped Gloria move* part of Harper's sentence. "So run to that tree over there and back."

Harper squinted at the pine tree at the trail mouth about two hundred yards away. "That's not very far. I want to run miles."

"You're not ready for miles yet, smart-ass. I'm going to check out your form and tell you how to do it better. Besides, for someone who sits at a desk and eats pizza all day, that tree is far enough."

Harper snorted. "You're missing a part of a leg, and you're already working on slow jogs on the treadmill. I think I can handle running to the tree and back with two regular legs."

His grin was sneaky. He couldn't wait to watch her puke. "Quit stalling. Run. I'll watch and judge mercilessly."

Harper stuck her tongue out at him and turned away. She took off at what was an ugly half sprint, half flail, and Aldo laughed. Her shoulders were hunched, her feet kicked out at odd angles behind her, and her entire torso twisted from side to side as she hurled herself across the terrain.

He'd never seen anyone worse at running before.

Her pace slowed as she approached the big pine and then slowed again as she turned around. Not so cocky now that she was realizing it was all uphill back to him, was she?

"Let's go, Harp!" he called. He could hear her wheezes from here.

Slowly, she shuffled her way back to him. "Please don't throw up. Please don't throw up," she chanted.

Aldo laughed.

"Agh!" She clutched at her side and finally stumbled back to him, collapsing in front of him. "That wasn't so bad," she rasped.

"You sound like a pack-a-day smoker, Harp."

"I think I have appendicitis. It hurts like a bitch," she hissed, her hand digging into her side.

"Welcome to your first side stitch."

"Side stitch?" she repeated on a wheeze.

"Come on," he said, nudging her with the running shoe on

his prosthesis. "Help me up, and I'll tell you all the things you did wrong."

"Like saying I wanted to learn to run?"

He gave her the basics while they worked their way through a series of stretches. *Don't swing your torso. Take smaller steps. Breathe in through the nose, out through the mouth.* Harper looked like she was taking mental notes.

"Let's take a little cool-down walk," Aldo suggested, pointing toward the glimmering waters of the lakefront.

"Cool," Harper said, mostly recovered from her disastrous run. "So how are you doing?" she asked.

He'd known she'd pry and couldn't say why he felt comfortable talking to her. Maybe it was knowing that her life hadn't always been all sunshine and rainbows. And that she knew pain too. Maybe it was that he didn't need anything from Harper but friendship.

"Good enough that I'm moving back to my place this weekend. The doc cleared it." It was his first back-to-real-life goal that he'd tackled and achieved.

"Aren't you going to miss your mom?" Harper teased.

"Me moving out is the only way we'll both live."

They picked their way down a short, rocky decline, and Aldo marveled that his muscles weren't screaming too loudly this time.

"Are you sleeping better?" Harper asked. "Is the pain still keeping you up?"

Aldo gave a shrug and debated answering. "Sometimes it's like my mind can't tell the difference between what's happening and what's happened. It's like this blur between past and present. And sometimes the only thing that clears it is pain."

"Maybe that's why you push your therapy so hard?" Harper mused.

"Maybe that's why I push everything so hard." He had a lot to prove. To himself first. He wouldn't say he was in the same mental swamp he'd been in when he first came home. The PT helped, and getting back to his own home would help more. But he still wasn't right in the head. He wasn't sure if he'd ever get right again.

He thought of Gloria. Wondered if she'd ever be able to accept him like this. Would she want him like this? Or would she recognize the wounds beneath the surface?

"So what's Gloria's apartment like?" he prodded. It was torture, gleaning information about Gloria from Harper. It was a little game they played. She knew why he was asking, but he played it off as casual conversation. He'd known she had moved. Knew where. Had even taken an after-midnight walk down Main Street her first night there to see if her lights were on.

"It's so perfect for her," Harper said. "She's already got everything unpacked and decorated, and you can just tell it makes her so happy. She's right there in the middle of everything too, which I think is good for her."

Aldo grunted.

"Speaking of, when are you going to stop avoiding everyone?" Harper demanded. They stopped at the lake's edge. The water made tiny, steady waves against the shore.

"I'm not avoiding everyone." He was. He hadn't been back to work yet. Hadn't gone out to eat in town. Hell, the only time he left his mother's house was for doctor appointments or late-night strolls—limps—when the walls were closing in on him.

She stopped him with a hand on his arm. "No one is going to think you're anything other than Aldo Moretta."

It wasn't true. But she couldn't possibly understand what it was like to have to face the fact that you were less than you used to be. That you were always going to be less than. And that everyone else would see it too.

"I really want to punch you in your face right now." Harper's words caught him off guard.

"What the hell, Harpsichord?"

"I can see you churning through this whole bullshit 'woe is me' garbage," she said, her voice raising and cutting through the summer noises of kids playing and squirrels arguing, birds chirping.

"I don't know how to make it stop. Okay? Happy?" He started to stalk off and was reasonably pleased when he was able to.

"Maybe you should talk to someone," she called after him.

"Maybe you should mind your own damn business," he said over his shoulder.

She snorted. "We both know that's not going to happen."

———

Another sleepless night. Some nights, it was worse than others. Tonight, every time he closed his eyes, all he saw was dust and blood. He heard the explosion. Saw from a distance as the truck he drove bounced on the shock wave. He watched Oluo crawl out of the passenger side as gunfire erupted. Fear. Pain. Darkness. Red. He wasn't dreaming. His brain had cobbled all accounts of the incident into a monster memory.

He pulled on a pair of gym shorts and a tank top. It was one in the morning. No one would be out and about. He was safe. The first few walks he'd taken, he'd worn pants in case he ran into anyone. But Benevolence was a town of early risers. Restaurants closed at nine, and downtown was a ghost town by ten.

He snuck through the kitchen, past the stairs to the front

door. Even here he could hear his mother's snores upstairs. "Fucking chainsaw," he muttered, stepping outside into the cool summer night. He didn't bother locking the door.

He shuffled off the porch and headed toward her. Always her.

Downtown Benevolence was, as expected, dead asleep. The traffic light blinked, coloring the night in a steady green, yellow, red. Dawson's Pizza was dark, but two floors above the restaurant, the lights were blazing. *What is she doing awake?* he wondered. Was she binge-watching TV? Reading? Was she upset about something? Didn't she feel safe enough to sleep either?

He stopped and stared up, willing her to appear in a window, hoping that she wouldn't.

He shouldn't be here. It wasn't fair to either of them.

What was he going to do when she moved on? When she finally met a nice guy? When he had to read her engagement announcement in the newspaper?

He turned his back on the building and walked on, leaving Gloria Parker behind him.

CHAPTER 33

The key slid in the lock, and Aldo pushed his front door open, waiting for the waft of stuffy, unlived air. Every time he came home from deployment, the first thing he did was open the windows in the entire house, letting the stale air out.

But when he stepped inside and dropped his duffel, all he smelled was the faint hints of lemon and cleaning products.

He frowned. Aldo knew damn well his mother wouldn't have thought to clean for him.

And if she had, nothing above her stocky five feet four inches would be dusted. The place was spotless. He'd never been a slob. But this—the spotless mantel, the neatly stacked mail, the charmingly arranged plants…

Gloria.

"Shit." Her presence was all over his house like a fingerprint. She'd repotted the plants that he'd purchased just so there would be a reason for her to be here.

He was going to have to get rid of them all.

Leaning against the wood of the front door, Aldo waited for the relief he'd expected to course through him. He could finally be alone. No one would be lurking in his kitchen or keeping up a running commentary over *The Price Is Right* or

Entertainment Tonight. No one to pretend for. He could sink into the misery in peace.

As soon as he removed all traces of Gloria from his house. Starting with those fucking cheerful plants. It was like she was here.

Hell, he could practically *hear* her. Singing.

When Gloria appeared on the stairs, lugging his vacuum cleaner down from the second floor and belting out "I Will Survive," Aldo was convinced he was hallucinating. He was back in that hallway in high school, watching the pretty girl in the spotlight.

And then she spotted him, shrieked, and dropped the vacuum cleaner the last half flight of stairs.

Gloria yanked the earbuds out of her ears. "What the hell are you doing here?"

Aldo blinked. "Me? I live here. What the hell are you doing here?"

"Your mother said you'd be moving back in this weekend."

His mother knew exactly when he was moving back home as she'd started a countdown on the refrigerator door last week when he told her.

"So you broke into my house to clean?" Asshole Aldo was rearing his ugly head. But he'd come home for peace and quiet. Not to have his sanctuary invaded by the very woman he was desperately trying to forget.

She looked fresh and pretty, and it made him hate himself even more.

"I used the key you gave me when you asked me to look after your place," Gloria said stiffly. She descended the rest of the way and stepped over the vacuum cleaner.

He stepped closer. "I don't need someone cleaning my place out of pity."

"And *I* don't need someone acting like an asshole when I was simply doing something nice," Gloria snapped back, eyes flashing.

For as long as he'd known her, Aldo had never seen a flash of temper from Gloria. It was impressive. And sexy.

She stomped around him, heading for the door, an impressive feat in flip-flops. He hadn't been this close to her for months. Every sense was alive and reporting back to him in emergency messages. She smelled like cookies and lemon. Her voice, that hint of huskiness, hit him in the chest while his eyes drank her in. She had her short hair pinned up and back, leaving her face unframed. Everything about her was still so delicate. The bone structure, the graceful curve of her slim neck.

The hand that snaked out and closed around her wrist surprised them both. He stared down at his fingers wrapped around her soft skin, wondering what in the hell possessed him to grab her like that.

"I just want to be left alone," he said quietly. Standing there, looking into the eyes of the woman he had some serious feelings for, Aldo realized exactly how Luke felt with Harper in his home. *Conflicted.*

Gloria tugged her hand free. "Welcome home, Aldo," she snapped, her tone indicating anything but welcome. "You're welcome for watering your damn plants and baking you a damn pie and cleaning your damn house. Rest assured it won't happen again." She opened his front door and glanced over her shoulder. "Oh, and you can pick up your own damn vacuum cleaner."

The slam of the front door had Aldo hanging his head. Alone. It was what he wanted. What he needed. And the sooner everyone else got used to it, the better.

His mind was an ugly place these days, and it was better for everyone if he kept to himself.

He pulled out his phone and dialed.

"Why the hell did you tell Gloria I was moving back this weekend?" Aldo demanded.

"Why? Was she there when you got there? Did you talk to her? Did you apologize for being a big, stupid asshole?" his mother demanded.

"You set this up!" He was going to have to either murder her or pack her shit and send her to Boca. Whatever it took to get this woman out of his life.

"Well, someone has to have your best interests at heart! If you don't snap out of this 'poor me' funk, you're going to stay there, and then no one will want to marry you, and I'll never get a grandchild."

Aldo swiped a hand through his hair. "Since when the hell do you want grandkids?" A family was now so far down his priority list it was almost laughable. He'd deployed with the intent of coming home and settling down. Now that he was home, the only thing he wanted was to be left the fuck alone.

"Since I thought you were finally settling down with a nice, smart girl who I don't hate. She brings me cookies, Aldo! Cookies!"

Leave it to his mother to play matchmaker over baked goods. "Stop interfering with my life!" he shouted into the phone.

"Stop interfering with my cookies!" she shouted back.

"I want to be left alone, Ma," Aldo enunciated slowly.

"Well, tough shit. Until you get right in the head, I'm going to make it my life's mission to guide you in the right direction."

"Stay out of it, Ma!"

"Make me, dumbass!"

CHAPTER 34

I should have said 'I deserve better.' No, wait. I should have demanded better." Gloria's bedroom ceiling was annoyingly impassive. She'd gone to bed early. But her thoughts were still roiling with all the things she could have, should have, said to Aldo Moretta earlier.

The stupid, sexy, haunted jerk.

One look at him, all scruffy and gruff, and she'd wanted to run down the stairs and jump into his arms. Then he'd had to open his mouth and be New Aldo. New, angry, wounded Aldo. He didn't want her anywhere near him. He'd made it abundantly clear on two occasions now.

She *should* just let it go.

"But he owes me an apology," she argued with the ceiling. And an explanation. Gloria wanted to hear the words explaining why he went from wanting to date her to wanting nothing to do with her. She wanted him to spell it out for her, and then she wanted her chance to tell him he was an ass.

She heard a knock on her front door and kicked the covers off.

Opening the door, she found Harper in the hallway.

"I know about Karen," Harper said.

Any imaginary arguments with Aldo immediately took a back seat in Gloria's brain.

Her friend's eyes were red and puffy. She was wearing pajama pants and a National Guard T-shirt four sizes too big.

"I didn't realize there was a time you didn't know," Gloria said, guiding Harper into the living room. Luke's wife, his high school sweetheart, had been killed in a car accident the day Luke's unit had returned home from a long deployment. She'd died on her way to pick him up. A travesty that, until recently, the entire town of Benevolence had assumed he'd never recover from.

"He was married, Gloria. *Married*, and he never said a word to me," Harper said, pacing the short distance between window and door. "He lost the love of his life in the most horrific way." She covered her face with her hands.

She was being called upon for comfort, Gloria realized. Tea. Wasn't that what people did to comfort hurt and tenderly care?

"I'll make tea," she announced.

"I'll sit here and wonder what it means that the man I love with every piece of my stupid heart didn't find it relevant to share the most important awful thing in his life with me," Harper said, falling down onto Gloria's couch with a noise between a sob and a sigh.

Gloria ripped open her beverage cabinet and debated tea flavors. Sleepytime, Energizing Citrus, or good ol' English Breakfast? Definitely Sleepytime.

She put a kettle on, chose two cheerful mugs, and returned to the living room to clumsily offer comfort.

Sitting next to Harper, Gloria patted her friend on the knee.

"I shared things with him. Ugly things," Harper said, sniffling.

Gloria handed over a box of tissues and said nothing.

"I told him about foster care and...and the abuse," Harper said. "I trusted him with *my* ugliness."

Wordlessly, Gloria squeezed her friend's wrist. *My ugliness.* That was exactly what it felt like to have those dark shadows inside her. Something terrible and ugly that needed to stay hidden so it wouldn't taint anyone else.

"What did he say to that?" Gloria asked. What would a man say to the woman he cared for when she talked of a pain he could never take away?

"Not much." Harper choked out a laugh. "Getting more than three words out of him at a time is physically exhausting. But he didn't make me feel ugly or damaged. Why didn't he trust me, Gloria?" Her eyes beseeched Gloria for a reason that wouldn't hurt, wouldn't bruise her heart even more than it already was.

The kettle whistled from the kitchen.

"I'll be back," Gloria said, patting Harper's hand. "Hang in there a minute."

She used the tea preparation to settle and collect her thoughts.

When she returned with a pretty tray of steaming tea and tiny cookies, Harper was blowing her nose and adding to the stack of tissues piled in front of her.

"Does this mean he doesn't love me?" Harper asked.

Gloria set the tray down on the ottoman. "No," she said definitively.

"He's never said it," Harper pointed out. "I assumed— hoped—he had a hard time saying it. But maybe it's because he doesn't feel that way about me?"

Gloria had never seen a man more in love with a woman than Luke Garrison. Whether he had the balls to admit it to himself or to Harper was another story.

"He cares. He asked you to stay."

"Maybe he just needed a house sitter?" Harper sniffled.

That was all Gloria had turned out to be for Aldo, wasn't it? *Shut up*, Gloria told herself. *This isn't your pity party.* She had important friend duties to attend to, and she wasn't going to mess this up.

"He cares for you, Harper. You know it. Don't let this doubt take that away from you. Believe in your gut."

"Then why would he keep this from me?"

Gloria shook her head. "The workings of the male mind are a mystery to me. If I had to guess, maybe he didn't want to hurt you or hurt himself by telling it. I've never heard him mention her name since. Maybe he can't? Was it hard for you to tell him about your...story?"

Harper blinked and thought. "Yeah. I guess so. I don't like talking about it. I don't want anyone to feel sorry for me or think that I'm some kind of victim."

"I get that," Gloria told her.

Harper looked at her and gave her hand a squeeze. "I'm sorry."

"Don't be weird. We both know what it's like, and we're both freaking fantastic women now who some lucky, handsome men are going to spend their lives being grateful for."

"I don't think he trusts me."

Gloria picked up her tea. "I don't agree with you. But I do agree this is a big problem. So what are you going to do about it?"

Harper reached for the plate of cookies. "I don't know. I don't think this is a 'you're a million miles away, so let's talk about our relationship' kind of conversation. I can't email him about this."

"No," Gloria agreed.

"So I guess I just try to process all of it until he comes home and then dump it on him like a bucket of ice water? 'Welcome home, Luke. Why the hell didn't you tell me about Karen?'"

"We'll work on your delivery."

Harper laughed and shoved a cookie in her mouth. "Thanks for being here for me."

"Anytime," Gloria said and meant it.

They sat in silence for a few minutes, feet tucked under them, sipping tea.

"How in the hell did no one in this big-mouthed little town spill the beans on this?" Harper wondered aloud.

Gloria gave a half smile. Benevolence was not known for its ability to keep quiet. "Well, I can't say for sure. I wasn't exactly in the loop when it all happened. But I think Luke took it very hard. Hard enough that his family worried they'd lose him too."

Harper closed her eyes, and a tear slid free.

"I'm sorry," Gloria said quickly.

"No, it's just… Ugh. I'm being selfish and a horrible person. Can I say it and you won't hold it against me?" Harper begged.

"Absolutely."

"He loved her that much. Does that mean that he can't love me at all? And am I willing to settle for scraps?"

"That doesn't make you a horrible person," Gloria said, nudging Harper with her bare foot. "That makes you a human being."

"I love him so much," Harper said quietly.

"I know you do. And you can do that no matter what happens. There's never anything wrong with loving someone," Gloria told her.

Harper let out a long, slow breath. "You're right. Thanks, Gloria."

"Do you want more tea?" Gloria offered.

"Do you have beer and chocolate?"

CHAPTER 35

S he should have been nervous. She should be trying to talk herself out of something she was most definitely going to regret. But for once in her whole life, Gloria had a full head of steam, and she was going to take it out on someone.

If Harper could find the guts to confront Luke when he came home, even if it meant jeopardizing her home, her job, and her relationship, then Gloria could march right up to Aldo's face and let him have a piece of her mind.

Ignoring the doorbell that she'd personally cleaned the cobwebs from yesterday, she lifted her fist and pounded on the door.

"For chrissake, Ma, use your damn key," Aldo bellowed from inside.

Gloria was not Ma, but she did have a key that she hadn't bothered returning yet.

She let herself in, glaring left and right, but the first floor was empty.

"I'll be down in a minute," Aldo groused from the second floor. But Gloria was already on the stairs.

She pushed his bedroom door open so hard it bounced off of the wall, and she had to shove it again to walk inside.

Aldo was speechless…and gloriously naked.

She sucked in a breath that sounded like a wheeze.

He was sitting on the edge of his bed, his prosthetic leg in hand. She'd seen him shirtless before. Had memorized the muscle and ink that covered his torso. He was leaner now, she noted. his cheeks more hollow above what was turning into a beard. There was an exhaustion in the slump of his shoulders. But he was still her Aldo.

It wasn't the brutal red scarring covering his knee and what remained of his left leg that drew her eye. No, it was the glimpse of long, girthy cock between his legs.

Holy shit. She'd only seen one other penis live and in person, and it wasn't even half the size of Aldo's…member. She felt a little dizzy. And a lot distracted.

"Jesus! Gloria?" he choked her name out and dove for his bedsheets.

From somewhere in her cock fog, Gloria noticed that he was more concerned with hiding his leg than he was his hypnotic penis. It was that glimpse of humiliation she saw in his eyes that had her turning around to face the open doorway.

"I have something to say," she told him, or rather the hallway.

There was a clunk behind her as his prosthesis hit the floor. Aldo swore under his breath.

"I'm happy you're home and that you're safe," she began.

He made a noise like he was going to interrupt, but she cut him off.

"Shut up. I'm not done. I'm glad you're home, but I'm very angry and disappointed with you. You made me feel like you saw a future with me. You let me get excited about that possibility. You made me think you believed in me…and now you want nothing to do with me. No explanations. No apologies. Just done."

"Gloria," he began quietly. She could hear the resignation. Years of dodging tempers had taught her how to be a reader of people.

"I don't know what's going on with you," she pressed on. "I don't know if you met someone else while you were deployed or you decided I wasn't what you wanted. But either way, you owe me the courtesy of an explanation. I deserve better than you having your mother slam the door in my face or you yelling at me when all I did was something nice for you. I expect you to be brave enough, man enough, to tell me why I'm not what you want."

She chanced a glance over her shoulder and found Aldo covered from the waist down in the sheets she'd washed for him. He was looking appropriately shamed, refusing to meet her gaze.

"Aldo," she continued softly. "You made me feel like I was nothing to you."

The sigh that rose from his chest seemed to take all his effort. "You're not nothing." He gritted out the words like they caused him pain.

"I'm done letting people do that. I'm not nothing. You'd be damn lucky to have me. Anyone would." She choked on the last word and cursed herself. She would not cry. She wouldn't be the victim here. Nope. She would go home and blubber like a baby. But she would not give Aldo a glimpse of the fresh hurt he'd caused her. Her newly rediscovered pride wouldn't allow it.

"What do you want me to do? Hop after you?" The bitterness in his words arrowed straight to her heart and broke a piece off.

"That's the stupidest fucking thing I've ever heard you say," Gloria snapped, and good Lord did it feel good to finally speak her mind. He didn't need her pity. He needed someone to slap him upside the head, give him a good shake.

He brought his head up.

"You don't know anything, Gloria." He spoke quietly and without heat.

She absorbed the words the way she would a blow. Waited for the burn of shame. But her anger, bright and sharp, shielded her.

Gloria looked down pointedly at where the sheet covered his left leg. "I know a lot more about wounds and healing than you might think. And I know they don't give anyone a license to be a dick—" An image of Aldo's appendage appeared before her eyes. "An asshole, I mean."

Those brown eyes of his flashed with anger, and Gloria patted herself on the back. At least there was something else besides self-pity there now.

"You owe me an explanation and an apology," she repeated. "I'll be waiting for both." On those victorious words, she shut his bedroom door behind her with a midgrade slam and stomped out of his house. But not before leaving his house key front and center on his dining table.

———

Gloria woke with a start. Her apartment was dark and quiet. Aldo's T-shirt, the one she'd liberated from his dresser, stuck to her face when she slowly sat up. She hadn't expected to feel so many emotions when taking this stand.

Her head hurt from the crying jag she'd allowed herself after confronting Aldo. Her eyes were swollen, but she felt liberated.

She had wanted to matter to him so much. She'd wanted that future he'd talked about. Desperately. But not with a man who didn't think she deserved an explanation. Not with the

Aldo Moretta who came home a stranger. He had shadows on his own soul now.

She checked her phone, telling herself it was only to see the time. But she still bit her lip when she saw there were no messages, no missed calls.

He was hurting. Not just physically. There was a hole in Aldo Moretta's spirit. She knew from experience that no one else could fix it. Not her mother, not a sharp-tongued doctor. She had to be the one to pull herself from the murk. Aldo had to do the same.

She stroked a hand over the T-shirt once and then, biting her lip, folded it neatly and stuffed it in the back of her second-hand dresser that she'd found on the cheap at a yard sale.

She'd put him away and focus on building this new life for herself. And she'd hope that Aldo would find the strength to heal from his own wounds.

Feeling a little extra lonely, Gloria padded into her kitchen to make a dinner for one.

CHAPTER 36

The Fourth of July dawned hot and humid with no thunderstorms in the forecast. And Benevolence was ready for it. Every inch of Main Street was decked out in patriotic bunting. The park was groomed within an inch of its life, ready for a few thousand people to tromp through it eating cotton candy and winning goldfish.

Three stories above it all, Gloria stared at her reflection in the mirror. "Do not freak out," she cautioned. "You worked hard and did the absolute best you could. If it's a total flop, you can slink out of town and start a new life under an assumed name."

Maybe Margot? She could sell insurance. Run a book club. Meet a nice guy named Todd or James and go to Applebee's every Tuesday for date night.

Plan B settled, Gloria tied a wide red bandana around her dark hair. She looked…ready.

Gloria couldn't remember looking in the mirror and liking what she saw more than she did in that moment. Her white shorts showed off bruise-free legs, and the navy-blue tank nicely showcased arms that were beginning to take shape. She looked strong, festive, and maybe even pretty. Inspired, Gloria dragged her makeup tote out from under the sink and skillfully applied a cat eye and subtle sparkle to her eyelids. She painted her lips a patriotic red with stain and then gloss.

"Happy Fourth of July," she whispered.

On her way out the door, she glanced at the letter on the table. She'd been too busy to open this one. That said something. She just didn't have the time to figure out what. The personal protection order was stalled until Glenn made some sort of overt threat. But the man was behind bars, and her focus was on giving her town the best Fourth of July celebration it had ever had.

Main Street Benevolence was a hive of activity. The finish line for the 5K race happened to be right in front of her building, and the judges' bandstand for the parade floats was set up across the street in front of the police station.

Gloria grabbed her phone and clipboard with her checklists, settled her sunglasses over her eyes, and took a deep breath. All the wheeling and dealing, the hand-holding, the hours of organizing and answering questions were about to come to fruition.

She was terrified.

What if it sucked? What if she'd organized the worst Fourth of July celebration in the town's history?

"Well, at least I won't be poor little Gloria Parker then," she reminded herself. "I'll be that idiot who ruined an entire holiday."

"Georgia Rae hasn't called me fourteen times this morning bitching and moaning about her damn parking space," Ty said, stepping up onto the curb to meet her. He tucked his thumbs into his utility belt. "Far as I'm concerned, this is the best Fourth we've ever had around here."

"You're only saying that because the fireworks didn't ignite the snow cone tiki hut yet. I should have moved it to the other side of the park. It's going to be a four-alarm blaze once the fireworks start," Gloria moaned.

Ty put a hand on her shoulder. "You did good, Parker. Deal with it."

"Thanks, Ty." She could tell him about the letter now. But tomorrow was soon enough. She had bigger fish to fry than Glenn Diller right now.

His radio squawked, and he grinned. "I'll see you around."

To-do list in hand, Gloria jogged off in the direction of the park to make sure everything was exactly right.

————

"I can't believe nothing's caught fire or a swarm of killer bees and locusts hasn't descended yet," Gloria said, unfolding one of the lawn chairs her mother brought.

"That's what I love about you, *mija*. Your incessant positivity," her mother said and snickered, taking the seat.

Everything was going according to plan, which made Gloria very, very nervous. She and her mom were front row at the curb so they could witness Harper's first, triumphant finish in the Red, White, and Blue 5K. Her friend had been training with Aldo for weeks.

Gloria appreciated Harper's ability to compartmentalize friendships. Aldo needed a friend right now, even if he had pissed Gloria off. And Gloria didn't need her best friend constantly running her mouth about the man who'd gotten away. Harper respectfully didn't discuss Aldo in more than broad, general statements.

That was how Gloria knew he'd be biking the 5K in a specially designed bike. Also how she *didn't* know how he felt about that. She was too busy to worry about it…mostly.

"Sit, Gloria. You're acting like a nervous pigeon," Sara teased, patting the chair next to her.

Technically, there was nothing more for her to do but sit back and enjoy the 5K and parade. Then she could frantically worry about the festival and fireworks.

She gave in to her already aching feet and sank down next to her mother.

"Good girl. Your friend Harper. She's running?" Sara asked.

"Yeah, she's been training hard," Gloria said with a smile, remembering last week when Harper had shown up on her doorstep sweaty and thirsty. "Lemonade me, for the love of God!" she'd begged.

Having a friend—a best friend—was a constant reminder that her life was completely different than it had been at the beginning of the year. Harper was one for the record books. After her crying jag the other night, Harper had not only met Luke's ex-mother-in-law, Joni, but befriended her. Joni had all but disappeared from Benevolence life after her daughter's accident. Seeing her with Harper gave Gloria a newfound faith in healing.

Perhaps there was hope for them all.

She very purposefully shoved Aldo from her thoughts.

"Hey, do you guys mind some company?" Sophie with Claire, Charlie, and little Josh in tow ambled down the sidewalk.

And just like that, Gloria was surrounded by friends, coworkers, and family. She'd never felt less alone in her life.

CHAPTER 37

He felt like a circus freak. The one-legged "hometown hero" on his goddamn hand cycle. It was like an adult version of a tricycle. And Aldo was the overgrown man-child in its seat. In his recumbent position, he only came up to Harper's torso as she nervously stretched next to him.

He didn't like being eye level with the crowd. It made him feel small, different.

But it was the only way his doctors would give permission for his participation in the Red, White, and Blue 5K.

So he sucked it up…mostly.

"I'm going to puke," Harper whispered, leaning down to stretch her hamstrings for the four hundredth time.

"If you puke on me, I'm going to run you over with this stupid tricycle," Aldo threatened.

She sucked in a nervous breath, and he took pity on her.

"Harpist, you're going to be fine. It's three miles. It'll be done and over with before you know it."

"I wish Luke was here," she confessed.

Aldo reached for her hand, gave it a bone-crushing squeeze. "Me too. But right now you're stuck with me, and you're not allowed to humiliate me. On second thought, if you're flailing around like an idiot beside me, no one will notice ol' Peg Leg Aldo on the freaking circus bike."

"Don't even pretend you're embarrassed. You're going to eat up all the attention." Harper poked him in the shoulder.

"It's kind of hard to impress a girl when you're acting like you're handicapped."

"Just take your shirt off, and no one will care if you're doing the race on a miniature pony. Is there any girl in particular you're trying to impress?"

He took a swig of water. "Maybe."

On the surface, he was smirking, but underneath he was scared shitless. This was his chance to prove to himself and the rest of the damn town that he was still a force to be reckoned with.

"I'm so nervous," Harper said, patting a hand to her chest. "Is it normal to be nervous?"

"It's not nerves. It's excitement." It was all a matter of perspective.

A guy weaved his way through the crowd to Aldo, offering his hand and a friendly "thanks for your service."

Aldo shook hands and nodded politely. He'd been inundated with thanks and well wishes since rolling up to the start line. It was overwhelming and embarrassing.

He'd never minded being the center of attention before. But now that it was for missing a fucking limb, he wasn't much of a fan. Today, that would change. Hopefully. Today was the first step in proving that he was still a damn man, and if he could prove that to himself, step two might be getting Gloria to forgive his dumb ass. She'd stood up for herself to him. He'd never in his life set out to be that guy. Amputation or not, he needed to find the strength to fight the slide into asshole territory.

"Ladies and gentlemen, please rise for our national anthem, sung by Peggy Ann Marsico."

Aldo climbed off the bike and stood at attention in a military salute.

He'd pledged life and literal limb for his country. And right now, surrounded by an ocean of his neighbors in red, white, and blue, he felt a shaky kind of pride. He'd made the promise, and yes, he hadn't really fully grasped what that sacrifice would feel like, what the reality of it would be. But he'd made the promise, and he'd lived up to it. That was something to be proud of.

It felt damn good to have an inch or two of his soul make room for something good and bright.

The race kicked off in style with Ty in his deputy uniform firing a blank into the air.

Aldo felt the familiar rush of adrenaline and basked in it. And then remembered it was his hands and not his feet that he had to move. Slowly, he and Harper lumbered off the starting line. The crowd thinned quickly with the sprinters—his former place of glory—taking off like greyhounds on the chase.

Aldo cursed his pedals and tried to keep pace with Harper, who still looked a little green around the gills.

"Just relax into it," he coached her. "We're just out here going for a nice quiet jog-slash-pedal in front of the entire town."

She snorted, but her feet picked up the pace a bit, a look of determination on her pretty face.

"Good job. Way to not suck," he told her.

"Shut up, man-beast."

———

"Oh my God. I'm dying. Aldo, I'm dying," Harper gasped.

"If you couldn't talk, I'd be concerned."

"You're not even out of breath," she muttered.

He flashed her a grin. He was Aldo "Fucking" Moretta. He didn't get out of breath...or at least he did everything to hide it. "You're fine. You've got a great pace." He waved from his bike at a group of kids cheering from the end of their driveway. Almost the entire course had been lined with Benevolence residents. It was the best turnout he could remember for a race he'd been running since high school. Everyone seemed to be in the spirit.

"Where's your mom?" Harper asked, pointing ahead at his mother's yard and the end of the block.

"Finish line probably," he told her. It was closer to the start of the parade, and Ina Moretta had an entire parade candy strategy honed from years of literally stealing candy from babies.

"How much farther?" Harper moaned. "I don't think I'm going to make it. Maybe I'll just wait here. You can come back and pick me up."

"Don't be so dramatic. Do you hear the yelling?"

"I can barely hear anything over the wheezing of my lungs."

"That's the finish line."

"Are you kidding? We're almost done?"

"Half mile to go."

"Seriously?" Harper perked up. "I think I can run that."

"I know you can. And so can I." He pulled the cycle into his mother's driveway.

Harper used the pause to bend at the waist and suck in air like a vacuum cleaner. "Aldo—"

He carefully stood, reaching down to adjust his blade. "Before you even start, I cleared it with Steers. A half mile at a slow jog. Are you up for that? We're not stopping until the finish line."

Her face lit up, and he knew there would be no stopping Harper Wilde on the final leg of their journey together. "Let's do it!"

They left the driveway at an easy jog and rejoined the race. Aldo's gait felt smooth on the carbon fiber running blade. It was his new toy, one that took him one step closer to the man he used to be.

He wanted to push. To sprint. To find his limits. But he owed the woman next to him a buddy finish. Harper had helped drag him from the darkest of the depression. Now that he could stand—hell, jog—on his own two feet, he could start making some changes.

"You make this look so easy," Harper puffed beside him.

"Believe me, it's anything but easy. But it's necessary."

They rounded the next corner together, and the noise level exploded. The finish line was only two blocks away, a straight shot down Main Street Benevolence. And the crowd was pulsing with good-natured pandemonium.

"They must think you're some kind of hero around here," Harper teased.

Aldo shot her a cocky grin. He was home. He was *back*.

He saw her, and his stride faltered for a second. Gloria in her little white shorts and that cute blue tank. Her dark hair pulled back under a red bandanna headband. She looked like everything he believed in, everything he'd signed up to fight for, to protect.

She was on her feet cheering. Sure, it was probably for Harper or any other runner in this race, but he wanted to think it was for him. He wanted her in his corner. And if he could do this, if he could finish this half mile strong, then he could make it a mile and then five. And then he could walk up to Gloria Parker and sweep her off her tiny feet.

The finish line banner loomed before them, and Aldo grabbed Harper's wrist, raising their joined hands high as they crossed the sidewalk chalk checkerboard line.

They'd done it. And it felt damn good.

Harper whooped in celebration. Two older veterans in their dress uniforms stepped in front of them with race medals in hand.

The two men, well into their seventies, snapped to attention and saluted Aldo.

"Thank you for your service, Lieutenant," one of them said.

Aldo saluted them back and accepted the medal. His throat felt tight with emotion.

"And here's one for you, young lady," the shorter of the two men said, placing a medal around Harper's neck.

Tickled, she leaned over and pressed an enthusiastic kiss to his cheek. "Thank you!"

"Luke is going to kick my ass if he sees I let you cast him aside for another soldier," Aldo teased, dragging her toward the water station.

They were intercepted by his mother and the entire Garrison clan.

Congratulations were doled out along with bottles of water and bananas. Aldo was searching the crowd for Gloria when Josh, Sophie and Ty's toddler, threw himself into his arms. Aldo swept him up.

"You sweaty too!" Josh crowed, patting Aldo's damp face.

"When are you gonna run a race, buddy?" Aldo asked him.

"I wanna be fast like you!" Josh pumped his arms back and forth. "Fast fast fast!"

Aldo chuckled. It was at that moment he spotted Gloria through the crowd. He set Josh on his feet. "Go find your mom and make sure you get a good spot for the parade, okay?"

"Okay!" Josh took off in the direction of Sophie, yelling, "Caaaaaaaandy!"

Man up, Moretta, he told himself.

One look at Gloria in her red, white, and blue, and he was toast. Burnt, crispy, throw-him-in-the-trash toast. He'd worked hard these last few weeks, talking himself into accepting the fact that he and Gloria were over before they'd begun. That the timing and circumstances were proof that they weren't meant to be.

But now?

A half mile was nothing to some men. To Aldo today, it was the world.

And now it was time to take his next step.

CHAPTER 38

H ere they come!" Sophie shrieked in Gloria's ear and took off toward the finish line with her phone set to record.

Gloria jumped to her feet to watch Harper round the corner onto Main Street, her cheeks flushed with exertion, her ponytail swinging rhythmically. The cheer Gloria had ready died in her throat when she saw the man next to her.

Aldo Moretta paced Harper on a gleaming running blade. He was sweating through his National Guard tank and grinning like a madman. He was running. On his own two legs.

Emotions hit her in a tidal wave. Pride and longing and that low-level anger stewed in her blood. He was magnificent. The entire crowd was on their feet, screaming their heads off as he and Harper loped toward the finish line.

Claire, tears streaming down her face, hollered at the duo. Charlie, always the quiet one, swallowed hard and clapped.

They hit the finish line together to raucous cheers.

Gloria lost sight of them as half the crowd spilled off the curb into the finish zone for congratulations. Runners were still finishing, neighbors still cheering. And Gloria was surprised to find a stray tear tracking down her cheeks.

That running fool looked more like the old Aldo than the man who'd come home in his place.

"Go give your congratulations," Sara said, reading her like a pop-up children's book.

Gloria nodded, not trusting her voice.

She found Harper sitting on the curb, sucking down water.

"Hey, Harper! That was some finish," Gloria called.

Harper, face flushed with exertion and victory, grinned. "You look gorgeous! I'd hug you, but I'd ruin your cute outfit."

Gloria laughed. "You can hug me after you shower. I wanted to see if everyone wanted to sit with me at the parade? You can't beat the seats." She pointed back to her front steps. "The parade goes right past."

Harper's eyes lit up at the idea of not having to walk any farther. "That would be great, thanks! What time does it start?"

"It starts after the last finisher of the 5K. They call it leading the parade," Gloria explained.

"Do you have room for one more? Maybe two? My mom's a sucker for parade candy."

Gloria jumped at the sound of Aldo's voice. Was he talking to her? She turned around slowly and felt her eyes pop out of her head.

He'd taken off his shirt and stood on the sidewalk in all his ripped, sweaty glory. She'd never seen a man look sexier or stronger. If she kept staring at him, she was going to pass out.

"Hi, Aldo," she said politely through her tight throat.

"Hi, Gloria. You look beautiful and festive."

She blinked, wondering if this really was Old Aldo that she was staring at. Or if New Aldo was playing a game. "Thank you. You look…good." Understatement of the year. But it was all he was getting from her.

He grinned, and her knees nearly gave out. "Do you mind if I join you for the parade?"

Gloria breathed in a little too sharply and choked on her own spit. She covered it with a cough. "Sure, I mean, not at all. The more the merrier." *No! Why was she saying that?* She would be perfectly within her rights to figuratively kick him to the curb. Or off it.

"Great. See you soon." He walked off.

It took Gloria a full ten seconds to notice she was fanning herself. "Oh my. What just happened? Did I pass out?"

Harper laughed and dragged herself to a standing position, delight written all over her flushed face. "I think this is Aldo coming around and pulling out all the stops. Prepare to be swept off your feet."

"I don't think I'm ready for that. Can't he just say hello to me once a week for a year or so until I get used to looking at him?"

"I don't think that's how he works. You'll be married in no time," Harper predicted.

"You're such a weirdo."

"You love me," Harper countered.

"Yeah, maybe." Gloria was still staring at the crowd where Aldo had disappeared.

She felt the weight of a stare and turned to face her mother.

Sara's eyebrows were an inch higher than usual. "And what do you want to say about that?" Sara asked quietly, nodding her head in the direction Aldo had gone.

"About what?" Gloria asked innocently.

"I might be your mother, but I am a woman first. I recognize that look. The handsome, sweaty athlete likes you."

Gloria laughed. "Yeah, he likes me today, and then tomorrow he'll be back to pretending I don't exist."

"Maybe he needs a good woman to help him find his way," Sara suggested pointedly.

"After the mess I just got out of, you want me to go running after another man?" Gloria rolled her eyes.

"*Mija*, if you don't run after that man, I'm going to check you for a pulse."

She couldn't help but laugh. "I don't see you putting yourself out there into the dating world."

"If it convinces you to spend some time getting to know that man biblically, I will find a date." Sara started scanning the crowd as if looking for an appropriate man. Gloria didn't doubt her mother's ability to snag a date on the street. She was beautiful, confident, and a smoky-eyed Latina. Basically irresistible.

"Mama! I might be ready for some biblical action. But I'm not sure if I'm ready to forgive him for acting like an ass. If I *was* ready, I don't know if *he's* ready to be what I want."

Sara's smile was bright. "I have great hopes for your future, Gloria. You're a smart girl. A strong girl. Maybe you'll have a little fun figuring things out."

A little fun. Gloria wasn't certain she remembered what that was. Sure she'd discovered how much she enjoyed hard work. But fun? And there was the fact that Aldo still owed her an explanation *and* an apology.

"Hey, Gloria, we've got a snafu with the entertainment tonight," Ricky Lesser called to her, waving the microphone she'd personally tested this morning.

Crap.

Not only did she have to make sure the rest of the day went perfectly, she also had to decide if she was going to give Aldo Moretta a toehold in her life.

CHAPTER 39

I'm not sure how we got talked into this," Gloria confessed to the woman next to her. Harper had somehow managed to convince Joni, Claire, and Gloria to help her run herd on Mrs. Agosta's three foster kids at the Fourth of July festival. Mrs. Agosta was a lovely woman in her early seventies who was absolutely worn out by three energetic kids.

"Harper can be very convincing," Joni said, looking fondly in Harper's direction. Harper was juggling Ava, the toddler, on her hip while Henry danced around her, listing all the festival food he wanted to eat. Robbie, the oldest, stood a few steps away from his younger siblings and pretended he didn't know them.

Biting her lip, Gloria overstepped her bounds. "I think it's wonderful that you two are getting to know each other," she confessed.

Joni sighed. "I wasted a lot of time grieving, blaming, and wishing things could have turned out differently. I missed out on a lot of living. Harper helped me see that."

"She's good at that, isn't she?" Gloria said with a smile.

"Gloria, there you are!" Kate Marshall jogged up, her two teenagers shuffling behind her. "You pulled it off," she said, sweeping an arm around the park. "I've been looking for you all day to tell you what a great job you did."

"Thank you. I really enjoyed it," Gloria said, flushing with pleasure. She remembered this feeling. Approval.

"Don't be surprised if I call you about Christmas." Kate gave her a wink and then hustled the kids off in the direction of the taco truck.

Gloria had to admit the carnival-like atmosphere was magic. Dusk was falling, and the lakefront park was lit up with neon lights and carnival music. There were rides and games and food stands everywhere. It looked as though the entire town had turned out for it.

Flying high on accomplishment and praise, she laughed while Claire and Joni fed the kids dollars to win the requisite carnival fish. "Guess you're going aquarium shopping tomorrow," Gloria teased Harper when Robbie's ping-pong ball splashed into the fishbowl.

"Crap!" Harper said in exasperation before perking up. "Laugh all you want, because here comes trouble for you."

Aldo Moretta, clean-shaven and sporting cargo shorts, boat shoes, and a navy-blue T-shirt that molded itself to his chest, was walking toward her. Not just walking. Striding. A man on a mission. An Italian god among mortals.

Gloria briefly considered dropping her funnel cake on the ground and running in the opposite direction. But his speed this morning had looked good as he crossed the finish. She wasn't sure she could outdistance him.

"Oh, God. Why do I have this reaction to him?" she whispered.

"Just enjoy it," Harper hissed at her. "Ask him if he wants to watch the fireworks with us." And with a helpful shove forward, her traitor friend disappeared back to the goldfish stand where the children in her care were racking up a school of fish.

"Hey," Aldo said, closing the distance between them.

Yep. He was definitely talking to her. On purpose. "Hi," Gloria croaked.

"Do you have a minute to talk?" he asked, nodding his head in the direction of the lake.

Big Chicken Gloria reared her terrified head for a minute. It was safer to be mad at him. Easier to keep her distance. She should brush him off like he'd done to her.

Her lack of response had him stepping a little closer. She could smell his soap. *Who knew soap could be sexy?*

"I believe I owe you both an apology and an explanation." His voice was low and a little rough. It stroked over her skin.

"You know, I don't think you really owe me anything—" she began.

He closed his eyes for a second. "Come on, Glo. Don't chicken out on me now. You have no idea what it took to get me here to you right now. The least you can do is listen to me before you decide to blow me off."

"Blow you off? Who blew who off?" she demanded, crossing her arms over her chest.

Aldo blinked, then grinned.

"And don't even think about making a blow job joke," she said, poking him in his chest with her finger.

Aldo captured her hand, engulfing it in his. Everything about him was so big, solid.

"I'm not making blow job jokes," he promised.

"Then what are you smiling at?" She pulled her hand back and was marginally disappointed when he let her have it.

"You're yelling at me," he said. "You're not apologizing."

"What do *I* have to apologize for?" She gasped, incensed.

Aldo winced. "I'm doing a really bad job of complimenting you."

"You're damn right you are." Gloria snorted. "Say something nice about my hair or my shoes or my eyes. Don't ask me why I'm not apologizing to you."

He stepped in on her while she was too incensed to notice the danger of a full-court press from Aldo Moretta. He slid his hand into her hair behind her ear, and her body went on sexy time alert. Holy hell. They were standing in the middle of the festival she'd organized, and she felt like they were alone in the summer night.

"Your hair is so soft, I spent hours every day while I was gone wondering what it would feel like to bury my hands and face in it."

"Oh," Gloria choked out.

"Your shoes are the sexiest thing I've ever seen. I've always had a thing for white tennis shoes."

Goose bumps, a bumper crop of them, had the hair on her arms standing straight up.

"And your eyes. Brown and gold." She could feel his breath on her face and realized her own had stopped. "I've never seen eyes like yours. They pull me in like a riptide. I could drown in them if you let me."

Could a woman pass out from compliments? Gloria had a feeling she was about to find out.

"Thank you." Through sheer force of will, Gloria managed to choke the words out.

"I'm just getting started, Glo. But first, I owe you. Can we talk?"

If he led her off into the dark, there were no guarantees that she'd keep her shorts on. In fact, signs were definitely leaning toward her ripping them off and twirling them over her head.

And she wasn't the sort of woman to get naked at public events. Especially not ones that she'd organized.

"Fine. Let's talk by the hot dog stand." She turned and headed in the direction of the obnoxious red and yellow neon. Nothing soured sexual feelings like hot dog water. She wasn't jumping to forgiveness. Not without a legitimate apology. She deserved that.

He caught up to her easily and walked next to her. Gloria wondered if they could be mistaken for any of the other number of normal couples strolling the park grounds. Couples, partners. Could she ever have that? Would she ever be normal?

She took a seat on the unoccupied park bench and was instantly bathed in the smell of hot dogs.

Aldo sat next to her, taking up space like it was his job. He crossed his left leg over his right and then, glancing down at the prosthesis, immediately uncrossed it.

"Does it bother you?" Gloria asked, looking at his left leg.

"Does it bother *you*?" he countered. His voice was gruff, earnest.

"It bothers me that you were hurt," she said carefully.

He ran his palms nervously over his knees and stared at the ground. "Could you still be with me…like this?"

"Like what?" Gloria wasn't sure where he was going with this.

He sighed, paused. "Damaged," he said finally.

"Are you talking about your leg or being an asshole?"

His gaze swiveled to her. "My leg."

"I have a much bigger problem with you being a jerk to me than I do you having one regular leg and one prosthetic one. Does losing a leg make you less of a man? Of course not. But does being a moody, self-absorbed asshole make you less attractive? In my book it does."

"You saw the scars," he began again.

Gloria turned sideways on the bench to face him and took his hand. "Aldo," she said softly. "I don't care if you're 'damaged,'" she said, throwing his own word back at him. "You and me? We're not wounded. We're scarred."

Closing his eyes, he brought their joined hands to his lips and kissed her knuckles.

"The thing about a scar?" Gloria continued. "It means we're healing. It means we're survivors. What you don't like is that you have to do your healing in front of everyone. Everyone gets a front row seat to your pain and your healing, and that's what you hate."

"Would it be weird if I told you I loved you and asked you to marry me right now?"

"No jokes," she admonished. "Talk to me."

"I'm having…trouble," Aldo confessed. She could tell the words cost him and stayed quiet. "There was pain. I mean, of course there was pain. I'm missing a fucking leg. But I couldn't sleep. Still don't sleep well. Every time I close my eyes, I'm back there at that moment. The explosion. Waking up in so much pain I thought I could die from it. Not knowing if everyone else was okay. My friend Steph. She was shot. Luke was so fucking lucky that he didn't take a bullet for me. I could have gotten them all killed."

Gloria squeezed his hand so tight her circulation complained.

"And then I come back, and I'm not me. I'm still alive, but I'm just going through the motions. Life goes on all around you, but you're left…"

"Sitting in your own pain," Gloria finished for him.

His jaw tightened, and Aldo swallowed hard. "Yeah. I had plans for when I came home. Plans that involved you. But you deserve someone who can protect you. Someone who can keep you safe for a change. You deserve that, Gloria."

With her free hand, Gloria pinched the bridge of her nose. "Are you saying you don't want to be with me because you lost a leg and you think I need a two-legged man to ride up and play the white knight? Because if you are, that's really, really stupid."

CHAPTER 40

D o you think *I'm* damaged?" Gloria was looking at him like she expected an answer. And Aldo had no idea what answer she wanted. "Do you think that me spending ten years in a controlling, abusive relationship damaged me? Made me unlovable? Made me more work than I'm worth?"

This was not going well, Aldo thought. He should have started with flowers and a nice apology card.

"Yoo-hoo! Gloria!" Georgia Rae beelined for them, double-fisting hot dogs. She was plump and festive in her American flag appliqué sleeveless sweater.

"Oh, sweet baby Jesus," Gloria whispered under her breath. She released his hand and scooted an inch away from him. And Aldo hated himself for feeling rejected. "Hi, Georgia Rae. Are you enjoying your Fourth?"

"You did a magnificent job, my dear," the woman said, gesturing wildly with said hot dogs. "I can't remember the last time I enjoyed a Fourth of July like this. I'm not just saying that because you took care of the crapper situation!"

Gloria choked on a laugh. "I'm glad you're having a good time."

"You did good." Georgia Rae nodded decisively. "And you!"

She shifted her attention to Aldo. "That was some race this morning. You had us all blubbering. Welcome home, honey."

"Thanks, Georgia Rae," Aldo said, feeling awkward and wanting desperately to get back to Gloria's question.

She blew them both kisses with hot dogs and fluttered off into the crowd.

But before he could steer the conversation back to the intimate, Linc Reed, the gargantuan fire chief, let out a wolf whistle. "Well, well, well. If it isn't Moretta. You know, man, I was kinda hoping that the whole leg thing would slow you down so I'd have a shot at the Jingle Bell 5K. But I'm not so sure about victory after this morning."

Aldo stood for the requisite handshake and shoulder slap. "Funny guy."

"And gorgeous Gloria," Linc said, shooting her an exaggerated wink. "You ready for another dance?"

Ah, shit. Linc and Gloria? Aldo kicked himself for not warning his friend off Gloria. Linc was a ladies' man, but he respected his friends.

"Hey, Linc," Gloria said. She gave him a friendly smile, but it didn't seem too friendly, too familiar. Not that it was any of his business. Not only had Aldo practically begged her to date while he was deployed, he'd also been a grade A dick when he came back. If she wanted to be with a golden god of debauchery with two working legs, Aldo technically had nothing to say. Her choices were her own.

"I don't know if you noticed, but this little lady pulled all this together," Linc told Aldo, waving a hand around the fairgrounds. "You should have seen her at the org meetings, answering questions, taking notes, wheelin' and dealin'."

Gloria was blushing now. And Aldo wanted to deck his friend. This was *his* shot at winning her back, not Linc's.

"Man, you look like you're gonna puke. Is it the hot dog smell?" Linc asked.

"I need you to go away. Far, far away," Aldo said in a low voice.

Linc's gaze flicked from Aldo to Gloria and back again. He grinned. "I think I hear some fresh-cut fries calling my name. You two have a nice night." He turned and lowered his voice so only Aldo could hear him. "Try not to fuck it up, man."

"Trying."

Linc wandered off, leaving the two of them alone again finally.

"You did a great job with all this," Aldo said, returning to the bench.

"Thanks," she said, almost shyly. "I wanted to do something. Show everyone I wasn't just poor little Gloria Parker."

"If they think that, they don't know you at all."

Gloria gave a dry laugh. "Isn't it ironic?"

"What?"

She tucked her hands between her knees. "You've spent your whole life being larger than life. Respected, admired. You're scared of losing that because your body is different. For me, all I've ever wanted is to be seen. To have people wave to me on the street. To belong. Damage makes you feel like you don't deserve it."

"You deserve everything good in this life." The vehemence in his tone surprised them both.

"I'm not so sure about that," she confessed. "But what I want to know is why would you assume that being an amputee makes you less worthy? If that line of thinking proves true, wouldn't it mean that me choosing to endure ten years of systemic abuse makes me unworthy of being loved?"

"You didn't choose it," he argued.

"I had more of a say in my shit than you did," she pointed out.

He hated that she felt that way. "You're here now," Aldo insisted.

"And so are you. Are we going to sit around and have a pissing match over scars? Or are we going to do something with this second chance we've both been gifted?"

He hoped to God that second chance that she mentioned was the relationship kind. "I don't want you to have to fight any more battles, Gloria."

"That's funny because I'm thinking the only way I'm going to grow is by fighting a few of my own battles."

He closed his eyes, the wisdom of her words washing over him. "I've waited so long for my chance with you, and I've done everything I can to fuck it all up."

"Well, at least I know you're human."

"I was an asshole. I was terrified, I still am, of what this new life is going to look like. What I can and can't do. I'm exhausted from trying to get back to where I started, and I'm so far from that."

"One step at a time," she reminded him.

His laugh was bitter. "I'm not a one-step kind of guy."

"Yeah. You're a balls-to-the-wall, sprint-a-marathon-and-then-bench-press-the-losers kind of guy." She bumped his shoulder, letting him know she was joking. "But look at it this way. If you come back from this, you've proved to yourself and everybody out there exactly how tough you are."

"I want to prove it to you."

"First, your explanation and apology," she insisted.

"When I came home, I was in a dark place. I thought you deserved better than a bitter, wounded vet. I want you to feel safe, and I don't see how you could feel like that with me."

"Safety doesn't come from being physically secure, Aldo. I'll feel safe with a man who I can count on to respect me."

He flinched. His reaction to her welcome home had been the exact opposite.

"I'm sorry for taking my shit out on you. I'm sorry for shutting you out and pushing you away."

"Are you going to do it again?" she pressed.

He shook his head. "I'll never do it *on purpose* again." He was nothing if not honest.

She looked him in the eye, nodded. "Okay then. You're forgiven. But if you feel like taking something out on me again, think twice. I don't let that happen anymore."

He couldn't help himself. Aldo slid his arm around her shoulders and held her against him. Her small body fit his like a puzzle piece. "I'm really proud of you, Glo."

"I'm pretty proud of you too," she said softly. She was looking at his mouth, her lids heavy, lips full. He could kiss her, right here on this bench as Benevolence celebrated around them. But when he moved in, she put a hand on his chest. "Aldo. Don't you think we should focus on being friends for a little while? I mean given how vulnerable we both are right now, we could both use a friend. Relationships can be… complicated."

Aldo couldn't calm the fear that kicked up inside him. The friend zone was not his final destination.

"I want more, Gloria. My feelings for you aren't just friendly. I don't want to pressure you, but I don't want to settle either."

"Aldo, we literally just made up. I don't know if I can trust you to not go back to New Aldo who can't stand me."

Aldo drummed his fingers on his knee. "Okay. How about a compromise? We date platonically."

"Like friends without benefits?" Gloria asked, looking at him like he'd lost his damn mind.

"Like we see each other exclusively. I prove to you I can be trusted, and you learn to date in a healthy relationship."

She frowned, considering. "I can't decide if this is the smartest idea I've ever heard or a really big mistake we're both about to make."

"'About to make' as in yes?" Aldo asked, hope so bright and fierce climbing into his throat.

She bit her lip, and he held his breath.

"Yes."

And just like that, Aldo got his second win of the day. And this one was much, much bigger than the first.

CHAPTER 41

The fireworks were a spectacular end to a day of surprises, Gloria decided. Her hand linked with Aldo's on the blanket. This newness was both overwhelming and thrilling.

Harper's charges, Henry and Robbie, were sprawled out with them. They'd peppered Aldo with questions about his leg and running and his tattoos. Aldo had answered them all without flinching.

Gloria could feel Harper's smug smile and chose to ignore her. She didn't want to explain that she'd forgiven but cautiously.

"Wow!" Henry gasped at a big, orange starburst in the sky.

Gloria smiled and let herself relax. All her weeks of work were over. She'd pulled together one hell of a Fourth of July. It was kind of like her own personal Independence Day. She'd shown the town something besides poor little Gloria Parker, and she'd stood up for herself to a man despite her very strong feelings for him. She'd drawn lines, set boundaries.

As the sky filled with color and sound, she allowed herself a minute to bask. Her hard work was starting to pay off. And for once in her life, she couldn't wait to see what tomorrow held.

The finale drew the expected oohs and aahs from the crowd as every firework known to man lit the dark canvas of sky.

Aldo leaned in. "You did good," he told her as the boys screeched their delight.

Gloria gave his hand a squeeze. "Thanks. You were pretty impressive today too."

The fireworks looked even better reflected in Aldo's brown eyes. She felt a delicious shiver travel up her spine.

———

"I'll walk you home," Aldo said quietly as Harper and her crew herded the kids toward the car.

"You don't have to do that," Gloria said automatically.

"I want to kiss you good night."

That thrill that had been buzzing up and down her spine turned into a full-on electric current.

"I just need to check on a few things first." *Before the kissing.*

The way his lips quirked, Gloria thought there was a good possibility he was thinking about that part of the evening too. "I'll help you check on a few things."

Together they tracked down Mack, factory maintenance worker by day and head of the Fourth of July cleanup crew by night. "You sure you don't need an extra hand?" Gloria asked. He'd told her he was in it for the fleet of golf carts made available to the cleanup crew.

"Tents are already down, food stands are packing it in, and we're halfway through the garbage pickup. We've got it," he promised.

"You're a dream, Mack." Gloria yawned. She hadn't realized how utterly exhausted she was until this minute.

"You did one helluva job, Gloria." With a little salute and a peek in Aldo's direction, he was peeling away in his electric golf cart into the night.

Aldo waited patiently at her side. They were giving Benevolence quite a bit to talk about tonight.

"I guess that's it," she said lightly.

He linked his fingers with hers. "I guess so."

In mere minutes, Aldo was going to kiss her good night. The perfect end to the perfect day. A new start.

She turned to lead them in the direction of her apartment and stopped in her tracks. Adrenaline dumped into her system, jacking her senses into DEFCON 1.

Linda Diller, Glenn's mother, stood in her path. Frail as ever, her shoulders rounded under a dingy white blouse. Her hair, mousy brown streaked with gray, hung limply around her face. She looked older than her fifty-five years. But years of abuse and poverty did that to a woman. Years of the belief that she deserved it.

"You!" She rasped, pointing at Gloria.

Gloria felt the weight of blame cast by that gnarled finger, those narrow, sunken eyes. She was painfully aware that the motion and activity around them stopped as neighbors paused to watch.

Another audience to another humiliation, Gloria thought bitterly. Would she ever escape?

"You're the reason my son is in jail!" Linda hissed. "The reason the light bill is late and the fridge is empty."

Glenn had sporadically provided for his mother. Groceries here and there. Sometimes cigarettes. Sometimes cash. And now there was no way for Glenn to provide for her behind bars.

"Please, not here," Gloria whispered to herself. Not when she'd worked so damn hard. Not when Benevolence had just started talking about her organizational skills instead of her black eyes or her limp.

"Here you are celebrating, cavorting, while my boy rots

behind bars because of you," Linda said, her thin voice shaking with whatever feelings she was still capable of.

The taste of shame was bitter on Gloria's tongue.

Aldo stepped up next to her. "Mrs. Diller—" he cut in, his voice cold with warning.

But Gloria stilled him with a hand on his arm. She could feel him vibrating beneath her touch.

Her battle.

"He fed you and clothed you and put a roof over your head for years, and this is the thanks he gets?" Linda was shouting now, and Gloria absorbed the humiliation as she'd been trained to do. All her work, everything she'd done to give her neighbors something else to see was wiped out. Was she always destined to be humiliated?

"Gloria," Aldo growled at her side. A warning that he was about to step into the fray to take care of things.

She shook her head.

"Mrs. Diller," she said, keeping her voice low. "I made my choice to leave. We're all responsible for our own choices."

"I didn't choose to have my son sent away! And now who suffers so you can be selfish?" Linda spat. "Me. My son. You ruined my family."

Gloria felt something else pushing at the edges of humiliation and guilt. Something harder and brighter. And she clung to it.

"I don't hold you responsible for your son's actions any more than you can hold me responsible for them. He's paying the price for his choices."

"You owe me," Linda hissed. "You owe him!"

"I owe you nothing. Glenn deserves to pay for his crimes."

"It's your word against his," Linda yowled in despair. "My son was good to you. But that wasn't good enough for you. No, you had to get rid of him so you could crawl into bed with this cripple!"

"Enough!" Gloria's voice rang out. "Not everyone has to stay with a man who beats them. Not everyone decides that scraps are good enough for them. I'm not going to let you make me feel guilty for not wanting to be beaten for the rest of my life."

"You're a whore! Nothing but a whore," Linda shouted. "And when my son comes home, he's going to make sure you pay for what you did."

Gloria felt her skin crawl. It was nearly word for word from one of Glenn's letters.

She heard the whispers of the crowd. Benevolence loved to witness a person's business. Now, they were getting a front row seat to the ugliness that had been her life for ten long years.

"You sound like your son," Gloria said sadly. "I feel sorry for you."

A police cruiser pulled up to the curb, and Ty climbed out. "There a problem here?" he asked.

"I think we're done here," Gloria told Ty.

She turned her back on Linda and walked away, shoulders hunched.

"I ain't done nothin' wrong," Linda announced to Ty.

"No one's sayin' you did, Mrs. Diller," Ty said in full-on authority mode.

Gloria slipped through the crowd, avoiding eye contact. One pitying look, and she'd break like fine china on concrete.

"Gloria," Aldo called after her.

But she kept walking.

He caught her on the steps to her apartment. "Say something," he said, reaching for her hand.

She let him have it because she wanted some sense of

kindness to warm the cold within. She knew what she needed. She only had to ask. And trust.

"Do you want to come upstairs and drink tea and watch *Pride and Prejudice* with me? Because I need a friend."

He grabbed her hands. "Is it the Colin Firth version or the Keira Knightley one?"

She felt the ghost of a smile play on her lips. "I have both."

CHAPTER 42

A kaleidoscope of color and pattern welcomed Aldo when he crossed the threshold into Gloria's apartment. As many times as he'd walked by in the late hours of the night, he'd never imagined her home to look like this.

The couch, the color of ripe eggplant, was nearly buried under a mound of throw pillows in every shade of green imaginable. The dining room table, a scarred and rickety find, was accessorized with a tablescape of fat pillar candles. She'd grouped bold art prints and framed family photos on the walls, which were painted a rich gray blue.

The throw rug was orange and white, which picked up the tangerines in the two upholstered chairs pushed under the bow window. They should have been hideous with their floral print and tufted backs, but somehow, as part of the whole, they were charming.

The environment, the sheer, colorful happiness of it took the edge off the anger he was riding from the confrontation in the park.

The door to what Aldo assumed was the bedroom was cracked open, and his curiosity was piqued. But she had asked him upstairs for comfort. And not the naked kind.

"You don't think it's too much?" She worried her lower lip between her teeth, looking at the room as if she'd never seen it before.

He thought of his own beige walls waiting for a paintbrush and personality. "Not at all. You did all this? It looks professional."

She brightened for him like the sun, and he vowed to do that again and again just to see that pride push out the shame in her eyes.

"You're forgiven. You don't have to kiss my ass," she teased nervously.

"I'm serious. It feels like you in here."

She studied him curiously for a minute. "So, um, ready for that tea?" she asked.

He flashed her a smile. "So ready."

Gloria took a step back and smacked into the small table inside the door, sending a stack of mail flying to the floor. "Sorry. I'm flustered," she said, fluttering her hands.

Aldo bent to pick up the envelopes. The one on top caught his eye. *Mailed from a state correctional institution.* He hadn't yet calmed down from the confrontation in the park, and the anger sparked back to life. It was Glenn. He knew it viscerally.

She was already heading toward the shoebox kitchen without any clue as to the ticking time bomb she'd left behind.

Shit. He was new to this boyfriend thing. What was more important? Being there for Gloria after what happened in the park? Or getting to the bottom of the letter?

Conflicted, he followed Gloria into the kitchen and watched her fuss over the tea. She poured a small amount of hot water into two mugs. "Preheating the mugs," she explained at his questioning look. She put the kettle back on the stove and rummaged through the cupboard for her collection of teas.

He said nothing, the letter still clutched in his hand.

She pretended he wasn't there, walking through the steps of what looked like a soothing ritual, dumping the hot water out of the mugs and replacing it with tea bags.

"How good of a new boyfriend are you prepared to be tonight, Aldo? Because I think I want to talk."

"I'm prepared to be whatever you need," he told her.

"Let's pretend for tonight that you're my best friend and I need to vent."

"Vent away. I'm here."

The kettle whistled, and he watched her pour the water over the tea, steam rising up from the mugs. She was silent for a long minute. "It was like living with a hard-to-please parent. My entire life revolved around not upsetting him. No makeup. No friends. Only the foods he liked. But no matter how good I got at reading him, I still did things he didn't like. I still got hit."

Aldo's fingers fisted, crushing the envelope.

"He controlled the finances, my car, where I could and couldn't go. I knew that I could go home to my mother, but I didn't trust that he wouldn't try to hurt us both if I left. He wasn't always awful. I think that's part of the cycle. The short fuse, the explosion, the apology, the sweetness. A week before I left, he brought me a stack of paperbacks by my favorite author from the library book sale. It wasn't all blood and bruises."

She looked up at him, gaze earnest, and handed him a mug.

"I had hope for so long that after every apology, this would be the time he changed. He was a victim too. His father beat him bloody every other week until he got big enough to fight back. He confided in me. He'd seen his father hurt his mother his entire life. It's what he knew. The physical brutality, that was one thing. I could mostly heal from that. It was the emotional side of things. Whittling away at my self-esteem, one snide comment, one accusation, at a time. He hated you for some reason," she confessed.

Aldo absorbed the statement, knowing the exact reason why Glenn Diller hated him.

"He accused me of having a crush on you, and I denied it. Even though it was true." She shot him a sidelong look.

"You did?" he asked.

Gloria nodded, remembering. "Who wouldn't have a crush on football star Aldo Moretta?"

Aldo needed desperately to move his body. To pace before the rage inside him erupted. Gloria stepped around him and led the way into the living room. She sat on the couch, gestured for him to do the same. He tucked the letter beside him on the cushion, still not sure how to approach it.

"I was shocked. Sure, looking back, there'd been warning signs. Times when he was rougher than the situation called for or making controlling demands that felt like love at the time. When he hit me, I pushed him. Called him a 'loser asshole,'" she recalled. "And he fell to his knees in front of me and cried. He begged me not to leave him. Apologized for hitting me. Said it was an accident, that he'd never do it again. He told me his story. That all he knew was violence. But he'd change for me. I felt…powerful. I had the choice to stay or go, and he was putting it in my hands."

"But he never changed," Aldo said quietly.

She took a sip of tea, and Aldo did the same. It was soft and floral, a gentleness removed from the ugliness of their conversation. "No. But he did give me hope. Weeks would go by, and things would be fine. He'd be working. We'd have a little money. He'd laugh at my jokes. Then I'd ask him to pick up onions on the way home from work, or I wouldn't wash his work shirt fast enough. Or he wouldn't even pretend to come up with an excuse that involved me."

Aldo suddenly got what true friendship was. As a man who was half in love with the woman bravely telling her story, hearing the details of her abuse was a kind of torture. But for Gloria, it was a cleansing. A healing. And that was more important than his own temper, his own discomfort. "Did he ever hurt you in other ways?"

"You mean rape," she said flatly.

He nodded.

"Once," she said quietly. "Though at the time, I didn't recognize it as rape. In recent years, I was more of a live-in housekeeper and cook."

Aldo forced himself to take another drink to soothe the ache in his throat. He put the tea down and took Gloria's hand. Squeezed.

"I stayed in hope and fear, in repeating cycles of both. I stayed because it was easier sometimes. Other times because I physically couldn't leave. And I have to live with that. I have to live with the fact that I wasn't strong enough to leave him the first time. I'm responsible for my choice to stay."

"It's not cut and dried like that, Gloria," he reminded her. "Brain scans show similarities between victims of abuse and soldiers on the battlefield."

She shifted to face him on the couch. "Do you wonder if that's part of our attraction? That we're both survivors?"

Aldo let go of her hand and squeezed her knee.

"I think our attraction is…complex," he ventured.

She looked at him, held his gaze. "So then maybe you get why Mrs. Diller coming at me tonight, airing all that ugliness, all my weaknesses in front of everyone I was trying so hard to impress, rocked me."

He stroked her knee. "You don't seem rocked."

"There's a lot going on beneath the surface," she admitted.

Aldo shifted and pulled her feet into his lap. He unlaced her shoes, tugged them off. When his thumb pressed into her arch, she let out a long sigh.

"I do get it. I was out there today doing my best to prove that I'm not a victim, to cover up my weaknesses."

Her fingers touched his shoulder, traced a pattern there as if branding him. "I'm tired of being a victim. That can't be all anyone sees when they look at me." Exhaustion colored her words.

Her words resonated so deep inside him Aldo thought he might split apart like an atom.

"It's not *all* they see. Yes," he began before she could cut him off, "your relationship history is something that they won't forget quickly. But there's so much more to you than that, Glo. So much more. And if you keep giving them glimpses of who you really are, eventually no one will remember that Gloria."

"Mrs. Diller will. Glenn will." Her gaze slid to the table inside the door.

He pulled the letter out, set it on the coffee table. "I saw this on the floor," he said.

She looked resigned, tired. "He's been writing from prison. Vague threats. Ty's pushing for a restraining order, but there isn't much to go on. He's behind bars, and he hasn't come out and said 'I'll beat you to within an inch of your life when I get out.'"

Aldo swore. Thanks to him and his fucking snit fit, he hadn't been there for her. He couldn't imagine how she felt with Glenn reaching out behind bars to still terrify and hurt her.

She gave him a sad smile. "That's pretty much how I feel. The legal system isn't designed to protect victims. It's there to punish criminals."

"That's bullshit."

"Speaking of bullshit, you don't have to watch this movie with me."

Aldo scoffed. "You can't dangle Mr. Darcy in front of me and then take him away like that. I'm staying."

Gloria laughed and left him to change. Aldo stared at his trembling hands. One day, he would get them on Glenn Diller. And when he did, the man would never so much as think of Gloria again.

"Sorry my TV doesn't compare to your gargantuan one," she teased, padding out of the bedroom barefoot. She had on a pair of cotton shorts and an original Benevolence High School sweatshirt.

"I'll get my binoculars," Aldo joked, trying not to memorize the way she moved around him to her side of the couch. She sank down, tucking her feet under her. He rested his arm on the back of the couch in welcome, and Gloria accepted the invitation, curling into his side.

Wielding the remote, she looked up at him. "Are you ready for this?"

CHAPTER 43

Gloria opened one bleary eye and saw the home screen for *Pride and Prejudice* still on her TV. Great. She'd fallen asleep on the couch again.

At least it was a full hour before she had to get up to get ready for work. Dawn was breaking outside her windows overlooking Main Street.

She'd felt. She'd purged. She'd slept. Therapy in action. And had it not been for Aldo, she probably would have stumbled home and sobbed herself to sleep.

A soft snore behind her startled her.

Holy. Fucking. Shit.

Aldo Moretta was curled behind her like a bear. His shirt was off. His wallet, keys, and cell phone were neatly lined up on her ottoman. His prosthetic leg was tucked in the corner at the end of the couch.

She felt the broad barrel of his chest rise against her back.

A riot of emotions erupted inside her.

He'd stayed. He'd stayed, listened to her word vomit, watched the sappiest of sappy movies with her, and held her when she needed a friend. A boyfriend.

Her heart limped slowly in her chest. Aldo Moretta was a real man.

She peeled her other eye open, lamenting through sticky mascara the fact that she hadn't washed her face before passing out on him. She should get up. Wash her face. Maybe start breakfast? What was the proper breakfast-related thank-you for being a good friend? Waffles. Although given the physique that she was sprawled against, he'd probably prefer something egg-whitey and chock-full of vegetables.

She'd make both. And strong coffee.

Another soft snore behind her. Damn it. Snoring wasn't cute. Yet the soft whistle from between Aldo's delectable lips was having the same effect on her as a litter of puppies. She shifted slowly so as not to wake him and studied him.

His lashes were thick, inky. Delicious stubble graced his jaw. His shoulders were barn-door broad, his chest wide and strong. He'd lost the gaunt shadows he'd returned home with, she noted.

She let her gaze slide over his pecs, noting the tattoos that covered his chest and part of his ribs. A tribal warrior, she thought, enjoying a peek at his abs. Real people didn't have six-packs. But Aldo Moretta was no mere mortal. The waistband of his shorts rode low, revealing the Calvin Klein branding on his underwear.

Gloria felt a quickening inside her. She tried to shove it aside. To ignore it. But Aldo chose that moment to rock against her in his sleep, and she felt every inch of what she knew, firsthand, up close, with visual confirmation, was a spectacular penis.

Oh. My. God.

She couldn't help herself. It was simple biology that had her cuddling her hips closer to him. He gave a little sigh and flexed against her again.

Was she this starved for physical contact that she was considering taking advantage of Aldo's morning wood that likely had nothing to do with her?

Slow. Slow. Slow. She chanted it to herself. They were taking things slowly. But the word did nothing to alleviate the dull throb between her thighs. She *wanted* him. Like puddle-of-lust wanted him.

She tried to peek farther under the blanket to the leg he'd hidden from her and then stopped herself.

They'd talked about her scars last night, but he hadn't opened up about his own to her. Until he did, his injury was his business.

She relaxed against him.

Yep. Up close, the truth was even more apparent. She'd never seen a more attractive man in her life. Including the Hemsworth brothers.

Aldo Moretta was something special. And he was *her* boyfriend. Her boyfriend who she was *this close* to dry humping in his sleep.

She closed her eyes and gave herself another moment to enjoy being wrapped up in strong arms that she thought could never harm her. Warmth, security, peace. She'd use this to steel herself against the day. Work would surely involve a rehashing of the Mrs. Diller confrontation. But for now, everything in the world was perfect. She was *safe. Happy.*

Gloria gave herself another ten minutes before slowly wriggling free of Aldo's grasp. His hold tightened on her and then relaxed as another little snore escaped his beautiful lips.

Gloria tiptoed into the bathroom to wash her face and comb her hair into a semblance of cuteness. She tied it back in a high topknot, leaving the rest loose, and snuck back out to the living room. She sat on the coffee table and watched him sleep, an arm thrown over his head, his big body sprawled across her couch, one foot poking free from the blanket.

"I can feel you staring," he murmured, eyes still closed.

"Good morning, sunshine."

He cracked an eye, rolled to his side.

"G'morning." His reply was muffled by the pillow he snuggled up to.

"Thank you for staying," Gloria said, rubbing her palms down her thighs.

"Mmm."

Morning Aldo was freaking adorable. And if Gloria didn't stop swooning over him, she would end up hungry and late for work.

"Breakfast?" she asked him.

He yawned mightily. "Yes, please."

She jumped to her feet, happy to have a task that would take her away from staring at his sexiness. "I'll make eggs. And bacon. And toast. Coffee too," she called over her shoulder.

She was in the midst of brewing coffee and layering bacon into her pan when Aldo came into the kitchen. He was fully dressed—to her great disappointment—and his prosthesis was attached.

"Does your couch emit carbon monoxide fumes?" he asked.

She laughed. "Why?"

"Because I haven't slept like that since before I left for Afghanistan."

"Definitely carbon monoxide," she told him.

"What can I help with?" he asked, eyeing her breakfast assembly line of toaster, plates, and utensils.

"You're a guest," she insisted.

"I'm the boyfriend," he shot back. "Boyfriends help cook breakfast after *Pride and Prejudice* sleepovers."

"Then you can be the toast master general," Gloria said, pointing at the bread. "So what did you think of Mr. Darcy and Elizabeth?"

"They wasted too much time being in their own way," he said, loading the toaster and then opening the refrigerator to hunt for butter.

"Maybe they needed that time to make sure they were right for each other," Gloria suggested.

Aldo grunted. "And maybe they were just chickenshit."

"Sometimes there's something to be said for being a chickenshit." She turned the burner off under the eggs she'd scrambled. "Thank you again for being here last night."

He shot her a smoldering look over the toaster. "Anything for you, Glo. Thanks for talking to me last night."

"Silence keeps it too powerful," she recited. "Or at least that's what my therapist says. Keeping it a secret that no one else knows gives it this unholy strength. But talking about it? It's ugly and hard, but it takes the power away."

"How do you feel today?" he asked, watching her carefully.

She thought about it as she shoveled eggs onto plates and divided the bacon between the two. "I feel okay. I know everyone's going to be gossiping about Mrs. Diller. But I made my choice, and I stood my ground. And I didn't cry in front of anyone last night."

"You're allowed to cry or do whatever the hell you want, Gloria. No one's here to make you do anything," Aldo reminded her, his voice rough enough around the edges that she felt it on her skin.

"I know." And then, "Thank you."

"Do you mind if I read the letter?"

Ah, the letter. She'd temporarily put the fact that Glenn was still pulling strings from a place where he physically couldn't touch her out of her mind.

Yes, she minded. Hadn't she given him enough of her garbage, her baggage, last night? Did he need this piece too?

"Please?" Aldo added. Her resolve crumbled like burnt toast.

She shrugged a shoulder. "Sure. Not that it'll do any good. Nothing actionable."

He didn't say anything but ambled out of the kitchen in the direction of the dining table. He'd have this part of her too now. But how else could she know if she could trust him?

CHAPTER 44

W ell, well, well. Look what the cat dragged in." Jamilah stretched in her ergonomic chair and crossed her arms over her chest.

Aldo leaned against the doorway. This was his first time stepping foot—ha—in the office since his return. Jamilah had called, texted, emailed, messaged, and even dropped by a few times before effectively giving up on her pissed-off, depressed partner. He couldn't blame her.

"Taking a trip down memory lane?" she asked. "Because I know you're not here to work. The last time I saw you and asked when you were coming back, you said when you fucking felt like it. Then I said 'Oh no. When *I* fucking feel like looking at your dumb face.'" She twirled in her chair, tapping a pen to her chin. "Do I feel like looking at your dumb face today?"

Aldo pulled his right hand from behind his back. Gloria, pretty in pink this morning, had whipped up a cheery apology bouquet for him. He had a lot of apologizing to do.

"Hmm," Jamilah said, eyeing the flowers.

He revealed the tray of coffee and the bakery bag he'd hidden in his other hand.

"If there's a raspberry tart in there, you can consider yourself mostly forgiven," she sniffed.

Aldo crossed to her, uncomfortably conscious of his slight limp. The race yesterday, while feeling like a tremendous personal accomplishment, had also served as a reminder that he wasn't who he once was. Yet.

He dropped the tray and bag on her table and handed her the flowers.

"I was an asshole," he began. He felt as if he'd been starting most of his sentences that way lately. At least he never had to apologize to his mother. She was a bigger asshole than he was, and they accepted each other's assholery.

"Yes. You were," Jamilah said without a hint of forgiveness. "And if you think you're going to use that shiny new limb you're hiding under a nice pair of Dockers as an excuse to be a dick around here, you are sadly mistaken."

"Excuse me, Jam?" A kid with shaggy bangs that hung in his eyes, requiring repeated head tosses to clear his vision, piped up from the desk inside the door.

"Yeah, Monty?"

"I've got Dave from Kleiborn Associates on line two. He's shouting and maybe crying a little."

"We've got a receptionist now?" Aldo asked.

"I can't do my work and your work *and* answer the phones," Jamilah said, shooting him a pointed look.

Aldo shoved his hands in his pockets. He wasn't great at begging. "I'm here now, and I promise not to be a dick. Or at least not much of one."

She rolled her dark eyes. "Fine. You can start by familiarizing yourself with the Jonestown bridge project in the OneDrive. They want to add a second lane of traffic and a pedestrian walkway. It's in downtown Jonestown and will be a huge pain in our ass." Jamilah swiveled in her chair and picked up her phone. "Dave," she said in a singsong voice. "How can I make your day better?"

Dismissed and properly shamed, Aldo took his coffee, his messenger bag, and his pride back to his desk. It, unlike every other flat surface in the office, was clean. Jam and their little band of associates had been busy picking up his slack. Granted, he wasn't scheduled to return until his deployment ended. However, he should have come back to work as soon as he was able.

Aldo sat down, relieved to be taking the weight off his leg, and booted up his computer. They'd be fine, he and Jamilah. They had a solid relationship that couldn't be derailed by either of them being a dick to the other for a few weeks.

There was a coating of dust on his monitors. He wiped them clean and took a breath. It was always hard coming back. To shift gears from life and death and the monotony of a war zone to pushing papers and dealing with the whims of an aggressively creative architect or wading into the murkiness of township ordinances. Always hard. Always surreal.

But this was the first time he'd sat down at his desk in his office with only one leg. The scars were on the outside this time.

His thoughts drifted to Gloria. To the confrontation last night. Her scars were on the outside now too, in the form of public embarrassment.

His hackles rose again, recalling Glenn's mother spewing her abuse in Gloria's face. He closed a fist around the arm of his chair. That family had their chance to tear her down for ten years. Enough was enough.

Mind made up, Aldo clicked on the icon for the network and got back to work.

Aldo glanced up from his monitor when a whistling uniformed deputy strolled into the office.

"Ya ready for lunch?" Ty called, his thumbs tucked into his belt.

"Bring me back a pastrami," Jamilah called from her desk.

Aldo shot her the pistol fingers on the way out. Together, he and Ty tromped down the stairs, and Aldo was suddenly grateful his injury hadn't been worse. He could still manage stairs, still access his office, his home.

He had a lot to be grateful for these days.

"So what's with the lunch date?" Ty asked, slipping his sunglasses on as they stepped outside into the summer heat. The man might talk slow and be affable as hell, but there was still a cop brain under the nice.

"Mrs. Diller," Aldo said.

"Had a feelin'."

"Do I need to worry about her?" Aldo asked as they turned down the block, heading toward the sub shop.

"I can tell you that I may have perused our records this morning. I wasn't in law enforcement when Glenn Diller Senior was alive and beating the hell out of her. According to records, she never put up much of a fuss then, and there were a lot of calls from neighbors."

"Didn't seem to have any qualms about standing up for herself last night," Aldo observed.

They stepped into the air-conditioned deli and got in line. Five minutes later, sandwiches in hand, they crossed the street to the edge of the park. Settling on a bench in the shade, they unwrapped their lunches and ate in silence for a minute.

"Sure you're not just upset that she yelled at your girlfriend?" Ty asked.

"She is my girlfriend, since you're fishing for info," Aldo told him. "And I'm not going to say I wasn't upset about it."

"From what I can tell, it was out of character for her to publicly confront Gloria," Ty said, taking a big bite of pepperoni and cheese.

"She doesn't look like she could physically do any damage," Aldo mused.

"But you're still worried," Ty finished for him.

"I think he's stirring her up," Aldo told him. "I think, in addition to sending vaguely threatening letters to Gloria, Glenn's writing home to his mother telling her that it's all Gloria's fault. He's her son. There's gotta be some kind of motherly bond."

If Ty was surprised that Gloria had confided in him about the letters, he didn't let it show. "But as long as he stays behind bars, she's safe," he pointed out.

"What if Mrs. Diller scrapes up his bail?"

Ty shook his head. "She's leveraged to the point of foreclosure. She's got nothing. Yeah, I checked on that too," he said before Aldo could ask. "That's why he's in the state prison. Couldn't come up with the bail, and county jail was full. There's a good chance he won't get out of there for twelve, fifteen years."

It wasn't enough, and they both knew it.

"He doesn't have some rich uncle who's going to sweep in with the money, does he?"

"If there was a rich uncle, he shoulda showed up a long time ago."

———

Aldo thought about the Diller family for the rest of the afternoon. He knocked off a little early when Jamilah informed him that overdoing it wouldn't be tolerated. He'd wanted to argue,

242

but she was right, and he wasn't quite as dumb as he had been in the past.

He took the opportunity to cruise through the south side of town. Benevolence was mostly cozy, single-family homes, tidy little duplexes, and a picturesque downtown. But there was a handful of blocks where the houses were a little shabbier, the landscaping a little more overgrown, and the shadows a little darker at night.

Relying on memory, Aldo cruised down Mrs. Diller's block. Once cozy, identical houses built on postage-stamp lawns, these remains showcased peeling paint and sagging porches. Mrs. Diller's house hadn't fared any better than her neighbors'. The once white clapboard siding was a rotting gray. The glass was cracked on two of the front windows. An ancient window unit air conditioner chugged away, dripping steadily on sodden porch planks.

The puke-green, rusty Buick sat in the gravel driveway on nearly flat tires. Weeds sprouted everywhere. It was the home of a woman who had depended on her men for everything before being abandoned.

The front door creaked open, and Mrs. Diller in a house apron stepped out onto the porch. Aldo sat and watched as she reached into her apron pocket and produced a pack of cigarettes. Her thin shoulders were rounded as if from years of tensing for a blow. She'd scraped her hair back in a tight bun, leaving her lined face bare. The skin on her neck sagged.

Her thin lips were pressed in a tight line of disapproval.

Life had not been kind to Mrs. Diller.

Deciding there was nothing more to see, Aldo drove on.

CHAPTER 45

That was one hell of a celebration yesterday," Claire announced, packing an arrangement of daisies and mini sunflowers into a white florist box. Their delivery driver, a crabby woman in her fifties whose standard comment was that no one had ever sent her flowers, would be making the second pickup in a few minutes. "You did good, kiddo."

They'd done a brisk enough business that morning that this was their first chance at conversation.

"Thanks. I'm pretty proud of myself," Gloria said, double-checking the orders in the computer and printing the delivery slips. It was a busy day for her. She had a full day of work, a therapy session scheduled over lunch, and a secret appointment that evening that she'd finally decided she deserved to make. To top it off, she was still riding the heady high of waking up in the arms of Aldo Moretta while processing her feelings about her confrontation with Linda Diller the night before.

It had been a complicated twenty-four hours.

"Rumor has it the town council wants to ask you to organize the Christmas festival," Claire pressed.

Gloria gave a noncommittal, "Hmm." They already had that morning. She had thought about the long hours, the endless meetings, the schmoozing of local business owners for sponsorships...and gave an emphatic yes.

At least Mrs. Diller's outburst hadn't completely ruined everything she'd worked toward, she thought. With care, she opened each of the four delivery boxes and smoothed back the tissue paper, double-checking the contents against the orders. Satisfied everything was perfect, Gloria stuck the peel-off delivery tags on each box.

Claire chattered on about how much Harper and the kids had enjoyed the fireworks and the festival while Gloria busied herself with the next item on her to-do list: snipping the stems of freesia to encourage the tight buds to open for their weekend centerpiece order.

"So Aldo..." Claire let his name hang in the air between them.

Gloria dunked the freesia into a plastic vase where they would stay until the blooms were ready for their arrangement. "What about him?" she asked innocently. She knew exactly what Claire was asking but decided it would be fun to make her work a little harder for the information.

"You left the festival with him last night, and he came to work with you this morning."

"Are you snooping on me, Claire?" Gloria asked, more amused than appalled.

"I happened to be perusing this morning's sales receipts and saw his name on the first one," Claire said, a picture of innocence.

"Hmm," Gloria said.

Claire threw herself down onto a stool dramatically. "You're killing me here. I feel like I'm talking to one of my kids when they were teenagers!"

A reluctant laugh escaped from Gloria. "We're giving the

dating thing a try," she admitted. "It's very new—as in not even twelve hours old—and I have no idea what I'm doing. Or how I'm going to screw it up before he does."

Claire clutched her hands to her heart. "I'm so proud of him and you. The idea of you two together makes me want to sprout wings."

Gloria laughed. "We haven't been on an official date yet," she said, managing expectations like it was her job.

"You forget. I have almost thirty-five years of marriage backing me. I know a real relationship when I see it."

"Don't you think it's a little soon? I mean, I just got out of a train wreck, and Aldo's still healing." Didn't she need more time to be better before she added someone else into the mix? Didn't she owe it to him to be the best she could be?

"Maybe you're meant to heal together?" Claire offered. "Maybe you can do a world of good for each other, and now is the perfect time?"

"I don't know," Gloria said honestly. She wasn't sure she was ready to think about that. She had enough trouble wrapping her head around whether she should call Aldo Moretta, high school football star and hometown hero, her boyfriend. She wondered what Aldo would think about the appointment she'd scheduled for herself tonight. The appointment that she was equally nervous and Christmas-morning excited for.

"Don't let one bitter apple make you doubt yourself," Claire advised.

"Heard about that too, did you?"

Claire gave a dainty shrug. "I have my sources."

"What's this one?" Gloria asked, picking up an order printout next to the register. "It says 'make it pretty.'"

"Oh, that was a phone order," Claire said, waving her hand. "They gave us an unlimited budget and said to make it beautiful. Why don't you work on that while I prep the foam and vases for the freesia?"

"Me?" Gloria blinked. She'd put together the occasional bouquet, small arrangements here and there like Aldo's order this morning for Jamilah. But she'd never had creative free rein. "I wouldn't even know where to start."

Claire lifted her eyebrows. "Make something you'd love. Don't overthink it."

Something she would love? What if no one else would love what she loved? What if she had horrible taste in floral arrangements?

"I can hear you overthinking it from here," Claire called from the back room.

"Make something I'd love," Gloria muttered under her breath. She could do this. And if she screwed it all up, Claire would fix it. Or Claire would be too worried about hurting her feelings and let Gloria send out a terrible arrangement that someone would hate.

"Omg, when's the last time someone complained about getting flowers?" she asked herself. She was overthinking and overpanicking.

She picked up the order and glanced out the front window. There was an old Buick just like Glenn's mother's idling across the street. Gloria thought of the letter that Aldo had read and promised to drop at the station with Ty. He didn't want it in her presence one second longer, and she appreciated that.

Gloria felt an invisible shadow creep over her. Anyone could watch her in here through the front windows. She felt exposed, unsettled.

"What is it?" Claire asked, poking her head out of the back room.

The Buick pulled away from the curb and disappeared around the corner. "Nothing. Just thought I saw something."

———

"Okay, give me your honest opinion," Gloria begged. She'd spent an hour and a half—in between the phone, the order system, and customers—on the mystery arrangement. She'd started with the hot-pink Matsumoto asters and gone crazy from there. It was happy and dramatic and whimsical...in her opinion.

To a normal human, it was probably a monstrosity.

"Do you love it?" Claire prodded.

Gloria studied the arrangement with a critical eye and then gave up. "I love the crap out of it. But I don't know if anyone else will."

"It's stunning. Happy and hopeful and beautiful," Claire surmised.

"Really?"

She patted Gloria on the shoulder. "Really. Now, what are you doing for a vase?"

Gloria chewed on her lower lip. "I was thinking about that pretty yellow terra-cotta pitcher, but…"

"Unlimited budget," Claire reminded her. "You've had your eye on that pitcher for weeks."

It was true. There was something sunshiny about the short, curvy piece of pottery. Maybe she was hesitating because she didn't want someone else to have it. But the pink asters and the peach roses would look amazing with it.

"Legitimately unlimited budget or 'I'm saying unlimited, but I really mean fifty bucks tops'?"

Claire laughed. "Legitimately unlimited."

"Who's getting this bad boy anyway?" Gloria asked. There was no buyer or recipient listed on the order form.

"Wasn't it on the order? Oh, the system must be glitching again," Claire said innocently. "It's a pickup, so don't worry about scheduling delivery."

Gloria was instantly suspicious. "Claire. Who is this for?"

"Is that my phone?" Claire said, patting her apron pockets. "Go get the vase, and I'll help you put it all together."

Gloria wiped her hands on her apron and walked into the shop. The yellow pitcher was currently playing home to a pretty tangle of exotic greenery. She transferred the greenery to a new concrete planter and brought the pitcher into the back.

Claire took over, filling the pitcher with filtered water and flower food before tucking the arrangement in place.

"Oh," Gloria sighed. It was perfect. And she had made it.

"Here's the card," Claire said, handing over the small envelope.

"Should I get one of the card holders—Why is my name on this?"

Claire beamed. "Surprise!"

"You're kidding me." Gloria stared down at the white paper in her hand, afraid to open it.

"Go on," Claire prodded. "Open it!"

Gloria slid her thumb under the flap.

Beautiful flowers for (and by) a beautiful woman.

Love,
Aldo

"You sneaky, underhanded…" But Gloria was out of adjectives. It was lovely and perfect and so very thoughtful.

"He signed it '*Love*, Aldo,'" Claire pointed out in case Gloria had missed that.

"I see that. I should be annoyed that he made me work for these," Gloria said.

"But you're not," Claire teased.

She wasn't. It was simply perfect.

"He snuck the card while you were working on Jamilah's arrangement today and hid it on a shelf, then texted me."

"Diabolical," Gloria said, fussing with an aster. "Absolutely diabolical." The smile on her face couldn't get any wider.

CHAPTER 46

I planned the entire Fourth of July celebration for my town. Everything down to what color the trash can buntings were. I made sure there were enough properly located porta potties. I helped with the permits for the food stands and vendors. Laid out the entire carnival map. Organized the parade order so there wouldn't be any fighting between the Kiwanis and the Lions Club.

I did a damn good job.

And what's everyone talking about? Glenn's mother calling me a whore.

I can't help asking: Am I ever going to get away from this? Am I always going to be tied to that situation, that family? Should I have moved to a new town where no one knows me? Or is there some value to living through this humiliation over and over again?

She called Aldo a cripple. I think that was the moment when I realized just how diseased this woman's perception is.

Diseased.

I used to be as sick as she is. But I'm not now. I may not be normal yet, but I'm not where she is.

Yes, I felt ashamed. Yes, I was embarrassed. But if she could stand there and call Aldo Moretta, a man who fights for his country and has a heart bigger than the moon, a cripple, then maybe she *didn't really see me either. Maybe I'm more than the ungrateful whore that she sees.*

I know. Her opinion of me shouldn't have any bearing on my own. But being embarrassed like that in front of everyone I'd tried so hard to prove myself to… It was like being stripped naked. It was a reminder that I can't outrun this shadow of shame. I have to face it. Live with it. Walk through it.

Maybe then I'll think more of myself, and eventually everyone else will follow suit. Or they'll keep whispering behind my back for all of eternity. Won't that be fun? Me in a rocking chair in the old folks' home with a bunch of white-haired gossips talking about how sixty years ago, I had an asshole boyfriend.

Aldo came home with me last night. Held my hand while I blurted out my life's story and didn't call me an idiot for staying. He held me while I slept. Made me feel safe.

And I know what you're going to say. It's too soon. I know it is. But he's waking up feelings that I didn't know I was capable of. Feelings I don't know if it's smart to feel. But I feel…good. I know everyone's going to be talking about Mrs. Diller. I know they're going to be rehashing every time they saw me in town with bruises. A few of the early birds in town are going to mention they saw Aldo leaving my apartment this morning. I have to be okay with it. I have to know my truth and believe in myself.

Aldo has his own scars. We haven't talked much about those.

Maybe he doesn't trust me yet. Or maybe he doesn't know what he's feeling. But he's my friend—my boyfriend—and I'll listen when he's ready to talk.

He sent me flowers. Actually, he did better than that. He ordered flowers, and I made the arrangement. He knew I'd get more out of it if I was trying to make something beautiful for someone else. He really seems to get me. Is that even possible? Can he really see beneath my scars? Can I see beneath my scars? I want to.

The letters? They're still coming. And I think he's feeding some of those threats to his mother. She came at me with a "he'll make you pay" threat. I don't doubt that he'll try to hurt me again if he gets out. He will. The only thing that's keeping me safe right now is the fact that he has no one to pay his bail.

That doesn't give me a sense of security. It feels like something big and dark hanging over my head ready to drop at any second.

But I can't live my life tensing for the next blowup, the next punch or slap. I have to move forward.

CHAPTER 47

Aldo pulled into the flower shop's parking lot and gave himself a minute to watch her through the window as she worked her way down the closing checklist. She was wearing navy-blue shorts and a cute little white blouse that still looked fresh and crisp even after a day of work. She was a breath of fresh air on a muggy summer day.

Gloria came out of the front door carrying a cheery bouquet of flowers in a sunshine-yellow vase. He grinned. She was taking the flowers home with her. He watched her juggle the flowers and dig for her keys in the depths of her bag.

Aldo slid out from behind the wheel and approached. "Nice flowers," he said, taking them from her and freeing her hands.

"Thanks and thanks," Gloria said, shooting him a shy smile. "What are you doing lurking in the parking lot?"

"I thought if I was cute enough while I lurked, you'd say yes to dinner tonight."

She gave him the once-over. "Well, you *are* pretty cute," she admitted. "But I already have plans."

"Can I be part of those plans, or would it be weird?" he pressed.

She studied him, debating. "Hmm."

"Is that a good hmm or a bad hmm?"

She tugged her lower lip between her teeth. "Fine. You can come with me," Gloria decided. She stopped him with a point of her finger. "But you don't get to have an opinion."

"An opinion on what?" Aldo asked, immediately intrigued. "You'll see."

He put her and the flowers in his truck and let her direct him across town to a little storefront with a few neon signs in the window.

"A tattoo parlor?" he asked. *Okay, this was a surprise.*

"No opinion," she reminded him, unfastening her seat belt.

"How about questions? Can I ask questions? What are you getting? Where are you getting it?" They got out of the truck and headed for the front door.

"You'll see," she said again primly.

He held the door for her, and she brushed past him into a small, artsy space. Aldo had enough ink done over the years to be a good judge of tattoo parlors. This shop was new to him but clean, bright. There were red vinyl armchairs arranged in an L on the black-and-white checkered floor of the waiting room. Instead of a TV on the wall, there was a bookcase stacked with worn paperbacks and magazines.

The guy behind the counter was tattooed from neck to wrist, but his T-shirt was fresh, his hair cut.

"Gloria," he said, reaching out a hand. "Good to see you again."

"Hi, Curtis," Gloria said, shaking his hand. "This is my friend Aldo. Aldo, this is Curtis."

"Nice place," Aldo told him.

"Thanks, man. Listen, I'm going to grab the stencil from the sketch if you guys want to go back. Room 2." He handed over a clipboard of the requisite "No, I won't sue you if I spell something wrong" paperwork.

Aldo hesitated, holding his breath and hoping. Gloria gave him another one of those long looks while she fiddled with the pen. "Okay. I guess you can come back with me."

He followed her behind the counter and down the bright hallway. There were art prints, black-and-white shots of tattooed skin on the walls. Tasteful, unique. Aldo didn't see a single rose tramp stamp or cartoony dragon-festooned bicep. He felt the familiar tickle, the desire for another design, and wondered what Gloria had chosen for her own stunning skin.

Gloria bypassed a room that was decked out with red walls and black leather furniture and stepped into one with cool blue paint and a white dentist-style chair. There was music in here, soft and spa-like. It was a small space but well organized.

She eyed the chair and straightened her shoulders. When she began unbuttoning her blouse, Aldo felt a strangled noise rise out of his throat. This was *not* how he'd imagined his first time seeing Gloria undress. He turned around abruptly to face the wall.

Her soft laugh had him peeking over his shoulder. She was wearing a thin-strapped camisole under her shirt, and he relaxed. But it was short-lived. "Where are you getting it?" he asked, his voice rough, picturing her sprawled out on the chair while Curtis worked on breasts Aldo hadn't been lucky enough to be invited to see yet.

She slid onto the chair and tapped the inside of her arm. "Here."

There was a scar there that he hadn't noticed before. An old one, silvered with age. Without thinking, he took her elbow and gently turned it to get a better look. Thin and jagged, it raced up the inside of her arm for three inches, and he wondered what had caused it, already knowing *who* had caused it.

"I wanted a permanent mark that I chose," she said softly.

Aldo's chest swelled with pride and repressed rage. He brushed his thumb over the scar.

"I wanted to take something ugly and make it beautiful," she said.

"There isn't anything on or about you that's ugly, Gloria."

She let out a breath. "So how bad is it going to hurt, Mr. Tattoos All Over My Body?"

"Not *all* over," he teased. "With everything you've been through? Walk in the park," he promised her.

She nodded, looking slightly less nervous. "Good. Okay. I can totally do this."

Aldo plopped down on the second rolling stool and wheeled it over to her chair. "I'll hold your hand," he offered.

She laced her fingers with his. "This is the weirdest first date."

"I'll take you out to dinner after," he offered.

"Let's see if I barf all over this poor guy first."

"Are you nervous?" He gave her hand a reassuring squeeze.

"Terrified. I've never *chosen* pain before."

He brought her hand to his mouth and laid his lips on her knuckles. "It's different when you choose it."

"So I'm not crazy for doing this?" Her eyes, wide and amber, pleaded.

"Not even close." He nodded to the exposed ink on his forearm where his shirtsleeve was rolled up. "Of course, I might be biased."

"I like your tattoos," Gloria confessed.

"And you're going to like yours too."

"Okay, Gloria," Curtis said, stepping into the room. "I've got your stencil here. Let's get started."

———

She held his hand in a tight grip but kept her eyes on the ink going on her skin. A tiny flock of birds in flight.

Simple. Classy. Meaningful.

She didn't have to tell Aldo what it represented. He knew. Freedom. Soaring. As Curtis worked his way up the sliver of scar, Gloria's smile got wider. As predicted, the pain was minimal compared to what she'd already endured.

Pride rose up in his chest, swift and fierce.

Aldo couldn't help it. He leaned in and pressed a kiss to her cheek. She dragged her gaze away from the work and focused on him. "Do you like it?" she asked shyly.

"Do you?" he countered.

She glanced back down at where the needle pressed into her skin. "Yeah. I love it."

"It's perfect," he told her. "I kind of want it."

Gloria laughed.

"I've got time," Curtis said without lifting his head from the subtle shading he was adding to a bird wing.

"You're not serious," Gloria said.

"Would it be weird for you? I've got the space…"

"We could do a variation on the design," Curtis suggested, reloading the tip in the ink cap. "If Gloria's okay with that."

She glanced back down at her arm and then up again at him. The connection he felt between them was solid, real.

"As long as he's not doing something stupid and putting my name on his body," she decided.

Little did she know how much of her was already indelibly etched into his skin.

CHAPTER 48

I can't believe we got matching tattoos on our first date," Gloria marveled, looking out the truck window. He'd gotten two of her birds tattooed on his chest, soaring above an existing piece that said *Serenity, Courage, Wisdom.*

"Think of how much fun it will be to tell our grandkids that story," Aldo suggested, reaching across the console and squeezing her hand.

She snorted and fought back a yawn. After their tattoos, Aldo had taken her out to dinner at a burger joint one town over to celebrate. She'd devoured the burger, fries, and chocolate shake like a woman starved while he plowed his way through a burger bowl—all the burger fun without those pesky extra carbs.

"You're sure you're okay with it?" Aldo asked, turning the truck toward Benevolence.

"Yeah. I mean, if I picked a design that's so amazing a tattoo veteran—pun intended—wanted it, that means I've got great taste, right?"

"Exactly. And now that we've got a memorable first date in the books, I need to confess something."

"Oh, God. What? You're seeing someone else? You don't

think we should see each other anymore? You're going to dump me now because you've rethought this entire thing and you don't like women with tattoos? Dammit, Aldo! You promised me tacos next week," she pretended to wail.

"All of that makes my confession a lot less weird."

"Let's get this over with," Gloria decided. "I want to make sure the liquor store is still open if I need a jug of wine to soothe my wounded soul."

"The tattoo below the birds?" he began.

"Yeah?"

"That one was my first. It was inspired by you too."

"What?" She would have been less surprised if he'd announced he was really into wearing women's underwear on the weekends.

He sighed, checking the mirror before changing lanes. "Let me start at the beginning. You want to know the exact moment that I decided you were going to be my girl?" he asked, playful now.

"Uh, yeah. I would really like to know that." Gloria freed her hand and poked him in the ribs. Touching him, being physically affectionate was easy with Aldo. It felt natural.

"I was walking down the hall to the locker room to change for practice. The auditorium doors were open down by the stage, and there was this beautiful girl on stage under a pink spotlight."

Gloria covered her face with her hands. "Oh, God. I don't think I can handle this."

"Shut up, I'm telling a story," Aldo said, steamrolling her in a most charming fashion. It was funny. Glenn had probably said those very words to her at some point over the course of their relationship, and Gloria's reaction to them would have been totally different. She would have clammed up, tensing at the warning that she'd gone too far. She'd pushed him too far.

Those same words from Aldo meant something entirely different. Because *he* was different.

"Anyway, there's this girl in a little denim skirt and a red-and-white striped T-shirt—"

"You remember what I was wearing?" This, right here, was officially the most romantic moment of Gloria Parker's life to date.

"Quit interrupting. I'm reminiscing here."

She giggled, an echo of the carefree sophomore she'd been. "Sorry. Please continue."

"This girl, in this sexy skirt, standing there in the spotlight. Then you opened your mouth."

His gaze was far away through the windshield as if he were remembering every detail of the moment.

"I sang… Oh my God! 'Hopelessly Devoted to You.' I was auditioning for the musical."

"I walked face-first into a set of lockers listening to you. It was like a fist to the heart. I was a goner."

She gasped. "Why didn't you say anything?"

"I was shy."

"Aldo Moretta doesn't have a shy bone in his body," Gloria pointed out.

"All right, I had to decide if you were too young. A senior and a sophomore? It mattered then. By the time I decided it didn't matter, I figured I'd play the game, show off for you a little, and then make my move."

"Make your move?" She twisted in the passenger seat. "Tell me."

"Well, you were always at the football games. I noticed, of course." Aldo stretched his arm across the back of the seat to toy with the ends of her hair. "I was going to wait until we had a really good game, one where I was clearly the hero."

Gloria snickered.

"And then I'd come up to you in the end zone where you and your friends would be celebrating."

Gloria held her breath, listening to this alternate ending for her teenage self. "And?"

"And I'd stroll up to you all confident and sweaty. And I'd give you the nod." Aldo glanced her way and jerked his chin at her, arching an eyebrow in the perfect imitation of a cocky high school jock. "Then I'd ask you if you were going to the bonfire or the diner or whatever that night. You would, of course, say yes all breathlessly and excited."

"Of course," Gloria said dryly.

"Then I'd show up with the thrill of victory still all over me and I'd say, 'Gloria Parker, I think it's about time I kissed you.'"

Gloria swooned on the inside. On the outside, she collapsed back against his arm. "Damn, that would have made my life."

"Mine too."

"Why didn't you?" she asked.

The fun went out of him. She could see it in the tensing of his shoulders, the single clench of his jaw as he stared straight ahead.

"You were already with Glenn."

"Oh." A short word in a tiny voice. A reminder of all that could have been but wasn't. And in its place, ten years of agony. She wanted to cry for them both.

"Gloria." His voice was rough, his eyes stormy. "I was the reason he hit you that first time," Aldo confessed.

The weight of the blame he'd carried for a decade opened up and bled like a fresh wound between them.

"What are you talking about?"

"The summer I graduated. The summer he graduated," Aldo added. "You were at a bonfire, and I talked to you. Glenn didn't like it. He pulled me aside, tried to be a big man and threaten me for talking to 'his woman.'"

Gloria swallowed hard. She remembered the bonfire. She hadn't known what had set him off. But she remembered talking to Aldo. A quick "Hey, how's it going?"

"It was innocent," she said quietly.

"Not for me, Gloria. It was never innocent for me. I wanted you, and he could see it."

"Aldo—"

"He told me he didn't like me talking to his woman. I told him I didn't like the way he was treating you. We got into a shoving match. Luke and Linc broke it up fast."

"I had no idea."

"He dragged you out of there by your arm." Aldo's voice was dangerous. "I made a point to run into you the next day, and you had a black eye. You said you fell at the bonfire."

Gloria couldn't look him in the eye. She stared down at her hands resting in her lap. It had been the first of many, many lies she'd told.

"You swore you were fine, laughed it off. But I could see that part of that sparkle, part of that shine from the spotlight, was already gone. He was already taking pieces of you."

She closed her eyes. "You tried to get me to break up with him. Told me he was trouble. Then I pretended like it was a joke, and I laughed."

"He hit you because of me. You got hurt because of me." The words poured out of him like water over Niagara Falls. They couldn't stop, even if Gloria wasn't ready to hear them. "I enlisted the next day."

"Oh my God, Aldo!"

"Luke had been talking about it, and I hadn't decided. But I knew if I didn't get away, I'd be the reason you got hurt again, and I couldn't live with that, Glo. So I enlisted, and I walked into the first tattoo parlor I could find in the phone book."

"It's the serenity prayer, isn't it?" Gloria asked. "Grant me the serenity to accept the things I can't change?"

He nodded.

"You had to accept that you couldn't change me." The man had marked his skin and enlisted in the military because of feelings he had for her that she'd never known about. He'd carried the burden of blame for something he had no responsibility in.

Had she left Glenn that first time, their story could have been completely different. The Gloria who left Glenn could have still been the Gloria who ended up with Aldo.

"I took every training, every assignment. I went to college. All just to get away from here. But I kept coming home. And I kept hoping."

She reached for him. Put her hand on his strong arm. "Aldo. He was always going to hit me. You were an excuse, not the reason."

He didn't move away from her touch, but he didn't try to hold her either. "When you didn't leave him... I didn't understand."

Her heart hurt. Another person she had disappointed, devastated.

"I hate this. I hate knowing that I let you down, Aldo."

"You didn't let me down. I didn't understand. I didn't get it. But I do now. I don't blame you for staying."

"I do. I blame myself every day. Aldo, what if I left him the first time it happened? What if you and I had that shot? My entire life would be different. I would have gone to college. I would have made something of myself. We might have kids and pets and soccer practice and lasagna for dinner."

Staring into the darkness beyond the windshield, she mourned the loss of things she'd never had.

"Or we would have been too young to know what a good thing we had and screwed it all up," Aldo pointed out. "I was eighteen. All I knew was football. The guard, college, all of that turned me into who I am today. I wouldn't be here now if it had gone down differently. I believe that, Gloria. I really do."

Maybe he had a point. But not enough to get her to stop wallowing. "I hate that I was a textbook battered woman."

"There are reasons why women don't leave," Aldo argued.

"And there are women who would never let themselves be put in that situation. Do you think Sophie would have ever let Ty hit her? Even once? No! She would put his balls in a pickle jar. But I didn't have that spine at sixteen. I didn't have that confidence. I was so hungry for attention I was willing to accept abuse and humiliation and isolation as the price to pay for it." Her voice was raised, and she didn't care. The words had been trapped inside her for too long. "I can't forgive myself any more than I can forgive him," she admitted. Her eyes were dry, but her heart was pounding in her head.

Aldo brought his fingers to the back of her neck where he stroked gently.

"This is a second chance for both of us. I'm going to try real hard not to blow it. But isn't the important thing not what you did or didn't do at sixteen but what you choose now as an adult? Isn't the point of all this that now you'll have that pickle jar, and you'll be ready to use it?"

"It terrifies me that I might not be ready. It shakes me to the bone to think that I might be exactly the same girl I was at sixteen, ready to make the same mistakes again. Still too hungry for attention. Too eager to please."

There. She'd said it. She'd voiced her greatest fear.

"I'm pretty sure you know that's bullshit, Glo," Aldo said, gently rubbing her neck.

Some days, she *was* sure. Other days, all she had to do was see Mrs. Diller and her carefully crafted confidence crumbled.

CHAPTER 49

They rode like that for long minutes of silence as street-lights shone intermittently through the windshield, neither of them inclined to speak. Their wounds were open, confessions made, and they were both still here. Aldo was here. Not running away from her baggage. Not blaming her for her choices. Not trying to control her reactions. Just letting her be.

She'd never felt more vulnerable, her truths all spilled and served up for someone else's consumption. In turn, she knew the weight he'd carried. He'd blamed himself for her being hurt.

"Did you know we had the same study hall together the year before?" she asked him quietly.

"We did not."

"We did. In Mr. Fink's biology classroom. You sat at one of the lab tables in the back with your jock buddies. I was the good girl up front shooting you looks of longing."

"I would have noticed you."

"You didn't. I was flat-chested and had braces."

He gave a gruff laugh and gave her neck another gentle squeeze.

Aldo pulled into the parking lot at Blooms and eased to a

stop next to Gloria's car. He unclipped his seat belt, and Gloria sighed.

"You don't have to get out and walk me to my car that is barely three feet away."

"I'm a gentleman," he insisted, flashing her a wolfish look. "Besides, I like kissing you without a console between us."

Swoon.

It was official. Tonight was going down in Gloria's book as the best night of her life.

She stepped out of the truck, and Aldo met her in the space between their vehicles, his broad chest and shoulders blocking out the night. She brought her hands to his pecs, mindful of his fresh ink.

"Thank you for the flowers," she said, pressing a kiss to the corner of his mouth. "Thank you for dinner." She kissed the other side. "And thank you for being honest."

She was moving in to capture his mouth full-on when he stopped her. Big, careful hands on her upper arms.

"Gloria. I need you to get in the truck." His eyes were hard and fixed on something behind her.

"What? Why?"

She turned and saw the scratches in the side of her car.

Whore.

"We'll go ahead and take some pictures that you can send to your insurance company, Gloria. In the meantime, is there anyone you can think of who isn't feeling particularly friendly toward you?" Sheriff Bodett asked.

"You know exactly who's responsible for this," Aldo growled. "Gloria's got two enemies in this entire town, and one of them is behind bars."

"Be that as it may," the sheriff said, unaffected by Aldo's temper, "there's still a procedure we have to follow."

Fuck the procedure. Aldo wanted Sheriff Bodett to pull up in front of Linda Diller's house with lights and sirens.

"I really don't want to make a big deal out of this," Gloria cut in. She rubbed her arms with her hands despite the fact that there was no chill in the July night air. Aldo tucked her into his side, wishing he could spirit her away and take care of this for her.

"She's being threatened by Diller, and last night, his mother confronted her publicly," he pointed out. "When is the 'procedure' going to start protecting Gloria from that family?"

This situation was the perfect shit show of everything Aldo hated in life: Glenn Diller and feeling helpless.

"I'm sure we'll get all this worked out," the sheriff said mildly. "Gloria, you go ahead and send these pictures over to your insurance company, and they'll take care of you." He bustled away with the notebook in which he hadn't written a damn thing.

Gloria stared glumly at the letters carved into her paint. "I have a thousand-dollar deductible."

"Don't worry about that," Aldo urged her. "I'll take care of it."

"Oh no, you won't." She rounded on him. Even though she was shooting the look at him, Aldo was glad to see some fire in her eyes.

"Why the hell not?"

"You're not paying my deductible. You're not paying my anything."

"It's not a big deal."

She shook her head. "It's a huge deal."

Aldo bit his tongue. Fuck. Glenn had held the purse strings

and likely wielded it over Gloria. For the first time in her life, she was responsible for herself financially.

He closed his eyes, changing tack. "Glo, this is like me being out of laundry detergent and you having some. You'd share your detergent with me, wouldn't you?"

"Aldo!" she said in exasperation. "Money is different. Money means power and control. And I'm not comfortable accepting money from you for my problem."

"Your problem is my problem," he reminded her, his voice steely.

But she didn't flinch. Instead, she rolled her eyes at him. "That's such an annoying alpha male thing to say."

Aldo prayed for patience. "What I meant to say is that we're in this together. My resources are your resources. My problems are your problems and vice versa." *Come on, woman. See the logic. Accept the help.*

"Aren't we a little early in this relationship to be talking about sharing resources?"

"Gloria, we got matching fucking tattoos tonight. We are not in a typical relationship. There's no use pretending that we are. We're dating. You don't want to be driving around town in a vandalized car. Let me fix this."

She crossed her arms over her chest. "I'm not taking your money," she hissed.

"Fine. I'll hire you."

"If you say you want me to water your plants, I am going to scream bloody murder, Aldo Moretta."

"Paint my house."

"What?"

"The walls, I mean. Everything is beige and off-white. I want some color in my life."

She stared at him, considering.

"Paint my house and the entire town won't be talking about what Glenn's mother did to your car."

It was the right button to push.

"Fine," she said grudgingly. "But let's not make this money thing a habit. You don't have that many walls."

CHAPTER 50

He fixed her car. Took her for tacos. Met her for lunch. Aldo did his best to dazzle Gloria in every way that a man can dazzle a woman. Except one.

In the course of their increasingly NC-17 good-night kisses, Aldo realized a new, awful fear. One that he wasn't sure he could share with her the way they'd shared the rest of their baggage.

Things between them were good. Great even. He loved their text messages throughout the day, their evening chats, the hours they set aside for each other.

Gloria's mouth beneath his was a slice of heaven that he couldn't get enough of. It was hard keeping these good-night kisses limited to just kisses. His body revved with long-forgotten need every time she opened for him, every time she made one of those little wild whimpers in the back of her throat.

She was the sexiest woman he'd ever known, he'd ever kissed.

And he couldn't pull the trigger.

Even now, Gloria was out of her seat belt and almost in his lap behind the wheel. That lithe tongue of hers was driving him in-fucking-sane. He wanted nothing more than to drag her all the way over the console into his lap and fog up the windows high school senior year style.

But he couldn't just throw the truck in gear and drag her caveman-style to his house. They both needed time.

He broke the kiss on a groan. It was getting harder and harder to say good night to Gloria. They'd been out three more times this week since the tattoos. And he was scared shitless.

"You should go in," he said, stroking his hands up her arms as if she could be cold with the smoldering furnace of unrequited physical lust that burned between them.

"I don't have a curfew, Aldo," she reminded him lightly.

"Yeah, but…" But what? It was a Saturday night. Neither one of them worked tomorrow, and all he really wanted was to take her home and make love to her until the sun came up. *But…*

She slid back into her seat and crossed her arms. "Okay, this slow thing was very respectful and admirable but, Aldo, don't you want to run the bases?"

He closed his fingers around the steering wheel in a death grip.

She was going to make him say it. Make him say the one thing that could never be taken back or forgotten…

"Gloria, I went through some trauma," he faltered. Jesus, was he really tap-dancing around this? Was he really about to admit to the woman he'd been hung up on forever that he was afraid that his dick didn't work anymore?

She was waiting for him to continue. But he had no idea how to get the words out without humiliating himself. It wasn't fair keeping this from her.

"Aldo. I told you I was raped. I was beaten. Then I confessed my gigantic crush on three of the members of 98 Degrees that I'm still not sure I'm over. Can what you're choking on be worse than all that?"

He couldn't look her in the eye. He stared through the windshield so hard he was surprised the glass didn't shatter. "I'm afraid I might not be able to...function in the way...that I used to before..."

"Your leg?" she asked, confusion etched on her face in the streetlight.

He shook his head. One quick jerky motion.

"Your—oh. *Oh!*"

He wanted to die on the spot. Wither up and turn to dust so he'd never have to look her in the eye again and see...pity? Disgust? Disappointment?

"Aldo."

He grunted.

"Aldo, look at me," she ordered, her voice firm.

It took everything he had to pick up his head and look Gloria in the eye.

"We'll take it slow," she said. "Okay? I won't force you into anything."

"I don't want to disappoint you. You deserve amazing. You deserve Old Aldo."

Gloria scoffed. "I don't know how someone can be so conceited and self-conscious in the same sentence."

"It's just that this recovery sometimes feels like I'm hanging on by my fingernails. If we try...*that*, and it doesn't work... I don't know if I could ever recover."

She pulled his right hand off the wheel and laced her fingers through his. "If we're talking about what I think we're talking about, allow me to one-up you. I've never had an orgasm."

It suddenly became imperative—the most important thing in the universe—that he, Aldo Moretta, give Gloria her first orgasm. And her last. And every single one in between.

He didn't know what to say. A gauntlet had been thrown.

273

One his competitive side couldn't ignore. But the wounded, damaged side was terrified he couldn't deliver. He would have to fight through this fear of failure, vanquish the beast, and give Gloria the satisfying sex life she deserved.

Oh, God. The pressure was going to kill him.

"That's a whole lot of inner monologue you've got going on in that pretty head of yours," Gloria teased.

"I don't know what to say."

"Just relax. Okay. Now that I know you're not physically repulsed by me, I can be patient," Gloria told him.

He looked at her, shocked. "You seriously thought that?"

"Uh, hello." She waved. "Damaged goods here. Don't you know that everything is because of me? Textbook battered woman trauma. We believe everything everyone does is because of us."

"You have a very healthy sense of humor, you know that?" he pointed out.

"That's what my therapist tells me. You could talk to her, you know. I mean, we already have matching tattoos. It probably wouldn't be any weirder if we saw the same therapist."

"It took me this long to work up the guts to tell you. You want me to turn around and tell a complete stranger?"

Gloria held up her hand. "It's only a suggestion. I'll remind you I spilled my guts to a complete stranger, and it maybe kind of helped."

Aldo dropped his forehead to the steering wheel. "Can we forget the last five minutes, please?" He knew how fucked up this was. Knew it was asinine of him to pursue her when he wasn't sure he could give her everything she needed, be everything she needed. But, God, he didn't want to miss his shot again. He was stuck between a rock and a hard place. The idea that, after all this time, he might disappoint Gloria was too much. But dammit, to be the first man to give her an orgasm? That was an honor he wasn't letting any other man attempt.

"Already forgotten," she promised.

They sat in awkward silence in the dark in front of Gloria's apartment building, each pretending everything was peachy keen.

"So you know you still get...hard," Gloria ventured.

He gripped the wheel again, waiting to die from embarrassment. He was hard as fucking steel right now. He had no problems getting hard around Gloria...it was the rest of the process he wasn't sure about.

"I mean, obviously you get...excited...at certain romantic moments," she soldiered on to his dismay. "And when you slept over on my couch that first time, you had some amazing action happening in your briefs...or boxers. Is it weird that I don't know what you wear?"

"Jesus, Gloria. Please stop," he pleaded.

"So you get hard," she reiterated. "But you haven't...you know...since before?"

"Oh my God. Are you trying to kill me? No. No, I haven't." But he would. He would find a way. Some way to give Gloria what she'd never had. "Can we please talk about something else? Anything. Anything at all?" he begged.

"You know, I could help you test it out," Gloria suggested. He could hear the smile in her voice and chanced a look at her.

She wasn't joking. She looked...enthusiastic as she stared at his raging hard-on that was fighting the confines of his pants.

"Gloria, the first orgasm between the two of us sure as hell isn't going to be mine."

CHAPTER 51

I t was Friday night, and Gloria was in her pajamas, loose shorts and a T-shirt, in Harper's kitchen pawing through takeout menus and debating which face mask she was going to try. It was sleepover night. Harper had invited Gloria, Sophie, and her friend from college, Hannah, for a night of full-frontal male nudity movies and pizza.

It was the perfect way to take her mind off everything else. And quite honestly, Gloria needed the break. On top of orders, deliveries, payroll, and twenty-two centerpieces for a wedding tomorrow, there had been nearly a dozen hang-up calls at the shop.

Either it was a rogue fax machine or someone with a lame sense of humor. But every time she answered to silence on the other end, Gloria's skin crawled. She couldn't help but think this had something to do with her.

Hannah, a tall, lovely woman with wide eyes and hair the color of pennies, was recounting an embarrassing college story involving Harper and a bio lab mix-up.

Gloria couldn't remember the last time she'd done something like this. the last time she'd had friends like this.

High school? Pre-Glenn. She'd deprived herself of so many things with that one choice.

Her phone buzzed in her pocket.

Aldo: Have fun tonight, Glo. You deserve it.

Seven words that banked a warm fire in her belly. She bit her lip. Could she believe that this choice was different, better than her last? All signs were pointing to a big, bright neon yes. The only niggling doubt she had was Aldo Moretta's braking ability. On one hand, she appreciated that he wasn't pushing for a fast, physical relationship. On the other, she'd gotten to the point where it felt like one more good-night kiss and she was going to spontaneously combust.

They talked on the phone, cuddled in front of the TV, went out, cooked dinner—which to Gloria was about as intimate as you could get with your clothes on. But there was still nothing happening on the naked front. He'd kissed her. Oh, had he kissed her. And she him. But every time she thought it was going somewhere, Aldo reached into his annoying well of self-control and hit the pause button.

She got it. He wasn't ready to chance a less-than-stellar performance. But at this point, Gloria would be properly grateful for even a C-minus performance.

Sophie stabbed the blender button and sent the margarita mix roiling.

"So what fat-free, calorie-free deliciousness are we ordering tonight?" Harper called over her shoulder as she let the dogs out the back door to romp around in the warm night air.

"We were thinking pizza and chicken bites from Dawson's," Sophie yelled over the whir of the blender.

"What about dessert?" the pretty Hannah wanted to know.

"I brought cookie dough," Gloria announced. "We can either make cookies or eat it raw." *Classic sleepover fare.*

"Best. Night. Ever," Harper sighed, lining up four pink plastic margarita cups on the counter.

Sophie brought the blender pitcher over and sloshed margaritas into the cups. Gloria doled out the lime wedges she'd cut, and Hannah rounded out the assembly line by plunking a straw into each cup.

"A toast, ladies," Sophie said, raising her glass. "To the lovely Harper. May she know how lucky we all are to know her."

"To Harper," Gloria echoed. She looked around their tight little circle and felt nothing but joy in the moment.

"You guys! My turn," Harper said, placing a hand over her heart. "To all of you. Thank you for being my family. I love each one of you so much."

A chorus of awws, a clink of plastic, and they all took their first sips.

"I approve you as a bartender," Hannah told Sophie.

Sophie winked.

"Well, let's get this party started," Harper said, dialing Dawson's and placing their order.

Gloria took the opportunity to fire off a quick text to Aldo with the kissy face emoji.

Hannah held up two DVDs. "So what do we want? Full frontal or rom-com?"

Harper dropped her phone on the counter and groaned. "You guys have full frontal at your beck and call. Let's not torture me with it when mine is on the other side of the world."

"Oooh! Let's talk about boys," Sophie said, clapping her hands.

"My 'boy' is your brother. Isn't that gross?" Harper laughed.

"For tonight, I'll pretend he's someone else's brother," Sophie said airily.

"Actually, there *is* a relationship I'm curious about." Harper grinned. "Gloria, what's the scoop on you and Aldo?"

Gloria choked on a frosty gulp of margarita.

"What makes you think there's anything to tell?" she asked innocently, pretending that it wasn't fodder for the whole town that they were dating.

"I have eyes and a brain," Harper teased. "I saw some patty-cake during the Fourth of July fireworks in the park," she explained to Sophie and Hannah.

"Hmm, Gloria Moretta. It's got a nice ring to it," Sophie mused.

Gloria felt her cheeks flame.

"You liiiiiike him!" Harper teased.

"Who is this Aldo, and is he Gloria-worthy?" Hannah demanded, sliding onto a barstool.

"Aldo is a muscly Italian stud who's had the hots for Gloria since high school," Harper supplied.

Muscly Italian stud. Aldo would love that description, Gloria thought.

Hannah snapped her fingers. "Luke's best friend, right? That's a long time to be carrying a torch," Hannah said. "You must be pretty great."

Gloria snorted.

"She really is," Harper agreed.

"You guys." Gloria laughed. "I'm still getting used to the idea."

"The idea of what?" Sophie prodded.

"Of Aldo…and me…dating."

Harper let out a whoop. "So it's official?"

Gloria let out a long breath and nodded. She hadn't been

sure when or how to tell her friends. She wasn't sure if she could handle their disapproval, if they showed any. "Official. I'm trying to take things slow, but boy, is he intense." She fanned herself with the takeout menu. Neither part of the statement was technically a lie. She *was* trying to take it slow, and Aldo Moretta *was* incredibly intense.

"I can't believe our little Aldo is finally all grown up," Sophie sighed.

"Do you have any pictures of this Italian stud?" Hannah asked.

Gloria blushed again and nodded. "I have some on my phone." They stuck their heads together over the screen, and Gloria felt herself glow while Hannah openly admired her boyfriend.

Sophie's hot-pink phone rang on the table. "Speaking of hot studs, it's the hubby." She took it into the dining room to answer. She returned a few seconds later, her forehead furrowed. She held her phone out to Harper. "It's Ty. He wants to talk to you. Sounds like he's in full-on cop mode."

Gloria's skin prickled again, and the hairs on the back of her neck stood up.

Harper raised her eyebrows and took the phone. "Hey, Ty, what's up? I thought you had the night off." She listened for a minute, her gaze falling on Gloria, and the color drained from her face.

CHAPTER 52

D o you think he'd come here?" Harper's question asked in staccato throbbed in Gloria's head. *No. This can't be happening. Not now.*

The hang-up calls. Was it him? Or had his mother been keeping tabs on her for him?

"Gloria's here with me and Soph and Hannah," Harper said into the phone. "We were just waiting on pizza, which has no bearing on the situation at all. I'm just nervous, and I'm going to shut up now."

Gloria's heart was hammering in her chest. Bile rose in her throat. No. No. No.

Harper hung up and stared at Gloria.

"What the hell is going on?" Sophie demanded.

"Glenn's out. Ty thinks he might be heading to Gloria's," Harper said, worry tight in her voice.

"Oh my God," Gloria whispered.

"It's going to be fine," Harper promised. "Ty is heading to your place now to check things out. The police know he's missing. They're looking for him. He's not going to get to you. No one is going to let that happen."

He was going to find her, and he was going to hurt her. She was putting her friends in danger just by being here.

"I think I'm going to text Aldo and let him know," Gloria said, fighting through the panic.

"Good idea," Sophie said, patting her on the hand.

She took her phone into the dining room and tried not to think about what could be lurking in the dark on the other side of those windows. She debated for a moment. This wasn't anyone's battle but her own. Not Harper's. Not Aldo's. But she didn't have to do this alone anymore.

She dialed Aldo before she could change her mind.

"Hey, Glo." His voice was warm, affectionate. "How's girls' night?"

"Glenn's out, Aldo," she said, happy that she kept the tremor out of her voice. "Ty called. They don't know where he is."

"I'm coming to you," he said. No hesitation. No questioning her fear. Aldo would be there for her.

Hannah hustled into the dining room and started checking the windows. She could hear Harper on the phone telling Mrs. Agosta to keep the kids inside. They were all on the same page. Glenn was coming after her.

"I don't want anyone to get hurt," Gloria whispered.

"Honey, the only one getting hurt is him if he tries to get anywhere near you," Aldo promised. She could hear his truck engine start.

Lola trotted into the room and leaned up against Gloria's leg. She wasn't alone, she realized. She wouldn't have to face this alone anymore. One way or another, it would end tonight.

"It's probably nothing. We're probably overreacting," Gloria told him, hoping it would be true. But she felt it coming. Trouble.

"I'm on my way now. Keep the doors locked, okay, Glo? I'll be there as soon as I can."

"Okay. I'm going to go tell the girls you're coming."

"I'll be there in a couple of minutes," he promised. "I'm going to call Ty, okay? Then I'll call you right back."

"Yeah. That sounds good," she said, taking a breath and then another one.

"I'll be there soon, sweetheart."

"Thank you," she whispered. She hung up and returned to the kitchen.

Lola jogged down the hallway to Harper, and Gloria heard the snick of the dead bolt.

"Sorry to be such a party pooper," Gloria said lamely. "Aldo's on his way."

"Ty too," Sophie told her. "He's checking your place and your mom's place first."

"Okay, good."

"So…who is this Glenn guy?" Hannah asked. "Because he sounds like a dick."

Sophie smirked, and Gloria let out a nervous titter. "Yeah, pretty much."

Before anyone could fill Hannah in on how much of a dick Glenn was, there was a crash of glass, followed by Harper's shriek.

Gloria's demon was here. She could feel him like a stain, a bruise, a dark mark that ruined everything.

"Oh, fuck!" Sophie lunged for the knife block and yanked out a boning knife.

"Everybody out!" Harper screamed from the dining room. "Go to Mrs. Agosta's!"

Hannah grabbed Gloria's wrist in a death grip.

"Go!" Sophie hissed at them, clutching the knife in both hands. "Get her out!"

Max's three legs skittered on the kitchen tile as Lola's warning growl sounded from the dining room.

"Shit." Hannah let go of Gloria and dove for the little dog before he could run straight into danger. Sophie opened the basement door, and Hannah set him on the top step before slamming the door.

"Gloria! Go!" Sophie shouted.

"Well, look who's home," a familiar voice cackled from the dining room, and Gloria's blood ran cold. The memory of a hundred beatings washed over her, freezing her to the spot. The inevitability of it broke her heart. It was always going to happen. No number of laws could protect her. No new boyfriend or new friends or new life could keep her safe.

Glenn was here. He came for her, and Harper was facing him alone...

"Gloria's gone. She's safe and calling the cops right now." Harper's words reached them in the kitchen. Sophie grabbed her phone.

"Get the fuck here now, Ty. Now!"

Gloria's phone vibrated against her leg.

"Gloria, you need to run," Hannah told her, pushing her toward the back door. "We're not going to let him hurt you."

Gloria watched her hand reach for the handle on the back door as if it belonged to someone else. Her worlds had collided. And she was supposed to run away? She was supposed to let him hurt them?

She heard shouting from the front room. Heard a growl and a scuffle and a sickening thump.

Hannah spotted the baseball bat leaning next to the back door and grabbed it, her fingers wrapping around it in a white-knuckled grip. "Sophie? You with me?"

Sophie, eyes blazing, held up the knife. "Let's get this fucker."

"Go," Hannah told Gloria again. She turned and ran with Sophie into the dining room.

Every cell in her body was screaming "run." Run out the back door and never stop. Run until she was someone else with no history. But she couldn't start this new life by running away. This was her mess. Her problem. And he was hurting her friends.

It was her turn to make a stand.

The realization unfroze her. She ran back to the kitchen and grabbed the first thing she saw—the cast iron skillet on the stove.

She didn't think, just let her feet carry her into the dining room. She took in the scene, not knowing if milliseconds or minutes passed.

Glenn was on top of Harper on the floor, a hunting knife to her throat. Hannah was winding up for another swing with the bat, and Sophie was kicking him in the ribs, screaming, "Drop the knife, you crazy fuck!" And then Gloria was flying in slow motion. Glenn lifted his gaze to hers. Their eyes locked for an eternity frozen in time. Years of history passed between them. Of victim and abuser. Of woman and man. Of all they never had. Gloria saw the sick hatred, the desire for violence in his dead eyes, and swung with all her might.

He wasn't human anymore. But she was. She deserved a life without a monster.

She didn't know she'd hit him until she felt the vibrations of cast iron hitting skull rolling up her arms as his body collapsed onto the floor.

Everyone was screaming except for her. She was unearthly calm.

"Holy fuck!" Sophie shouted.

"Oh my God. Oh my God. Oh my God," Hannah chanted.

"Get him off me!" Harper groaned, her voice raspy. "He's crushing me."

Still numb, Gloria grabbed Glenn by the collar and, with Hannah's help, shoved his deadweight onto the dining room rug.

Lola belly crawled up to Harper. "My sweet girl," Harper whispered, stroking the dog's fur, causing her rear end to wiggle.

Gloria stared down at Glenn's unmoving body, the knife now harmless on the floor. There was a thin line of blood on Harper's throat. One more second. One more millimeter.

"Tape him up!" Sophie ordered, producing a roll of camo duct tape from God knows where.

Hannah bravely straddled the monster and yanked his arms behind his back.

"Get it up higher into his arm hair," Gloria suggested. Her breath returned, coming in short, ragged gasps. She collapsed against the wall, the skillet still in her hand.

Harper rolled to look at her, and their eyes met. The first giggle slipped out, and there was no stopping it. It was contagious. One by one, they all slid to the floor in a loose pile, shaking with laughter and adrenaline. Lola limped over, pausing to lick each one of them, reassuring herself that they were all okay.

The front door exploded off its hinges and crashed to the floor, narrowly missing Sophie. Aldo and Ty tumbled through the door, Ty with his gun drawn and Aldo with rage in his eyes.

They all froze. Aldo's gaze found her, and Gloria felt it like a force field surrounding her. Safe. She was safe.

"You could have come in through the window," Harper wheezed.

It was deathly silent for two seconds that felt like minutes. And then Sophie and Harper exploded in peals of hysterical laughter. Ty clambered over them to kick the knife away from Glenn's still body.

Gloria wondered if she'd actually killed him. Was she a murderer? Was she going to go to jail now? Oh, the irony.

Her downward mental spiral was abruptly cut off by strong arms banding around her like steel. She relaxed into the safety of Aldo's grasp. He was here. He'd showed up when she needed him most. And so had she.

"Are you okay?" His voice was rough with emotion. She could feel his heart racing in his massive chest.

She let the pan slide from her hand and fall to the floor, wrapping her arms around Aldo.

"I'm good. So good."

CHAPTER 53

The big bastard was awake and fighting his restraints with the desperation of a man who knew he'd never again see daylight.

Bellowing like a wounded bear, Glenn lowered his shoulder and lumbered at Ty. Ty let the man hit him like a limping freight train.

Aldo saw the opening and didn't question it. He threw a roundhouse to Glenn's jaw, knocking the big man back into the wall, where he slid to the floor. Ty got up, brushed himself off. "That's all you get, my friend." He stepped between Aldo and the dazed Glenn.

"It's not enough," Aldo rasped.

"No, it's not. But now we get to add resisting arrest and assaulting an officer to the charges." Ty hauled Glenn up to his feet and handed him over to a pair of uniforms. "Get this asshole outta my sight."

Glenn howled with rage on his way out the front.

Aldo watched from the porch as the man who'd tortured the woman he loved for years was hauled off in the back seat of a cop car, out of their lives forever.

The woman he loved. If he'd had any doubt, tonight had

brought things into crystal clear clarity. He loved Gloria Rosemarie Parker.

He flexed his fingers, relishing the pain. Glenn Diller deserved a hell of a lot more than one quick shot to the mouth, and Aldo knew he'd have to live with the regret for the rest of his life. Sometimes karma didn't let you be the instrument you longed to be. Aldo knew he would also spend the rest of his life reliving the moment he and Ty knocked the door down together. He still wasn't convinced she was safe.

She was inside, surrounded by first responders, giving a statement to the state police. She was safe. But he couldn't tell his body that. Not when it was in the midst of a full-blown adrenaline dump. His heart hammered in his chest as if he'd just sprinted a marathon. Blood rushed in and out of his head, his breath coming in short stabs. He felt like he was underwater and fighting for oxygen.

"Little Gloria Parker knocked 'em out cold with a fry pan," an EMT was saying to one of the neighbors who had lined up on the sidewalk, eager to witness the gruesome spectacle of domestic violence.

Through the sea of adrenaline that separated him from everyone and everything, Aldo thought that Gloria would appreciate the fact that she hadn't been referred to as "*poor* little Gloria Parker" this time. One home run swing of a cast iron skillet had banished that adjective forever.

She'd taken the stand she'd needed to. But Aldo couldn't forgive himself for being late. He hadn't been here when she needed him most.

And he didn't care how alpha or selfish it sounded, he'd wanted to be the one to end Glenn Diller's reign of terror.

But he hadn't.

Gloria had.

He went to her, needing to reassure himself that she was okay, that she was still here.

His heart hammered in his chest, an uneven stuttering. His insides were electrified. Blue and red lights flashed hypnotically through the glass. The only thing he could see clearly was her face. She was listening to the detective, nodding earnestly. Calm and collected. But when her gaze caught him, she changed. She was reaching for him, and he was closing the distance.

He could have lost her.

That thought rattled around in his mind, wreaking havoc on his system. He knew what this was, had seen it before in soldiers after violent attacks. But even seeing Gloria safe and unharmed, holding her to him, wasn't enough to reassure him that everything was okay. The clawing panic inside him was raking his guts to shreds.

Ty and Harper were arguing over who was going to call Luke and break the news to him. Harper's friend Hannah was on the phone with her husband, and Sophie was forking over cash to the pizza delivery guy.

"Is he gone?" Gloria asked him.

"Yeah, honey. He's gone." Aldo's own voice sounded like it was miles away.

He pulled her into the kitchen away from the lights, the badges, the questions. Opening the back door, they slipped outside into the night.

He needed a minute, ten minutes, a lifetime with her.

"Aldo." Her voice was steady, soothing.

But nothing short of murder could soothe the beast that raged in him.

Never again, he vowed. Never again would Gloria be left alone to face her demons.

He didn't realize how tightly he was holding her when he

backed her into the wall next to the door. The siding bit into his knuckles. Aldo wanted to be gentle, wanted to stroke and comfort. But he wasn't in control.

Gloria's hands came up between them, but instead of pushing him away, her fingers dug into his chest, holding on tight.

"I'm okay, Aldo," she whispered.

He crowded into her, pressing her against the wall of the house, trying to reassure his body that she was safe. His cock, raging hard, found the juncture of her thighs. He searched out her mouth with his own as he thrust against her.

With a whimper, she wrapped her arms around his neck, locking him to her, craving the contact as much as he was. She kissed him, lips devouring his with a hunger that matched his own.

He should slow down. Stop. She'd had enough violence in her life. He didn't need to be manhandling her to calm himself down. She needed sweetness on satin sheets, not a ham-handed mauling in a dark backyard.

But then Gloria was moaning against his mouth. "Yes. Yes. Yes. Aldo." His name. Her lips. A perfect combination. She was surrendering to him as if she knew instinctively what he needed.

He rocked his hips into hers, and she gave a breathy little moan. He had one hand in her hair, the other roaming the slim curve of her hip. His fingers kneaded the soft skin under the hem of her shirt.

And then she was reaching between them and cupping the painful length of his shaft, and he lost his damn mind. He rutted into her, rocking and thrusting as if they were naked. As if there were no barriers between them.

"Oh my God," she gasped against his mouth.

He needed to stop. Needed to take care of her. But he couldn't stop taking.

"Gloria."

Her slim hand was slipping under the waistband of his shorts, fingers wrapping around his goddamn aching dick, and his world went black for a minute. She pulled him free, lined the head of his cock up between her legs, just under the hem of her loose shorts. There was one more layer between them, and Aldo tried to hang on to that. He had to stop this.

But his body had other ideas. He thrust himself into her grip.

"God, yes," she breathed, biting his lower lip.

His fingers decided two could play her game and dove under her shorts into her panties. He growled when he felt the wet.

"Do you want this? Do you want me like this?" He needed the yes. Needed it more than oxygen and water and sunshine. He needed Gloria's surrender.

"Touch me, Aldo," she demanded.

He obliged, sliding two fingers through her slit, sinking into her welcoming flesh. He groaned, an unholy sound. Trauma. Violence. Adrenaline. Together they were feeding on it. It couldn't be healthy. But he couldn't stop.

"Don't you fucking stop, Aldo," she breathed against his neck, using her teeth to drive the message home.

Her fingers tightened on his shaft, skimming over the sensitive head that was already leaking in anticipation of a release so intense it could level him. Not like this. Not like this. He didn't want it to be like this.

He fucked her with his fingers, wishing it was his tongue, his dick. Wishing he was worshipping her as he'd always planned. Slow and soft and sweet.

She opened her mouth just as he felt her quickening around his fingers, and he clapped a hand over her lips to keep her silent. She rocked her hips against him, eagerly riding his hand, her eyes wide.

Fuck yes. It was so wrong, what he was doing. But he couldn't fucking stop. She was a drug, and he was a junkie. She tightened her grip on him, and he felt the electricity in his balls shoot up the base of his spine. He dragged her underwear to the side and lined himself up with that beautiful slit.

In the dark, in the shadows, Aldo dragged the crown of his cock over Gloria's sweet clit. She bit his palm as those inner walls clamped down on his fingers, exploding around him. He pinned her to the wall with his body and fucked her hand, her slit, coming with her. A saw-toothed release that carved him out with each tremor, each jagged explosion.

They stared into each other's souls, hearts slamming together, bodies trembling, pleasure so bright it burned fire through their veins.

CHAPTER 54

I'm sorry. I'm so sorry."

Gloria couldn't quite hear him over the persistent buzzing in her ears. Was that a normal side effect of a mega orgasm? She had nothing to compare it to but was willing to throw herself into extensive research of the effect. Her body was molten liquid held together by nothing but Aldo's arms of steel.

"Wow. Wow."

"What?" Aldo was peering into her face. "Glo? Are you okay?"

She laughed, a breathy, desperate sound. "*Okay?* Okay is *not* the word I would use. Miraculous. Mind-exploding. Life-changing. Stunning. Holy. Fucking. Amazing." She could feel herself glowing, lit from the pleasure that Aldo Moretta had delivered. "This is the best night of my life."

"Are you insane? Have you completely lost your mind? You *almost died!*"

"I've come closer to dying crossing the parking lot on dollar taco night at Uncle Tito's," she scoffed.

But Aldo wasn't in a joking mood. He was hanging on by one tenuous thread. Grasping the situation, Gloria changed tacks. She took his shaking hands in hers, put them on her.

"Aldo, tonight I vanquished my own personal demon. He's not getting back out. The detective told me the charges. Attempted murder, assault, breaking and entering, stalking, harassment. Unless he breaks out of jail—and let's face it, he's not smart enough for that—that chapter of my life is officially over."

"Gloria, he broke into a house with a hunting knife to get to you."

"He never got past Harper. He never got near me."

"She was between you and him. He had to get through her to—"

"Stop. Stop it." Gloria stroked her palms over Aldo's chest. "It didn't happen. He didn't get to me. Now, he'll *never* get to me. Harper's okay. I'm okay. Everything is good."

He was shaking.

"I didn't want him to have any part in...this," Aldo said, his voice mechanical as he looked down at their bodies.

"Don't you shut down on me, Aldo. Don't make what we just did something ugly. It was incredible. Beautiful. It was just you and me." Gloria pulled one of his big hands to her mouth and rained kisses down over his knuckles.

"You and me," he repeated. "You and me."

"Please don't regret this. I don't think my heart could take it."

"I wanted it to be special."

"Aldo. You made me feel like you were wild with desire for me. There is nothing more special than that. It was like...hell, I don't know. Like I was finally realizing my potential. Aldo, it was beautiful. I'd also like to point out that there's plenty left that we didn't do. That was no home run."

"Fuck. Okay. Okay." He rested his forehead against hers, squeezed his eyes shut tight. "I want to make everything perfect for you. Everything. Every day. Forever."

If she hadn't been in love with Aldo Moretta before that sentence, she was totally, irrevocably, little-hearts-orbiting-her-head in love with him now.

"Would it be wrong to point out that you, ah…performed admirably just now?"

He snorted, but she could sense a lightening in him. Aldo nuzzled into her neck.

"I'd also like to point out that we were very physical, and I didn't shatter into tiny pieces."

She felt his lips on the juncture of her neck and shoulder.

"I'm glad you're safe," he whispered against her skin.

"I'm glad you're here. Now, what are we going to do with the…um…evidence?"

"There's a garden hose back here somewhere—"

"Aldo! You are not hosing me off!"

———

Ty called an emergency vet to check on Lola, who was given a clean bill of health and a prescription for as much steak as her heroic wiggle butt wanted. The Dawsons' delivery driver returned with a dozen pizzas at about the same time that Luke's foreman, Angry Frank, showed up with a three-man crew to board up the window and door. An hour later, Hannah's husband, Finn, burst into the house dressed like a mountain man. Luke's younger brother, James, arrived shortly after that.

Harper declared it to be a sleepover since no one was keen on anyone being left alone. Aldo didn't leave Gloria's side. Sometime around 4:00 a.m., they all collapsed in the living room. She was curled up on the couch, Aldo at her back, his arms wrapped around her as if he couldn't bear to let her go.

She closed her eyes and checked in. She didn't feel like a victim of violence tonight. No. She felt a little tiny bit like a hero. Her very own hero. She'd vanquished her own demon. And yeah, it had been terrifying. But she did it anyway.

She snuggled back against Aldo, reminding herself that he was there, so solidly there. This was what it felt like to win. She was going to hang on to this feeling for a very long time.

"Psst. Gloria?"

Gloria lifted her head to look at Harper, who was sprawled out on the floor with the dogs in the dark.

"Yeah?"

"You were awesome tonight."

Gloria grinned. "You too. Thanks for fighting a psychopath for me."

"Thanks for braining him with a frying pan and saving my life. You're my hero."

Aldo squeezed her once around the waist, echoing Harper's sentiment.

CHAPTER 55

L ittle Gloria Parker beaned that asshole with a fry pan." That's
what they're saying around town. They're still talking about
it, but no one's calling me poor anymore. There's no pity there. And
you know what? As long as I'm not pitying myself, then no one
else has any room to do it either. Lesson learned. So many lessons
learned.

I know I should be curled into a ball sobbing somewhere
having flashbacks, but I have never felt stronger. Or more sure of
myself. I did it. I saved myself. I am my own hero.

And I was from the minute I walked away from him. I just
didn't know it.

But I do now.

I know Aldo wishes it could have been him. He hasn't said it.
But he's got his own baggage when it comes to Glenn. He's got this
real-life action hero thing going. So having to take a step back and
let someone he cares about take care of themselves is hard for him.
But he's doing it.

He didn't get the closure I did that night. But he's so proud of
me, and that feels incredible.

I think I might love him.

I haven't told him yet. I want to hang on to it a little longer, *figure out if it's the truth. But I know whatever I'm feeling for him is real.*

I'm doing this. I'm living. I'm normal. And I'm going to take advantage of every second I get.

Thank you. For listening. For guiding. For everything.

CHAPTER 56

Gloria woke in a rush, her heart beating against her ribs. But it wasn't because of her nightmares anymore. Those had stopped the minute Glenn Diller had been hauled away in the back seat of a cop car, feeling the effects of the concussion she'd dealt him.

These nightmares were Aldo's.

She'd had her suspicions. Post-traumatic stress. Panic attacks. He covered them well. But he couldn't hide it from her in his sleep.

Aldo was wrapped around her, tensed as if to strike, his body trembling. She thought he'd sleep better in his own bed, had insisted they move their sleepovers to his house for the weekend. But the nightmares still found him.

Gloria rolled over and wrapped her arms around him, pulling him close. In his sleep, Aldo buried his face in her tank-top-covered breasts.

They hadn't spent a night apart since the incident with Glenn. They also still hadn't had sex.

Two weeks had passed since the trauma that had unlocked Gloria from her prison. But it had had the opposite effect on Aldo.

After their *moment*—their mind-blowing, life-altering *moment*—in Harper's backyard, Gloria thought that a physical relationship would bloom naturally between them. However, it seemed that the sexiest moment of her life had only encouraged Aldo to put sex on the back burner...in someone else's kitchen...in a town across the country.

She got it. She did. To a man like Aldo, pride was wired into his DNA. If he tried and failed at something like the sex that they'd both built up to be the be-all and end-all of orgasmic experiences? Well, the progress he'd made since coming home could come to a screeching halt.

Not knowing was better than knowing.

Unfortunately, now that she knew what an orgasm was, waking up to Aldo's raging morning wood was a special kind of torture. But he'd been patient with her. She could return the favor. But if he made her wait ten years, she'd have to get creative with her seduction techniques.

"Aldo," she whispered.

His body stiffened against her, but she held on tighter.

"Wake up, *mi león*."

Aldo woke instantly with an uncanny perception of his surroundings. Without even opening his eyes, the man forced himself to relax, to pretend he hadn't been in the throes of a nightmare.

"What does that mean?" he asked, pulling Gloria tight to him.

She could feel his heart still pounding against her cheek. "My lion."

He grunted, approving the nickname.

"Was it the explosion or Harper's house?" Gloria asked.

Of course, it was neither and both. Dreams, especially ones that were shaded by post-traumatic stress, weren't usually an exact replay of real life. Gloria knew this from experience. But the feelings they left in their wake were.

"I was lost in the woods, looking for you," he murmured against her hair. "Couldn't find you. Then someone started shooting."

She was so grateful that he talked to her. That he didn't go full-blown testosterone-fueled "don't worry your pretty little head about it." He was trying. But maybe it was time they looked for some answers outside themselves. She had a few ideas.

Relaxing back against him, she reached up and threaded her fingers through his unruly hair. "You okay to meet up with Harper and the gang for breakfast?"

"Yeah," Aldo said gruffly, cuddling her closer.

———

She was already regretting her decision. The box bounced and scrabbled in her grip as tiny claws tried to shred the cardboard like a Tasmanian devil.

"Hang on. One more minute. Please, please, please, be cute and sweet and not horrible," Gloria whispered to the box. "Oh my God. This was the worst idea I've ever had."

But it was too late, the bell was rung, and Aldo was opening his front door.

Thank God there was also pie. Or there would be.

His face lit up when he saw her on his doorstep, and Gloria clung to the hope that he wouldn't think this was the stupidest thing she'd ever done. His hair was ruffled like he'd just woken up, and she could hear the TV inside. They'd parted ways after breakfast with the Garrisons, Harper, and Luke's former mother-in-law, Joni, to handle Sunday errands.

Gloria's errand running had slipped into the overstepping boundaries zone.

"Hey, Glo. Whatcha got there?"

The box trembled in her grasp, and an impressive yowl sounded from inside.

"Oh, shit," Aldo said, staring at the box.

"I got you something," she said, shoving it into his hands and picking up the grocery bag at her feet. "And no matter how dumb or awful it is, focus on the fact that I'm going to bake you a pie."

The box shuddered and screeched. "Apple pie?" he asked.

She nodded and stepped inside, shutting the door behind her.

Aldo pried the lid off the ventilated box, and all hell broke loose.

The kitten, all one pound of him, exploded out of the box and launched himself at Aldo, hooking those claws into his shirt.

"What the—Ow!"

Terrified or incensed by Aldo's yelp, the cat dislodged himself, landing on the floor before Aldo or Gloria could catch him, and took off for the couch.

"I think he ripped my nipple off," Aldo said, peeking under his shirt.

"I don't know what I was thinking," Gloria began. She was cut off when the ball of gray tabby hurtled across the living room floor and wrapped itself in the drapes on the front window. "He's a boy. Nine weeks old and blind in his left eye."

The curtain rod came tumbling down, drapes landing in a heap, startling the cat.

They danced out of the way as the one-eyed fur monster sprinted back and jumped onto the coffee table, sending magazines and mail in all directions.

He was meowing and growling and hissing and making

other odd grunting noises. "I went with Harper to get Lola's eye drops at the shelter, and there was a litter of kittens, and you live alone, and I thought having a sweet little kitten to cuddle with would be—"

The kitten wiggled its chubby butt and tried to make the jump from coffee table to recliner, falling short by about a foot. To exact his revenge, he sunk his front claws into the recliner's footstool.

"No! Bad!" Gloria chased after the deceiving fluff ball, but he avoided her with freakish, ninja-like skills.

Aldo dodged left and dove right, capturing a handful of fur. He plucked the kitten from the floor and held it aloft.

Wrapped in his big hands, the kitten paused his war of destruction. The big man and the little cat blinked at each other.

"Mew!"

"Shit. He's kinda cute."

"Mew!"

The longer the man and cat stared at each other, the wider the bounds of Gloria's heart stretched. Her big, burly boyfriend, with his ruffled hair and Sunday stubble, peering into the fluffy face of a terrified, horribly behaved kitten.

Gloria was a goner.

The cat—dubbed Ivan the Terrible—ate too much cat food, threw up on the kitchen floor, showered kitty litter all over the laundry room, and was now curled up, sound asleep in the crook of his new owner's muscled arm.

Aldo was perched on a stool, resting his good leg, and watching Gloria commandeer his kitchen. She peeled and sliced and measured while he cuddled the cat.

"You don't have to keep him," she reminded him, fishing a bowl out of a cabinet and moving on to level off a cup of flour.

In his kitty coma, Ivan snored against Aldo's forearm.

Aldo chuckled softly.

"I thought that it might be nice for you to have someone—" Her gaze slid to the cat, adorably snuggled into him. "Something to talk to around the house. So you aren't alone."

He was watching her softly. "You talk to yourself," Aldo observed.

She gave him a shy smile over the pie crust. "I do. I was my only company for a long time."

He rose and crossed to her.

Aldo wrapped his free arm around her waist from behind. She leaned back into his chest and felt as content as the napping kitten.

———

For Gloria's next intervention, she enlisted Mrs. Moretta's help. Procuring the information she needed only cost her two dozen peanut butter chip brownies and a car wash. It was worth it to get the necessary intel.

She carefully put the next steps of Operation Help Aldo Heal into motion via email and phone call.

CHAPTER 57

A ldo? Can you answer that for me?" Gloria called out from the kitchen. She was in the midst of a baking frenzy that smelled amazing and had banned him from the room unless he wanted to be enlisted. He only ventured in to make her a fresh cup of tea or to drag Ivan out of the bag of flour. Twice.

Her laptop had signaled an incoming video call. He didn't feel right answering for her. "What if it's your mother and I'm not wearing a shirt?" he yelled back.

"It's not my mother, and you are wearing a shirt," she reminded him.

Reluctantly, he clicked to answer.

"Doc Dreamy?" His flight trauma surgeon's face filled the screen.

"How's it going, Lieutenant?" Her smile was warmer than it had been when he'd been a world away and on the brink. She'd come to visit him after surgery, and they'd talked on the phone when he'd been shipped off to Germany.

She'd saved his life. Kept him from bleeding out.

Seeing her now, grinning at him from a background with palm trees and turquoise water, gave him a new appreciation of where he was.

Gloria poked her head out of the kitchen with a sweet smile. The sneaky little woman had set him up.

"It's going well," he said, pulling up his pant leg to knock on his prosthesis.

"Very nice," she commented.

"That doesn't look like Bagram," he said as a man jogged past her and dove into the surf.

"Still sandy," she quipped. "I came home three weeks ago, cleaned off the inch of dust in my apartment, and then hopped on a plane here."

He thought of all she'd seen as part of a forward surgical team. All the blood and loss. The trauma and the fear. "You deserve it."

"I like to think so," she said, brushing off the compliment. "So how's the healing going?"

"All healed up," he insisted.

"You know, not all wounds are on the outside."

Aldo's gaze slid up to meet Gloria's. His girlfriend was suddenly needed on urgent kitchen business and ducked away. He didn't know how to feel about Gloria going behind his back to dig up the doc. Not trusting him to work through it on his own.

"Very subtle, Doc."

She shrugged nonchalantly and looked over her shoulder at the bluest swath of ocean Aldo had ever seen. "Look, just make sure you're doing as much work for your mental state as you are your physical state, and you'll be fine. That's all I'm saying."

"Who says I'm not fine?" he challenged.

"Those big-ass circles under your eyes," she noted.

Where everyone else cautiously tiptoed, Doc Dreamy stomped in and pointed right at the damn elephant in the room.

"Look," she said. "I'd hate to see you screw up my very fine lifesaving work by ignoring the most important part of recovery. Think about it, talk it out, do the damn work."

"Yes, ma'am," Aldo shot back.

She jerked a thumb in the direction of the water. "I come here for mental health breaks. Otherwise I'd crack under the pressure. Find your blue water, Lieutenant, and keep working."

He was embarrassed, annoyed to know that he hadn't been hiding his struggle as well as he thought he'd been. "Will do, Doc. Will do."

"Good. I gotta go. I've got a rum punch with an umbrella headed my way."

"Enjoy, Doc. And thanks for everything."

She threw him a salute and clicked off.

Gloria was singing in the kitchen, giving him his space while she ran interference on his life.

The laptop lit up again, signaling another video call.

"Can you get that?" his interfering girlfriend called sweetly.

"We need to have a talk about boundaries, Gloria."

"After you answer the call," she said flippantly.

Stephanie Oluo's face popped up. "LT!" she crowed.

"Oluo! What the hell are you doing calling my girlfriend? Are you trying to steal her away?"

Steph laughed. "Gloria is a lovely woman, but I've got my hands full." She tugged another woman on screen. "Meet Mrs. Oluo." They held up matching wedding bands.

"No shit? Congratulations!" It did his heart good to see his friend, his fellow wounded compatriot, so happy.

"Life's too short not to go for it, man," Steph said, watching as her wife walked off-screen. "She's pregnant. Four weeks. We're keeping it quiet for a while, but I wanted you to know you're going to be an uncle."

"Shit, Steph. That's amazing."

"Not too shabby for lying in the dirt bleeding a few months ago, eh?"

"Not at all," Aldo agreed.

"So how are you? You sleeping yet?"

Of course she'd know. She'd been there, lived it. Survived it.

He glanced toward the kitchen where Gloria was disentangling Ivan from a dish towel he'd tried to steal. "Not great," he admitted.

"Been there."

"You sleeping?" he asked.

She flashed that white-toothed, shit-eating grin through the screen. "Like a baby. Now."

Aldo sighed. She was going to make him ask. "How'd you do it?"

"So glad you asked," she smirked. "I talked to someone. I was rattling around feeling like a skeleton among the living. Little things setting me off, scaring the hell out of me, not sleeping. And when I did sleep—"

"Nightmares," Aldo filled in.

She nodded. "Yeah. Still have them sometimes. But not as bad. Talk to someone. Get it out. If you keep it in, it'll eat at you from the inside out."

It was something he'd planned to avoid. He could power through this on his own like he did everything else. Only this time, it wasn't working.

They chatted for a few more minutes about old wounds and new plans. When they disconnected, Aldo stared at the desktop wallpaper on the screen and drummed his fingers on his knees. It was a picture of him and Gloria out to dinner. The waiter had taken it, and they were both grinning at each other like idiots over gyros.

Didn't he owe it to them both to get all the way better? To give it his all?

He stood up, stretched, and ambled into the kitchen where the scents of caramel and apples and home wafted.

He wrapped his arms around Gloria from behind and nuzzled into her neck.

"You can lecture me about boundaries now," she said sunnily.

"Thank you for not respecting mine."

She laughed lightly and turned in his arms. "I want things to be good for you. As good as they can be."

"With you here, making—what the hell is that?"

"Caramel apple pie."

"With you here, making caramel apple pie, and this furry little asshole climbing up my leg, things are pretty damn good."

CHAPTER 58

I don't really know how this works. It was Gloria's suggestion. I get that you have to look at me blankly like that when I say her name because of HIPAA bullshit. But I know you know who I mean when I say Gloria.

I'd do anything for that woman, including spill my guts to a complete stranger. Lucky you.

How am I doing? I could have lost her. I don't know how I'm dealing with it. I guess not well. I wasn't in the best place before this. It was better but still not normal.

I think Gloria's worried that this whole thing with that asshole is making me backslide. She got me a kitten. Or a monster that looks like a kitten. But it's nice to have something else in the house with me. It's nice not being alone.

I had… I don't know. Something like a panic attack right after Diller broke in.

I wasn't there when she needed me. And don't give me any of the "how could I have known she was in danger?" I should have known. I should have been there. I wasn't. I failed her. Again. I failed her when she was sixteen years old, and I failed her again now.

But she saved herself. She didn't need me.

And that makes me so fucking proud of her. Sorry.

I'm all mixed up about it. I wasn't there. I failed her. In the end, she didn't need me.

It still hurts. My leg. I'm tired. I used to never get tired. I get that it's going to take time, but I don't know if I'm ever going to feel normal again. I don't know if I'm going to ever pull on a pair of shorts without thinking that I used to have two legs. Or not be exhausted after a full day of work. I don't know if I'm ever going to be able to close my eyes and not see that explosion or Gloria holding a fucking frying pan with eyes as big as coasters.

Life feels…darker. Less certain. Everything feels vaguely unsettling. Except for Gloria. She's like this beautiful bright spot in my day. There are things I want to give her…but I don't know if I'm ready. And if I'm not ready, if I fail her again…

I'm pushing myself physically because it's what I do. I'm making progress there. But maybe not so much emotionally. I have a closet full of left and right shoes and only one foot. I can still feel my toes that aren't there. Sometimes I can't tell the difference between real pain and ghost pain. And that's what's going on in my brain. I can't tell the difference between real fear and ghost fear.

I don't feel strong, and I was always strong. I was always the best. The hardest worker. I don't know if I can get back to that. What am I if I'm not the strongest? The best?

I want to move forward with Gloria. But I'm stuck in this valley of fear, paralyzed.

I wasn't there. But she didn't need me.

If she doesn't need a hero, what can I be to her? If I'm not a hero, what am I?

CHAPTER 59

"What is so important that you dragged me away from my very boring life of missing my deployed boyfriend?" Harper asked, skipping into Gloria's apartment on a Saturday morning. Lola and Max, leashes tangled, stampeded inside and made a dive for Gloria's couch.

"I need your help seducing Aldo."

Harper's iced coffee slipped from her grasp and fell to the floor. "Shit! Shit! Sorry!" She scrambled for the cup. "You were saying?"

"We haven't had sex yet."

"But all the smoldering! You two practically set things on fire when you're together."

"I know! But I can't get him to pull the metaphorical trigger," Gloria lamented, grabbing paper towels to clean up the spill.

"I seriously thought you guys were basically naked at all times." Harper flopped down on the couch next to Lola and gave the dog a face squish. "Can you believe Auntie Gloria and Uncle Aldo aren't banging like bunnies? Lola can't believe it either."

Max, sensing a human without a dog, launched himself off

the couch and danced at Gloria's feet. She picked him up and snuggled the little dog to her chest.

"I think he's scared," Gloria confessed.

Harper blinked. "Aldo? Aldo Moretta?"

"That's the one."

"Well, knock me over with a feather and call me Sally."

"Well, Sally, I put my ex-abuser in prison for the next twenty years or so—with a stop off at the hospital for a concussion. I'm renowned through town for being a goddamn hero. I just got a raise at work for completing my probationary period. So I'm ready for my happily ever after. And that involves orgasms. Dozens of them. Hundreds. Thousands. For that to happen, we need to move Aldo off first base."

"Have you done anything?" Harper asked, looking morbidly curious.

"Oh yeah. And it was magnificent. And he immediately shut down. And I want more. I'm seeing him tonight, and if he doesn't end up naked and spread-eagle on my bed, I. Will. Die."

"Got it. Okay. What time's he coming over?"

"Six."

"So we've got eight hours to destroy Aldo's vow of chastity," Harper mused.

Gloria chewed on her lip. "Can it be done?"

"G, I've seen the way he looks at you like you're the last cupcake on the buffet. He wants to devour that cupcake. We're going to push him over the edge."

———

Seven hours and thirty-two minutes later, Gloria was ready for battle. She was wearing a tight black blouse that was unbuttoned low enough to show a peek of new and very flattering black lace beneath, cropped pants that made her ass "look like its begging to be bitten" as Harper promised, and red, sky-high heels.

Her nails were done a deep red that matched her lipstick. She'd gone smoky on the eyes and light on the perfume.

She poured herself a glass of wine and surveyed the space. Dinner was ready. Grilled chicken, Caesar salads, and oven-roasted vegetables. And for dessert: whipped cream.

Aldo Moretta didn't stand a chance.

She hit Play on her phone, and low, bluesy music played softly through the little wireless speaker she'd borrowed from Harper. The sheets on the bed were freshly laundered. She'd even sprung for new pillows in case dessert turned into an all-night feeding frenzy.

There were candles ready for lighting if the mood needed a little boost and more wine for nerves.

Harper was a diabolical genius. Gloria had no problem seeing how she'd landed the reluctant, reclusive Luke. No one could withstand her. She was glad Harper was on her side.

The knock at her door startled her, stirring up her nerves again. It was showtime. Aldo Moretta had no idea how lucky he was about to get.

She opened the door with a flirty smile. "Hi, handsome. Right on time."

"Wow."

That was exactly the right reaction, she decided, pressing a kiss to the corner of his mouth. "Are you hungry?"

She watched his eyes dip into her underwire-aided cleavage. "Aldo?"

"Huh? I mean, yeah?" He already looked dazed, and Gloria hadn't even gotten started. *Whew. Okay.* She could do this. She could seduce a man for the first time in her life.

"Listen, about tonight," she began. "I have an ulterior motive for asking you to dinner." She turned away from him. "Would you like a glass of wine?"

She could feel his gaze on her butt and resisted the embarrassing urge to shake it.

"Wine would be good. What's your ulterior motive?" he called after her.

"Have a seat," she told him from the kitchen and then took her time pouring him a glass. When she returned to where he sat nervously on the couch, doing her best saunter, he licked his lips.

"Isn't it obvious?" She handed him the wine. "I'm seducing you."

He went rigid. Gloria thought about straddling him but decided she should get his consent loud and clear without physical coercion. She sat next to him and smiled.

"Gloria. I don't think that's a good idea," he began nervously. She was surprised he didn't start inching away from her on the couch. "This relationship is so new."

"Ten years is a long time to wait for anything, don't you think?" she asked conversationally.

"Yeah. But this is moving pretty fast, and I want us both to be sure."

Gloria rolled her eyes. If she got any more sure, her pants would catch fire from the smoldering happening down below. "Is this an 'I don't find you attractive' rejection or an 'I have a legitimate concern about moving our relationship forward' rejection?"

"It's not a rejection," he said, putting his wine down abruptly and wiping his hands on his shorts. "It's not. I swear."

"Aldo. I want to have sex with you. I don't know how to be more clear than that. If we don't have sex tonight, it's because one of us—you—didn't want to."

"Jesus. Of course I want to!"

"I feel compelled to remind you that we promised to be honest with each other at all times."

"I am being honest. I want to be with you. I want to make love to you until neither one of us can walk or move or breathe."

"That sounds like a good start. Let's do that." She unbuttoned the first button on her blouse and watched Aldo's pupils dilate.

"I want it to be right," he said, wetting his lips again in a gesture she found ridiculously sexy.

"Are you still worried about your...function?" she asked. He'd proven exactly how well his talented cock worked up against the back of Harper's house. If that hadn't reassured him, Gloria—with her limited sexual experience—wasn't sure she could help him with whatever was bothering him. "Or do you just not want to function with me?"

He grabbed his wine and took a fortifying gulp. "I'm making a mess of this. Gloria, I swear I used to be smoother, more confident. I would have walked in here and rocked your world and never had an ounce of self-doubt."

"What's different from that Aldo to this one?" she asked.

"I'm terrified of letting you down. Yeah, my cock worked. Yeah, I had a wicked orgasm wrapped in your sexy fist. And yeah, I've gotten myself off every fucking night since then thinking about that moment when you came on my fingers."

Gloria wasn't sure if she was still seated or if she'd melted into a puddle of gooey lust on her rug. Never had sexier sentences been strung together.

Her eyes were at half-mast imagining him gripping his raging hard cock. Fuck.

"But there's a lot more to sex than just my dick doing its job."

317

"Care to demonstrate?"

"Gloria! Sweetheart, I want everything to be perfect for you. I want you to have the most amazing sexual experience of your life, and I want to be responsible for it."

She undid another button. Slid another inch closer. "The way I look at it, you already did give me the most amazing sexual experience of my life, and we haven't even had sex yet."

"I'm scarred, Gloria. Hideous, ugly scars. How are you supposed to look at my fucking leg and stay in the goddamn mood?"

"Oh, baby." Gloria breathed at the vulnerability, the pain, laced in his words. "Is that what this is?"

He stared at his glass of wine, jaw tight. "You might not know this, but I'm a vain, shallow excuse of a man."

She slid off the couch and knelt between his legs. "Look at me, handsome."

It took him a moment, but he did as he was told.

"Most of my ugly scars are on the inside, and I've presented every last one of them to you. You're still here. I think you owe me the same chance. Show me your scars, Aldo."

CHAPTER 60

She doesn't know what she's asking for, Aldo told himself. This beautiful creature should never be touched by violence again. And that was exactly what was branded onto his skin, into his DNA. A permanent, physical reminder of the sins human beings were capable of inflicting on each other.

He wanted nothing but beauty and softness and perfection for Gloria.

But she begged for the brutal truth.

Ever so gently, she skimmed her palms under the hem of his shorts and stroked his thighs. "Show me, Aldo. Please?"

It was her plea that he was powerless against. He'd give Gloria anything, anything in this world. Even if it broke his own heart.

Silently, he rose. She stayed where she was on her knees in front of him. Slowly, he slid his shorts down. Eagerly, Gloria helped him step out of them. He sat again, thumbs slipping into the compression sleeve that covered his stump just below the knee. He closed his eyes, teetering on the edge of doing what she wanted and being a complete coward.

Then her hands were on his, and together, they carefully worked the sleeve down his skin.

He didn't want to look at his leg. He'd already seen it a few hundred times, and it still jarred him sometimes. The brutality that was so far from "normal." He watched her face instead, studying it for any signs of revulsion, rejection.

But she merely set his prosthesis aside and returned her gaze to the very worst part of him.

Then she was touching him, so gently. Like the rush of air beneath a bird in flight. Those lovely, capable hands skimming scar tissue and pain. His breath caught in his throat. His eyes burned.

"Is this okay?" she whispered.

Never had he felt more vulnerable. He was ripped open, stripped bare, and the woman he loved was staring into his soul.

Terror. Lust. Need. It all rolled through him.

He was rock-hard and careening toward a breakdown or a breakthrough. Words failed him. Gloria leaned forward and pressed her lips to the worst of the scars, jagged and nasty beneath the sweetness of her mouth.

He didn't want to taint that. Didn't want his ugliness leaving its stain on her.

She looked up at him, but it wasn't pity or fear that he saw in those golden-brown depths. It was glassy lust. Could she possibly want him like this? Scarred and broken. Damaged.

Yet she was worshipping him. With lips and tongue. Tasting his scars.

Something like tears and fear clawed at the back of his throat.

"You're beautiful," she whispered.

"Gloria." All he had was her name, her touch anchoring him to this place. And that was everything.

"So beautiful," she murmured. With one hand still gently stroking his mangled leg, she reached into his boxer briefs and brought her mouth to his cock.

His heart shattered into a thousand tiny slivers that carved his chest open. Light and heat rushed in like a door flying open on a summer day.

She was touching him with love, with lust. Everything he worried he wasn't worthy of.

"Is this okay?" she asked again, her breath hot on the crown of his dick. He ached for more. More softness, more words, more of her beautiful mouth.

Aldo nodded. He slipped his hands into her hair, gently rubbing her scalp as those magical lips closed around the tip of his erection again.

Fuck. The pleasure from her mouth taking him in one inch at a time was going to break him. This wasn't sex. This was a spiritual experience. Two souls opening to one another, the most vulnerable they could be. Together.

She was an angel, absolving him of his pain. She welcomed him to a place where there was only room for pleasure and awe as two bodies worshipped each other.

Gloria moaned as his hands stroked her neck, her shoulders. He needed to honor her, to touch her, to give her pleasure with every touch. There were dark fingerprints on her that she was trusting him to erase. He wouldn't take that responsibility lightly.

Keeping one hand on his knee, Gloria used her free hand to grip him at the root of his thick cock, pumping.

A fire lit in his balls as they tensed and pulled up against him. If he didn't stop it now, it would turn into a raging wildfire. Aldo was so far from being done with her. He had a decade's worth of fantasies stored up. So much pleasure to give.

Her head bobbed between his legs, and Aldo's eyes rolled back in his head. Tongue and teeth and lips were being used against him as weapons of destruction. "Gloria," he growled.

When she didn't listen, when she continued her measured torture, he slid his hands under her arms and pulled her up.

His hard-on popped free of her mouth and immediately began to ache for more of Gloria's touch.

"I want you in bed," he confessed.

"Okay."

"I can't walk there," he told her, eyes sliding to his prosthesis.

"Lean on me." She stood, offering him her hand. When he stood, when she slid her shoulder under his arm and he placed his weight on her, he knew humility.

The walk to the bed was short, and once they arrived, Gloria seemed to not know what to do next. He kissed her, long and deep, tasting her, teasing her. "Lie on the bed, beautiful."

She did as she was told, reclining dead center on the mattress. He watched her as he undressed, pulling his shirt off over his head. He balanced on his good leg and slid his boxer briefs down.

Her gasp. Her earthy, lusty, glazed-eye delight kindled a desire in him so powerful that he didn't care if he didn't survive it. He would do whatever was in his power to please her. To heal her the way she was healing him.

"Oh my God. You're perfection," she murmured.

He shook his head. "You look at me like…like I'm something incredible," he said, sliding onto the mattress. He lifted her feet in his hands, kissed her ankles. "You look at me like I'm a hero."

"You are, Aldo. You're my hero."

He slid the straps of her sexy as fuck shoes off and gently removed them, brushing kisses over the arches of her feet. She moaned, and it was a symphony to his ears.

Aldo started on her pants next. He unhooked the clasp, slid the zipper down, and gently tugged them from her body one leg at a time. Dear God. The peekaboo black lace under her shirt matched what was under her pants, scraps barely obscuring the skin beneath. He'd hardly touched her, and already he was certain she'd taken him to heaven.

"You're so fucking beautiful, Gloria. So fucking everything to me."

He let his fingers, big, blunt instruments, stroke over the flat of her stomach, the gentle curves of her hips, enjoying the tease of lace that acted as speed bumps, warning him to slow down and savor what was beneath.

Her breath was shallow. "I can't catch my breath, Aldo."

He paused, thumbs resting under her belly button while his palms splayed out over her stomach and waist. His cock hung heavily, dipping toward that black lace between her spread legs.

She had scars too. Tiny ones, silvered with age. Symbols of trauma survived. Adversity conquered. And a tattoo that marked her victory. She was his hero.

"Don't you dare stop," Gloria gasped. "I don't care if I have oxygen. I just want you. *All* of you. Every piece, every scar, every millimeter of flawed perfection. You're mine, Aldo. Please make me yours."

He went a little blind and a little deaf. His hands shook as they moved up her torso to the last three buttons that kept her hidden from him. One. Two. Three. He worked them open, and the sound that rose from his throat when she was bared to him was like a desperate man's plea.

He *was* desperate. He'd told himself he could wait. Could find a way to make it perfect. But perfect wasn't what Gloria wanted. She wanted him, flaws and all.

Lowering down slowly, his cock brushing the inside of one silky thigh, Aldo pressed his lips to her heart.

"Oh my God." She was chanting now, and there were tears in her eyes. Or maybe those were his tears in his eyes.

He lifted up and filled his hands with her breasts, thumbs stroking the tender points beneath the lace. She bucked against him, and his cock twitched in anticipation. "Get me out of this thing," she breathed, tugging at the straps of her bra.

With pleasure.

One-handed, he found the clasp at the back and released it.

"Show-off," she teased.

But he couldn't joke. He couldn't smile. His body was consumed by what was happening under him. Her breasts spilled free, and he looked his fill, brushing his fingers lightly over the round flesh. Her nipples were dark and hard, and there was no way in hell he could do anything but lower his mouth to those tender points and taste.

One brush of tongue, the fastening of his lips around her peak, and Gloria's hips bridged off the mattress, pinning his cock between their bodies.

"Fuck. Oh my God. Oh my. I'm going to die and I don't care—" She lost her breath and her words when he started to suck, pulling the point into his mouth.

She rocked against his erection, begging with her body. He wanted to be buried inside her, wanted to feel her walls quicken around him as he rode her to an orgasm so explosive they'd be melded together for eternity. He needed to join their bodies. Just the thought of being buried in her had precum leaking from his tip like a faucet turned on, soaking the front of her lace panties.

He switched to her neglected breast and feasted there while she moaned and writhed beneath him. Gloria tried to wriggle her way out of her underwear, and it drove him mad. He'd never been wanted like this. Desired. Craved.

He nuzzled at her breast and slid his fingers into the front of her underwear. God. She was wet and beyond ready. The heat between her legs called to him, a siren's song he heard in his blood.

"Glo, I don't have a condom."

"I'm clean. I'm tested." She whispered the words between peppering kisses and bites across his chest.

"What about birth control?"

"I'm on it. And there is nothing that I want to feel more than your bare cock inside me."

Everything went black for a second or two, and then he was yanking her underwear down her legs. It got tangled up on an ankle, but it didn't matter. The promised land was before him.

He couldn't help himself. Aldo gripped his cock and guided it through her slit, letting their arousals mingle. Flesh to flesh. Nothing had ever felt this decadent, this good, this right before.

Gloria hitched her knees up higher.

"Aldo, if you wait one second longer, I'm going to die right here, unfulfilled."

"I'd do anything for you, Gloria. Anything." And with that vow, Aldo drove himself into her.

CHAPTER 61

Gloria wasn't clear on the physics of it all. However, she had been operating on the assumption that there was no way that Aldo Moretta's magnificent cock should have fit inside her. But fit it did. And even stretched right up to and maybe just a bit beyond her limits, she was hurtling toward the second orgasm of her life, and he hadn't even moved a damn muscle yet.

"Oh, sweet Jesus," Aldo gasped into her neck and shoulder.

He was sheathed in her. Bound to her. Just that joining, that scrape of his chest hair over her sensitive nipples, his expletive-laden gasp of joy, made her come.

She felt it rise up in her like a prayer lifting to the heavens and then break around them in a dazzling array of fireworks. She felt it in her fingertips, her toes, the roots of her hair. She was coming so hard Gloria couldn't tell if her eyes were open or closed because there was nothing but fireworks.

Aldo grunted dark, dirty words of praise as she clamped around his cock like a vise. Then he moved. She didn't know enough about orgasms to know if this was the same one or round two. But either way, if she could have told Aldo "I told you so," she would have.

As it was, she'd lost the power of speech.

His breath was hot on her cheek, his soft grunts as he withdrew only to sink back into her welcoming flesh sinfully erotic. For a woman who had only experienced mediocre sex with a lousy lover, Aldo Moretta was a sex god. He used those long, slow thrusts to drive her insane. Gloria writhed beneath him, joyfully accepting his weight on her. She hitched her hips up higher, begging for more speed.

He was making love to her. Honoring her with his body.

"There's so much I want to show you, give you," he said, pressing kisses to her neck, her jaw, as he moved inside her. "This isn't enough."

Her eyes fluttered open. "We have all night."

"Still not enough." He caught her lower lip between his teeth. "I want to show you all the ways you can come. I want to taste you, every single inch of you. I want to belong to you."

"Oh, God, Aldo." Her teeth chattered. Those delicate inner walls were already tremoring again at his words. "Don't stop!" she hissed.

Oh, God. She was yelling orders at her lover while he was inside her. Two orgasms, and she'd turned into some needy dominatrix.

He cracked a half grin. "Say it again, and I'll move," he promised.

Aldo gave her a teasing half thrust. And it worked.

"Gah! Aldo!"

Master of self-control Aldo lazily increased his speed, taking his time so Gloria could feel every ridge and vein of his shaft as he pumped her toward her next orgasm. She wanted to memorize this moment. The feel of his chest pressing against hers, flattening her breasts to him. The sweat that slicked both their bodies was evidence of their desperate need for each other. He glided into her, stretching her tight around him.

Gloria felt every nerve ending in her body wake up and start firing. Her body had one purpose: to climax or die trying. That miraculous quickening tickled her core as he drove into her once more. He was so careful with her. So gentle. And it was beautiful. Their bodies were a work of art, a constellation of scars and strength and grit. Together they made something beautiful.

"Aldo." She couldn't close her eyes on his gaze. Not when it enhanced the connection of their bodies.

"I feel you, Gloria," he gritted out. "I feel you getting tighter, sweetheart." He swore, sweat dotting his forehead as he carried them both toward the finish line.

"Can you...with me?" She tried to pry the words out around a tortured moan of pleasure.

His breathing tripped up, and she felt the change in him, letting a tiny bit of control go. He stared into her as his cock flexed inside her.

They groaned together. Gloria dug her heels into Aldo's very firm ass cheeks. She wanted to bite them, wondered if that was weird, and decided she didn't care.

His dark words whispered against her throat told her he liked it. And when he sank into her again, he lifted her hips with those strong, callused hands.

Something caught fire inside her, ignited. She clenched around him, fingers stabbing into those broad shoulders. Her entire body went rigid as the first wave of the orgasm paralyzed her.

"Aldo!" She screamed his name, and he was right there with her.

She felt the first jet of his release explode deep inside her, and her world went bright. *Yes. Perfection.*

His breath stopped, heart stopped, body frozen for one

heartbeat, and then they were coming together. His release, the mingling of their bodies' arousals was a baptism of sorts for Gloria. This was what sex should be. This bonding, this joining. This wall of pleasure and beauty that they built together only to be buried under.

This was love.

"I think we should get married," Aldo gasped out.

Gloria laughed, unwittingly clamping down on the penis still buried inside her. He groaned and shifted his hips against her.

"Are you okay?" Aldo asked, pressing his lips to her hair. He sounded...beautifully wrecked.

"What's better than okay?" she asked, nuzzling into his chest. With one finger, she traced the outline of her birds that he'd put on his skin.

"Good? Great? Perfect?" he teased.

"Amazed," she decided. "Amazed and humbled and happy and glowing."

"That's a lot better than okay," he teased, tracing a finger over her lower lip. "There's so much more I want to show you."

"There's more? I might need some food and some oxygen and maybe some celebratory wine first. But I'm yours tonight."

"And tomorrow?" he asked. He was still half hard inside her. Still wholly dangerous.

"Tomorrow too," she said magnanimously. As far as she was concerned, the man could have her body for the rest of both their lives. "Oh, hey. Asking for a friend," she said lightly. "Are guys freaked out when a girl cries after sex?"

"Depends on why she's crying," he said gruffly, his own voice tight with emotion.

"Because you made her feel like a goddess."

Aldo let out a shaky breath. "You're my fucking miracle, Gloria."

"And you're mine." She grinned up at him, started to pull him down for a kiss. But he paused, his eyes dancing with mischief.

"I am pretty incredible, aren't I?"

Old Aldo was back.

CHAPTER 62

W hy do you have my laundry basket?" Gloria asked when Aldo whistled his way out of her bedroom with a week's worth of laundry.

Ivan launched himself off the back of Gloria's couch to pounce on something on the rug only visible to insane kittens.

She was still getting used to having Aldo around her place. Sometimes she glanced up and found him half-naked, reading reports on his laptop, and she would inwardly swoon. He made everything normal seem sexy and fascinating.

That one-night seduction had driven their relationship directly into the fast lane. They spent every night together, whether it was here at her place or in Aldo's house. Where the walls were now that perfect hunter green she'd once fantasized about.

His broad shoulders heaved up, then dropped. "I'm doing laundry today. Figured I'd save you a trip to the laundromat."

Gloria stopped fiddling with the coffee maker and stared at him. It was as simple and as devastating as that. She was in love with the man.

The realization nearly took her out at the knees. It was a menial, domestic task. One that she'd been doing herself since junior high. Glenn didn't know where the laundromat was, let alone how to operate a washing machine. In all their years together, he had never once thanked her for all the clean shirts and pants she'd neatly stowed for him.

"Why do you look like you're going to cry?" Aldo asked, suddenly concerned.

Ivan raced over and attacked her bare foot. She shook him off and threw one of the cat's four million stuffed mice across the floor. He darted after it, a dangerous, fluffy hunter on the loose.

"You're really going to do my laundry?" she asked. He'd even stripped the sheets that they'd nearly shredded last night from the bed.

"I have a washer and dryer at my place. It's stupid for you to lose a whole afternoon going across town to the laundromat."

Little pink hearts had to be exploding out of her eyes.

"Aldo, I think I—"

Her spontaneous confession of affection was cut off by a staccato knock at the door.

"I got it," Aldo said, dropping the basket and beating her to the door. Ever the protector. "Gloria, there's a goofy cop asking for donuts."

He stepped back to let the uniformed Ty into the apartment.

"Moretta, don't you ever wear clothes?" Ty asked.

Aldo flexed for him and winked at Gloria. Yep. The Old Aldo was back. And Gloria realized that for the first time in a long time, she hadn't compared her life to Other Gloria. The Gloria Who Left Glenn the First Time might have been sweating her way through a Pilates class before brunch, but she hadn't spent all night making love to Aldo. It was a win for the record books.

"I was just making some coffee," Gloria said. "Do you want a cup?"

"If it's no trouble. I have some news for you about Diller."

Gloria turned her back on the men and stepped into the kitchen. There was one fucking person who could ruin everything for her. For them.

She sent up a silent prayer as she poured two mugs. *Please don't let him touch this life.*

Ty thanked her for the coffee, and Aldo tucked her under his arm. "Spit it out, Adler. What's the latest?"

"He pled guilty."

Gloria felt her eyebrows climb her forehead. "He did?"

Ty nodded, blew at the steam rising from his mug.

"That means no trial?" Aldo pressed.

"No trial. Do not pass go. Go straight to jail. Attempted murder, stalking, assault, handful of other charges. Third-time offender thanks to that DUI a few years ago. Adds up to about twenty years and change."

For the second time that morning, Gloria felt her knees go a little weak.

"So that's it. He's out of my life."

"You've also got a nice shiny piece of paper that forbids him from contacting you. And makes it awfully uncomfortable if his mama gets within fifty feet of you."

Aldo dropped a kiss on the top of her head.

"Oh my God. I don't know what to say." The monster was gone. She was free to live her life. Free to tell Aldo she loved him. Free to go to work and make plans and have a future. There was nothing standing in her way. No shadows left to block out the light.

"Diller had her keeping tabs so he'd know where to find you as soon as he got out. She admitted that much. But still didn't fess up to vandalizing your car. You can press charges, and we'll have a go at her," Ty offered.

But Gloria shook her head. "No. I'm done with that family."

Aldo squeezed her arm in agreement. They were done with Glenn. Done with the sordid past. They had a whole big, bright future to look forward to.

CHAPTER 63

"Well, well. If it isn't my own personal hero," Aldo said, answering the video call that popped up on his desktop screen.

Luke's face grinned back at him. "If it isn't my vertebra-dislocating, deadweight friend."

"You called all the way from Afghanistan to tell me I'm a lard ass?" Aldo kicked back in his desk chair and smoothed his tie. He was in the office early this morning before the hordes—his partner and their associates and interns—descended with fancy coffees, endless chitchat, and smartphones that never shut the fuck up.

He hadn't stepped back into his role at work so much as dove in headfirst. It was sink or swim. They'd landed a contract for a massive, state-wide bridge study and replacement project. It meant at least a couple of years of consistent work—and huge volumes of red tape. Today alone, he had an on-site inspection and two zoning board meetings in addition to his actual normal work.

"Well, that, and to tell you I'm coming home."

Aldo sat up. "No shit? It's about damn time."

Luke rubbed a hand over his head. "Yeah, two weeks, and I'll be able to see your lard ass in person."

"I can't believe Harpist didn't spill her guts," Aldo said, thinking of their morning run. They'd worked their way up slowly but surely and now met up several mornings a week to run through the quiet, sleeping town. He was proud of her... and pissed that she'd keep her lips zipped about Luke.

"Well, that's kinda the thing. Harper doesn't know." Luke grinned.

"And you want to surprise our little ray of sunshine," Aldo said, catching on.

"Exactly."

Well, well. Luke Garrison planning a surprise homecoming. There was hope for him yet.

They talked strategy for a few minutes with Luke nixing every big, public spectacle idea that Aldo threw at him just to annoy him.

"Let's keep it simple. Private," Luke said. "And don't tell anyone. That town has bigger mouths than a lake full of bass."

"I'll have to tell Gloria. She'd murder me in my sleep if I kept a secret like this from her. Plus, she's a good organizer."

"How are things there?" Luke prodded.

"Good, good," Aldo said, playing it cool. The first person to find out he was in love with Gloria Parker was not going to be Luke. "Diller's in prison for a long-ass time. Gloria and I are...seeing each other." He was a gentleman after all. Plus it would be plain mean to tell Luke about his explosive sex life while his friend had nothing but miles of desert and his hand.

"So how's everything else going?" Luke asked. It was bro code for "how's life with only one leg?"

"Oh, you know. Living the dream. Sleeping in a real bed,

taking hot showers, sleeping late on Sundays." He could stick it to Luke just a little.

Luke sighed. "I can't wait to come home."

"You better make it quick. I saw Linc chatting up Harper at the bar the other night."

"What?" Luke's general dislike of Lincoln Reed was still alive and well.

Aldo chuckled. "Relax. I'm just messing with you."

"You're such an ass. Why are we friends again?"

"Because no one else will put up with your surly ass."

"Right. I forgot."

Aldo ignored the steady stream of emails pouring into his inbox as clients around the tricounty region started panicking at the start of their business day. "Given any more thought to retirement?" he asked. Aldo knew the idea would be more tempting at this stage of deployment: close enough to home to taste his mama's apple pie and his girlfriend's sweet mouth.

"Yeah." Luke nodded. "I'm thinking about it a lot. We'll see how things go when I get home. Talk it over with Harper."

Luke Garrison wanted to talk his future plans over with a woman. It was about fucking time. Maybe Luke didn't realize it, but Aldo could see the truth written plainly on his friend's face. Luke was in love with Harper. And that also was about fucking time.

CHAPTER 64

*T*hings *are good. Really good. I'm sleeping. I'm…doing other things that a healthy adult does in bed. Ivan finally stopped trying to claw my eyes out.*

And Gloria is everything.

I'm happy. Happier than before I deployed. I'm better than I was with two fucking—sorry—legs. I never thought I'd get to this point. I'm still working my way back to where I was in some areas. But overall, this is the best time in my entire life.

I didn't realize how much I wanted someone to come home to. Instead of hanging out at work, clearing a few hundred things off my list when everyone else leaves, I'm leading the pack out the door so I can see her face faster, get that smile fixed on me sooner.

She's doing great. She's planning the hell out of the town Christmas festival and light show. Things at work are going well for her. It's like she's this flower that's finally bloomed. I think she's surprised by how far she's come. But I'm not. It was always in her.

I want to move things in a more permanent direction. You know? Like more than just swapping house keys and sleepovers. I want to ask her to move in. But I don't want to spook her. Not when things are this good.

She's been there for me. Even when I didn't deserve her. Even when I was trying to fix everything myself. She stood by me, nudged me when I needed it. I want a hell of a lot more than just living together. I want a life together.

One step at a time. One foot in front of the other. Right?

CHAPTER 65

Things were practically perfect exactly the way they were. For the first time in her adult life, Gloria felt comfortable, secure, appreciated. Work was challenging and interesting. She'd survived an online QuickBooks course and thoroughly enjoyed a weekend workshop on floral design. Her apartment was the cozy home she'd always wanted. And Aldo was…Aldo. He was the burliest, brightest part of every day.

There was just one teeny, tiny thing.

He'd been holding back on her. Keeping her up on that sky-high pedestal, drowning her in romance and sweetness. She wasn't complaining. She wasn't a monster, for God's sake. But every glimpse she got of the darker side of sex, she wanted to explore it more. And she wanted Aldo to take her there.

He made her feel safe. Because of that, she could trust him to make her feel *craved*.

They'd enjoyed a flirty dinner together. Teasing, private touches. Long, warm glances. And it was about to pay off.

Aldo pushed in the front door with more brute force than finesse, stripping her of her sweater before the door was even closed.

Ivan scrambled off the back of the couch and rocketed across the room in the direction of his food dish.

"Damn cat," Aldo muttered before he crushed his mouth to Gloria's.

This was where she usually lost the battle. He'd dig deep, pull back, and make very civilized, careful, beautiful love to her. It was incredible. But she'd had tastes of what he held back, and Gloria wanted all of him.

"Here," she told him.

She saw it in the flaring of his nostrils. The immediate denial, the need to control the situation. To take care. Biting her lip, Gloria unclasped her bra and slid the straps from her shoulders. She took pleasure in the automatic clench of his jaw, the way his hands tightened to fists at his sides.

"Gloria."

"I'm not just a good girl, Aldo. I want you to show me everything." She tucked her thumbs in the waistband of her skirt and watched him as she slid it down her thighs, revealing the fact that she'd neglected to wear underwear.

He came at her, a shark locking on to its victim. She prayed he'd never regain his legendary control because the way he was looking at her right now stole her breath.

"Pants," she said, surprised by the sharp tone.

One hand on her naked body, Aldo worked his belt free, and Gloria lent him a hand with the rest. Pants, socks, sexy-ass red boxer briefs. Everything landed on the floor. Muscle, ink, hard, hot body. His cock was already hard for *her*.

Aldo was a spectacular specimen, and she wondered how he could see anything else in the mirror.

"God, you're hot," she breathed.

But there was no time for conversation because he was taking her down to the floor in a desperate embrace turned tackle. The hardwood bit into her palms and knees.

"I need you to be sure," he told her, his voice a gravel road.

"I'm sure, Aldo. I trust you."

He swore. "If you change your mind, tell me to stop, and I will."

"Trust me not to break." She was bared to him, her back arched, her core begging for attention.

He ran his hand down her from neck to hip in one long sweep of heat. It felt so good she purred like a damn cat.

"Okay?" he asked.

"If you ask me that again, I'm putting my clothes back on, going home, and buying a shower massager."

He growled from behind her. And then she felt the delicious stroke of his tongue between her legs, the press of his face against her ass. She was so vulnerable in this position. He pushed her knees wider as his tongue probed and danced over her neediest flesh.

Her legs trembled, quaking as desire woke.

"You look so fucking sexy, so ready for me," he murmured, brushing kisses along the insides of her thighs, over the round cheeks of her ass.

He went back to tasting her, quick thrusts of his magic tongue between her folds, nudging at her clit, her entrance. She was seeing static and shadows.

She could come like this, if he let her. She could come on her hands and knees, his face between her thighs. And she felt no shame.

Gloria gasped, shaking harder when she felt the velvet tip of his tongue dip between her cheeks to the secret puckered rim that no one had ever touched.

It felt...so good and so wrong. She wanted more and told him so with a rock of her hips.

He gave another grumble low in his chest. "Have you ever...?" He didn't finish the question, merely replaced his tongue with the tip of his finger.

"No," she squeaked at the gentle pressure. But for Aldo, she would. She wanted it *all*.

"Do you want to?" His voice was barely a rasp now.

"Yes."

He stroked both hands down her sides, over her hips, gripping her there. She could feel him deciding.

"Everywhere that you touch me, you erase something dark," Gloria whispered.

His lips brushed the curve of her hip. Then his teeth grazed her flesh. The sensation was so new and carnal that Gloria's skin pebbled.

"You like that." A statement, not a question. For the first time, Gloria felt like Aldo was a willing participant in this exploration.

"Yes." She peeked down between her legs to where his erection hung heavily, brushing the inside of her thighs. A drop of precum appeared and dripped down to the floor. She shuddered with the thrill of it. "Let me be your fantasy, Aldo," she pleaded. "Like you're mine."

"Fuck, sweetheart. When you say things like that, how can I deny you anything?"

"Why would you want to?" she whispered, submitting to the slow, steady stroke of his hands down her body and back up. Over and over again until her skin was aflame.

"I want to be careful with you."

"I won't break," she argued.

"God." On that mournful word, Aldo slammed home into her wet, begging channel.

It stole the breath from her lungs, and Gloria gasped for air. With one hand, he reached under her to grip her breast, kneading it as he pulled out and sank back into her. He tugged at her nipple over and over again while he jerked her hips back into him. She could hear the steady slap of his balls against her and felt dizzy with desire.

It had never been like this. And she didn't want to miss a second of it for the rest of her life.

He gave a guttural grunt as she flexed around him. "Already, baby?"

Still gripping her breast, Aldo used his other hand to find that needy bundle of nerves between her legs.

"Oh my god, Aldo!" She was incoherent as he fucked into her tight body with the power she knew his body possessed.

He was using her for his own pleasure, and that dark thought that once might have disgusted her now liberated her.

She felt the shiver start at the bud beneath his talented fingers, felt it spread like a halo encompassing her entire body. She came, exploding around him, clamping down on that thick cock that he buried inside her.

He rode out her orgasm, swearing and sweating and bucking into her as her hungry little muscles clutched him. When she was done and trembling, he stopped, fully sheathed in her. His hands slipped over her slick skin to stroke.

"Why are you stopping?" she breathed.

"Need a minute or else this is going to be over too fast."

As if echoing Aldo's point, his cock jerked inside her once. Reflexively, Gloria closed around it.

Aldo growled. "Behave yourself, sweetheart."

"What if I don't feel like behaving?" She did it again, and he surprised them both by swatting her ass. The connection of his palm on her flesh did weird and wonderful things to Gloria.

Then he was moving again, slowly, methodically pulling all the way out and pushing in to the hilt. Lazily fucking her as if they had forever.

She could feel the fabric of his compression sleeve against

her, wondered how they looked naked on the living room floor. Then she felt his fingers, damp and searching, slide up the cleft of her ass until they found what they were looking for. Back and forth, dragging the wet with them.

"Yes?" he asked, his thrusts coming stronger, a little faster. Just the way she liked them.

Gloria nodded.

"Say it, Gloria."

"Yes."

He stilled, and there was pressure as he pushed, discomfort as he slid in, and then a relaxation of sorts as his finger slid past the barrier. Then he was moving in her again. His cock and his finger worked her together, taking Gloria past anything she'd ever known in bed.

She was safe. She was treasured. She was craved.

"Aldo, I think I'm going to come again," she gasped.

"Touch yourself, Glo," he ordered.

It took only a few delicious, excruciating seconds, and Gloria was coming and slamming her hips back against him, urging him on. He thrust into her, cock and finger, faster, harder, feeling her orgasm build and break.

He shouted as he let biology take over, let himself rut into her body as his own orgasm exploded. She felt it when he released his load inside her as deep as he could go. She looked down between her legs and watched his semen-soaked cock plunge into her body over and over again as they both trembled over the crest.

"Yes, Aldo!" She was with him, still coming.

CHAPTER 66

I'm impressed, Harpsichord," Aldo whistled through his teeth as they rounded a corner on the path in the frigid morning air. "A few months ago, you couldn't run the length of a football field. Now, look at you."

Harper rolled her eyes at the nickname and tossed a smug look over her shoulder. "I could say the same about you," she teased, increasing her speed to keep up with the pace he set. Their footsteps echoed quietly on the ground beneath them.

"Yeah, but I'm a perfect physical specimen. I'm designed to run no matter how many legs I have. You were a late-sleeping desk potato."

He smirked at her gasp that turned silver in the frosty air. "Desk potato?"

"Someone who doesn't watch a lot of TV but spends all their time sitting at a desk."

"Where do you come up with this stuff?"

He tapped a finger to his temple, his breath steady. "It's all up here. All the secrets of the universe."

"Let's see if those secrets of the universe help you move a little faster." She picked up the pace and shot him a haughty look over her shoulder.

They'd worked their way up to five miles together. Every step, every mile, a hard-fought battle. That made every run all the sweeter. He ran most mornings alone, slipping out of the house or Gloria's bed when she left for early mornings at work. But a few times a week, he and Harper hit the park together. And today, today was going to be a memorable one.

He let his loose joints gear up and speed past her on the trail.

"Now you're just showing off," she laughed. "Don't let your leg fall off!"

"Gotta get there before sunrise," Aldo called. The lake at sunrise was the second-best way to start the day. The first being waking up naked with Gloria.

He listened for her footfalls behind him and grinned when she caught up with him. "So you ready for Luke to come home?" he asked. "Next week, right?"

He saw the sparkle in her eyes. "I'm trying not to think about it too much, so only every half second or so. We didn't have much time before he left, but I still feel like I've been missing a limb—no offense—for the last six months. I'm excited and terrified and everything in between."

"Terrified?"

"Our relationship has lasted seven months. Six of those, he was on the other side of the world. What if he doesn't like me anymore? What if everything is different? What if I can't handle the reason he didn't tell me about Karen?"

Aldo stopped, put a hand on her arm.

"What's wrong? You need a break?"

He smirked and meant it. "Do I look like I need a break?"

She gave him a slow appraisal. "No," she decided. "You look like you could breeze through a half marathon if you wanted to."

"Damn right. And stop worrying. You two have what it takes to make it."

"I love you, Aldo." The out-of-the-blue statement hit him like a fist to the chest. He stared dumbly at her.

"Not like that," she corrected, rolling her eyes. "You're the closest thing to a brother that I've ever had, and I love you."

"Well, shit. I love you too, Harpsichord," he said gruffly.

"Don't say it because I said it." She punched him in the arm.

Aldo retaliated the way any good big brother would and put Harper in a headlock, ruffling her hair. "I didn't, dummy. You're the little sister I never wanted."

Laughing, they worked their way back up to speed. "So are you planning to surprise Luke when he comes home?" Aldo asked, enjoying being diabolical.

Harper snorted. "Can you think of anything he'd hate more? No. In fact, he told me he doesn't even want me to meet the bus. He wants to meet me at the house."

"You know why he wants it that way," Aldo reminded her. Thinking of Karen. Of that day. Of the years that followed.

"I do. But it still hurts my heart to think of him coming home with no one there to greet him. It's been so long. I don't want to waste the time it would take him to drive home. Ever since he told me that he's coming home, every second feels like half an hour. I just want him here. I want to look into his eyes and…"

The sun was peeking over the trees as they broke through the woods. A lone figure in camouflage stood facing them, his back to the lake and the sunrise.

"No," Harper gasped. "I…"

Captain Luke Garrison opened his arms, and damned if

Aldo didn't feel himself get a little teary-eyed as he watched Harper run into those arms. They collided in midair. Luke boosted her up and wrapped his arms around her.

Aldo heard the first sob from Harper, and then they were kissing. He pulled his phone out of his pocket and snapped a shot of them, backed by the sunrise, their new beginning on the horizon. He gave them their moment until it looked like their moment might turn X-rated and cleared his throat as he walked up.

"You guys are ruining my view of a perfect sunrise," Aldo teased.

Luke let Harper slide down to the ground but kept her anchored to his side. And Aldo knew his friend was in love.

"You knew, and you didn't say a freaking word!" Harper reached out to smack Aldo in the arm.

"Surprise!"

"Thanks, man," Luke said, stepping forward to wrap Aldo in a one-armed hug.

Aldo clapped his best friend on the back, and then they were hugging, the crushing embrace of brothers. "You look good, Moretta," Luke said, pulling back to ruffle Aldo's hair.

"I feel good. Check out the hardware." Aldo tugged up his pant leg. He saw the hard swallow, the tightening of the jaw, and knew Luke was struggling with memories. Aldo clapped him on the shoulder. "Hey, I'm good. I'm better than good."

Luke gave a tight nod and then pulled him back for another hard hug. "I'm sorry, man," he whispered.

Aldo smacked him on the back of the head, joining the manly battle against tears that threatened them both. "Shut up. There's nothing to be sorry for. Asshole."

Luke gave him a grin and a shove. "Dick."

Toying with his victim, Aldo wobbled, flailing his arms,

and when Luke reached out to steady him, Aldo danced a little jig. "Psych! Solid as a rock. Thanks to your girl there."

Luke reached out to Harper, and she snuggled into his side. "She took good care of you?" he asked.

"She even got me a woman."

Harper rolled her eyes. "Don't make Gloria sound like a prostitute!"

Aldo checked his watch. "Love to stay and chat, but speaking of my woman, she's waiting for me. That gives you two about forty-five minutes before you have to be at the diner."

"The diner?" Luke gave Harper a confused look.

Understanding dawned bright in Harper's eyes. "Oh, you're good," she said. "Does anyone else know?"

Aldo winked. "Nope." He tossed Luke a set of keys. "Your truck is in the lot on the other side of the trees."

"How did you get his truck here?"

Aldo shrugged. "Gloria and I stole it from the garage last night. You're one sound sleeper."

"You riding back with us?" Luke asked.

"Nope. Gloria's waiting with my truck. I'll see you soon. Glad to have you home, Luke. Later, Harpsichord!"

And with that, he loped off toward the parking lot and his own beautiful girl.

CHAPTER 67

Now did it go?" Gloria bounced up and down next to his truck in sweats and a winter coat. Winter was coming. The crisp, frosty morning felt like it was practically here, but she was too excited to hear about Luke's surprise to wait in the warm cab.

Aldo jogged up and surprised her by picking her up and swinging her around in a dizzying circle. He kissed her firmly on the lips, and she invited his warmth to steal over her. Sweaty, happy Aldo was her favorite of all the Aldos. He was particularly irresistible.

"Love is in the air," he pronounced, kissing her again before setting her on her feet. "They're coming to the diner for breakfast."

"Oh! Good! Wait, what about Joni?" Gloria asked, pausing mid celebration. "Luke doesn't know Harper knows about Karen. He doesn't know that Joni and Harper are friends."

Aldo shook his head. "Luke's got to face the past sooner or later. Otherwise there's no going forward. Harper's his chance."

"I hope they can survive this. They've both been through so much already," Gloria said, worried.

Aldo settled an arm around her shoulders. "Sometimes you

just have to believe that love will win." He passed her his phone. "And love looks a lot like this."

Gloria glanced at the picture on the screen of Luke and Harper's embrace. "Oh, wow. You definitely need to save that for their wedding."

His laugh boomed out over the empty parking lot. Aldo kissed the top of her head. "I'd take you back to them, but if I was reading the signs right, they're getting naked in the woods right now."

"We'll give them some space."

———

Gloria was practically giddy. It felt like Christmas morning watching the Garrison clan settle in for breakfast without a clue of what was about to walk through the diner door. Aldo kept shooting her knowing looks while he carried on a conversation with Luke and Sophie's brother, James.

Sophie and Ty were wrangling Josh, who kept diving for the maple syrup. "The last thing you need is a pint of sugar," Sophie told her son. Uncle James snuck another puddle of syrup on Josh's plate every time Sophie turned her attention elsewhere. Claire and Charlie were arguing over whether Charlie could have a chocolate milk or if he should get the healthier orange juice with his egg white omelet.

"The woman will make me a vegan before I'm dead," Charlie complained.

The diner door opened, and Gloria dug her hand into Aldo's thigh. "Sorry I'm late!" Harper called cheerfully. "Do we have room for another?"

Claire was the first to notice the man behind Harper. "Oh my—"

Sophie shrieked and climbed over Ty and Josh. Claire

shoved back her chair, almost tripping Sophie as they fought to get to Luke first.

"For Pete's sake, you just saw the girl two days ago. What's all the…" Charlie trailed off, turning in his seat.

Gloria's throat tightened, and she blinked back tears.

James jumped into the action, hugging his brother as the diner patrons broke out into applause.

"Best surprise ever," Gloria whispered to Aldo. He laced his fingers through hers and brought their joined hands to his lips.

"Second only to Ivan the Terrible," he corrected.

"Of course," Gloria scoffed. "But I don't think Luke is going to go home and wreck the house and wake Harper up at four in the morning by jumping on her face."

Aldo rubbed the faded scratch on his cheek. "I don't know. They might be into that kind of stuff."

Charlie was hugging Luke now as his wife and daughter cried happy tears next to them. Gloria nudged Aldo. Joni was standing, hands folded in front of her. She saw the flash of shock pass over Luke's face when he spotted Joni waiting to greet him. His gaze flew to Harper's face and back to Joni.

Gloria held her breath, and then Joni opened her arms to embrace Luke. Gloria could feel the riot of emotions crackling off Luke. Then he was putting his arms carefully around Joni and Harper was tearing up.

"All good," Aldo whispered to her. "They've got this."

But Gloria wasn't so sure. Harper's love was written all over her pretty face. But when Gloria looked at Luke, his expression was unreadable.

CHAPTER 68

D on't be nervous," Aldo coached Gloria.

"Nervous? What's there to be nervous about?" She sounded like she was being strangled.

Gloria was gripping the door handle and Aldo's hand with white knuckles. She wasn't fooling him at all. Sara Parker had issued a summons to dinner—which included Aldo's mother— and Gloria was freaking out.

It was adorable.

Sure, dinner with the parents was a big deal. It meant that Sara Parker was ready to take this relationship seriously. But Aldo was ready for the challenge. He planned to turn on the charm and win Sara over with his thoughtful hostess gift and his obvious feelings for her daughter.

Gloria, on the other hand, looked like she wanted to jump out of the truck window.

"What's the thing that's scaring you the most right now?" he asked, rubbing a thumb over hers.

"If I say it, you're going to think I'm a big, dumb baby."

"How about I promise to think of you as a petite, pretty baby?" he offered.

"I'm twenty-seven years old, and I still want my mom's approval," she confessed.

"I will get you your mother's approval if I have to steam clean her carpets every month for the rest of her life," Aldo promised.

Gloria graced him with a laugh. "It's not you I'm worried about. Hello, war hero, business owner, all-around great guy. It's me who needs the approving. I spent a lot of years letting her down. I'd really like to turn that around."

"Need I point out that you chose the war hero, business owner, all-around great guy to bring to dinner? I think that says a lot about your taste, maturity, and good sense."

"I don't want her thinking I'm making a mistake or moving too fast," Gloria said, and he felt the nerves in her words.

"Glo, look at what you've done with your life in the last seven months. You're a miracle, and anybody would be proud of you."

"Thank you. I'm sure it will be fine," she lied.

Her thoughts were clearly a mile away, probably running through every possible negative scenario that could happen.

Aldo laughed and squeezed her hand, not buying her bravado for a minute. "How about I promise to keep my mother in line, and you handle yours? Divide and conquer."

Gloria nodded. "Okay. We can do this. It probably won't be terrible. I mean the food will be good at least, even if they hate each other and get into a screaming match over European soccer teams."

"Does your mom watch soccer?" Aldo asked.

"No."

Aldo laughed.

She was quiet for another minute and then said, "We should have brought Ivan. He could have distracted them from fighting with total house destruction."

They picked up his mother, who insisted on sitting in the back seat and then complained the whole way to Gloria's mother's house about the lack of leg room. Gloria, trying to be accommodating, rode the rest of the way with her knees in the dashboard.

"Ma, shut up," Aldo told Ina in the rearview mirror.

"I bet you don't talk to your mother with such disrespect," she sniffed to Gloria.

"Her mom doesn't have the manners of a child raised by wolves," Aldo pointed out.

"What's in the bag?" she demanded, rooting through the gift bag Aldo had on the floor behind his seat.

"Get out of the bag, Ma! It's for Gloria's mom."

Gloria looked surprised and delighted.

"Why don't I get a present?" his mother said and pouted.

"Isn't being my mother gift enough?" Aldo joked.

Ina thought that was pretty funny and laughed the rest of the way to their destination.

———

The introductions went well, in Aldo's opinion. His mother didn't say the f-word, and the fashionista Sara didn't make any comments about or stare too long at Ina's god-awful gravy-brown sweater and matching polyester pants.

They were on a first-name basis, and there was alcohol. Aldo considered it a win.

It was time to turn up the charm. "Mrs. Parker, Gloria tells me you make a mean margarita," Aldo said.

"Call me Sara. And yes, I do," she said, eyes twinkling as she winked at her daughter.

They made a picture, Gloria and Sara together. Both dark hair and dark eyes, the same smile.

Aldo handed over the gift bag. "I thought these might come in handy next time you're mixing."

Eagerly, Sara unpackaged the glass set. He'd found the handblown bubble margarita glasses in the window of a gift shop when he was rushing between meetings. He'd been ten minutes late to his appointment with the architect, but Sara's approving look made it worth it.

Gloria stood on tiptoe and kissed his cheek. "Nice going, kiss-ass," she whispered. She was relaxing, finally. Trusting him not to let her down.

He poked her in the ribs, and Gloria laughed, wrapping her arms around his waist. "I'm a catch," he whispered back.

"A very nice gift," Sara decided. "We will see if you are also a very nice man." But the twinkle told Aldo which way she was leaning in that judgment.

"You got a lotta color in here," Ina announced at full volume, carrying her glass of sangria into the living room. Of course, anything a shade deeper than beige was a lot of color for his mother's tastes.

They dined on pork chops, colorful vegetables, and wine around Sara's round table. Music, something bright and Latin, played in the background.

Aldo felt a foot on his shin, and Gloria sent him a slow wink. She was relaxed and enjoying herself. He loved seeing her this way. Carefree and happy. He wanted more nights like this, more dinners like this. More of everything with her.

"So, Sara, what are a couple of hot single moms like us doing dateless on a Saturday night?" Mrs. Moretta wondered at stadium volume.

"Sometimes the world makes no sense," Sara pointed out, topping off Ina's glass of wine.

"Maybe we should sign ourselves up for that speed dating thing down at the lodge next week?"

———

Aldo insisted on helping clean up while Gloria showed his mother the flower garden in the backyard. He could sense his mother's garden envy and prayed she'd hire a professional with a rototiller this time instead of enlisting him to expand her own flower beds.

Sara took the plates he rinsed and stacked them neatly in the dishwasher. "Thank you for helping with the cleanup. I can't decide if you're polite or just kissing up."

He really liked her. "Let's call it a combination of both."

She picked up her wine and sampled it. "I like your honesty."

"I love your daughter."

Her smile was slow and knowing. "Good. You will marry her and make sure she is safe and happy for the rest of her life then."

"That's where my head is at," Aldo acknowledged. Saying the words, admitting what he really wanted, felt…good. He'd been dancing around it long enough.

Sara gave him another hard-won smile of approval over the rim of her glass. "I hope she doesn't make you work too hard for it."

"I can be patient," he said. And he would.

"Thank you for showing my daughter what a real man is," Sara said, pressing a quick kiss to both his cheeks.

He felt himself flush at the praise.

"Now, pour yourself a little more wine and go kiss my daughter in the dark. Give her a little romance."

CHAPTER 69

I f he had an older brother, I would take him dancing. Does he have an older brother?" That was how Sara Parker gave Gloria her blessing on the subject of Aldo. And Gloria— between busy work hours and long, cozy nights with Aldo— breathed a sigh of relief.

She knew it was silly to be an adult and still crave her mother's approval. But seeing as how she'd done nothing but disappoint the woman for a decade, it felt like a very large, very satisfying win.

Especially since winning involved having a mysterious date with Aldo tonight. He'd given her no details, only the instruction "Prepare to be wowed." Gloria couldn't be giddier if a litter of puppies appeared at her feet.

She was climbing the final steps on the third flight of stairs to her apartment, still thinking about what she should wear, when she spotted it on her door. A big, glittery heart taped to the center.

Pick you up at 7.

Exactly what kind of date was this going to be, she

wondered, fingering the lacy edge of the heart. She couldn't wait to find out. Digging through her purse, Gloria pulled out her phone and snapped a picture of the heart.

Gloria: What's a girl supposed to wear to a glitter heart date?

He responded as she was unlocking her front door.

Aldo: I hope you don't mind, but I took care of that too. Look inside.

Gloria couldn't get the door open fast enough. She'd given him a key as much for romantic relationship purposes as for convenience's sake. Apparently, it had paid off big.

There was a garment bag hanging from her bedroom door with another red heart.

Wear me, please.

Giddy ramped up into ecstasy. Gloria dumped her purse and coat in a heap on the floor and ran to her bedroom. "What are you?" she asked, unzipping the bag so fast that she could have lost a finger. "Oh, my!" Chiffon, in a lovely soft rose, exploded out of the bag. Gloria worked the dress off the hanger and nearly swooned. The skirt was chiffon and light as air, but the bodice glittered like diamonds with hundreds of silver sequins over a sheer lining.

It was breathtaking and, with a quick peek at the tag, her size.

On a girlish squeal of delight, Gloria wrestled her sweater over her head and headed in the direction of her bathroom, the dress clutched to her chest.

"Where are you taking me?" she demanded, opening the door before Aldo could even knock. She didn't know if he answered her or not because she'd been struck dumb by the man in the tuxedo. "Holy crap," she breathed.

"You look incredible," Aldo said, taking her in. She indulged them both with a little twirl.

Her phone pinged.

Harper: Where is he taking you???

It pinged again.

Sophie: I want a detailed timeline of everything you two do tonight! With pictures! And video!

Another ping.

Mom: What shoes are you wearing?

Her lady posse was on red alert tonight. Gloria turned her phone off and dumped it on the table inside the door. "Um, come in. You look like James Bond. Only hotter." And she was doling out awkward compliments like she was a shy sixteen-year-old.

Aldo took her hand and twirled her once more. "You take my breath away."

There went the swooning again. Gloria had to lock her knees in place so the traitors wouldn't give out on her again.

"Thank you." She managed to get the words out without choking on them. "Could you help me zip my dress? I couldn't quite reach."

He took his time turning her away from him, and she melted at the decadent touch of his palm gliding over bare skin. Slowly, he tugged the zipper up, holding her by the waist with his other hand. Every touch was a seduction. And Gloria was more than willing to be seduced.

"We could stay in," she suggested, running her hands over his lapels.

Who knew she had a thing for tuxes?

He grinned at her, and her panties went up in flames. She couldn't wait to get into the dress, and now she was ready to beg him to take it off her.

"I didn't lint roll my pants three times to get all the cat fur off them just to stay in tonight," he said, dipping his head. His lips brushed hers gently. The sound that came from the back of her throat was positively carnal.

Aldo took a deep breath and a step back. He scraped a hand over his jaw, his erection straining at the front of his trousers. It was the sexiest thing Gloria had ever witnessed in her life. Impressive, considering she'd seen the man naked on multiple occasions.

"Where could we possibly be going dressed like this?" Gloria laughed, fluffing her skirt.

"Ah, but you're not quite dressed yet," Aldo countered. He produced a small box from his pocket and, with a quirk of his lips, popped the lid.

Diamonds glittered on satin. At least she thought they were diamonds. Glass didn't shine like that. Earrings, each with five spokes that wrapped around and under the ear from a single point.

"Oh my God," she breathed.

"Do you like them?" he asked.

She nodded, eyes wide, not sure words would do her gratitude justice.

"I saw them, and they reminded me of you. Cool, classic, with a lot of sparkle."

"Aldo, I don't know what to say. No one's ever…" Of course no one had ever given her anything like that. They both knew it. "It's too much. I don't want you bankrupting yourself to give me things."

His snort caught her attention.

"What?" she demanded.

"Glo, money isn't an issue."

"I know you have your business," Gloria said. "But you don't need to be spending it all on me."

"I'm a partner in a comfortably successful business. Luke and I happen to hold the patent on a fancy little joist system that turns a decent profit."

"Decent profit?" But she was waving her hands. "Never mind. I don't want to know. It's none of my business."

"I want you to have beautiful things, Glo. I hope you're okay with accepting gifts because this was the most fun I've ever had shopping. I pictured you looking just like you do now." His voice was rough, but the words felt like a caress.

"Aldo." Gloria clutched a hand to her heart. "You make it hard to breathe."

He beamed at her, that boyish grin that she recognized from her ninth-grade study hall. She wasn't that girl anymore. She wasn't the broken woman anymore either. She was someone new.

CHAPTER 70

He'd worried that the limo was too over-the-top, but when Gloria gasped and grabbed his arm, his regrets went out the window. Then she'd insisted he take a picture of her hanging out the sunroof, and he knew he'd done good.

They drank champagne behind tinted windows and talked about their days as if it was common for them to spend their Friday night in the back of a limo. Gloria reveled in pushing each and every button she could find, opening and closing the sunroof, opening and closing the minibar, changing the lighting from white to purple to swirling disco.

And Aldo enjoyed every second of it.

She'd never had a prom. Another rite of passage stolen from her. Another memory for him to make with her. When Sara suggested romance, Aldo put some serious thought into it. He'd never been a big romance guy. Had never gotten serious enough with someone where romance was required. But Gloria deserved this. And seeing her enjoy herself, seeing her bloom with happiness, made him wish he'd thought to do this sooner.

They arrived at their destination, and Aldo helped her out of the back seat.

"Thank you," Gloria said to the driver, who held the door. "Where are we?" she asked, studying the building before them.

Aldo gave a nod to the driver, who winked at him.

"This is the Breeches Creek Mill," Aldo said, tucking her hand through his arm and leading them up three short steps to the door. He turned the knob. "It's being renovated for event space. I happen to know the owner, who owes me a favor. So their first event is your prom."

He had to give them credit. He'd stolen every associate and intern his firm had, paid them each an extra hundred bucks for the day, and given them an unlimited decorating budget. Jamilah had groused about an entire day's worth of work lost until Aldo sent her off to the massage and pedicure he'd scheduled for her.

She'd texted him hours later after too many complimentary champagnes to tell him he was the best business partner in the world.

"This. Is. Insane." Wide-eyed and slack-jawed, Gloria stepped inside.

There were fairy lights roped around the thick, rustic beams above them. Flowy white panels hung from the rafters to the oak floor. There was music playing softly on a speaker tucked away between potted palms and pines. A fire crackled in the stone fireplace on the far wall, and a pretty sign that said simply *PROM* rested on the mantel.

A table, also swathed in white, was set for two with more champagne chilling in a bucket. On one of the plates sat a sparkling tiara.

"Aldo…" It was as far as she got because she was crying.

"Sweetheart." Gently he pushed her into the chair and pulled out a handkerchief to dab her eyes. "Please don't cry."

"This is the nicest thing anyone has ever done for me," she said, eyes glistening. "I love you for it. Screw it. I love you. I've

been not saying it for a while now—since the laundry—and…
now…" She gestured around them. "I just love you. I love you
so much."

Aldo found himself in the predicament of feeling a little
choked up too. Okay, a lot choked up.

They'd come so far, the two of them. He wanted to ask her
right then and there. To talk about the future, make decisions,
set goals.

But Gloria deserved this night of no strings.

He cleared his throat, trying to dislodge the lump. When
he opened his mouth, no sound came out.

"Oh, hell. It's too soon," she said, covering her face with
her hands. "Shit. You did this amazing thing, and I screw it all
up by being all 'I love you.' And now I made it weird—"

"Gloria, will you please shut up so I can tell you that I don't
remember ever not loving you?"

"What?"

"I love you, Gloria. I'm *in* love with you."

"Really?" she squeaked. The tears were back again. "Because
if you're messing with me or saying it back because I said it first,
I'm going to kill you. Like run you over with a limo kill you."

"How could I not love you after a threat like that?" He
kissed her, his mouth eagerly seeking hers out, branding his lips
to hers. She kissed him back like she was starving for him.

"Wait, wait." He pulled back.

"What is it?" Her lids were heavy, lips plump, and Aldo
couldn't remember ever seeing anything sexier in his life.

"This." He plucked the tiara off the plate and settled it on
her dark hair. She went from bewitching fairy to seductive queen.

She looked at him for a beat, lips parted. "Aldo, take your
pants off."

They stripped with more speed than finesse. But when

Gloria straddled his lap on the chair wearing nothing but the tiara, Aldo knew lust. And when she positioned his cock at her entrance and sank down on him, taking him in inch by fucking inch, he knew love.

She watched him through pleasure-heavy eyes as she rode him by fire and fairy light. Gentle, smooth strokes. He touched her everywhere, wanting to memorize the feel of the moment as much as the look of it. The kisses he pressed to her lips, her jaw, her breasts, weren't enough.

The feel of her skin under his palms and busy fingers wasn't enough. Every time she rose, he felt desolate only to be plunged into ecstasy, completeness, when she took him back in. She rode him leisurely, loved him decadently. And he worshipped her.

He tasted the tip of her breast, stroked the side of her face, her neck. He felt it build between them. The pulse in her throat hammered away. Aldo lifted her arm, tracing his thumb over the birds in flight. He knew what they were flying toward, what they were migrating to.

She touched the birds over his heart with two fingers, traced them as her breath grew shallow.

He loved her. She loved him. It was that simple. Their bodies loved and moved together with one mind, one purpose.

He wanted to devour her and be devoured. He wanted to give Gloria a piece of his soul. And then he realized he already had.

She was tightening around him, sighing into his mouth, and he felt it welling up inside him, climbing his spine. Pleasure and love intertwined into something different, something invincible, something that burned brighter than history and carved a way into the future.

Their lips met, their bodies shook, their hearts blended.

And when they finally shared their first dance much, much later, it was naked in the firelight.

CHAPTER 71

Thanksgiving was here and giving Gloria big, mixed feelings. On one hand, she was looking forward to her first real holiday with Aldo. Halloween didn't count. Not when they'd spent the evening judging the jack-o'-lantern carving contest on Main Street. On the other, her mother was out of town on her annual Caribbean cruise with friends, a tradition that Gloria realized had started to help Sara forget about her estranged, abused daughter and the holiday they should have been enjoying together.

"I promise to change the date next year, *mija*," her mother swore when Gloria dropped her off at the airport.

"Don't you worry about me," Gloria told her. "We'll celebrate when you get back."

While Gloria would have preferred a cheerful, cozy Thanksgiving at her mother's house, she was willing to settle for second prize: Thanksgiving at Harper and Luke's.

Her first real-life big, family holiday. Gloria was honest enough with herself to be glad someone else was hosting. Sure, she'd fantasized about being the hostess with the mostest someday, but that day was *not* today. Harper, however, felt no such qualms about hosting a million people for her first time cooking for the holiday. Where lots of things still made Gloria nervous, nothing scared Harper.

They arrived bearing gifts. Gloria had the pretty floral centerpiece she'd made of short orange and peach roses arranged in neat rows, planted garden-style in a low, rectangular box and accented with glossy greenery. Mrs. Moretta carried a box of wine under one arm, and sweet, thoughtful Aldo brought up the rear with an array of specialty dog biscuits for Max and Lola.

Ivan the Terrible was at home with a belly full of special turkey treats and his new stuffed drumstick.

They disbanded at the doorstep, Gloria and Mrs. Moretta following Joni back to the kitchen where female voices were raised and the heavenly scent of comfort food wafted. With a wink and a kiss, Aldo peeled off to the living room for football and beer with the menfolk, who included Ty, James, Charlie, and Luke.

Gloria found Harper in the midst of chaos. She wore an apron and snapped orders like a chef in a wildly popular Manhattan restaurant on a Saturday night. Claire was running a hand mixer through an obscenely big bowl of potatoes. Sophie was wrapping foil packets of vegetables to roast on the grill. Harper was directing everything else.

"Joni, baste the turkey! Gloria, those flowers are gorgeous. Put them on the table. Mrs. Moretta, I need wine stat!"

Gloria headed into the dining room to admire the table. It was funny. The last time she'd been in this room, a man had tried to kill her friend. A man who'd been there because of her. She looked down at the floor, the spot where she'd hit him and he'd gone limp. It hadn't been the first time she fought back, the first time she'd hit him. But it would be the last.

"They did a good job with the door and window."

She turned, spotted Luke in the doorway holding a bottle of beer loosely in his fingers.

The dining room window, the heavy front door, had both been replaced. "It was a scary night," she admitted.

"Sometimes the past catches up with us," he said hollowly.

It was an odd thing for him to say. Like he had something else entirely on his mind. "Yeah. I guess so," she agreed.

Luke looked...weary. Not at all like a man who was surrounded by family and friends. A man home for good with the people he loved the most. He looked tortured. Lola rumbled into the room and leaned heavily against Luke's leg. He leaned down to give her a good scruff behind the ears. "Pretty girl," he murmured.

Lola sneezed in appreciation.

"Listen, Gloria," Luke said, straightening up to his full height. "Can I give you some advice?"

He was drunk, she realized. Or buzzed enough to slur a little.

She nodded, wondering what would make Luke Garrison drink to excess when he was living what to so many others was only a dream.

"Don't make the same mistake twice. What's the definition of insanity? Doing the same thing over and over and then expecting a different result? Sooner or later, everyone has to face facts. A mistake is a mistake. No matter how good everyone else tries to tell you it is."

There was a burst of laughter from the kitchen, and Luke's expression darkened. His exit was as abrupt as his entrance.

"What the hell was that?" Gloria murmured to herself.

———

Gloria doubted anyone else noticed it, but Luke and Harper sat at opposite ends of the table. Harper spent more time pushing the food she'd worked so hard on around her plate than eating it. Gloria pushed it out of her mind and focused on the rest of the festive guests. Laughing when Aldo spoon-fed her stuffing and when Mrs. Moretta and Sophie argued about organic vegetables. James and Ty made a show of going back to the kitchen for seconds *and* thirds.

The food was good. The company—most of it, at least—was even better. Aldo squeezed her leg under the table. The spark in his eyes told her he had plans for dessert later. She surprised them both by leaning over and kissing him on the cheek.

"What's that for?" he asked.

Gloria gave a little shrug. "Guess I'm feeling thankful for you."

As the action died down around the table, Joni cleared her throat. "I just wanted to thank Harper and Luke for inviting me today. It's been a hard few years, and it means so much that you still treat me like family. It's good to be reminded of what's really important in life, and you all have done that for me. So thank you for that. And Happy Thanksgiving!" She raised her wineglass.

Everyone raised their wineglasses. "To family," Charlie said, winking at Harper.

"To family," everyone echoed.

Everyone except Luke, who stared morosely into his empty glass. Gloria nudged Aldo and nodded in Luke's direction. "What's going on with Luke?" she asked in his ear.

Aldo watched his friend for a beat, shrugged. "Dunno."

"Maybe I should talk to Harper?" Gloria ventured.

But Aldo was closing his hand over hers. "Come with me."

He pulled her away from the table, telling everyone they were going to browse the desserts, and proceeded to drag her straight out the back door.

Once on the porch, he took his time backing her against the wall. Gloria suddenly couldn't remember what they were talking about. "What's this for?" she asked when he kissed her sweetly.

"To soften the blow when I tell you that you're not responsible for the mood of the room."

"What are you talking about? I just have a bad feeling about what's going on between them."

"Glo, listen to me." He put his hands on her shoulders, squeezed gently. "Whatever's going on, it's not your job to fix it or make it better. It's not your job to make everybody happy."

"That's not what... Well, hell." That was exactly what she'd been doing. What she always did.

"I get it," Aldo pressed on. "You take responsibility for how other people feel because those feelings were taken out on you again and again. But you aren't responsible for other people's happiness. You're in charge of your own, and you're doing a damn good job with it. But you can't go in that house and make Harper and Luke happy."

"But there's something clearly going on with them," she argued. Aldo was taking apart the way she lived her life, the way she interacted with everyone she met. She thought back, recalling her parents' fights. Remembering how she'd draw them special pictures of their family, holding hands and smiling like she wanted them to. If she could just get better grades or score that goal in soccer...they'd be happy. They'd be proud. If she could just get dinner on the table faster or fold the laundry the way he liked it, he'd be happy.

"Honey." Aldo cupped her face. "None of it's your fault. And it's not your job to fix it."

She closed her eyes and let out a long, slow breath. "That's a lot to process."

"When you try to fix things for other people, you're basically saying you don't believe in their ability to fix it themselves. You're telling them you don't believe in them. Respect them. Trust them."

"But what if they don't fix it? What if they keep making mistakes?" Luke's words in the dining room came back to her.

"That's on them. What are they going to learn if they just do what you tell them to do?"

"Huh." Gloria blinked, processed. "That makes an odd amount of sense."

He laughed. "You can't control everything and everyone. You can't make everything perfect and everyone happy. *You* can be happy and make good choices for yourself."

She felt the weight of a thousand burdens slide off her shoulders and land on the porch boards at her feet. "I really don't have to fix everything?"

He shook his head. "Only the things you break."

CHAPTER 72

They unanimously decided to leave the dishes for later and run off some of the food with a friendly game of football. As with all Garrison games, the friendly pickup fun quickly turned into a skirmish.

Aldo was used to the way things operated. He hoped that a quick game of flag football would help pull Harper and Luke out of whatever funk they were in. Not just because he didn't want to see them at odds with each other but because it bothered Gloria. If he wasn't careful, he'd start running in front of Gloria trying to neaten and tidy everything and everyone up.

Aldo, Gloria, Luke, and Harper squared off in the backyard against Ty, Sophie, and James. He and Luke quickly fell back into the groove of calling plays and dodging defenders. Gloria and Harper were laughing at Sophie's trash talk.

Claire was safely out of earshot, so the siblings let loose all the "fucks" they'd kept bottled up during the nice family meal. With the trash talking, the action intensified too. After Luke criticized Harper's lackluster defense, she jumped on James's back and hung on for dear life as he caught the long bomb Ty threw.

James, always one to show off, spun her around to his front

and tossed Harper over his shoulder, running the length of the "field" with Harper laughing and threatening to throw up on him.

The fun ended there. When James put Harper on her feet, Luke hit him full speed.

"What the hell, man?" James shoved back. In the span of a second, they were on the ground wrestling.

"Fuck," Aldo muttered.

"Luke!" Harper's sharp tone didn't register to the grown men acting like idiots grappling on the ground.

Sophie smacked Ty in the chest. "What are you waiting for, Mr. Law and Order? Get in there and break it up."

"Soph," he said mournfully. "I just ate three plates of turkey. I can't bend over."

Aldo took one look at Gloria's stricken face and waded in. "Knock it off," he ordered, dragging Luke off his brother and shoving him toward the patio. "Cool off before you make a bigger ass of yourself."

"What's your problem?" James called after his brother, looking more confused than pissed off. Aldo pulled him to his feet.

Harper crossed her arms against the November chill, and Gloria put an arm around her friend's shoulders. "He's been drinking. A lot," Harper told them. "I don't know what's going on with him."

Sophie shook her head. "You better find out before Mom catches wind of this. She'll want to hook him up with a therapist next."

"That's way worse than a spanking," Aldo said, winking at Gloria. If it worked for her and him, it would probably work for Luke. Maybe he'd feel him out, browbeat him if necessary. But for now, he was taking Gloria home.

"Best Thanksgiving ever," Gloria said, reaching up to spoon-feed Aldo a bite of pumpkin pie. He reciprocated by spraying a dollop of whipped cream directly into her mouth. Ivan pranced over, swatted at the pie plate, and then flopped over to bite the rug.

The fire burned low where they lounged naked under blankets and pillows in front of it. The November chill and Harper and Luke's problems were far, far away. He himself had also come quite far, he realized, noting his prosthesis propped against the ottoman.

"Agreed," Aldo said, sliding a hand down Gloria's bare back. He wondered if he'd ever have his fill of touching her, of learning her body. His fingers found the small scar on the curve of her hip and danced over it before skating back up her ribs.

"I wondered what your plan was when you asked me to make pie and then told me to leave it here," Gloria said, stretching her arms over her head and sighing.

"From now on, this is how I want to end every Thanksgiving," Aldo announced. "A new tradition."

"Is that so?" Gloria purred. She reached out to ruffle Ivan's fur and snickered when the cat tried to eat her hand. Ivan puffed up and then turned tail, running up the stairs and sounding like a small pony.

"I think it would be a little easier if you lived here though. Or we could move into your apartment. Or buy a different house," Aldo mused.

Gloria went still and quiet in his arms.

"I'm trying to be really suave and romantic and ask you to move in with me," he said after a few more seconds of silence.

"Me? Us? Move in together?"

"You don't have to decide now. You can think about it."

This was not how he'd pictured it going. He should have practiced what he was going to say, not blurted it out between gobs of whipped cream.

"Yes."

"Yes, you want to think about it?"

"No. Yes, I want to move in with you."

"Wait, there was a no and a yes in there." It was very important that Gloria clarify exactly what she meant.

She twisted in his arms, pressing her breasts to his chest as they tipped backward. "Yes, I want to move in with you. I love you. I love this house. I even love that monster parading as a kitten."

Holding her to him, he rolled her onto her back. "You're not just saying that to make me happy, are you?"

She grinned at him, and his heart picked up the pace. He was going to marry this woman and make a family with her here within the walls he'd built and she'd painted. But first, he was going to lick whipped cream off every inch of her body.

CHAPTER 73

L uke broke up with Harper, and no one knows where she is."
Sophie's announcement upon sweeping into Blooms
had the effect of a record scratch to Gloria. All the glow of
Thanksgiving and Aldo's invitation to move in disappeared like
a bubble popping.

"I'm going to have to call you back," Della, her boss, said
into the phone.

"What? What happened?" Gloria asked. "Things seemed
strained yesterday but not this bad."

"According to my chickenshit asshat of a brother, it wasn't
working out, and they wanted different things."

"Oh my God. This is awful," Gloria said. "And he doesn't
know where she is?"

"He basically kicked her out last night. On Thanksgiving!
We need to find her. Once we do, I'm going to kill my brother
and make Harper fall in love with James so I can keep her in
the family."

Gloria fished her phone out of her apron pocket. No
messages from Harper.

"I'll call Hannah. Maybe Harper went there," she told
Sophie.

"Good thinking. I'm going to do another loop around town. See if she ran out of gas in any parking lots." It was how Harper came to Benevolence and how she'd happened to save Gloria's life. Now it was Gloria's turn to find her friend and help her.

"Della?" Gloria turned to her boss.

"You go on now. Go help your friend. I'll close up tonight."

"Thank you," Gloria said, already dialing Hannah's number.

Hannah hadn't heard from Harper in a few days and was as shocked about the breakup as the rest of them. After making Hannah promise to call her if she heard anything, Gloria got in her car to do what Sophie was doing.

She fired off a quick text to Aldo and prayed that he'd at least heard from Harper in the last twenty-four hours.

When her phone rang, she answered it immediately. "Hello?"

"Gloria? Hi, it's Joni. Harper gave me your number."

"Harper?"

"I didn't want you all to worry. She's here at my house. She's going to stay with me until…well, until she figures out what she wants to do."

Gloria closed her eyes, allowing the panic to seep from her body. "Is she okay?"

"Oh, honey. She's hanging in there. She's, well, devastated is a strong word. But she'd hung a lot of hopes and dreams on Luke."

"She loves him," Gloria said, half to herself.

"And I'll be honest. I think he loves her too."

If they loved each other, how could it not be enough?

"Is there anything she needs?" Gloria asked, clearing her throat.

"She showed up with one little bag. So I imagine she'll need a few things from home...Luke's house. But for now, she's okay. She hasn't gotten out of bed yet. Poor thing. But she didn't want you worrying about her."

"Tell her it's not working. I'm very worried."

Joni chuckled. "I'll pass that message along. She told me to tell you that she'll let you know when she's ready to talk."

"Okay. Please tell her I love her and I'm here for her. Anything she needs. No matter what."

———

With no one to search for, Gloria adjusted her course, steering her car toward Chickenshit Luke's house.

"I'm not fixing things," she told herself as she pulled into the driveway and stomped on the brake behind his pickup truck.

Her phone was ringing. Aldo. But she ignored it for now.

She climbed the front porch steps under a full head of steam and barged right in the front door. The dogs came scrambling to greet her from the living room, warning barks turning to happy yips and the tap dance of dog nails.

Luke was sitting on the couch staring at the TV that wasn't on. There was a beer in his hand and two more on the coffee table. She shot him a good hard look, letting him know without words exactly what she thought of him, and stormed up the stairs.

"Gloria!" he called after her. "Did you talk to her? Do you know where she is?"

She heard him on the stairs behind her, but she ignored him, veering off into the bedroom he'd shared with her best friend until the night before. She opened a dresser drawer and found only men's T-shirts. Another one was all sweats and gym shorts. She left the drawers open and stalked to the closet.

"Gloria?" Luke entered the room behind her, and she spun around, finger pointing.

"Don't talk to me. I don't like you very much right now."

"I had to do it, Gloria," he called after her when she ducked back into the closet.

She grabbed a few sweaters and sweatshirts, some bras, and underwear that she found in a drawer.

"She'll understand eventually," Luke said.

"You keep telling yourself that if it helps you sleep at night," she muttered to him, brushing past him to throw her clothing haul on the bed. She stomped into the bathroom and rifled through the vanity, pulling out everything that looked remotely feminine. In an immature and thoroughly satisfying move, she added Luke's deodorant and toothbrush to the heist.

Back in the bedroom, she crossed to the other dresser in the room and found Harper's gym clothes and pajamas. The pile on the bed was growing.

Luke walked into the closet and came back with a duffel bag. "Here," he said.

She snatched it out of his hands and started stuffing clothing inside. "I want to know why," she said. "Why did you have to hurt my friend like that?"

"If I didn't hurt her now, imagine how much worse it would be a year from now."

"She loves you!"

Lola, unhappy with the shouting, stuffed her head under the bed.

"I'm damaged. You don't love something damaged. You try to fix it. But I can't be fixed," Luke snapped. "After Karen... There's no recovering from something like that. No getting back to normal."

"Is that why you didn't tell her about Karen?" Gloria demanded, zipping the bag shut.

"I was selfish. I tried to pretend that I wasn't this scarred, broken person. Harper brightens every room she walks into, and I fell for that…for a while. But I can't love her. Not the way a normal man can."

"Just because you're damaged doesn't mean you can't live happily ever after." Gloria's lip was trembling, and she didn't know why.

"That's exactly what it means. It means I'm not capable of loving her the way she needs me to. I had to let her go so she can find that with someone who can."

"That's bullshit," Gloria said, fighting back tears that had snuck up on her. "You're making excuses for being a chickenshit." She pushed past him, hauling the bag with her into the hallway.

"What is it with women calling me a chickenshit?"

"Get used to it!" she called over her shoulder.

"Just…wait!" He started down the stairs after her. "Is she okay? Is she safe?"

"What do you care?" Gloria demanded, rounding on him at the foot of the stairs.

"Just because I'm a monster doesn't mean I don't care."

"She's safe, no thanks to you."

"She needs money. Let me give you—"

"Harper doesn't need your guilty payout. She's got friends who love her." And with that, Gloria slammed the door in his face. She didn't want to let his words dig their barbs into her. Didn't want to let them damage what she was building with Aldo. But, God. What if Luke was right?

She pushed the ugly doubt away and hurried down the walk.

Back in her car, she saw Aldo was calling again. She hit Ignore and dialed Sophie instead.

"Joni called. Harper is with her. And I just broke into your brother's house, stole a bunch of Harper's stuff, and called him a chickenshit."

"Do I need to send Ty over to deal with the body?"

CHAPTER 74

Gloria trudged through Aldo's front door. She stopped short, avoiding Ivan's mad streak in front of her, a toy mouse half his size bouncing in his mouth.

It had been a long, ugly day. It started around 4:00 a.m. with a nightmare that hadn't plagued her in weeks. Glenn was chasing her. She was in a dark, unfamiliar house, and every door she tried was locked. She'd terrified herself awake and had been unable to get back to sleep. Her therapist had warned that there would be setbacks along the way. But after months of happiness, of a consistent sense of security, Harper and Luke's breakup and the ensuing nightmare left her feeling queasy and unsettled.

So she'd gone into work early and promptly screwed up an order that may or may not have ruined a bridal shower. She rounded out the day with a visit to see Harper.

"I've had my arm and ribs broken in foster care," Harper had said. "This hurts more."

Seeing her friend gaunt and pale with circles the size of hubcaps under her eyes had been her undoing. Gloria had cried in her car for twenty minutes before making the short drive to Aldo's house. They hadn't been the cleansing tears that arrived unprovoked in the early weeks after leaving Glenn. No, this was grief.

"Hey, Glo! I know declawing is inhumane, but what about detoothing?" Aldo called from the kitchen.

She was supposed to laugh but didn't have it in her. She didn't have anything in her.

With a feeling of detachment, she glanced around the living room. They'd been progressing without her really noticing it. Painting her color choice on the walls, stocking the kitchen with her favorite cookware, rearranging the dining room furniture.

Aldo was making space for her here. He was trusting her to be a good, healthy partner. Believing that she could overcome her past.

And there he was, greeting her with a glass of wine and a kiss. She turned her head at the last second, so his lips landed on the corner of her mouth.

She felt...defeated. As much as she'd tried to ignore Luke's words, his prophecy that there were no happy endings for the broken, she couldn't stop hearing them.

"How was Harper?" Aldo asked, taking her coat and bag, hanging both in the closet but not before getting her phone out and setting it on the charging station on the console table they'd picked out together.

Gloria took a sip of wine and tasted bitterness. "Not good."

Aldo swore quietly. "What does she need?"

Gloria shook her head and sank down on the couch.

Harper *loved* Luke. She'd trusted him with her heart, her scars. And look where that had gotten her. Alone. With a broken heart.

"I don't know."

Aldo sat next to her, absentmindedly stroked a hand over her hair. "I'm going to have to kick his ass."

"You can't make him love her. He said it himself. He's not capable of loving anyone after Karen."

Ivan dashed downstairs and hurled himself into Aldo's lap, curling up and falling asleep in less than a second.

"That's bullshit," Aldo said. "He didn't lose the ability to love when Karen died. He lost the ability to be brave. It's gotta stop. He's throwing away a lifetime of happiness. A future. All because he's scared."

Gloria spun the stem of the wineglass in her hand. "He's not scared. He's sure. He's positive that he can't love her, and he wants her to find someone who will. It's kind of... I don't know. Noble in a sad, twisted way."

"Don't tell me you buy that crap he sold you. That's fear, Gloria," Aldo insisted. "He's scared to get hurt again. He's scared to lose again."

"He's damaged. You said yourself you can't fix someone else. Harper can't fix Luke," Gloria reminded him.

You can't fix me. The thought rose up and bloomed between them, getting bigger and uglier. It felt like the truth.

She took a shaky breath and pressed on. "And he doesn't want her to make a mistake trying to love him. That's why it's so hard for him to be around Joni. She's a reminder of what happened. That's how I feel every time I see Mrs. Diller. That woman will be a permanent reminder to me of all the mistakes I made just because we share a town."

Aldo, still cradling Ivan in one arm, turned to look at her. God, he was so handsome it hurt to look at him. Low-slung sweatpants, a tissue-thin T-shirt that looked about a decade old. His hair, dark and curling, and that scruff of beard over his jaw. She loved him so much. At least, she thought she did.

Maybe this wasn't love. Maybe this was some misguided attempt to be whole again. She felt sick again.

"Hey. You sound stressed. How about a bath? I'll run one for you. Candles, music. No cat. You go up there and shut out the world for a while. I'll order a pizza, and we'll call it a night."

Goddammit. Why was he so good to her? Did she even deserve it? Or was she wasting his time the way Luke had wasted Harper's?

The difference was Luke was sure he didn't love anyone, and Gloria was no longer sure what love was.

"I think I should go," she said, setting the glass of wine down and rising.

"Go? Why?"

"I just...I need some time alone to think."

Aldo put the cat down on the couch and came to his feet. "Talk to me, Gloria."

She stepped away from him, cognizant of the fact that if he touched her, if he pulled her against that broad, safe chest of his, she'd never be able to leave. Never be able to do the right thing.

"Harper's devastated. Like she's a shadow of the Harper we love. It's like someone flipped a switch and all the light went out of her. It's because she fell for someone too broken to love her back."

There were tears blurring her vision.

"You're upset because your friend is hurt. I get that," Aldo said carefully.

But it was more than that. So much more. Gloria had never seen anyone love as freely as Harper. And if that kind of love couldn't be reciprocated, what did that say about Gloria's future? Was she like Luke and too damaged to ever be in a healthy relationship? Did her scars run too deep?

Or was she like Harper and chasing a love that wasn't real?

Looking at Aldo, in the dim glow of lamps, she couldn't be sure. She needed to think. Needed to figure out if she was making a mistake or if she'd already made it.

Because now she knew that love wasn't enough.

"I'm sorry, Aldo. I think I need some time. Some space."

"Spell it out for me, Glo. Because you're scaring the shit out of me right now. Are we talking about just tonight?"

She swallowed hard and shook her head. "No. We're not. I'm not. I think all this might have been a mistake."

"Sweetheart, if you want to back off on the moving in together thing, that's fine. I don't want to rush you. I love you. I love being with you. I'll be as patient as you need me to be... *if* you're in this."

The *if.* She didn't know the answer. Didn't know if she should be in it. Shouldn't this be easy? Shouldn't she know? Maybe that was her answer.

"I think I made a mistake, Aldo."

"No, Glo. No." He reached for her, but she shied away, and she saw the pain flicker across his face.

She knew he wouldn't hurt her. Not like that. Never like that.

"I'm sorry," she said lamely. "But I need time. And space. And I need you to give me both. You said you'd give me anything."

"Anything," he repeated.

"Then give me this." And with those parting words, she walked to the closet. She got her coat, bag, and phone. And then she left.

CHAPTER 75

The pounding on her front door had Gloria leaping out of her bed and running barefoot into the living room. She hadn't slept. Her decision the night before hadn't given her the peace she sought.

"Aldo?" she called, flinging the door open. Maybe he could fix this for her. Help her figure it out.

But it wasn't Aldo. It was a wild-eyed Sophie who brushed past her, pushing a to-go coffee into Gloria's hands.

"We need to brainstorm," she said, hustling into the apartment.

Disappointment pushed Gloria further into her shame spiral. There was no reason Aldo would be showing up on her doorstep. Not with the ultimatum she'd given him. She'd done this to herself, pulling her head and heart back into a protective shell. Now, not only was she *not* happy, she was fucking miserable.

If this was what safe felt like, it was total crap.

"Brainstorm what?" she asked with zero enthusiasm.

But Sophie was too far gone in her plotting drama to notice.

She unwound a scarf from her neck and dropped her coat

over the back of the dining chair before dramatically flopping down on Gloria's couch.

"How to get Luke and Harper back together," she announced. "I schemed them together in the first place, and now my services are desperately needed again."

"I don't think I'm the right person to be scheming with," Gloria said, sitting down next to Sophie and hugging a pillow to her chest.

Sophie stared at her for a long beat. "Oh, for fuck's sake! You too? What the hell is wrong with you people? Are you running against my brother for mayor of Chickenshitville?"

"How do you know it was me?" Gloria asked.

"You have that 'I made a huge mistake' look written all over your puppy-dog eyes," Sophie said, pointing a finger in her face. "And for the fucking record, you did make a huge mistake if you're telling me that you and Aldo broke up."

"Well, we did. Not that it's any of your business," Gloria said primly.

"Don't get all fussy with me. I should take that coffee back," she said, eyeing Gloria's cup.

"I will slap the daylights out of you if you try."

But instead of laughing, Sophie stood up. "Is Aldo okay? Or are you just like my brother and pretending you never knew the man?"

"Aldo is going to be fine." Gloria thought of the look on his face when she'd walked out. The hurt. The utter agony. She closed her eyes. "This is the only way he's not going to get hurt in the long run."

"I'm going to hurt you in the short run, Gloria. I don't even feel bad about threatening an abuse victim with more violence. That's how mad you're making me."

"Sophie, not everyone is as strong as you are. Okay?" Gloria said wearily. "Not everyone is lucky enough to know who they are, what they want, and how to get it. Some of us are damaged and won't ever be fixed."

"Bull. Shit. You think because you went through some shit in your life that you're unlovable or incapable of love? Between you and my brother, I don't know who I want to slap more. It doesn't matter what happens to you. In the end, all we are is our ability to love. That never gets taken away or diminished. It's dumb chickenshits like you two who try to hide from it. You're as capable of loving as I am."

"Jeez, don't hold back or anything," Gloria said, getting to her feet.

"The whole damn world has gone insane," Sophie snapped, stomping toward the door. "You know what I'm going to do? I'm going to go crawl back in bed with my husband and show him all the ways I'm so grateful he isn't half the dumbass you all are!"

With a slam of the door, Sophie was gone, and Gloria was alone again.

CHAPTER 76

He asked you to move in with him?" Gloria's mother patted a hand over her heart. "I'm so happy for you, Gloria! He is a good man." In celebration, she stabbed the button on the blender, working her magic on a pitcher of strawberry margaritas, the glasses that Aldo had thoughtfully chosen lined up next to it.

Gloria sucked in a breath and finished the rest of the miserable story. "I told him I needed some space. Some time to think," she said loudly over the blender.

Her mother turned off the blender abruptly. Sara's long, quiet look communicated quite a lot. So did her "hmm."

"What?" Gloria felt defensive now. She shouldn't be so quick to jump into such a serious relationship. She needed time to heal, time to grow on her own. She was being *responsible*. She slid off the stool to pace. "I'm not rushing into a commitment. Again," she said, ignoring the fact that she had already rushed into the commitment and then promptly backed out of it.

"You were sixteen, *mija*. No sixteen-year-old is equipped to make good, informed decisions. You're all hormones and angst and 'my mother doesn't understand me.'"

In a lot of ways, Gloria felt like she was still sixteen,

standing in her mother's kitchen defending her life's decisions. "Mama." She rolled her eyes. "I know what I'm doing. It isn't the right time."

"I am listening to your words and not believing them. I don't think you believe them either," Sara pointed out, crossing her arms over her chest. Her earrings, delicate silver bells, danced from her lobes as if shivering from the judgment Sara was firing in her direction.

"It seems like we're moving too fast. We're both coming out of difficult situations, and now we're spending Thanksgiving together, and he's asking me to move in. What's next? An engagement? Marriage? Kids?"

"If that's what you want, yes! Is it what you want?"

"Of course! But when the time is right. Not when I'm less than a year out of a nightmare."

"Okay. What is enough time? A year? Three? Ten? How much more time do you want to waste because of Glenn Diller?"

That hurt. Gloria felt it like a wound on her already dented heart.

"This isn't because of Glenn, Mama! Yes, I'm being more cautious now because of the lessons I learned. Isn't that what being an adult is? Learning from your mistakes? Doing better?" It was suddenly imperative to Gloria that she make her mother understand.

"So what then? Do you wait to find a partner until you are perfect?"

"Of course not, Mama." *Broken people are never perfect.*

"No. You choose a man—or woman—who will grow and change with you. Who will support you as you grow and change, not force you to stay the same."

They squared off on opposite sides of the peninsula. The blender of frozen happiness between them had lost its cheer.

"I don't know if I can be what he needs me to be, okay?" Gloria snapped.

"What does he want you to be other than happy?"

"Who spends ten years in a relationship where they're treated like garbage? Who stays? I'm damaged, Mama. I'm walking around with an entire set of baggage!"

Sara blinked at her coolly. Empathy had never been her mother's strong suit.

"That is a steaming load of bullshit," Sara finally commented. "You're not damaged. You're scared. You are acting like a coward."

"I'm being cautious, not cowardly!"

"Do you know how many people would do anything for a love like this? For even an ounce of what you two found in each other? Do you know how many would fight and claw and beg for this? And you throw it away like it's replaceable?"

"I didn't throw it away!" She didn't. She had respectfully announced her need for time and space…and then insinuated that if Aldo didn't give her both, he never cared about her in the first place. This wasn't making her feel more confident in her decision. She was heading for a tailspin now, doubting her motives. She might as well be back in the trailer, lying on the threadbare carpet after another fight.

"Are you still dating?" Sara demanded.

"Not at the moment," Gloria said grudgingly.

Her mother threw her hands up in the air. Sara Parker was born without a poker face and launched into some very colorful Spanish.

"I thought you'd be proud of me. You never made the same mistake after Dad left. You never jumped into another relationship—"

"Because I am *waiting* until I find a man who looks at me

the way Aldo looks at you. Do you really not know how very lucky you are? How rare that is? I would love to be in a relationship, maybe even a marriage, with a man who loves and respects me. I'm holding out for what you were so quick to dismiss."

Her mother was never one to pull punches, and Gloria felt every single one of her words as if it were a physical blow.

"I'm trying to do the right thing, the thing that makes the most sense."

"*Mija*, sometimes the thing that makes the most sense is *wrong*. Don't hide away, trying to protect yourself from ever getting hurt again. It will be a sad and colorless life. Without pain, there is no joy."

"We were moving too fast." Stubbornly, she stuck to her guns though her stance was wavering.

"How can you doubt your feelings? I saw the way you looked at him. You loved him. You love him now, and you stand here and pretend you don't. You were looking for an excuse."

"I wasn't looking for an excuse! I don't know how I feel!"

Sara shook her head, pursed her lips. "You don't trust yourself. And you never will until you jump in and try hard and deal with the consequences. But first, you must believe. You don't have to believe that everything will work out and be perfect. You have to believe that you will survive it. You have to know, in your heart, that you will do whatever it takes to chase down your happiness."

Did she know that? Was she fighting for her happiness, or was she fighting for safety? There was a time in her life when safe meant happy. Did that still hold true now?

"My job is to respect your decisions. I am not here to hold your hand and guide you in life. You are an adult. I will respect this decision, but I will be very disappointed in you."

"That's not fair, Mama. I'm doing what's best for me."

"You are doing what you think is safest. Safe and best are rarely the same thing." Sara looked at her and shook her head sadly. "I have never once said this or felt this before, but today I am disappointed in you."

And with that, her mother swept from the kitchen, leaving behind her a quiet blender and a cloud of disapproval.

CHAPTER 77

He wasn't sure what day it was. All Aldo knew was the pavement blurred beneath his feet. His new running blade, made from carbon fiber–reinforced polymer, was a dream to run on. But the rest of his life felt like a fucking nightmare.

Gloria left, taking the light out of his house…and leaving him with a bad-tempered kitten hell-bent on world domination.

Everything sucked. And he couldn't fight his way toward what he wanted. Not this time. He didn't understand where it all went wrong. What had pushed Gloria to embrace the doubts.

They were going to move in together. He'd been planning to propose. Maybe after she moved in, making things more official. Now, he had a damn ring and no Gloria.

The gloomy winter morning was looking gloomier by the second. But if he called off work again, Jamilah would make good on her threat to show up at his door with the entire office staff so they could all work from his home.

So he'd suited up and headed out for a head-clearing, frosty morning run, the ring tucked carefully in the inner pocket of his windbreaker. He felt stupid for it, but he believed Gloria would come around. She'd tell him what was wrong, they'd fix it together, and get back to their joint happily ever after. He felt it in his gut.

But these days without her were starting to chip away at that hope, that faith.

"Moretta!"

Linc jogged up to Aldo from a side street and fell into step with him. "What the hell happened to your face?" Aldo asked.

"You didn't hear? Me and your BFF Garrison got into it in the beverage cooler at the grocery store."

"You fucking with me?" Aldo asked, his breath puffing out in a silvery cloud.

Linc snorted. "Nope. I was in there keeping Harper warm—"

"I bet you were."

"Ha. Poor girl is pretty broke up about him. I was hiding Harper from Garrison. Then doesn't the son of a bitch poke his head in the door?" Linc shook his head ruefully.

"He look as bad as you?" Aldo asked.

Linc grinned. "'Bout the same. But if he's out getting into bar fights in the grocery store, you might want to have a talk with him."

Aldo had been neglecting his friend duties, sinking into his own depression.

"Harper break up the fight?"

"Nope. Bunch of people called Deputy Do-Right. He got to pop Luke one right in the jaw." Linc mimed a punch.

"Fuck," Aldo sighed.

"Just thought you should know."

"Yeah, thanks."

———

Aldo went in to work an hour early, burying himself in schematics and ordinances and five hundred emails until noon.

He worked with the fervor and focus of a man who didn't want to think about anything else in his life.

The interns and the associates, probably under Jamilah's orders, kept to themselves, the entire office buzzing away in silence.

Finally, he switched off his monitor and stretched his arms over his head. "J, I'm taking a long lunch."

She raised a thumb over her head without taking her eyes off her screen.

He made the drive to Luke's house, noting how most of the leaves were off the trees. Christmas was coming up fast, and he had no desire or drive to put even the minimum effort forth. He had a guest bedroom closet stashed with gifts he'd already bought for Gloria, a few for her mother, one or two for his own. But his holiday spirit had died when Gloria walked out. However, that was no excuse for abandoning his friend—dumbass or not—in his time of need.

He spotted Luke's truck in the driveway and pulled in behind it. Knocking once, Aldo let himself in. "Hey, you home?" he called.

His gaze flicked to the dining room where a dozen boxes were stacked neatly and labeled "Harper."

"In here," Luke answered from the living room. The dogs vaulted off him to dance around Aldo. He stooped and doled out pats and scratches.

"What are you doing home in the middle of the day?" Aldo asked.

Luke peeled himself off the couch. He looked like shit. Unshaven, bruised, exhausted.

"What are you doing in my house in the middle of the day? And do you want a beer?"

Aldo shrugged. "Sure. Why not?" He followed Luke into the kitchen.

"So to what do I owe the pleasure?" Luke asked, opening the refrigerator and pulling out two beers. Beer was the only thing in Luke's fridge.

Aldo popped the top and took a sip. "You're probably gonna want to open yours before I say what I have to say."

Luke's sigh was ragged. "We're doing this now?"

"Yeah. So what the hell is your problem?"

"I don't have a problem," Luke said.

"You have a huge problem," Aldo countered, jerking his thumb at the boxes in the dining room. "Is this what you think Karen wants?"

Luke hated nothing more than being blindsided by his dead wife's name.

"What the fuck are you talking about?"

"Do you think Karen would have wanted you to spend your life miserable and alone?"

Luke made a noise like a growl and strangled his beer.

"I don't care that we're not supposed to mention her name around poor, delicate Luke. You're being a dumbass. As your friend, it's my job to knock you on your ass when you're being a dumbass."

"You don't know what you're talking about." Luke drilled a finger into Aldo's chest. Aldo shoved it away.

"Let's say you died. You're dead. Karen's still alive. What kind of life would you want her to have without you? Would your stupid fucking ghost be happy to see her locking herself away from everyone who loves her? Burying herself in work? Coming home to an empty house every night to relive her misery?"

Luke dropped the beer on the counter and put his hands on his head. "Of course not."

"Then why the hell would you do that to Harper?"

"I didn't do that to Harper! She was the one who built this whole pretend life—"

"Pretend?" Aldo spat out the word. "So she didn't love you? She didn't love us? She didn't love this whole fucking town?"

"Of course she did."

"Then why did you take that away from her? For Karen? For you?"

Luke dropped his hands to his hips and stared at the floor. He didn't answer.

"It's a completely different story if you didn't love her, Luke. But if you love her and threw away that life that she built for both of you, you're a fucking idiot."

Silence reigned for a tick of the clock. "Of course I love her. How could I not?" His voice was gravel. "I just don't know how to be with someone who isn't Karen."

Finally, the fuckhead was making some sense.

Aldo grabbed him in a bear hug and slapped him on the back. "You're such a stupid asshole," he said warmly.

"Learned it from watching you."

Aldo released him but kept a hand on Luke's shoulder. "It doesn't have to be one or the other. Do you know that Harp puts flowers on Karen's grave every week?"

Luke blinked. "That's Harper doing that?"

Aldo nodded. "You aren't choosing between them or replacing Karen with Harp. You're allowed to love them both. How do you think parents have more than one kid? They don't only love the first one."

"I just assumed that's what my parents did," Luke joked.

"No, if they would have stopped at one perfect child like mine did, then you'd be right. The human heart can love more than one person. You love your parents, don't you?"

Luke nodded.

"Soph? Josh? James? Obviously you love me. Otherwise, you wouldn't idolize the shit out of me. You have room. And just because you love someone else doesn't mean you're wiping the slate clean."

Luke sighed out a breath. "Thanks, Moretta. Sometimes you're not a complete idiot."

"No need to be a dick."

They shot the shit for another half hour, eating leftover cold pizza, Luke filling him in on the cooler fight and what he and Ty had discovered about Harper.

"So Harper's ex-foster father, the one she put in prison for child abuse, used Glenn to get to her?" Aldo asked, crumpling his paper towel.

"It's fucked up, man," Luke sighed, absently rubbing the knuckles of his right hand. "But that bastard is never getting out, and he's never getting near her again. Took care of it with Ty and another cop today."

At least one of them had the pleasure of ending their woman's nightmare. Aldo would always regret not being able to do more than take that one swing at Glenn. But he hadn't. Now, he was alone again. Except for his friends, his family, and his god-awful cat. But he missed Gloria with a fierceness that took his breath. He was giving her the time she'd asked for, but every beat of his heart was like a prayer offered up that she would come back.

When Aldo left, he felt a little lighter, more hopeful.

Luke would win Harper back. And if his dipshit best friend could make love work, then there was hope for him and Gloria.

Gloria. He checked his phone again, then tossed it on the seat next to him. Still nothing from her. He'd promised her space. But damn it, this was feeling more like a void, a vacuum.

There wasn't anything he could do to convince her to

come back. But there was something he could do to make her life a little better. He turned away from the office, and as he drummed his fingers on the steering wheel, his first smile in days curved his lips.

CHAPTER 78

She'd fucked up. Big time.

Gloria woke up that morning—after yet another mostly sleepless night—with the clarity she'd been seeking. Waking up in this small bed with no big Aldo was the exact opposite of what she wanted.

Damn it all to hell. She was an idiot.

She'd let fear and self-doubt creep in and whisper in her ears. Luke's damage wasn't hers. Harper's broken heart wasn't hers.

But that big, glowing love for Aldo Moretta that started in the center of her chest and worked its way out to her fingertips and toes and roots of her hair? That was all hers.

And she was going to fix it. Somehow, she decided, opening her makeup drawer. Most of her good stuff was at Aldo's. The man had made the mistake of giving her a Sephora gift card that disappeared so fast he'd given her another one the very next day.

Yes, she'd fix this mess she'd made.

But first, she was going to fix herself.

———

The prison smelled like bleach and mothballs, a musty kind of chemical scent that overpowered Gloria's floral perfume. She sat on one side of the glass and tapped a nail to the stainless-steel counter, wondering if she'd lost her damn mind.

The fluorescent light above her flickered, drawing her attention. A steel door on the other side of the glass opened. Gloria craned her neck to see through the small window. It was him. Glenn Diller in a baggy, orange jumpsuit.

She didn't know if it was the glass between them or the vacant look on his hangdog face, but she didn't feel a lick of fear. There was no threat here anymore.

He stared at her through the dingy, thick glass. Gloria picked up the phone on her side, waited. Glenn took his time lighting a cigarette, taking a drag. Finally, he picked up the receiver on his side.

"Hi, Glenn," she said, her voice steady as she marveled at this newfound strength.

"What do you want?" he grunted.

"Closure."

"You wanna come in here and look at me like I'm some kind of animal at the zoo? That it?" The anger that always bubbled just beneath his surface seemed more habit than anything now.

"Something like that," she admitted. "See, I'm moving on. Sometimes in order to do that, you have to remember where you came from."

"You'll always remember me," Glenn said darkly.

"I will. But probably not the way you want."

"I fed you. I put a roof over your head. This is the thanks I get?"

It was an old song, and Gloria didn't feel like dancing anymore. "You beat me. You tried to break me. Maybe you didn't know any better. Maybe you're just a sad, broken product of your childhood. But you were never my problem to fix."

"I'm no victim." He stared at her through the glass, anger flashing briefly in his eyes. He looked so much older than his age. Ancient really.

Gloria gave a small smile. "Neither am I. We're both responsible for our choices. You don't get to hurt me anymore."

"You think you're going to run off and be happy with someone else?" He snorted.

"Actually, I'm going to be happy on my own and then run off with someone else."

He sneered at her, taking another drag from the cigarette. "Just remember who touched you first. Who owned you first. You'll never forget me!"

"I think it's you who won't forget me. Me and that cast iron frying pan."

He coughed, a brutal hacking sound. "Someone should teach you a lesson," he hissed.

"Well, that someone isn't going to be you anymore. I'm walking out of here today, and you will never see me again. I'm not afraid of you anymore."

He slapped a big hand to the window. "Big talk coming from someone on the other side of bulletproof glass."

"Goodbye, Glenn." She started to rise, started to replace the receiver.

"Wait! Wait!" She could hear the words from the phone, see the urgency as he mouthed them through the glass. "Don't go. Don't leave. I'm sorry!"

The definition of insanity, Gloria thought.

"I wasn't there to kill you."

His words were clear as day. She snatched the receiver back. "What did you say?"

"I wasn't there to kill you. I was put up to it. I was supposed to kill your blond friend. He paid my bail. You're mine, Gloria. I would never hurt you like that. You have to believe me."

"You were there for Harper?"

Glenn nodded his bloated head. "Her foster dad or some shit's in here. She put him in here. He wanted to put her in the ground. But you gotta believe I'd never do that to you. I told the cops everything. You're mine. I take care of what's mine."

With disgust and pity, Gloria stared at him one last time. "I'm not yours. I never was."

She hung up and, without a look back, walked out of the visitation room, oblivious to the guards rushing him as he railed against the glass.

She'd crossed one Diller off her list. But there was a second one who was a constant reminder of her ugly past. What could she do about Mrs. Diller? The restraining order was good for a while. But they shared a town. Would she have to see this woman for the rest of her life and be reminded forever?

Gloria pulled up in front of the little clapboard house, still not sure what she was doing. She could offer her money if the woman promised not to try to act out any Glenn-fueled revenge. But the thousand dollars she'd saved seemed like it wasn't enough. Perhaps she could at least buy a temporary truce. Some purchased goodwill.

The weeds of summer had shriveled up and died in the first lick of winter, leaving behind colorless corpses against the front porch and sidewalk. There was a For Sale sign with a bright, bold Sold sticker. A pile of boxes towered on the front porch, and a new-ish sedan was parked in the gravel driveway.

Mrs. Diller's puke-green Buick was nowhere to be found.

Gloria debated for a moment and slid out from behind the

wheel. She knocked and shoved her hands in the pockets of her coat, hunching her shoulders against the cold.

The inner door opened, and Mrs. Diller glared at her. "You can tell your boyfriend I'm leaving tomorrow," the woman snapped.

Boyfriend? Leaving tomorrow? Gloria was at a loss. "Where are you going?" she asked.

Mrs. Diller huffed. "My sister. She lives in Illinois. Her husband died last spring of the lung cancer."

"So you're moving out there?" Gloria couldn't believe her luck, her bright, beautiful luck. All she'd needed to do was figure out what she really wanted, and everything fell magically into place.

"Like you don't know," Mrs. Diller sniffed, stuffing her hands into the dirty apron she wore over her shabby sweater. "Your big boyfriend thinks I'm a charity case. Threatening the impoverished is what I say it was. Buys my house and pays off my mortgages on the condition I leave town? That's a threat. I have half a mind to stay to spite him."

Aldo Moretta was her magic, her bright, beautiful luck. And Gloria wasn't the least bit surprised. "Aldo bought your house."

"Wasn't much cash leftover," Mrs. Diller said disdainfully. "Enough for a car that won't rust out on me for a while, maybe a security deposit on a new place. Shoulda asked for more. He had me follow you, you know," Mrs. Diller said. "Glenn did."

"I know," Gloria said.

"I did it, and I'm not sorry. But I'm guessing I don't owe him anything else anymore." She looked down at the cigarette in her hand.

"I'm guessing you don't. It's a fresh start for us both."

Mrs. Diller gave her a jerky nod. "Yeah, well. Reckon you

408

should get off my property while it's still mine till tomorrow. And the restraining order and all."

Gloria nodded. "Good luck, Mrs. Diller."

The woman gave a tight nod and slammed the door.

Two Dillers down. One Moretta to go.

CHAPTER 79

He wasn't at his house or his office. It took Gloria a good ten minutes and a dozen cookies to pry it out of Mrs. Moretta, who was not happy that Gloria had broken her boy's heart.

Gloria dragged the tiny wheels of her suitcase over the frozen ground, cresting the hill. His truck was here. He had to be here somewhere. She was losing the daylight, tromping around a field lugging a bright purple bag. The handful of people here were looking at her, and she didn't give a crap.

Because there, lying on the ground, saw in hand, was Aldo Moretta in jeans, a thermal shirt, and a vest, cutting down a Christmas tree.

The world came to a screeching halt as Gloria drank it in. This was love. And she was going to do everything in her power to hang on to it with both hands…and maybe her feet and teeth too. Whatever it took to make it up to Aldo, to convince him that she was ready.

He was swearing a blue streak as the tree stubbornly refused to topple.

"Come on, you motherfucking son of a bitch tree. You're coming home with me so my fucking cat can destroy you."

Gloria cleared her throat and set her suitcase neatly in front of her.

He turned his head, the tree choosing that moment to fall on him.

"Oh my God!" Gloria trotted forward, and together they pushed the tree off him.

Carefully, Aldo climbed to his feet and brushed at the sap and needles that covered him. He glanced at her suitcase and back at her, expressionless. "Going somewhere?"

She nodded, and his face fell.

"I'm moving in," she said quickly. "Well, I mean, if you'll still have me, I'm moving in with you." Lord, she was nervous. It wasn't the cold that had her hands shaking. It was straight-up nerves. But she pressed on. "This is my literal and metaphorical baggage," she explained, pointing at the bag.

"You're bringing me your baggage," he said slowly, sliding his hands in the back pockets of his jeans.

Gloria nodded. "We all have baggage. Some of us have more of it than others. But you loved me before I freaked out, and now that I know exactly what my baggage is, I hope you can love me again. Or still." Her voice broke, but she rallied.

Damn it. She was doing this and doing it right. Pride be damned.

"Aldo, I screwed up. I let fear get in the way of what I was feeling. I let it make me doubt myself."

"And you're not afraid now?" he asked softly.

"I'm freaking terrified," she corrected him. "I'm scared you won't be able to forgive me. I'm scared that I wrecked the best thing that happened to me because I thought it was too good to be true. That someone like me didn't deserve to be loved by someone like you. I'm scared that I'm not going to be able to fix it."

"Gloria, that's the stupidest thing I've ever heard."

She laughed, hot tears bubbling up.

"I thought I was too damaged to know what real love was. But I was wrong. I know what it is because of my scars, because of my past. I know what love is. I know that I love you and that I'll spend the rest of my life loving you if you let me." Her voice trembled. "Hell, I'll spend the rest of my life loving you even if you don't let me."

"You and your baggage," he confirmed.

She nodded. "Unfortunately, it comes with me. But maybe between the two of us we can whittle it down to a carry-on."

He looked at her, then looked at the ground.

"Do you still love me?" she asked in a tiny voice.

"Of course I do, Gloria. But, Jesus, woman. You walked out on me."

"I didn't know how to be happy when she was sad," Gloria blurted out.

"Harper?" he asked, looking at her again.

Gloria nodded. "She was so hurt, Aldo. And all I could think of is that that's how it was going to end up for us."

"We aren't them," Aldo said softly.

We. We. We. He said *we*. He bought Mrs. Diller's house to get the woman out of Benevolence, away from her. They could make this work. He just needed to believe in her.

"No, we're not. We make our own mistakes—mostly me and mine—and have our own baggage, and, Aldo, I'm probably going to screw up again. I'm really new at this healthy relationship thing. So I'm not always going to do or say the right thing, but I want to try. I want to try so hard with you. Please, at least think about it?"

He nodded slowly and then knelt down next to the tree.

Gloria hung her head and turned back to her suitcase. She'd said her piece. He'd listened. She shouldn't have expected him to jump at the chance to bring her crazy back into his life. Now she was going to have to do the walk of shame back down the hill of the tree farm with a fucking piece of luggage. Thank God she hadn't actually packed anything in it.

"Gloria."

She turned back to him, swiping a knuckle under her nose, and then froze.

Aldo Moretta was down on one knee holding what looked to her teary eyes like either a diamond ring or a piece of star that had fallen from the sky.

"In case you haven't noticed, I'm far from perfect too. And I never stopped loving you. Would you and your baggage do me and mine the great honor of marrying me?"

"Wha?" She couldn't even get the whole word out. She was hallucinating, wasn't she? Mrs. Diller had hit her in the head with a frying pan to show her how it felt, and she was imagining this entire scenario. That explanation seemed more plausible than Aldo Moretta proposing marriage after she'd so carelessly cut out his heart and stomped on it.

He flashed her that devilish grin that sparked a thousand memories spanning more than a decade. "Gloria Parker, will you marry me and move in with me and have a family with me? Will you forgive me when I'm an ass and love me like I love you until the day I die? Will you bake pies and smell like flowers and paint my life with all the color you bring?"

"I think I'm having some kind of hallucination," she whispered. She reached out, pinched his arm. He was real. So very real. And he was hers. All she had to do was say…

"Yes!"

She launched herself at him, tripping and falling into his waiting arms. They landed on the fallen tree. Then she was kissing him with the urgency of a lifetime.

"Put the ring on before I lose it," he demanded, breaking the kiss long enough to shove the stunning solitaire onto her finger.

"Why are you carrying an engagement ring with you?" she asked, kissing him again.

"In case I ran into you at a Christmas tree farm."

"Aldo!" She laughed.

"I believe in us, Glo. I believe in you. I was sure. I just needed you to be sure."

"I'm so sure! So sure. Let's get married tomorrow!"

He shook his head. "Huh-uh. I've waited this long. We're doing it right. White dress, big party, tux."

"Mmm, I love you in a tux."

She kissed him softly this time, not even minding that there were branches and sap and needles everywhere.

"Did you really buy Mrs. Diller's house?"

"Technically, it's in your name. We can fix it up, flip it. Or I thought maybe you'd want to rent it out. Maybe to women or families who are down on their luck? Need a fresh start?"

She pulled back to look at him. To drink him in. Her beautiful, perfect man who she'd almost thrown away. "Every time I think I can't possibly love you any more, you go and do a thing like that. I don't know if I deserve you, Aldo Moretta. But I don't care. I'm going to spend my life loving you whether I've earned you or not."

When his lips met hers, when she sighed her breath into his mouth, when their hearts beat together, Gloria knew she was absolutely ready for the rest of her life.

EPILOGUE

The knock at the door came ten minutes on the right side of orgasmic bliss. Gloria and Aldo had returned to her apartment to do a preliminary round of packing and gotten blissfully distracted in the bedroom…and the kitchen. And then again in the bedroom.

Gloria dragged on Aldo's huge National Guard sweatshirt over the leggings that she'd found wrapped around her bedside lamp and padded to the door.

"Harper! What a nice surprise! Come on in." Gloria made sure to pull the sleeve of the sweatshirt down over her beautiful new diamond. They had plans for the announcement.

Her mother knew already, of course. Nothing got by Sara Parker. Unlike Ina, Sara could keep her mouth shut for a day or two. But the rest of the world was going to have to wait just a little longer.

Harper looked tired and sad, her MO since the breakup.

"Am I interrupting?" Harper asked wearily.

Gloria stepped aside, waving Harper in. "No. Aldo's in the kitchen making grilled cheese sandwiches and trying not to burn the place down."

"Are you sure I'm not interrupting?" Harper looked

pointedly at Gloria's sex-smushed hair. Her unpainted lips curved just a little.

Gloria laughed. "Ten minutes earlier, and you would have been." She winked.

Instead of laughing, Harper wrapped her friend in a tight hug. "I'm so happy for you, Gloria. I really am."

Gloria returned the hug. "Me too. I owe it all to you, you know."

Harper released her. "Don't be silly. You got yourself here in a real home with a sexy man making you grilled cheese. You deserve every bit of it."

Gloria couldn't help it. Her heart was singing. She had to share just a little. "I'm so happy, Harper. I never imagined life could be like this." She hugged Aldo's sweatshirt closer. "Enough gushing. Can I interest you in a half-burnt grilled cheese?"

"Is that my old pal Harpoon out there?" Aldo poked his shirtless torso out of the kitchen, and Gloria felt the familiar pitter-patter of affection and lust curl in her belly.

Harper laughed weakly. "Hey, sport. I haven't seen you in a while."

"When are we hitting the trails again? Got a new blade that'll leave you in my dust."

"Nice," Harper said, threading a hand through her hair. She looked nervous, resigned. "I actually wanted to let you both know that I'm, uh, leaving."

"Vacation leaving?" Gloria asked, her brow furrowed. Harper couldn't leave. Not with Luke finally ready to make amends. This was her friend's shot at her own happily ever after.

Harper shook her head.

"Happy trails leaving?" Aldo pressed. He was always calm in a crisis. Yet another thing Gloria loved about the man.

"Happy trails. Or just reasonably okay trails at this point," Harper joked.

"It's not because of Luke and Linc's fight to the death in the grocery store, is it?" Gloria asked.

"I heard they were both banned for life after they destroyed the bread aisle," Aldo interjected. "Buns and loaves everywhere."

Harper rolled her eyes. "Well, the small-town rumors are one thing I won't miss."

"Are you giving up on him?" Gloria asked, her heart aching for her friend.

"I have to. For my sake. For his. I can't change him. And I can't stay here either."

"You have friends here," Gloria reminded her.

"And I'm so grateful to have you all in my life. But Benevolence is Luke's home, and me staying here is just going to be a painful reminder to both of us of what was."

Gloria weighed her words carefully. "I disagree with you, but as your friend, I will support your decision. As long as you promise to let us come visit you," Gloria said. She felt her panic level rising. If Harper left before Friday, everything would be ruined.

"Of course," Harper said with a teary smile.

"So where exactly will we be visiting you?" Aldo asked, hands on hips, still clutching a spatula. His gaze skated to Gloria, telegraphing the same feelings. *She needs to hang in just a little longer.*

"I'm not really sure yet. I'm leaving Saturday, so obviously I have to have a plan then. I'll let you know." Harper bit her lip.

Gloria breathed a sigh of relief. Harper wouldn't be leaving Saturday. She wouldn't be leaving ever if everything went according to plan.

"Listen, when I do tell you where I am, do you promise not to let anyone know?" Harper asked.

"Anyone meaning Luke?" Aldo crossed his arms.

Harper shook her head. "No. Just anyone who doesn't need to know. Like if a stranger asks you…or something." She was fumbling this, making a mess.

"Are you in trouble?" Gloria asked. She knew exactly what kind of trouble Harper had been in. The man who had abused her and countless other children in foster care had gone to prison thanks in large part to Harper. He'd been sending her threatening letters and had escalated things by tasking Glenn with the job of killing Harper. It still made Gloria shake when she thought about how their monsters had overlapped.

But Luke had fixed it. There would be no parole for Harper's monster. And obviously she didn't know that yet.

Oh, hell. Things were going to get messy if Luke didn't make his move.

"Everything's fine. I just wanted to tell you both personally. You've been such good friends to me. I'm really going to miss you." Harper's voice cracked. "I love you guys so much."

Gloria wrapped Harper into a hug again. "I wish I could talk you into staying."

"Is there room for me in there?" Aldo grabbed them both and squeezed.

"One joke about a threesome, and I'll smack you with that spatula," Harper threatened.

Gloria giggled. "Promise me you won't give up on love."

"I promise." Harper nodded.

Gloria recognized the lie. Her friend had already given up, and it hurt Gloria's heart. But soon, everything would be perfect.

When Harper left, Gloria looked at Aldo.

"She has no idea, does she?" Aldo asked gleefully.

"That Luke made sure her evil shadow will never get out

of prison? That he's planning the biggest, craziest grand gesture to win her back? That you spent nine hours yesterday helping Luke decorate the house for Christmas? Nope. No clue." Gloria grinned.

She went to him and wrapped her arms around his neck, and together they laughed diabolically.

Ivan raced by and dove head-first into an open moving box.

———

"I didn't know until right this second that I had a thing for Cher," Aldo whispered into Gloria's ear, his fingers stroking through her long, black wig.

"And I didn't realize how sexy you could make a ridiculous mustache look," Gloria said, pushing on the fur lining Aldo's upper lip. He also made tie-dye look pretty damn hot too. Of course, Gloria had given the T-shirt a little extra Sonny Bono by cutting a deep, '70s-style V in it. Her own matching tie-dye was knotted sassily on her hip.

She tossed her long, fake hair over her shoulder.

They were crammed asses to elbows with the Garrison family and a handful of other townsfolk in the storage room at Remo's just off the greasy kitchen. Word had spread about Luke's plan to win back Harper, and the entire town had turned out to show their support.

Gloria's mother was out there with a glass of wine and a table full of girlfriends, including Ina Moretta. The two had become fast, odd friends.

Aldo made a show of kissing Gloria and tickling her with the fake 'stache. "We're definitely going to hang on to the costumes. I've got plans for later," he told her.

Gloria laughed and squeezed him in a tight hug. For the rest of her life, she had plans for later.

"Love is in the air tonight," Claire said next to them as she snuggled a little closer to her husband, Charlie. They were both wearing hideous Christmas sweaters.

Gloria prodded Aldo in his ribs and nodded to where Luke stood in the corner studying a sheet of lyrics.

Aldo rolled his eyes. "Go ahead and fix him. But just this once. Since it's a special occasion." He ran his thumb over the diamond on her finger.

Gloria kissed him lightly on the cheek before wriggling around bodies to get to Luke. His lips were moving, carefully forming each word on the page.

"Are you ready for this?" Gloria asked him. It wasn't the ideal place for an intimate conversation. Not with a dozen nervously enthusiastic friends and family getting ready for the surprise of Harper's life.

Luke blew out a breath. "Is it enough? Is this enough?" he asked, jerking his chin at the chaos in the glorified closet.

"Do you love her?" Gloria asked.

She watched his Adam's apple work in his throat. "Yeah." Luke's voice was a rasp. "Yeah, I do."

"Then that's enough."

The corner of his mouth quirked. "That's it? That easy?"

Gloria glanced over her shoulder at Aldo. The love of her life. The man who brought her into the light. Who put a promise of forever on her finger.

"Nobody said anything about easy. But it is so worth it," Gloria promised. She thought about her purple suitcase and the Christmas tree—the tree they'd already had to stand back up twice, thanks to Ivan. She thought about the boxes that had already made their way to Aldo's house. *Their* house. "Just make sure the apology is always bigger than the screwup. And I'm pretty sure you blew it out of the water with tonight."

"I'm asking her to marry me." Luke said the words so quietly Gloria almost didn't catch them. "Not here. But at home. If she forgives me."

Gloria was having trouble seeing him through the tears that threatened to spill over. If Harper could forgive, she'd be getting her own happily ever after tonight. And knowing her friend's gigantic heart, Luke had a very good chance at a lifetime of happiness in front of him.

"We'll celebrate tomorrow," Gloria said quietly. She raised her left hand, just enough so that the diamond caught his eye.

"No shit?" Luke beamed at her, then over the heads that separated him and Aldo.

"Tomorrow we celebrate. Tonight's your night," Gloria said, patting him on the arm. "Oh, and if all goes well, I owe you a stick of deodorant and a toothbrush."

Sophie Garrison, wearing a matching Garrison Christmas sweater and a mile-wide grin, ducked her head in the door. "Showtime, guys!"

———

Angry Frank and his lady backup singers kicked things off with a rousing rendition of "With a Little Help from My Friends." Gloria couldn't see Harper through the crowd from her vantage point hugging the wall near the service bar, but she had a feeling the festive vibes of the crowd would have her friend smiling.

Aldo was crowded up against Gloria's side. Everything, even a night at Remo's, was different with him next to her.

Nerves shimmered in her belly.

She'd spent the better part of this year putting herself out there, but this was taking it to a new level.

The crowd cheered as Frank and his cohorts exited the stage, and Gloria's stomach churned.

"Do you think Cher ever gets stage fright?" Gloria asked Aldo.

He brought her hand to his lips and fake mustache. "Sweetheart, with everything you've faced down this year, a little karaoke is nothing."

Fred, the bar's owner, was back on the stage calling for quiet. "It's gonna be an old-school night, folks. Put your hands together for our next act, Sonny and Cher."

Aldo gave her hand a squeeze and flashed her that charmer's smile. And the stage suddenly didn't seem so high, the lights not quite as blinding. Nothing was as scary with him by her side. He led the way onto the pencil-thin stage, bounding up the step. And there sat Harper, front and center, her cheeks flushed, the glee of the community overriding her sadness for the night. Harper clapped a hand over her mouth when she got a good look at their getups.

Hand in hand, they approached the mic. Aldo leaned in, his big, booming voice carrying over the bar noise. "Thank you, ladies and gentlemen. Gloria and I would like to dedicate this song to the woman we owe everything to. This one's for you, Harper."

"We love you," Gloria said, blowing Harper a kiss.

The music started, and with a shared laugh, Aldo and Gloria swayed together to the beat. Gloria broke into "I Got You Babe" in the singing voice she hadn't used since that high school musical.

"Oh my God," Harper mouthed from her little table.

Aldo crooned, Gloria tossed her hair Cher style, and the entire bar hummed and swayed along.

The moment was coming. Their own little sparkling second in an evening overflowing with love. Gloria knew Harper would be over the moon. That was what friends did. They loved and cheered for each other no matter what was going on in their own lives.

She watched her friend's face carefully as Aldo sang about giving her his ring. And when he held up Gloria's hand, when the lights hit the ring just right, Gloria felt Harper's joy as sharp and swift as if it were her own. She felt the crowd's too when the entire bar got to its feet. They were cheering for her. For the happily ever after that she'd earned.

Harper jumped up, eyes shining bright, and blew them a kiss. It was the perfect moment.

They finished with a flourish, and then Aldo was bending her over backward and laying a kiss on her that had the crowd roaring. Or maybe that was just the blood in her head, the joy in her system.

There was no more "poor little Gloria Parker" here. No more Gloria who left Glenn after the first time. Only Gloria Parker, the luckiest woman in town.

———

Gloria hopped off the stage, and Harper dove for her hand. The diamond sparkled like the bright, shiny promise it was. They wrapped each other in a fierce hug. "I am so happy for you two." Harper's voice quavered with feeling.

Gloria cupped her friend's cheek in her hand. But words failed her.

"We wouldn't be here without you, Harp," Aldo yelled over the noise, moving in for his own hug.

"We're hoping you'll agree to be our maid of honor," Gloria said, clasping her hands together. She was planning a wedding. Dear Lord help her. She needed her best friend by her side.

"Are you serious?" Harper yelped. "Oh, you guys! I would be honored!"

Gloria hugged her again. "Mind if we join you?"

"Please! Sophie disappeared. I can't believe she's missing this."

Gloria and Aldo shared a mischievous look.

Someone produced a third chair, and they all crowded around the tiny table. The excitement of the moment, of what was to come, gave Gloria goose bumps.

Harper leaned in. "This is a pretty incredible send-off," she whispered with a sad smile.

Gloria bit her lip and smiled. She didn't trust herself not to shout "Just you wait!"

Aldo dug into the nachos. "I was too nervous to eat dinner tonight," he confessed.

Harper laughed. "You guys were great."

"Wait until you see the next act." Gloria winked.

She didn't have long to wait. They were already taking the stage.

The Garrisons. And Joni.

Sophie was front and center with Claire and Joni flanking her. Charlie, James, Uncle Stu, and Ty crowded in behind them. They were all wearing ugly Christmas sweaters that said Garrison Xmas.

The funky '70s beat of Sister Sledge's "We Are Family" filled the bar. The women moved toward the mic in unison.

They pointed to Harper and sang to her about family. And Gloria felt goose bumps rise on her arms. She and Harper would start families together here in Benevolence. They would raise children together and host book clubs and bake sales and work long hours. They would come home to men who loved them, treated them as partners. Their future was so bright and shiny that Gloria couldn't see through the tears for a moment.

Aldo, reading her thoughts, reached under the table and

squeezed her knee. She blinked back the tears, and he mouthed the words that had changed her life.

I love you.

She squeezed his hand back, realizing she had so much more to say to him.

The Garrisons' number ended, and the entire family paraded off the stage, pausing to hug and kiss Harper. And then Gloria felt the shift in the air.

Luke stood alone in front of the mic, hands in his pockets.

Aldo squeezed her knee again.

Luke cleared his throat, and the noise around the bar died down. "I'd like to dedicate this song to one of the women I've been lucky enough to love in this lifetime. I don't deserve you, Harper, but I hope you won't hold that against me because I love you with every piece of me."

Harper squeaked out a sound, her mouth open in shock.

It was Gloria's heart's turn to burst with happiness for her friend. Luke had barely begun "Angel Eyes," and Gloria could see that Harper had already forgiven him. Harper was crying. Gloria was crying. Even Aldo's eyes looked a little extra glossy.

There was so much love in this room that Gloria thought her heart might not be able to take it. When Luke pulled Harper up onstage, when he kissed her like it was the first and last time, Gloria tugged Aldo to his feet.

Together, they wove their way through the crowd, shaking hands, accepting hugs and congratulations. When they finally made it to the door, Gloria pushed it open and sighed into the quiet night.

Christmas was coming, and the entire town was decked out. Even Remo's had icicle lights dripping from its porch roof. The night air was crisp and cold and full of promise.

"Is everything okay?" Aldo asked as she pulled him toward

the far end of the parking lot. She found the spot in the gravel where her life had almost ended before it began and turned to face him and took a breath.

"More than okay," she said, watching the worry ease from his handsome face. "Everything is perfect."

"You're going to freeze to death out here, Glo," Aldo said, rubbing her arms with his hands.

"Nothing could freeze what's inside me tonight," she told him. "You glued on a fake mustache and got onstage in tie-dye to support a friend. You didn't care if you looked silly or if someone would make fun of you. You did it because you love your friend and you wanted him to be happy."

"Also the mustache. I'm totally digging it."

"I love how big your heart is, Aldo."

His hands slowed their motion on her skin. His gaze turned serious. But she knew that he understood that she had things to say.

"You love so big, Aldo. And that's what makes you strong. Your love makes me stronger and braver than I ever thought I could be." She looked down at the gravel under their feet. At the spot where it had begun...and ended. "This is where it all started. This exact spot where my life almost ended. And now I'm standing here with you, and everything is just beginning. I can see us years into the future. I can see babies and football and Sunday brunches and that damn cat. I can see college visits and Mediterranean cruises. Wrinkles and doctor appointments, retirement accounts. Quiet nights with nothing but your skin on mine. I see a life with you, Aldo. Not just the good pieces."

He reached up and cupped her face in his hands.

"I'm going to spend the rest of my life loving you, trusting you, supporting you," she promised. "And this, right here, is just the beginning."

She kissed him. Softly, sweetly, with all the hope and joy that threatened to burst free from the tetherings of her soul.

He held her like she was precious and strong and infinitely perfect. Kissed her like he'd never have enough. And together they loved bolder than pain, fiercer than history, and brighter than all the Christmas lights.

BONUS EPILOGUE

Eight years later

Aldo pulled into one of the visitor spots in the elementary school parking lot and cut the engine. Receiving a personal invitation from the principal to his kid's school was not how he'd planned on using his lunch hour.

In fact, he and his wife had some very non-kid-friendly plans. Every Wednesday, they both blocked out a ninety-minute lunch and then proceeded to make excellent, naked use of those ninety minutes.

Unfortunately, urgent calls from the principal took precedence.

He slid out from behind the wheel, adjusting his pant leg over his boot. He looked down and paused for a moment. Somewhere between walking down the aisle with Gloria Parker, adopting their oldest, and watching his wife power through labor with their second, he'd forgotten he was an amputee. The label had simply peeled off, fluttered away, and life was normal. Beautifully, blissfully normal.

Until your seven-year-old daughter's principal demands your presence in the middle of the day. Parental concern and guilt twined together in his gut. He'd help Lucia fix this, whatever it was. He just hoped it wasn't his fault.

Aldo had just reached the door when he heard his name. He spotted her, dark hair catching the autumn breeze, lips pursed in maternal worry. She was beautiful as always. He never got used to it. The feeling would sneak up and sucker punch him every time he looked up and saw Gloria Parker—Gloria Parker-Moretta—stroll into the room. She was his, and he was hers. It was as simple and as beautiful as that.

"Hey," she said, leaning up to kiss him on the corner of the mouth. "Did they give you any idea what this is about?"

Aldo tucked a strand of hair behind her ear, tickling the diamond earring he'd given her years ago.

"Nope. I think it's part of the requisite psychological parent torture. They want us to assume the worst when really Lucia won some kind of geography award or something."

"Lucia wouldn't know how to find her way out of our driveway," Gloria said dryly. Their seven-year-old was smart, outspoken, and athletic. But her sense of direction—or lack thereof—was a running joke in the family.

"She would if we got her the new iPhone that Tiffy Hernandez's parents got Tiffy," Aldo teased.

Gloria rolled her eyes and tucked her arm through his. "After all these years, I still feel poorly equipped to parent. And Tiffy's 'here, have everything you ever wanted' parents are making it even harder."

"They'll thank us someday," Aldo said optimistically. Lucia and Avery had it pretty damned good. Both he and Gloria saw to that.

She grinned up at him. "You're a great dad."

"I know," he said airily. "You're a pretty great mom too." She was a phenomenal mother. An incredible wife. And an even better woman. She'd never lost herself to any of those roles. Not when Della and Fred had retired and sold her the business. Not when she'd fallen in love with owning a rental property and had proudly housed seven families that desperately needed a chance. And not when she'd become a wife and a mother.

"Are we just telling ourselves that so it doesn't hurt as much when the principal accuses us of helicoptering or neglect?" Gloria wondered.

"Glo, we've got this. We're going to make this mystery meeting our bitch, and then we're going to have a quickie in my truck."

She considered for a moment. "Not on school grounds."

"Of course not," Aldo snorted. "We're parents, not hormonal teenagers."

Together, as a team, they marched down the hallway in the direction of the administration office.

———

"Lucia got into a fight on the playground," Principal Tucker said. His voice lacked the trademark sternness that administrators in Aldo's school career had all possessed. And with wire-rimmed glasses and his reddish hair brushed to one side, he looked more like everyone's favorite cousin than a disciplinarian.

"A fight?" Gloria repeated. "A physical fight?"

"He started it, Mom," Lucia piped up. Her skinny arms were crossed defiantly over her chest. She had dirt on her face and grass stains on the knees of her jeans. One of her braids had come loose. Aldo wasn't sure if the damage was from the fight or just life. His daughter lived life hard.

At age five, Lucia had announced she wanted to play football like daddy. Two years later, and Aldo was a peewee football coach, and his daughter had the best kicker's leg in the division.

Lucia was Vietnamese and adopted, but no one doubted she was 100 percent Moretta. She had Aldo's swagger and Gloria's knack for reading people...and then working around them. They were going to be in serious trouble when she hit her teens. He couldn't freaking wait.

"I don't care who started it, Lucia," Gloria said in well-worn mom language. "Fighting is never the answer." She softened the rebuke by stroking her hand down Lucia's long dark ponytail.

They were treading on marshy ground. Violence had left such a mark on Gloria's life that she feared their daughters would face the same dangers. The worry kept both of them up some nights.

Principal Tucker pushed his glasses up the bridge of his nose. "We're just trying to get to the bottom of what happened. We're not looking to make someone the bad guy here."

"Who were you fighting with, Lu?" Aldo asked.

"Toby Potts."

Shit. The kid was on the football team. He was trouble on and off the field. Bigger than the rest of the kids, he didn't give a shit about authority unless it was his grumpy-ass father who rarely made it to games, and when he did, he shouted his disappointment from the sidelines.

"Why were you fighting with Toby?" Gloria asked.

Aldo could hear the tension in his wife's voice.

"He told my friend Janicka that she had to be his girlfriend. She said no, but he said she had to. I told him boys can't make girls be their girlfriends if they don't want to, and he shouldn't take it personally. And then he told me to shut up." Lucia paused to take a breath. "So I told him that *he* should shut up, which I know is against our code of conduct. But, Mr. Tucker,

Toby was so *annoying*." Lucia rolled her eyes dramatically, and Aldo had to cough to cover his laugh.

Gloria stepped on his foot, but he could see the amusement in her eyes too. They had to look away from each other to maintain the appropriate level of parental disappointment. At this stage of the game, they were professionals at not laughing at funny things.

"Anyway, so we said shut up a couple of times, and then he tried to grab Janicka's hand. And I was like *no!*" Lucia demonstrated a sweeping karate chop through the air. "And I hit his hand away just like that."

Aldo made a note to review proper technique with Lucia again.

"My mom and dad both say that people shouldn't hurt each other unless they absolutely have to and they're defending someone," Lucia lectured Mr. Tucker.

Aldo breathed a sigh of relief.

"Janicka was scared, and Toby was being mean. He doesn't get to tell her she has to be his girlfriend. Right, Mom?" Lucia looked up, eyes pleading with her mother.

"You're right," Gloria said. She put her hands on the back of Lucia's chair and gave the principal a look that dared him to argue with her. "That's definitely not okay."

"I am in complete agreement," Mr. Tucker said, interlacing his fingers on the desk. "But Mrs. McKnight said that you were, um…sitting on him, stuffing dirt in his face."

Aldo choked, and Gloria elbowed him in the side. Parenting was a balancing act between teaching your kids the exact right thing to do and letting them get away with something every once in a while. Aldo was leaning heavily toward letting Lucia get away with making Toby Potts eat dirt.

Lucia looked down at her lap. "I maybe got a little carried

away. He pushed me first. Called me a stupid girl. And then he grabbed me here, real hard," she said, holding up her tiny arm where a bruise was already developing.

Aldo knew rage. It was immediate and fierce. Someone had laid hands on his little girl, had tried to physically hurt her. That kid was going to run laps until he dropped dead for the rest of football season. He'd talk to the father too. Lay it out very clearly. He'd talk to Lucia again, a refresher course in Girl Power 101. Avery was old enough too. Four was old enough, right?

Gloria gripped his arm, fingernails digging into his skin until he started breathing again. She knew him so well. And if stuffing a seven-year-old boy in a trash can after school was the right thing to do, Gloria would hold the lid for him.

"What did you do when he grabbed you, sweetie?" Gloria asked, careful to keep her tone neutral. But Aldo could see the anxiety in her eyes.

"I pushed him, and he fell on his b-u-t-t, and I jumped on him. I told him he doesn't get to hurt people just because his feelings are hurt. Just like you said, Mom."

"I didn't tell you to stuff dirt in someone's face when you said it," Gloria reminded her, shooting a guilty look at Mr. Tucker.

"I improvised that part," Lucia said proudly. "I have some questions. Am I in trouble? I was just standing up for my friend. And Toby was mean. Really mean. Also, why isn't Toby in here? Why is it just me? Is it because I'm a girl? Am I in more trouble because I'm supposed to be nice and sugary sweet, and I made someone eat dirt?"

Gloria's jaw opened and then closed with a snap. Aldo squeezed her shoulder as they both basked in unabashed pride in their daughter, the budding feminist.

"I don't think you're going to be in trouble," Mr. Tucker predicted. "But I would like to talk to your parents for a minute, Lucia. Can you wait out in the office for us?"

"Okay." She rose reluctantly and eyed all three adults. "I didn't do anything wrong." And with that, she headed for the door. Aldo stopped her with a hand on her shoulder. He was about to burst with pride. And yeah, maybe they'd have to navigate some sticky areas of self-defense and the etiquette of dirt stuffing, but Lucia was going to be just fine out there in the world.

He held up his fist. She looked up at him and back at the fist before bumping it with her own. She gave him a nod worthy of a cocky NFL quarterback and strutted from the room.

"Please, sit," Mr. Tucker said, indicating the chairs in front of his desk. Warily, ready to leap to the defense of their daughter, they sat. The principal took his glasses off and pulled a cleaning cloth from his desk drawer. "Allow me to be candid. This is not the first time Toby has been involved in a physical altercation. We have reason to believe that there are issues at home, which is why I'm hesitant to respond in the typical disciplinarian fashion."

"So this kid just gets to walk around getting physical with classmates?" Aldo demanded.

Mr. Tucker put his glasses back on and smiled benignly. "Not at all. Our school has a pilot counseling program that provides students—and families—with access to professional therapists. And we will be encouraging Toby's family to partake. Toby will have his own sessions at school, and if he attends them and participates, he won't be punished for this incident. If we can turn this into a teaching moment, we have the opportunity to put students like him on an entirely different path."

Aldo stewed on that for a minute.

"Kids like Toby are considered at risk for repeating patterns learned at home," Mr. Tucker said cryptically. "We take these situations very seriously. These kids are young, and they can still learn to change those patterns. But we need as much help as we can get."

"What can we do?" Gloria asked. His bighearted, public-serving wife was constantly getting him roped into volunteering and giving back. It was one of the things he loved most about her.

"Well, I was thinking since your husband is Toby's football coach, maybe some time spent with a healthy male role model—a hometown hero, if you will—would help. This is a really essential time in childhood development. Kids are interacting in their own world with what they've learned at home. If a boy learns that he can get what he wants with violence now, it's much harder to change that pattern later in life. The same as if a child learns that standing up for themselves gets them hurt."

Aldo felt Gloria shudder next to him.

"You two have raised a bright, smart, strong little girl who is utterly fearless. I wish I had a school of Lucias."

"No, you don't," Aldo and Gloria said together. They laughed, and the tension broke.

"I guess what I'm saying is we're a community here, and if we all work together, these kids are going to have a brighter, healthier future."

———

"Did I just volunteer to mentor the kid who bruised our daughter?" Aldo asked with disbelief when they stepped out into the sunshine.

"Welcome to my world," Gloria said wryly. "What's Uncle Luke going to say when you tell him you wrangled him into it too?"

"Already figured that out. I'll have Harp do it."

"Smart. I imagine the grandmothers will celebrate Lucia's dirt stuffing with baked goods and nail polish tomorrow night at dinner."

"What's on your mind, Glo?" he asked, reading her like a well-loved book. He turned her to face him, settling his hands on her slim shoulders.

"That our daughter is so much stronger than I was at that age. And how happy and proud and sad that makes me. That Glenn never had an Aldo Moretta to look up to. That our beautiful, sweet, smart girl is seeing this at seven. *Seven*, Aldo. I thought we had more time."

He pulled her into his chest and wrapped his arms around her.

The scars were still there under the happy, the busy. The scars were what made them love so deeply. "You raised a little girl who just stood up to a bully and then a bunch of adults who might have thought about holding her responsible for it. You did that, Gloria Parker-Moretta. She's living up to your beautiful, kick-ass, shining example."

She blinked back a tear and looked up at him. "I just wish the world was different for our girls."

He stroked a hand over her smooth cheek. "We're making it different, one kid at a time."

She sighed out the tension and worry and angst on one long breath. "I love you so damn much, Aldo. Thank you for being my partner in all this."

"Thanks for choosing me."

"Thank you for being an excellent father and a brilliant husband, Mr. Hometown Hero."

"It's a great life, Glo."

"Yeah, it is." She looked down between them. "So how fast do you think you can get out of those pants?"

It turned out he was able to get out of his pants pretty damn fast. They were parked against the tree line at the far end of the lakefront parking lot. And as he shoved up the skirt of Gloria's pretty blue dress, as he held her just over the tip of his needy erection, he knew a love so fierce it carved his chest open.

She was his. And he was hers.

Gloria brought her mouth to his as she settled onto him, over him, their bodies recognizing the familiar push and pull of lust born from love.

It was a great life. One brightened by the color and laughter of their daughters. Shaded by the constant presence of friends, family, and community. And filled with a love so deep and abiding that old wounds healed and new confidence marched them forward into the beautiful future.

Author's Note

Dear Reader,

I literally don't know what to say right now besides thank you for reading *Finally Mine*! This book was a very long time in the making, and I hope you found the wait worth it. So far, Aldo is my favorite book hero to date, and Gloria's character arc was one of the most challenging and rewarding I've ever written.

Gloria's story was so important to me to tell. Many of you have your own stories. And whether you share them or not, I hope you know you're not alone. Gloria wasn't. I wasn't. You aren't. And I sincerely hope you feel that.

Whew, okay! Let's talk about what a trip it was to revisit Benevolence and Luke and Harper! I had written *Pretend You're Mine* as a standalone. But y'all kept emailing me. And messaging me. And posting comments. For *three years*. It took me a long time before I was ready—and I originally thought Gloria and Aldo would be a novella. Ha! Over 108,000 words later, thank you for forcing me to write this book.

If you loved Gloria and Aldo (and of course Mrs. Moretta), please consider leaving an embarrassingly glowing review and telling a few hundred of your closest friends who enjoy reading contemporary romance and eating tacos.

Want to hang out and be book pals? Follow me on Facebook and join me in my reader's group: Lucy Score's Binge Readers Anonymous. I'm also on Instagram. And if you want first dibs on preorders and sales and awesome bonus content, sign up for my newsletter! You will be dazzled by my sparkling wit and fart jokes. #classy

Xoxo,
Lucy

Acknowledgments

It takes a freakin' army to keep me on task and get a book from blank page to your hands. Thank you, from the bottom of my cold, dead heart, to:

- My readers, who begged, pleaded, and threatened me for three years before I finally delivered this book. Now you can stop.
- Andrea for being brave and beautiful, raw and real while sharing her story with me and making sure that Gloria shined.
- Joyce and Tammy for being the best damn admins in the whole damn world.
- The maker of fuzzy blankets. You make me feel loved because my cat will only sit on me if I'm under a fuzzy blanket.
- Dawn, Amanda, and Jessica for finding all my misplaced commas and bringing to my attention such questions as "Is she on her back or her knees?"
- Mr. Lucy for bringing me to the beach to work and feeding me tacos and martinis. Also for doing all the work that I don't want to do. You're a good man.

- The beta readers who bravely stepped into this story before it was polished and pretty.
- Carlina for suggesting I write this particular story.
- My author posse without whom/who (crap, I already paid the editors off at this point) my life would be empty and sad and waaaaay less distracting.

About the Author

Lucy Score is a *New York Times* and *USA Today* bestselling author. She grew up in a literary family who insisted that the dinner table was for reading and earned a degree in journalism. She writes full-time from the Pennsylvania home she and Mr. Lucy share with their obnoxious cat, Cleo. When not spending hours crafting heartbreaker heroes and kick-ass heroines, Lucy can be found on the couch, in the kitchen, or at the gym. She hopes to someday write from a sailboat, oceanfront condo, or tropical island with reliable Wi-Fi.

Sign up for her newsletter by scanning the QR code below and stay up on all the latest Lucy book news. You can also follow her here:

Website: lucyscore.net
Facebook: lucyscorewrites
Instagram: scorelucy
TikTok: @lucyferscore
Binge Books: bingebooks.com/author/lucy-score
Readers Group: facebook.com/groups/
BingeReadersAnonymous
Newsletter signup: